GHOST MONTH

GHOST MONTH
ED LIN

Published by Soho Press, Inc.
853 Broadway
New York, NY 10003

Library of Congress Cataloging-in-Publication Data

Lin, Ed.
Ghost month / Ed Lin.
p. cm
ISBN 978-1-61695-326-3
eISBN 978-1-61695-327-0
Street vendors—Taiwan—Taipei—Fiction. 2. Young women—Crimes
against—Fiction. 3. Murder—Investigation—Fiction.
4. Taipei (Taiwan)—Fiction. I. Title.
PS3562.I4677G48 2014
813'.54—dc23   2014003810

Interior design by Janine Agro, Soho Press, Inc.

Printed in the United States of America

10 9 8 7 6 5 4 3 2 1

For my parents.

There is no crime greater than having too many desires;
There is no disaster greater than not being content;
There is no misfortune greater than being covetous.

—TAO TE CHING

CHAPTER ONE

When I found out the girl I was going to marry had been murdered, I was sitting on a foldout stool at a sidewalk noodle shop in Taipei's Da'an District. My mouth went dry, my eyes blurred and I couldn't stop shaking. It was the hottest day in July, and the island's humidity was draped over me like a mourning veil, yet my body went cold and sweaty. Even my skin was crying.

I was somehow able to hold the newspaper still in my hands while reading and rereading the entire story of Julia Huang. It was only three paragraphs long. She had been shot in the head. She hadn't been wearing much. She had been working at an unlicensed betel-nut stand in Hsinchu City, an hour outside of Taipei. The surveillance camera—Taiwan's top crime-fighting tool—had malfunctioned, and no footage of the crime had been recorded.

I sighed and slumped over. I wished it hadn't been my Julia. I wished it had been almost anybody else. I thought about some of our old classmates I didn't care for. Why not one of them? But it was definitely my Julia. I touched the three Chinese characters of her name as I read them. Her name, Huang Zheng-lian, meant "positive light." Everything she did I'd always seen in a positive light.

I hadn't seen her in seven years, when I had left for UCLA and she for NYU. I hadn't even known she was here in Taipei.

The two of us had grown up together, Jing-nan and Zheng-lian, who became Johnny and Julia, two Taiwanese sweethearts with the same American dream. Our families had been friends for at least three generations, so it had been predestined that we would be close. As soon as Julia and I could talk, we talked to each other. We went to the same school and the same cheap cram schools and worked at our respective family night-market stalls, which changed locations over the years but were always near each other.

We did everything together. *Everything*. We knew we were in love by third grade. We knew we were going to get married by the fifth.

NEXT DOOR TO THE noodle shop where I sat with my paper, in a store that sold altars, gods and goods for the next world, a man set up burning incense sticks at the feet of several deities. He brought a folding table out to the sidewalk, and I watched him set up offerings for human spirits: a three-layer pyramid of oranges, a bulk pack of instant noodles, a six-pack of Coca-Cola, a six-pack of Sprite and boxes of cookies and crackers. He slid a plastic bucket of water and a small towel underneath the table, so the ghosts could wash up before and after eating. He lit up incense for the table and sneezed hard twice. Finally, he touched his lighter to a sheaf of paper and dropped it in a metal bucket to the right of the table. Black smoke from the burning money for the dead snaked toward me.

A motorcycle-repair shop on the north side of the noodle shop simultaneously set up its offerings table. Judging by the outsized table and offerings, the owner was either less lucky or more fearful than the guy who ran the gods store. Incense smoke as thick as a movie special effect streamed out of a censer on his table.

The makeshift offering tables were meant to appease not only the spirits of one's ancestors, but also those of people who died with no heirs. Supposedly if no one was around to pray for you and offer money and food throughout the year, you really suffered in the afterlife. You might be pierced with hooks, hung upside down and set on fire, depending on what your specific beliefs were. After eleven months of pain and hunger, these ghosts were looking to take out their wrath on anybody alive.

I looked over at the gods next door and choked on the spiced air.

THIS MORNING, EACH OF the seven twenty-four-hour news channels had been going off on the betel-nut girl who was shot and killed, replaying computer-animated reenactments of the crime. If the surveillance-camera footage had been available, that would have been played in endless loops, too.

I had watched the cartoon shooting with indifference, numbed to the over-the-top violence, sex and sexual violence the news channels served up to compete for eyeballs. The woman in the animated reenactment looked more like a strung-out Marge Simpson than Julia. One version featured the gunman killing the woman and then spitting betel-nut juice on her face as a final act of indecency.

The girls who work at betel-nut stalls are usually in tough circumstances. It pays well and doesn't require a college degree. You just have to be willing to wear next to nothing and to let the occasional big tipper conduct your breast exam.

How many disgusting men with ugly, red-stained teeth drove up to the stand and tried to grab you when you handed them their betel-nut chew, Julia? Did you fight back? Is that why he shot you?

Betel nut, or *binlang*, is a stimulant grubby Taiwanese men can't get enough of. *Binlang* is utterly unacceptable in most social settings—even in easygoing Taipei—because users constantly spit out the bloody juice as it collects in the mouth, staining the teeth and gums. If you want to chew *binlang*, you have to not care what you look like.

There are many benefits to chewing *binlang*, though. It's better than coffee at keeping drivers alert, which is why it's so often associated with taxi, bus and truck drivers. It has a flavor that outlasts any gum, and it tops cigarettes in terms of effectively delivering mouth cancer to its users.

Best of all are the barely legal, barely dressed women who work at the betel-nut stands, the "betel-nut beauties," or *binlang xishi*. Community standards and furious wives have kept betel-nut stands outside the city limits, relegating them to highways and off-and on-ramps. At night drivers will see stretches of young women in swimsuits and lingerie in their glass-enclosed stands. Visitors to Taiwan think all the women are prostitutes. As I understand it, only the less reputable stands are fronts for hookers, who also sell illegal drugs.

Nonetheless, religious and political leaders have often called for regulation in the industry. A Christian coalition called for the women to completely cover the three Bs: breasts, butts and bellies. But then the tips wouldn't be as good. Anyway, some of the privileged young women at Taipei's throbbing nightclubs weren't dressed that differently from socially and educationally disadvantaged betel-nut beauties.

Are the *binlang xishi* exploited or are they empowered? Maybe a combination of the two? It's hard to say. Many of the women who work at the stands are from broken and poor families. Some stands employ aboriginal girls for a touch of the exotic. The income they earn is on the high side, but they are typically supporting an entire household. One thing is quite clear, though. There is money in it, and the *binlang* stands have a steady inflow from lonely betel-nut addicts. Drugs, tits and asses are recession-proof, and even the most forlorn *binlang* outposts are always hiring. I didn't chew *binlang*, I didn't go to the stands and I hadn't cared about the undeniably seedy world that they operated in.

How could Julia, the valedictorian of our high school and the love of my life, have ended up working as a betel-nut girl? What the hell had happened?

The newspaper article was thin on details of Julia's murder and ended with a call to shut down unlicensed betel-nut stands. I checked my phone to see if the story had been updated, but there was nothing new.

I dropped my phone in my shirt pocket and rubbed my thighs. A truck going by hit a pothole, and the vibration caused some of my soup to dribble over the side of the plastic bowl. I had eaten exactly one bite before I saw Julia's name.

The woman who ran the noodle shop came out from behind the counter, and we regarded each other. She was maybe sixty-five years old and had once been the young bride of a retired soldier from the mainland, who started this beef-noodle-soup stand. Her face was still smooth but had some spots that were only getting darker. She wore Buddhist counting beads and a Taoist pendant around her neck, which had three long and deep scoops taken out of the flesh.

She noticed my puffy eyelids and tear-stained face.

"Ah," she said. "I told you spicy was too spicy for you! And you said you could handle it because you sell spicy food at the Shilin Night Market!"

"I do," I said to one of her spots. "Well, not everything's spicy."

"Look, you didn't even eat any of it and you're crying your eyes out! Let me make you one without chili peppers."

"That's all right. I'm not hungry."

"A young man like you should always be eating."

"I should be going now." I stood up and towered over her.

"Hey, before you go, could you please help me? My son was supposed to be here an hour ago, and it's getting late to set up the offerings for the good brothers. We use the table in the back, but it's too heavy for me to carry. Could you please bring it to the sidewalk for me?"

"No," I whispered.

"No?"

"I can't."

"Do you want your money back? Is that the problem?"

"I have to go."

She grabbed my arm. "This will only take a moment, and I need your help. Don't deny an old woman!"

"Listen," I said, a lot harder than I meant to. "I'm not going to help you set up your stupid little table for your stupid little ghosts!" I was shaking, and I cracked my neck in an attempt to settle down.

"How can you say that?" she said, her eyes brimming with tears.

Part of me felt sorry for her. Another part of me was nauseated, maybe from all the incense. I reached out and touched the woman's left elbow. "Your son will be here soon," I told her before leaving.

In both directions of Jianguo Road, the sidewalks were crowded with offering tables and streaming rivulets of smoke. I couldn't handle it, not right now anyway. Luckily, Da'an Forest Park was nearby. I crossed the northbound lane of the street and walked under the Jianguo Elevated Road, listening to car tires moaning overhead like mournful spirits.

Why had Julia come back to this horrible island? Why was I stuck here now? We didn't belong. After all, neither of us believed in religion or astrology, and Taiwanese are the most superstitious people in the industrialized world. For example, the Da'an District is home to the country's top universities and brightest professors and young people. Yet these supposedly educated people would chuck their books and degrees into the fire if it made them more pious for Ghost Month.

Essentially, Ghost Month is the entire seventh lunar month of the year, when everybody on the island spends nearly five weeks indulging every crazy belief they hold about the spirit world. Supposedly the gates of the underworld are opened and spirits of the dead are allowed to walk among the living once again. It feels like hell's doors have been opened, as the festival usually straddles the two hottest months of the year—July and August.

Why the hell did we need to appease spirits and idols? We Taiwanese are capable of so many miraculous things on our little rocky island, such as building the tallest building on earth and operating the world's largest semiconductor plant. Yet we are also held back by our bizarre beliefs.

Car and house sales fall off during Ghost Month because Taiwanese stay away from big-ticket items out of fear that ancestors would feel they were being neglected. The ghosts could also "claim" such purchases by cursing them. Cesarean delivery rates go up the month before. It's unlucky to give birth during Ghost Month, and if you're unfortunate enough to be born during it, nobody will celebrate your birthday out of fear of offending jealous spirits.

All year round, Taiwanese avoid the number four because it sounds like "death" but love the number eight because it sounds like "luck." Buildings lack fourth floors, and it's not possible to get a license plate with a "4" digit. The way people drive in Taipei, you need all the luck you can get.

Taiwanese also believe China would attack the island should

we formally declare independence, mainly because Beijing vowed to. So we maintain a flimsy fiction to the international community that we are citizens of a wayward Chinese province. In the Olympics, we marched as "Chinese Taipei." How embarrassing. We were like the perennial kid in the playground whose mother made him wear a sweater in the summer—only in our case, if we didn't wear the sweater, she was going to invade and kill indiscriminately.

I FELT A DULL throbbing in my head as I waited for a spot to open up so I could cross the southbound lane of Jianguo Road and enter the park. Traffic was nuts.

All my plans, hopes and dreams collapsed into each other like sections of a blurry telescope being slammed shut. I realized the futility of the stupid life plan I had set for us. How Julia and I were going to live the American Dream and leave behind all the backward thinking and backward politics of Taiwan.

We loved America because it was the kind of place where religion and superstition didn't dictate the culture. The US president didn't burn incense to gods, bow down to idols in temples and worship his ancestors. The Taiwanese president did.

America also didn't have the "black gold" problem that Taiwan had. *Heijin*—the practice of politicians working with the criminal underworld—was an embarrassment to any Taiwanese who truly believed in democracy. Vote buying was rampant. Gangsters openly ran for seats in public office—and won titles and immunity from prosecution while serving.

We didn't think America was perfect, but it was better. It was a country with ambitious people doing great things, not a tiny island that was getting more crowded and dirty every day.

Tens of thousands of Taiwanese attend college in the US. A lot of them intend to come home and become big-shot bankers, lawyers and politicians. In fact, the last three Taiwanese presidents were all Ivy Leaguers. That wasn't our thinking at all, though. Julia and I were done with Taiwan. We thought we were as destined to settle down in America as we were destined to be together forever.

Now, and only now, I realized that it was the stupid teenage dream of a stupid teenager. I was just another in a long line of men in Taiwan talking big and delivering nothing.

Generalissimo Chiang Kai-shek said he'd regroup his military and retake the Chinese mainland. He ended up dying here in exile.

Chen Shui-bian promised he'd fight corruption. Now the former president was in jail for embezzlement and bribery.

I had promised Julia we'd be happy and somewhat successful in America. But in the end, she had been reduced to working at a betel-nut stand, and I was running my family's crummy food stall at the Shilin Night Market.

I checked my phone again. Two more details had been added to the story. Julia hadn't graduated from college, and she had apparently returned to Taiwan a few years ago.

So neither of us had finished school. Damn.

How could she not have graduated? Julia had been the smartest person in high school and possessed an intuition about things that can't be taught. For example, she could guess the number of beans in a glass jar with a single glance. Too bad she hadn't been able to see that I was missing a few marbles.

I punched myself several times in the stomach as I continued pacing on the corner.

"Stupid, stupid!" I yelled. People edged away from me. If a cop were here, he might try to shout some sense into me.

I had bigger things to worry about, like what was I going to do now?

Until I'd learned about Julia, I had been working on Plan B. I was going to return to the US, finish my degree at UCLA, get a great job and then we'd get married. The details of the plan were always a little murky.

Now both of our lives were over. There was no future and the dream was dead. Like my father and my father's father, I was an uneducated yokel cooking up skewers at the night market.

The only girl I'd ever loved was dead, and there wasn't a thing I could do about it. I couldn't even cross the fucking road.

CHAPTER TWO

A phalanx of mopeds and motorcycles that had formed at the last light blasted by as the traffic signal was finally winding down. Businessman riders wore dress shirts or short-sleeved polos. Young and elderly people wore hoodies. Some vehicles carried two people, some carried fully packed plastic crates and many of them carried more than what was probably a safe weight for steering or braking in time. It didn't matter. As long as you wore a helmet, the cops would leave you alone.

When Jianguo Road was mostly clear, I shuffled across the street and entered Da'an Forest Park. On a superficial level, I registered that it was a beautiful place as I walked among the maple and camphor trees. I should come here more often. If I had a better nose, I could probably pick up the magnolia and jasmine scents, but years of grill grease and smoke from the night-market stall have destroyed my ability to smell anything but a customer.

It's a fairly big park considering it's in the middle of Taipei, about sixty-four acres. I had entered at the northern border, Xinyi, right where the MRT stop is. A group of melting Australian pensioners had tentatively entered the park and couldn't decide whether to explore more or enter the subway.

"Pardon me," I interjected. "Are you all lost, mates?" I looked from face to face. About a dozen of them. I searched for the one with the biggest smile. She was wearing a traditional Taiwanese farmer's hat, which featured a wide brim topped with a cone.

"It's our first day here," she said. "Do you think we should spend it in the park or go to Taipei 101?" We all looked up and to the east. Taipei 101, which had been the tallest building in the world from 2004 until 2010, loomed in the distance, a jade pendant hanging down from the sky.

"I think you should be ambitious, since your flight wasn't that long—not as long as it takes the Yanks to get here," I said, pausing for the laughs I knew would come. "Go to Taipei 101, take the elevator up and see Taipei from all directions. Get your bearings and enjoy the air conditioning. You can come back to the park some other time, when you're used to the humidity."

"That's what we'll do, then!"

"Oh, by the way, tonight or any night, you should come to the Shilin Night Market and check out my stand, Unknown Pleasures." I dealt my card out. "My name's Johnny and I've got the best food in Taipei. Follow the map on the back."

"We will definitely stop by," she pledged. I gave it a fifty–fifty chance.

"Please come by," I said, adding, "I'll put a shrimp on the barbie for ya!" They laughed again. Maybe it was fifty-one–forty-nine now.

I waved goodbye. Ah, the happy-go-lucky Johnny Taipei persona. Cultivated over years of calling out and bringing people in like a sideshow barker. Johnny was everybody's best friend. As Jing-nan, I didn't have any friends. Johnny loved being out with people, but Jing-nan wanted to be alone. Johnny was Mr. I Love Taipei. Jing-nan was distant and lost in his thoughts.

With Julia's death, I felt that much more removed from my Johnny personality, even as I slipped him off. I coughed and wiped my mouth. There. Now I was sad again.

I WALKED BY THE children's playground. The multicolored slides and tunnels made it look like a giant board game, big enough to climb over and crawl under. The kids in the sandpit tried to form mountains and monsters before pulverizing them to look for buried treasure.

I continued walking south. The park was just like any in Los Angeles. Palm trees. Big bald spots in the grassy areas. Elderly men playing Chinese instruments.

I came across the open amphitheater near the center of the park. When I was a kid, I'd seen an Elvis imitator on this stage. I remembered that when he spoke English he seemed to have a Filipino accent, but when he sang he sounded just like the recordings.

I looked at the people hanging out on the benches before the barren stage. All the guys seemed to be with their girlfriends or families. I didn't have either anymore. As an orphan I had more in common with the squatters and homeless old soldiers who'd been thrown off the land to make the park.

Somewhere in the park was a Buddha statue that a typical Taiwanese in my distressed state would probably seek out to pray to. I decided that I'd rather see animals than a good-for-nothing statue, so I headed northwest to the giant lotus pond. I leaned against the railing and listened to hidden insects make whirring sounds. The egrets seemed to be out to lunch. I looked over the floating green muck and found a group of turtles doing nothing. It seemed to be a life free of worries.

To my left, three older men in baggy slacks sprawled on top of a bench, mirroring the turtles in the pond. They spoke in a Chinese dialect I didn't know. Maybe they were soldiers who'd been stranded in Taiwan after the Chinese Civil War ended sixty years ago. More likely, younger relatives had brought them over more recently from rural China, thinking they'd be better off in a modern city. The men didn't look or sound too happy to be here. Content Chinese people do tai chi in the park. Bitter Chinese people complain until the sun goes down.

It was a common story, that elderly Chinese couldn't enjoy the urban conveniences of Taipei. They could have anything they wanted except for the foods, places and people they had left behind—which was all they wanted. I know what it's like to be unhappy where you are.

I STILL RUE THE day five years ago when I came back to Taiwan from UCLA because my father was diagnosed with terminal cancer.

My mother was killed in a car accident on the way to the airport to pick me up. After that my father lived only three more weeks.

It was the hardest thing in the world for me to tell my father that his wife was dead. He burst into tears, and the rare display of emotion created an uncomfortable situation for both of us. Then he told me that it was up to me now to keep the food stall going after he was gone. There was an old gambling debt my grandfather had accumulated that had never gone away, and those people had to be paid. I'd known about it, but I hadn't realized how large it was and how little of it we had whittled down over the years. Selling everything my family owned would cover maybe a quarter of the debt. If I tried to return to UCLA, leaving the country without repayment would put a price on my head.

Just like that, my American sojourn was over. I didn't even get to finish my sophomore year.

If only I had taken a different flight or not come home at all, my mother would still be here, I would have an American job and Julia would be alive. Maybe she'd be sunning in her bikini on a California beach with me instead of being shot dead in her bikini at a highway betel-nut stand.

Before we left for college, we had both known that carrying on a long-distance relationship would only distract us from our schoolwork. It would hurt our grades and therefore our prospects for American jobs.

We promised ourselves to each other in the nicest love hotel we could afford, and I told her that while I wouldn't be in touch, I would come for her when I was fully set up in the US.

"I'll just show up at your door with my best suit on, and we'll head to the city hall and get married," I had told her.

"That would be so romantic!" she had said. "You don't have to wear a suit. I know you hate dressing up."

"I have to for the photos! For the kids to see."

"You're so stubborn. I know that's exactly what you'll do."

Now when I remember that exchange, I see her eyes flicker with doubt, her eyebrows twisted with concern. She knew even then I wouldn't come through.

A turtle plopped into the water and startled me. How pathetic was I? I was taken by surprise by one of the planet's slowest-moving creatures.

I checked my phone. No more news on the murder, but I got a text from the *Daily Times*, noting that I might be interested in a related story. I knew there'd be a drawback to registering for updates. The new offering was a story about how an incarcerated member of the infamous Black Sea gang was making allegations that the American Central Intelligence Agency was helping them smuggle in heroin and other drugs on American vessels that weren't subject to search by Taiwanese authorities.

Who cares? I deleted the message. Damn, it was getting late. Almost three o'clock.

In my haste to get back to Jianguo Road, I inadvertently walked by the Buddha I had wanted to avoid. *So you got me after all, huh?*

At least it wasn't the fat, happy guy my parents had prayed to. This statue was of Guanyin, the bodhisattva of compassion. She stood with a serene expression on her face, eyes closed, her dress flowing down in smiling folds.

I WAS STRAPPING ON a helmet when a bus swerved to a stop just inches from my face. A stern-looking man—apparently a shipwreck survivor, judging by his tattered clothes—held a thick rope in one hand and with the other thrust a bottle of cologne at me. "LA Calling."

LA certainly had come calling, and I had gone. Now I was stuck back in Taipei. Pride had kept me from calling Julia and telling her of the change in plan. After all, I might still someday make it back to UCLA, and then everything would be back on track. All I had to do was find a buyer for the night-market stall, and then I could pay off the debt and fly back to Los Angeles. The recession killed that plan, though.

I never heard from Julia when my parents passed away, even though she must have known. I admired her discipline and how she could stick to a promise. Sometimes I was angry she hadn't broken down and called me, but I always loved her for it. Every day I didn't hear from her meant we still had a chance.

Why did we want to be Americans so badly? We were both

smart and ambitious. Not that people who wanted to stay in Taiwan weren't. But whenever there was a global event and Taiwan was allowed by China to take part in it, our national flag was banned, along with our name. It was embarrassing. Especially since we were one of the most advanced economies and societies in the world. Taiwan's continuing strange and strained estrangement from China wasn't going to end anytime soon, and it sure wasn't going to end well—certainly not for the island.

The US didn't take shit like that. The Americans stood up for themselves.

I had wanted to be an American since July 1, 1998. That was when American President Bill Clinton, while on a formal visit to China, said there was only one China and that Taiwan was a part of China. The *Daily Yam*, Taiwan's most inflammatory tabloid, ran a huge headline on its front page: US TO TAIWAN: DROP DEAD.

I showed the newspaper to my father and he said what he always said: "doesn't matter." When I showed him a perfect test score, when I pointed out that another stall in the night market was charging more or less for the same items, when I told him I was going to marry Julia someday.

"Doesn't matter. Doesn't matter. Doesn't matter!"

I wanted to live a life that did matter, and maybe it would in America, because it sure didn't seem to here in Taiwan.

My father was right, though. It didn't matter what I wanted. I was trapped living the same life he had, cutting, cooking and skewering meat for most of the night, a shadowy existence in a shadowy country the US didn't even formally recognize. I had no time for friendship or love, and if I'd had a family, I wouldn't have had time for them, either. My life in Taipei was exactly what I had been afraid it would be—exactly what I'd sworn I'd never be—except when I'd sworn that I'd thought my parents would both be alive until I was old.

Now, I was twenty-five, and my sense of smell was grilled out. But my sensory receptors had compensated by deepening my hearing function, making music more meaningful. My little house was filled with the sound of music, almost always Joy Division. I liked to start the day with a studio or rehearsal recording and end

the day with a live album, to hear and be part of an audience providing visceral reactions—something the band was always able to
provoke.

Joy Division's music captured what Taipei looked and sounded
like. Martial beats of constant construction. The detached vocals
of automatic announcements. Blocks and blocks of dreary, grey
concrete walls scrolling by. The paranoia of closed-circuit cameras
everywhere. Some people say that the songs are depressing, but I
think that they represent life as it is. Here, anyway.

I STARTED UP MY moped, checked both ways on Jianguo Road
and headed north. I went by the noodle stand and saw the offering
table was all set up. It made me feel less bad about being a jerk to
the woman.

At every intersection, the looming Taipei 101 skyscraper to
the east regarded me silently, as the Buddhist statue had. When
I reached Xinyi Road I could see the building in full profile, and
the segments of its body. Driving east on Xinyi Road would bring
me out of the Da'an District and into the Xinyi District, where
the building stood. On the other end of Xinyi Road, to the west
in Zhongzheng District, was the Chiang Kai-shek Memorial Hall
complex. When my class visited the hall, I must have been six years
old. I stood in front of the giant, seated Chiang Kai-shek statue,
scared out of my wits. I couldn't move. Even though he was smiling, I intuitively knew this man was capable of doing horrific things
to his perceived enemies. The Generalissimo, after all, demanded
complete loyalty. Sure, many fathers were that way, but they didn't
have a network of spies and secret police ready to round up and
"disappear" perceived enemies of the people.

I do not believe in spirits, but there are some seriously bad vibes
in that hall. I will never go there again.

The haunted past and the hopeful future of Taiwan shared Xinyi
Road but stood at opposite ends. The sun rises in the east, lighting
up Taipei 101 until the green exterior of the building glows white-
hot like a giant joss stick. The evening sees the Chiang Kai-shek
Memorial Hall lit in red, orange and yellow by the primordial gas
cloud that passes for dusk in Taipei.

Facing west, the homesick statue of the Generalissimo gazes beyond the sunset, toward China.

Chiang Kai-shek was once the face of Taiwan, or Republic of China, as he would have insisted on calling the island. Now every tourist guide to Taiwan had to feature Taipei 101 on the cover. It took the tallest building in the world to replace the Generalissimo.

Caught between the past and the future on Xinyi Road was the famous Din Tai Fung, the *xiaolongbao* restaurant that constantly had lines out the door. The juicy little pork soup dumplings, or "little-basket buns," they made were famous in their now worldwide outlets, but the restaurant on Xinyi was the original location and was everything that an eatery should be—great kitchen, lousy seats.

The preparation area was featured prominently in the window with the staff dressed in immaculate uniforms and wearing face-masks. Making *xiaolongbao* is a precise undertaking, as much as assembling cell phones—each bun has eighteen folds.

The seating area was rather plain and cramped. All the pleasure was in the eating. I'd eaten upstairs a few times with Julia, and we'd always count out the folds of the buns before biting them open to drink the meat-gelatin-and-soup base. One time we ate there, a Japanese film director and his crew were eating near us, becoming progressively louder and drunker. I saw him on a talk show the next day, looking extremely sad. Makeup couldn't cover up his bloodshot eyes. That was the first time I realized how big Din Tai Fung was, and how small my family's business was.

The last meal I'd had at Din Tai Fung was with Julia, so it'd been more than seven years. Shit.

I CROSSED XINYI ROAD, which was choked with traffic. Half the road was being torn up for the construction of an MRT line, and men in hard hats and flip-flops directed traffic to merge. I watched out for frustrated motorists who might try to tear onto Jianguo Road to get by.

I only managed to go a few blocks before stopping for a red light. I put my feet on the ground and sighed. Seven years. All that time felt like my own personal Cold War for love, in that nothing had actually happened. No face-to-face meetings, no negotiations and no quarter given, certainly not to myself. In the face of harsh reality, I'd never doubted my delusion that I was still going to make it out of here and win all my battles. I had been cocky. Now I hunkered down over the handlebars, trying to hide from everything and everybody.

I turned my head and stared at the corner of Jianguo Road and Shimin Boulevard and thought, Julia and I went to that place in junior high, when that 7-Eleven was merely a 7-Eleven knockoff. Our history was disappearing in the present.

Across Shimin Boulevard, I regarded the lobby of Miramar Garden Taipei, a fairly new hotel. That hadn't been there, either, back then. I saw a young woman in a white dress standing just outside the lobby with her back to me. She flipped her chin-length hair with her right hand the way Julia used to. But a lot of girls did that. She looked about Julia's height and the more that I looked at her stance, the more I thought that it could be her.

I wanted to see her face. While I stared at her, waiting for the light to change, she would sometimes turn her head, but not enough. Of course, as soon as the light changed and I took off, she slowly turned to where I could have seen her in full.

She shrank and slid into the chipped lower right corner of my rearview mirror. Had she just stared right at me? I suddenly had to swerve to avoid slamming into the back of a motorcycle carrying two passengers. I don't think they noticed how close I came to hitting them.

What a strange and awful day. I continued north and passed by the trees lining the street at Zhongshan Girls' High School. I thought about my brief walk in the park, going by the children's playground, the pond and the bodhisattva. I sat up in my seat. I'd honestly thought that I'd forgotten where the Guanyin statue was, but maybe subconsciously I had wanted to go there to pray for Julia's soul.

No. She was gone. She didn't have a spirit or a soul. Still, for her to die on the eve of a big holiday for the dead seemed more than coincidental.

I sank back down over my handlebars. Why dwell on it? Why think of anything, anyway? I could hear my father saying "doesn't matter" on repeat. He was right. Nothing mattered in the end.

CHAPTER THREE

In high school we read *A Tale of Two Cities* by Charles Dickens. In the book, Jerry Cruncher derisively refers to his wife's praying for his salvation as "flopping." I thought that was a perfect way to describe the act of *baibai*, bowing to an altar while brandishing a lit joss stick.

Students, who should be the least traditional segment of society, were out in force, *baibai*-ing at the temples like it was a contest. I felt bad for them. Most of them were taking their summer classes, studying their brains out for that senior high school test at the end of ninth grade. I know how hellish it is. Maybe they didn't want to jinx themselves by pissing off the undead.

BOTH MY PARENTS AND the Huangs had loved to go flopping. Julia and I were dragged into temples and forced to inhale the fumes of burning incense, burning fake money and the cigars smoked by the odd folk-religion shaman between prophecies. But Julia's mother was way worse than mine.

For years her mother prayed for a lighter color for Julia's skin. She acted like her daughter was an obsidian idol when in reality Julia was the same beige shade as a generic PC. Mrs. Huang had some herb from a Buddhist monk that she scrubbed over Julia's face to remove the sins from a past life. Her mother hired shamans—*jitong* in Mandarin, although I prefer the Taiwanese *danki*—to perform rituals to continue cleaning Julia's soul and checked in with fortune-tellers at the temples to monitor progress.

I wondered what Mrs. Huang thought about souls and past lives now.

If I allowed myself to believe even for half a second in the superstitions surrounding Ghost Month, I would be terrified for Julia's spirit. It was the worst possible time to die, because with the gates of hell opened and spirits pouring out, the recently departed might become confused and be doomed to wander the earth without rest forever.

But I didn't believe in such things. I believed in facts, science and, every once in a while, human beings.

Ghost Month was also nicknamed National Pollution Month, because of the amount of ash generated by people burning fake money, paper-and-foil houses and cars in braziers and coffee cans to send to the dead. We appeased animal spirits, too. Buddhist monks presided over ceremonies at the pet columbaria for people to send Xiong Xiong the late Chow a nice house complete with dining-table set.

Buddhists believe in the cycle of life, death and reincarnation, so in what realm would these material goods be enjoyed by the loved one? Taiwanese like to cover all the bases. Maybe the cycle of life and death slowed at times, or didn't exist at all. Maybe Xiong Xiong would want to catch a nap under that new dining table.

Religion was stupid and so was belief in a spirit world, I told myself. Julia wasn't a ghost now. She was gone. That was what we believed. No. It was what we *knew*. I shouldn't miss her but I did. I wished I didn't have to feel anything.

I MANAGED TO STEEL myself and stuff down my emotions as I drove to work. It helped that my moped seat was worn and the ride almost always put my ass to sleep.

As the Shilin Night Market came into view, I thankfully felt myself shifting into work mode, Johnny mode. Fake mode. Uncaring mode. Just like I was to those Australian tourists. Put on a smile and a show.

The outdoor market turned the streets into blocks and blocks of everything and anything for sale. All the buildings had ground-floor establishments—sit-down restaurants, clothing stores with changing rooms. The streets themselves were crammed with stands that would soon be dishing out fried, frozen, grilled and raw foods.

The market was devoid of customers, and the continuous bare-metal frames of the unadorned stalls looked like a skeletal dragon splayed out across the length and breadth of the market. Vendors unpacked cardboard boxes and plastic crates. Apart from their usual goods, tonight many of them brought small folding tables to set up rickety altars for the first night of Ghost Month. Shilin Night Market was huge but too crowded to make burning large amounts of fake money feasible. I saw a few ashtray stands for accommodating petty cash offerings to the spirits.

I slowed my moped to a crawl to wriggle through a small flock of bumpkins blocking the road with their two vehicles. Both were half motorcycles welded to oxcarts. With riders in place, they looked like ugly mechanical centaurs fighting each other.

And they *were* fighting. You know the story. An extended family or group of close friends decides to invest together and start a night-market business. After a few weeks, the stand still doesn't come close to breaking even, much less earning money. The distrust sets in. Each investor sends a representative to make sure nobody's pocketing cash. The contempt for the struggling business turns into outright disdain for cheap customers who never buy enough. Before long everything falls apart and the other vendors buy up the used equipment for next to nothing, and the space itself is quickly rented to someone else.

The centaurs were yelling at each other and each other's passengers to dismount and unpack first. I exchanged a few knowing looks with their amused neighbors. One of the drivers relented and drew his contraption back, giving me an opportunity to waddle through on my moped.

DON'T THINK OF MY food stall as a restaurant. I don't. But it is bigger than most of my competition, and I like to think it serves better-quality food.

Shilin District is a residential area, and most of the people who live there stroll in for a snack or two at least once a week. A large population of foreigners lives here, too. A "red hair"—*hong mao* in Mandarin, or if you're down with Taiwanese, *ang mo*—who resides in the neighborhood may not literally have red hair, but she or he can probably speak our language. Their kids can eat grosser things than any American-born Chinese who come through the Shilin Night Market.

Everybody comes here, not just the ABCs and tourists. This night market isn't one of those five-block-long, locals-only rinky-dink operations. It's the biggest one in Taiwan, and the best. All the tourist brochures tell people how to get here in general, but I'll tell you how to get to my specific flavor emporium, Unknown Pleasures.

Here's what you do. Take the red line of the Taipei Metro—the MRT—to Jiantan Station. The stench of stinky tofu should swaddle you even before you leave the elevated station. I suggest bearing east up Dadong Road, away from Bailing High School, unless you want to see mischievous boys trying to swat each other in the nuts and devious girls egging them on.

Yes, continue walking past the large indoor market—sure, there's great food in there, but there's amazing food throughout. Be adventurous! Marvel at the stand that makes sponge cakes in the shape of erect penises that the guy calls "gaykes." Recoil at the thought of eating "frog eggs." (Despite what the stand signs say in English, the dessert jelly *aiyu* is actually made from fig seeds.) Flip through the racks of cheap leather handbags. No brand knockoffs here—this isn't China.

The crowds talk loudly, eat loudly and belch loudly, but they aren't ever pushy. If you're not Asian, people will probably stare openly at you. Take note of what they're wearing and what they're eating. Ask them where they got that cute shirt or those warm blocks of peanut candy and they'll point out the stand. If they say they're eating the best meat skewers ever, then you're probably getting closer to my stall.

Don't let the loud music deter you. That's just a DJ a group of pot-sticker vendors hired to drum up more business. Make a left at the stand that sells underwear with superheroes from Japanese cartoons. If you hit the circle with the OK Mart, you've gone too far. Backtrack through Dadong Road and make a right on Dabei Road, also known as Jeremy Lin Lane because of the shirts, shorts and book bags adorning the merchandise racks there. One of the indoor stores proudly displays in its window a laminated printout of an email from the Jeremy Lin Foundation, thanking a donor for a $50 gift.

You'll find Unknown Pleasures, my food joint, at the northwest intersection of Dabei and Daxi.

Maybe it's a little corny, but I had the interior walls painted black and scraped out the white radio waves that appear on the cover of Joy Division's first album, *Unknown Pleasures*. Some people mistake them for subsea mountain ranges. It looks so cool, and I can't help but think less of people who ask me what the artwork is all about.

Look up at the only non-cluttered sign in the entire market: UNKNOWN PLEASURES is spelled out in English, horizontally, in all capital letters across a back-lit plastic panel, just like it is on the back of the album. A vertical sign in stained wood, lit by the light of the English sign, contains the two characters of the stand's original name, given by my grandfather: *Ke Kou,* or "Tastes Good" in Mandarin.

Phonetically it also sounds like the two characters for "embezzle," or "withholding money." My grandfather had felt that society had robbed him of opportunity, and to scrape by he had to resort to selling skewers made with scrap meat. It's hard to imagine the business's lowly beginnings now.

Incidentally, the first two syllables of Coca-Cola's Chinese name are the same two characters as *Ke Kou.* The soda company has never contacted us, and my father told me we've had the name longer, in case the Americans want to sue us for trademark infringement.

Unlike most joints in the Shilin Night Market, Unknown Pleasures has five solid tables set up with sturdy chairs, all under a roof. The dining area in other places is usually unsteady stools at wobbly foldout tables under cheap umbrella stands that collapse in a sudden windy Taipei downpour.

Please come by and get some skewers to go, or step inside and order a spicy stew from Dwayne, the big guy who mans the counter. Point to the pictures of what you want and you're good. Order more than you think you can eat. Come early during your stay in Taipei so you can come back and eventually try everything on the menu. I need the money.

I PARKED MY MOPED around the corner from Unknown Pleasures, but I couldn't go directly to work. I had to see an old friend first, Dancing Jenny at Belle Amour. She caught me trying to rush by one day and slapped my arm hard. "I know you think I'm just an ugly old woman, but you still have to respect me!" she cried.

Belle Amour's huge illuminated sign dominates our intersection of Dabei Road and Daxi Road and features a full-length curvy silhouette of a woman leaning against the words, one hand holding her ponytail erect. Located on the southeast corner, the store is stocked with upscale dresses and costumes made by up-and-coming Taiwanese and Japanese designers. Jenny Lung Ming-tai is the proprietor of the store and model of the sign. She is prone to wearing leotards from time to time, so everyone calls her Dancing Jenny even though she doesn't dance.

The northeast corner of the intersection is Song Kuilan's dumpling and soup joint, Big Shot Hot Pot. In Chinese characters, the sign says "Big Man Hot Pot." It's right across the street, but none of our offerings compete directly. Kuilan runs the place with her beaten-down husband. Recently she's been able to rope in her petty-criminal son, Ah-tien.

In the span of my memory, our three stores are the lone originals left. Stores too many to count have come and gone. An available stall never lasts long. There's always a cart business that wants to move to a fixed stall on the street next to a storefront, and there's always a fixed stall that wants to move into a storefront. The storefront stores are angling on a corner location. Going back to the beginning, there's always a new cart rolling in with a kid with a vision or a lonely retiree trying to feel useful.

The southeast corner of the intersection is where Julia's family last had a store. Ever since they sold the location there more than a decade ago, there hasn't been a business that has lasted more than two years on the corner. The current business is a sci-fi toy store called Beyond Human.

When we were still kids, I wrote our initials as small as I could in a wet concrete patch on the corner and enclosed them in a tiny lopsided heart. It was visible for less than a year before that part of the sidewalk was tiled over, chipped out and paved over again. Building materials don't endure in Taipei's heat, rain and humidity. Only human flesh does.

AT THE DOORSTEP OF Belle Amour, I took a deep breath and exhaled. I tried to forget everything. It was show time.

"Jenny!" I called out as I stepped into her store. "Where's my favorite vendor in the whole market?" I have to be fully in my Johnny-night-market persona when I see her. When I act shy, she pinches my nipples.

A motion-activated alarm announced my arrival, playing the chorus to "Lady Marmalade." The inside of her store was lit with a series of vintage-style filament light bulbs, which gave the place a filtered-lens, Instagram-inspired feel. Her offerings were divided into three aisles of double-decker racks. Most of the floor was bamboo wood, but the two dressing rooms in the back were carpeted—some customers wanted to make sure they were able to get down on their hands and knees comfortably while wearing certain outfits.

"Ah, Jing-nan!" Jenny cried as she came out of the middle and narrowest aisle. She set aside a bundle of dresses on the counter and kissed my cheek. For me, being extroverted is an act, but Dancing Jenny was genuinely flirty and flashy, her fingers and lips brushing your skin. Some said she was that way because she had been abroad. Some said she was into broads.

She was in her late thirties and stood a little shorter than me. Her arched eyebrows taken alone were severe, but her soft eyes and small smile gave her face an inviting look overall. Anybody who obsessed over the silhouette in her sign wouldn't be disappointed upon seeing her.

Jenny opened up the place by herself when she was a teenager, and she was the first woman I ever saw wearing an exposed corset. My father slapped me upside my head because I wouldn't stop staring. Her outfits are a lot less risqué these days, but a lot of boys and men still like to ogle her. Some women, too.

She pulled back and turned to her side, exposing the slit in a paisley skirt that seemed too short to have a slit.

"What do you think?" Jenny asked. Her hands came together at her waist and she instinctively picked at her cuticles.

"It seems way too short. I like it."

Visibly relieved, she fixed her hair. "I'm glad you do, Jing-nan. This designer has been such a pain in the ass to work with. But she does such great stuff!" She retreated back down the aisle. I heard a zipping sound and her feet shuffling. "Do you think we'll have a big crowd tonight?" Jenny yelled.

"How can we not? The holiday's about to start, and foreigners are pouring in."

"I hope they feel like buying stuff. This economic downturn has them acting all cocky. I swear, the white people never tried to bargain so hard until Wall Street bit it."

"Let them! They're celebrating Taiwanese night-market culture when they bargain."

Jenny came from behind a rack of designer shirts and gave me a little push. "Whose side are you on?" She had changed into a pair of form-fitting denim shorts, a short, beaded shirt that exposed her midriff and a trucker hat with nonsensical graffiti in English sprayed across the front foam panel.

"Always on your side, Jenny! It's the only safe side!" I held up my hand and we did a high five. "Have a great night," I said.

"You, too," she called out as I left.

My next stop was Big Shot Hot Pot.

Kuilan's son, Ah-tien, was at the front counter, seasoning a spicy soup base and a sour soup base. When he saw me, he gave the smallest nod and yelled out for his mother before assuming a sullen and resentful look. The son and I had never really hit it off. He was a bit of a delinquent and seemed to regard people who finished high school as sellouts. I shuffled my feet as the silence between us swirled and thickened like the soup.

Ah-tien was thirty, five years older than me, and still wore the buzz cut left over from conscription. He probably hated me because I'd been able to defer the mandatory military service, and then had been excluded from it because I was an orphan and running a business that employed others.

His black tank top showed off tattoos of tigers as well as a *ba gua*, the octagon-shaped Taoist symbol with a black-and-white yin-yang swirl in the middle. The collar was low enough to expose the face of a dragon with lobster-like eyestalks. He noticed me looking and puffed his chest out more.

I had never done anything to make him hate me, but I'm sure his mom had beaten him over the head with my good example of what a son should be. I had heard Kuilan talk about Ah-tien, always in a disparaging way, for years before I actually met him. I thought she was doing the overly modest thing parents do. Maybe this supposed "bad kid" was really the class salutatorian and not the valedictorian, merely an above-average pianist and not a virtuoso. Maybe the "trouble" Ah-tien was having with the cops was just an argument about a parking ticket.

Ah-tien's slouching form showed up at the night market about two years ago. The first time I saw him, with his tattoos, wild eyes and suspiciously crooked fingers, I had no idea who he was. This man I didn't know was counting money and smoking in the men's restroom in the indoor part of the night market. I looked at him, not accusingly, but with curiosity.

He straightened up and seemed pleased he was taller than I was. Thinking that I was focused on the cash, Ah-tien stuffed the wad partially in his front pocket. Try to take it, kid, his smirk seemed to say. Then he coolly rubbed out his cigarette on the plastic No Smoking sign and left without saying a word.

Less than an hour later, Kuilan brought him over to Unknown Pleasures and introduced him to me.

"Jing-nan is a *good* young man!" she emphasized, to my horror.

I got my hand to him as quickly as possible and we shook. I'd never met anyone with scars on their palm before.

"Hello," he said in a quietly furious voice.

From now on, Kuilan said, Ah-tien was going to be working at her stall, and he and I were going to be best friends. I nodded and faked a smile. Ah-tien was better at it than me. We hadn't had a substantial exchange of facial expressions since.

KUILAN GREETED ME WITH her hands on her hips and a nod. She had to be in her early sixties now, but she still looked the same as when I first saw her two decades ago. Kuilan often cited her Mongolian blood for her strength and slightly heavier-than-average build.

"Jing-nan, I forgot my hat today," she said. "All this flour in the air is going to turn my hair even more grey!"

"That's the only way I can tell the difference between you and Dancing Jenny," I said.

She rubbed her ears. "You're just a kidder! I know I look like her father. Say, have you heard about that new rumor going around? The district is going to pass a law that we're all going to have to close by midnight!"

I laughed out loud, but too heartily for the beginning of Ghost Month, so I dialed it back a little. "There's no way they could do that! Midnight is when Taiwanese first get hunger pangs."

"It's the tourists they're thinking about. The image of Taipei is that we're too morally loose, eating so many hours after the sun has gone down. Christians think it's a sin! I know because my sister married a Christian. They call it 'gluttony.'"

"The problem is that your soups taste too good!"

Kuilan's son had had enough of our small talk. He wiped his hands on his apron, jammed a cigarette in his mouth and headed outside.

"Hey, Ah-tien!" his mother snapped at him. "You haven't finished yet!"

He didn't bother to remove the cigarette to talk back. "They have to simmer now. Do you expect me to make time go faster?"

"Why can't you be like Jing-nan? Look how nice he is. Everybody likes him, and he's never in trouble." Luckily Ah-tien was out of earshot before she was even halfway done talking. She sighed and said to me, "I just hope the tourists and not the good brothers are hungry for our food. I'll set another table outside for them."

I didn't want to, but I thought of Julia. I imagined her in pain and confused, wandering about with no relief, covered in blood.

"Do you want some water, Jing-nan?"

"No, thank you."

"You're swallowing a lot."

"Your soup smells so good."

"Such a kidder! So funny! How come you're not married yet?"

I laughed soundlessly, feeling a cutting motion across my guts. "It's not time yet."

"Are you kidding me? When I was your age, I was already picking out baby names!" At that remark, Kuilan's rarely seen husband, Bert, poked his head out from the kitchen in the back. He seemed to be sitting on a stool, and his hands were dutifully twisting dumpling skins over ground-pork fillings.

"Kuilan, looking at your husband reminds me that I should get my own show on the road. Don't sell so many that you fill up my customers!"

"Bert!" Kuilan chastised him. "You didn't say hi to Jing-nan the entire time he was standing here, and now he's leaving!"

"Uh?" Bert looked up at her in awe before focusing on me. "Yes, hello, Jing-nan. You're a good worker and a testament to what a good son is."

I walked out just in time. Ah-tien was coming up Dabei Road, wearing a big pair of noise-canceling headphones.

I APPROACHED UNKNOWN PLEASURES with more than the usual dread. I was an actor who had lost his motivation. I wasn't fully confident I could pull off the role tonight.

My two employees—colleagues, really—were prepping for the evening's business.

Dwayne, the half aborigine who cooked and did pretty much everything else at the indoor counter, ran out and grabbed me around my arms. He didn't use his customarily tight grip. It was soft. Caring, even. It brought me back to reality.

"I read all about Julia," he said. "I'm so sorry."

Shit. Dancing Jenny and Song Kuilan didn't pay attention to the news and Dwayne did?

I slumped a little. Dwayne led me inside to a metal prep table next to the sink in the corner. I sat down and lay my head sideways on top of my folded arms. Dwayne slid over a serving of spicy entrails stew in a ceramic bowl.

It looked and smelled exactly how my grandfather and father used to make it. The pig intestines and the pudding-like, coagulated lumps of duck blood were in the same proportion. We hadn't slipped at all. If I didn't hate my life completely at this moment, I'd say that I was rather pleased.

"Eat up, Jing-nan. Best thing you can do," Dwayne said. He pulled out a chair and sat on it backward so he could perch his upper body on the backrest. He was close enough for me to see the red lightning-bolt veins radiating from his pupils. "This is terrible news, but we need you to be functional tonight, boss."

He tilted his head down and regarded me over his cracking knuckles. You couldn't tell he was part Amis. Dwayne looked like just another dark-skinned Taiwanese man in his late thirties, albeit on the heavier-built side. He fought back against his receding hairline by maintaining a crew cut.

I watched my hands turn the bowl of soup clockwise ninety degrees. "You remember Julia well, don't you, Dwayne?"

"'Course I do. Me and the Cat both remember her. Wonderful little girl. Real nice and smart and pretty."

From the other prep table on the other side of the sink, Frankie the Cat closed his eyes and nodded to us. Frankie was in his seventies, but he was ageless and silent in his appearance and movements. As always, he wore a clean, white long-sleeved kitchen uniform in spite of the humidity. With his big smile and oversized eyeglass lenses, he looked like the Cheshire Cat. Now, though, his mouth had sobered into two sad earthworms.

Dwayne and Frankie. Those were not their given names, but like a lot of people at the night market, such as Jenny, they were on their second or third chance at life. I was at a disadvantage here because I only knew certain episodes from their pasts, but Dwayne and Jenny had known me for most of my life, and Frankie, all of it. I couldn't pretend to be someone different around them; that's why they called me Jing-nan and not Johnny.

My right hand picked up a pair of chopsticks, and I watched red oblong shapes of hot oil stretch and slide into the hollow of the soup spoon my left hand was pushing into the soup. Steam lightly scorched my forehead as I bent down and ate mechanically.

"You and the Huangs haven't been close in a few years, right?" Dwayne asked.

"I think the last time I saw Julia's parents was at the funeral," I said. "The funerals, I mean. Those were the last conversations I had with them. They sure sold their stall at the right time, when the economy was good."

"What about Julia? You never . . . talked?"

The evening was getting a little too real for me. I had hoped to grieve inside and keep everything I felt in that soundproof darkroom with no doorknob. But Dwayne had kicked in that door and turned on the lights. I wasn't used to talking to him in this way, either. We both had these playfully antagonistic, guy-guy personalities that we wore during work hours. When my parents died, he had mercifully said next to nothing. Now he wanted me to talk things out?

I scooped a few peppercorns from the stew into my mouth and crunched them one by one, feeling a burst of hurt every time.

"It was so stupid, Dwayne," I said to a shaky reflection of myself in a shimmering oval of chili oil. I slurped up a stretch of chewy intestine. It broke easily in my mouth, with just the right amount of give. The ginger flavor had burst through the spicy firewall and became prominent in my mouth. "You knew about my plan, right?" I asked when my mouth was empty enough.

"Sure I did. You guys were going to ignore each other for a few years and then you were going to swoop in one day like a prince on a horse. Just like *Sleeping Beauty*."

"Not quite *Sleeping Beauty*." I stirred the stew and watched a cloud of pickled cabbage surface briefly. I picked out a dried chili that looked like a little devil's tongue. I chewed it but didn't swallow. "More like *Snow White* without the prince showing up. I couldn't pull it off, Dwayne."

"You tried. It was beyond your control."

That set me off, because I wasn't ready to stop blaming myself yet. "Beyond my control! Everything's beyond my control! Look at me. Still doing the same shit my parents and grandfather—"

Dwayne stood up and kicked the chair across the tile floor. Frankie simply lifted his leg and clamped the chair down before it could fly into the street.

"Hey, you watch your mouth, Jing-nan!" said Dwayne. "This is a respectful business and one of the best restaurants in the market. Your grandfather, rest his spirit, and your parents, rest their spirits, put everything they had into this to make life better for you. For us, too."

"I'm sorry, Dwayne. I didn't mean to insult you. You too, Frankie."

"Don't apologize to me and the Cat. We can take it. You apologize to your ancestors and set up an offering table for them. You have to. It's bad enough that you took out the Guan Gong altar when you redesigned the place." Like most Chinese gods, Guan Gong was based on an actual person, a famous general, in fact. He's the red-faced guy holding a giant sword with a blade that looks like a lobster claw.

"No more fake gods here," I said, my throat raw from the spices and anger.

"The previous management would be appalled!"

"It doesn't matter, because I'm in charge now!"

"You lousy Han Chinese," Dwayne said. "You destroyed my culture and you don't even respect your own!"

Finally. We were both going back into work mode. Dwayne was the indignant native Taiwanese and I was the super-upbeat Johnny Taipei. Wrestling was definitely on the menu tonight. Frankie the Cat was going to go on being his silent self as he kept the stews fully stocked and fresh ingredients prepped throughout the night. The guy runs in the background like security software on a computer network.

I charged back into the stew with renewed vigor, never once letting go of my chopsticks or spoon. I wiped my forehead with the back of my right forearm and ate until there was nothing but pepper grit at the bottom of my bowl. I heard a scraping sound. Frankie was pushing out the front grill—Johnny Taipei's pulpit—to the street. I stood up and put my bowl and utensils in the sink.

"Be happy," I told Dwayne. "It's the first day of you-know-what and we're going to make a lot of money."

"Oh, I know. Your restless undead are up and walking, trampling upon my people's graves."

"There's no rest for us because we're going to have customers in two seconds, my good *Pangcah*."

"You don't get to call me that! Only Amis get to call each other that. The way you say it, you murder my language."

"Then how do you say it?"

Dwayne snickered and wiped his face. He went to the big back grill and tossed more wood chips and charcoal under it.

At some point Frankie had cleared out the sink, and now he was washing out pig and cow intestines, stomachs and chicken butts. The water washed down through a tube to a metal vent in the street curb. Who knew where that went to. The air smelled like wet feces and blood. It was comforting and felt like home.

I strode out to the front grill, feeling brand-new.

"That's my boy, Johnny," said Dwayne softly.

I set up the smaller skewers in a display behind my sneeze guard, to catch the eyes of people walking by. When they got hooked, people could move on to the larger skewers inside. Frankie brought over a tub of marinated, chopped-up meats and entrails. We each gathered a handful of wet bamboo skewers and began to spike them until they were full. As I stood shoulder-to-shoulder with Frankie, he regained his full smile.

I remember making my first skewer, setting it on the grill and watching it burst into flames—I didn't know the skewers had to be soaked in water first. It was good for a laugh for my grandfather and parents, but Frankie came over with tongs, tossed out the burned skewer and showed me how to do one properly. This was before Dwayne came on the scene and years before I'd be working there.

I looked at Frankie's fast fingers. He had trained to be a soldier as a child, and that rigid discipline was still there.

Down the street, someone had set off fireworks. They were supposed to be banned in the night market. They always bend the rules a little around holidays.

Foot traffic was going to be heavy tonight. Some Taiwanese would be staying in for the night, but an influx of tourists would more than make up for the loss. There would also be ICLP and MTC students coming off the summer semesters, looking to blow off steam. Kids in the International Chinese Language Program and Missionary Training Center and other classes come from all over the world, and they're into eating and buying night-market food.

A cloud of smoke and grease anointed my face. My worries and cares were sliding away. Jing-nan was the guy who had just lost his one and only love for good. Johnny was the hawker who always had a good time, was the life of the party and loved to show off his English to the foreigners. Johnny didn't care about the dead. He lived life to the fullest.

Johnny made the most of the night market even before it was fully dark out.

He noticed a group of young white girls reading the stand's sign and talking among themselves from a safe range.

"Hey, you," I yelled out in English to the tallest one. "You're an American, right?"

"What else could I be?" she said, laughing. She approached, and five of her friends followed in a tight formation. First time in Taiwan. Probably first time in Asia. The girls' sunburned faces showed that they had already been here for a few days.

"You could be other things," I said. "People come to Taipei from all over the world. But you and your friends talk like Yanks."

"We thought the night market would be busier, but there's, like, hardly anybody here."

"You guys are early! The sun's still out, people are just getting up right now!"

The women laughed. They say white people all look the same, but that's not true at all. Their skin tones were all different, even with the sunburns, and their faces were all distinctive. They don't all smile like Kate Hudson and Naomi Watts.

"Your English is really good," the tallest woman said. "I knew there was something special about this stand because it was named Unknown Pleasures."

"I love Joy Division, and that's one of my favorite CDs." I'd changed the English name from Tastes Good to Unknown Pleasures five years ago, when it was clear that I'd be stuck here for the fore-seeable future. I'd meant it mostly as a tribute to Joy Division, but another meaning for me was that the word "unknown" indicated that I wasn't sure what I was doing, and I certainly didn't know if it would be "pleasurable." I also figured a lot of cool people would be into it.

The American said, "I've never really listened to Joy Division. But we're from Pittsburgh and there's a store with the same name that sells sex toys."

"The Pittsburgh Pirates!" I said, wielding an imaginary bat and swinging. "Well, we sell food, not toys. But if you want to try some sheep penis, I can help you!"

Her friends squealed in horror and fascination.

The American partially extended her index finger and tentatively pointed to some well-done mini pork and chicken sausages.

"What are those?"

"Sausages. Just pork and chicken. Nothing strange, I promise."

"Are they good?"

"They're the best in the whole world!" I plucked them from the grill with my tongs and released them into a crystalline bag. "Use this toothpick," I told her. "Just eat it out of the bag."

All the other women wanted the same exact things. I was only able to convince one of them to try a skewer of grilled pig intes-tines, and I think she planned to pose for pictures with it. I busied myself with bagging up sausages.

I was glad they didn't want sit-down food. I could tell they were old friends who hadn't seen each other in a while and they would linger for a long time.

"What's your name?" the tall American asked. Her eyes gleamed with newfound interest, since the language barrier wasn't an issue.

"Please call me Johnny," I said, not pausing one second in my bagging motions. "What's your name?"

I realized I was taking a huge risk by opening this door. Ameri-cans love to talk about problems they're having and issues in their families with people they don't even know. I was willing to take the extra step to make them feel more comfortable. After all, I had wanted to be an American, and a big part of being American was that you couldn't be shy about physical contact with the people you met. Everybody wanted to hug.

"My name is Megan." She extended a hand. I shook it briefly, pushed a sausage-filled bag into her palm and patted her knuckles lightly with my fingers.

"Please pass this to your friend," I said.

I had met several women named "Megan" at UCLA. Me-gan. It sounded like "not dry yet" in Mandarin.

"I'm here for the ghost celebrations," Not Dry Yet said.

I glanced at the other people in her group. They stood nearby, anxious to get their food and pleased they could buy it from someone fluent in English. Otherwise, they wouldn't trust that the food was safe for eating.

"Be careful!" I warned the woman. "You can't say the word 'ghost.' It's bad luck. Call them 'good brothers.'"

"Oh, no! I've been saying it all day!"

"It's all right," I said. She was safe. No gluttonous spirits would try to possess an American body. Too many food allergies. "Also, don't whistle, Megan. That attracts good brothers." I handed the remaining bags out to Megan's friends.

"But what do I do if I see a really cute guy?"

"Then just go up and talk to him," I said, laughing uncomfortably. "I saw some cute guys go around the corner over there."

She and her friends had paid and were already nibbling. Sure enough, one woman was posing for pictures with the intestine skewer poised over her extended, studded tongue. I wished they would all just keep walking.

"The whole thing is a Taoist holiday, right?" Megan asked. "Some other people were calling it Buddhist, and I was correcting them."

"All of you are right. In the seventh lunar month both Buddhists and Taoists celebrate their ancestors, so it's all mixed. Everybody celebrates—well, not 'celebrates'—let's say 'participates in' the holidays."

"Are all Taiwanese people as nice as you?" she asked, playing with her right earring.

I looked directly at Megan. She seemed to be sincere. I think she liked me, too. I knew she did. But that wasn't enough of a reason for us to open up and start talking about the island's problems and what I hated about Taiwan.

After all, I was fully conscious that underneath this persona, I was crying my eyes out over Julia.

I nodded at Megan and gave a big, platonic smile. "Oh, yes," I said. "Everybody in Taiwan is very nice."

"I'm going to be here for a few days," she said. "Maybe you can show me around a little."

"I think you would find a taxi tour very interesting."

Dwayne didn't understand much English, but he read the woman's big smile and the tilt of her head.

"Tell her you're married!" he yelled out in Taiwanese. "Say your wife keeps a padlock around your cock and you don't know where she hides the key!"

Frankie the Cat's smile curled up tighter at the ends.

Fearfully, I looked at Megan, but she hadn't understood. Most tourists, if they spoke anything other than English, only knew the official and formal Mandarin dialect.

I looked directly at Megan's chin and said, "My boss says my wife will be really jealous if she sees us talking."

"You're married? I thought you were like twenty!"

"No," I said, not smiling. "I'm a very old man." I glanced over at potential customers buzzing near the stall, hoping she would get the hint to leave. Her friends had already moved on to Dancing Jenny's Belle Amour.

Megan brushed her hair back over her ears and said, "Anyway, happy holiday, Johnny!"

"Thank you, Megan," I said, sounding as sincere as possible and nodding perfunctorily.

Three Asian men in their thirties stood a few footsteps away. They looked like guys who had stepped out of the office early. I could tell they were on the fence.

In Taiwanese, I said, "Better get your food now and go home early before the brothers come out and get you!"

They chuckled and came over. They ended up getting some appetizers up front and stews inside. People say it takes money to make money. It also takes customers to make customers. A small line had formed to sit inside, and that generated more interest. I was running out of skewers on the front display grill, so Dwayne transferred over a few tubs of partially cooked skewers.

"Thank you, Megan," he said in a high-pitched whine. I kicked him lightly with my right heel.

DURING A SMALL SLOW period around 11:30 P.M., Dwayne caught me offguard. I should have been ready. When there are no customers, it's high school guy-guy time, and my ass was pretty much up for grabs, along with my private parts. In school, when the teacher's back was turned, you had to practically cover your crotch with one hand. Taiwanese boys punch and kick each other in the balls just for laughs.

Dwayne snuck up behind me and pinned my arms back. The smell of his sweaty arms and neck, smeared with burned fat and grease and blood and shit from dirty intestines, would have made me gag if I didn't smell so strongly of all those things myself.

"That's it, you lousy Han Chinese people," Dwayne grunted with pleasure. "We're taking revenge for all the years that you people have mistreated our tribes."

"We gave you the Great Warmth a few years ago," I said, referring to the stimulus bill that targeted disadvantaged populations, including those of aboriginal descent. I struggled to find the weak spot in Dwayne's grip.

"You gave us the Great Warmth of your farts," spat Dwayne.

Frankie the Cat sat on a plastic stool, put his back against a wall and lit up a cigarette.

"The English, Dutch and Japanese murdered you off, too," I said dryly.

"We'll get to them soon enough, you dirty Han! It's only because your parents were kind to me that I will spare your life and also the life of one potential mate. Now pick one!"

"So we're going to play this game again, huh?"

"Hey, how about Dancing Jenny? I know you think of her when you beat off!"

"Yeah, but I haven't since last week."

"What about her?" Dwayne still had me swaddled in his grip. He turned my entire body and pointed my face at a woman in a low-cut dress sucking on a frozen melon pop.

"She's not quite my type."

"Don't tell me her tits aren't your type!"

"I look for many things in a woman, not just her body parts."

"I think you like her," growled Dwayne. While trying to keep a firm hold of my waist, he worked his hands down my stomach to my crotch. "I'm going to check if your dick's hard."

He was trying to do too much at once. This was my chance.

I turned to my side and dug into his chest with my right elbow until he had to let go.

"I'm going to put a skewer in my boxers so the next time you reach in for my cock you'll shish kabob your fingers!" I told Dwayne.

"Your thing's so small, it's already a skewer!" We clasped right hands and Dwayne cradled my head with his left hand. "I'll make you a warrior yet!" he told me.

Frankie dropped his cigarette and clapped his hands. "C'mon, boys!" he yelled. "Customers!"

CROWDS BEGAN TO TAIL off shortly after one in the morning, and market stalls began to close around one thirty. Sometimes it's later, sometimes it's earlier. A few savvy people rushed around to get great last-second deals at stands. To the south, on the other side of the night market, the secondary stalls opened up in the little lanes between Dadong Road and Wenlin Road. This is where the people who work at the Shilin Night Market come to relax after a long night, eat soup noodles and omelets, chew betel nut and play mahjongg. If you are a tourist, do not go to the after-market. Non-vendors are not welcome. After all, this is their safe space, where they can stretch and complain about people like you, in addition to life in general. I didn't go there, either. For one thing, I didn't want to hang out any longer than I had to at the market.

I was cleaning the counters when Dancing Jenny stopped by. All she had to do to close was roll down her metal gates and padlock them. She was now wearing a blue linen blouse and matching skirt that went past her knees.

"Jing-nan," she said, "I'm going to Cixian Temple. Do you want to come?"

The temple was less than two blocks away. Supposedly the night market grew out of stands that sold snacks to worshippers more than a century ago.

"I'm not going, Jenny. You know I don't believe in that stuff."

"I don't really believe, either, but why take a chance?"

"He's taking a chance going the other way," said Dwayne. "I'll see you there, Jenny."

"Don't take too long," she told him before turning back to me. "It will just take a minute, Jing-nan. Just light some incense. That's all."

"I'm not going."

"Even if you don't believe, your ancestors did, so do it for them."

"I'm already running this stand for them. Jenny, please. Don't ask again."

"Frankie, are you going to talk some sense into him?"

Frankie briefly looked up from scrubbing the grill surfaces and shrugged. "He's my boss. I can't tell him what to do."

Jenny sighed. "I'll see you tomorrow, Jing-nan."

"I have some leftover skewers, if you're hungry, Jenny," I said.

"Not for me, I'm vegetarian for the month."

After she left, Dwayne poured a watered-down detergent on the floor and scrubbed a stiff brush over the tiles. As he worked, a light foam built up on the floor. It looked like a toothpaste commercial with a close-up of the toothbrush cleaning the teeth.

I sorted and counted up the cash.

"It was a good night again, gentlemen," I said.

"Of course it was," said Dwayne. "You got the two best workers in the world here. Frankie, how about we unionize? That way the little bastard will pay us a fair salary."

Frankie's face twitched, looking like he checked a sneeze.

The work night ended with me paying out Dwayne and Frankie, and giving Frankie some more to shop for tomorrow's ingredients.

Dwayne got up close to me and warned, "I'm going to say prayers for Julia. I don't care what you think."

I'd had my phone charging the whole night and hadn't had a chance to check it. There was no more news about Julia, but I had an update on the supposedly related story. The incarcerated Black Sea member had made a new allegation: the American CIA was operating fronts owned by the gang. An anonymous senior member of the Legislative Yuan, our parliament, said the allegation was ridiculous and that the CIA hadn't been in Taiwan "since the Cold War ended."

Doesn't matter, I thought as I slid on my helmet.

CHAPTER FOUR

Driving southwest along the grimy Tamsui River on my moped, I felt Johnny peel away like sunburned skin. I allowed myself to picture Julia for the first time in hours and felt my heart slowly fossilize.

I was driving the same route our families used to drive back home from the night market. Some of my earliest memories were of riding in the open air on the back of a pickup truck. Julia and I, still aged in the single digits, sat on loose cushions and held on to each other while our mothers grabbed rope holds on either side of the truck bed and shouted over the engine about how much better the other's stall was doing. Our fathers sat in the cab together in silence, blowing trails of cigarette smoke out of either side.

I don't remember talking to Julia much during those rides home, because usually we were barely awake. I yawned a lot, yielding tears that turned cold when whipped by the wind. On the night of my ninth birthday, Julia leaned in and kissed my cheek, and I quickly kissed her back on the forehead. We held each other tighter. Blood was rushing past my ears and I couldn't hear a sound, not even what our amused mothers were saying.

I SHOOK MY HEAD to adjust my helmet and regarded the Tamsui for a few seconds. It looked like two rivers—one of black water near the banks flowing south, with a multicolored midstream sliding north.

The road was notably less crowded than usual. Many people thought it was important to avoid going near or into the water during Ghost Month. The spirits of people who perished at sea are sure to possess you, as they are wont to do. Considering Taiwan's long history of harboring Japanese and Chinese pirates in its coves, there must be scores of soggy, angry souls.

But I wasn't going to change my route and avoid the river for the sake of superstition. If I had it my way, and if I wasn't still a bit of a coward, I wouldn't even light up the incense at home for my ancestors.

I wondered if I should have gone to the temple for Julia. She would have hated it.

An idea took form in my head. Maybe the murdered girl wasn't her. Maybe it was a case of mistaken identity. Of course. I took a deep breath. The only way I could be certain that it was Julia was to visit her parents.

It would be rude to simply call the Huangs, considering how close our families had been and how many years it had been since I'd seen them. I had to show up in person. The thought made me feel helpless, afraid of what I'd find. I could understand why one would seek solace in charms and temples. Suffering sucks.

I slouched to my right side and regarded the river again, this time in despair.

My gut felt like a friend at the other end of the seesaw jumped off and my ass slammed on the ground. Thinking about that playground made me think of school. Thinking of school made me think of Julia. Thinking of Julia made me want to die.

I took my hands off the handlebars and folded my arms over my windbreaker. Julia, I thought, if you're dead and can somehow hear me, please come and knock me into the river. Right now. I could accept it from you. Do it! Now! We can be together again!

Suddenly I panicked and brought my hands back down. How foolish would it be to get in an accident for such a silly stunt? It certainly didn't make sense to tempt fate when I had already taken the precaution of wearing a helmet. In order to fight superstition one had to be practical, and it was practical to keep both hands on the handlebars.

My eyes drifted over to the river again. It was a little unnerving to see my reflection in the water followed by two small blobs of white light. Streetlamps? My parents?

Stop looking.

I turned as the road followed a bend in the river. The buildings on the other bank scrolled by with the curvature. At night all cities looked the same from the highway. What I saw now could easily pass for LA.

If only my father had been healthy for two more years, I could have finished college.

Time was the cruelest change agent. Back then, two years would have meant the world. Without them, the last unremarkable seven years had gone by as fast and as meaningless as oncoming traffic.

Ten years from now, I could be driving the same dark route home—I hoped on a better moped, at least. Where would I be in my life at that point? Married? A father? Maybe still lonely?

What a pathetic turnaround from being Johnny. I chuckled to myself darkly. One minute he's chatting up tourists and they're hitting on him. The next, he's ready to kill himself.

Julia might be gone for good now, but I hadn't spoken to her or even seen the woman in years. You can't be hurting for someone whom you've been out of touch with for this long, can you?

I always felt that she was near, though. Sometimes even as a physical presence. Some nights I slept on one side of the bed to make room for her, and I saw her in my dreams at least once a week.

I dropped my head and wiped my nose with my right shoulder.

It was best that Julia never saw what became of me. What woman would want a man who came home late seven nights a week, smellier than a fried chicken ass and tired as shit?

I knew that not getting married and having kids as soon as possible was an affront to my ancestors. Ghost Month was supposed to be the time to show what a good descendant you were, but I showed my filial piety all year round by keeping the food stand going. I didn't need to fanatically burn heaps of incense. The smell rising up from the main pit stoked by Dwayne was strong enough to reach the spirits of my mother, father and grandfather even if their ethereal sinuses were stuffed with ectoplasm.

SOON ENOUGH I WAS back in the Wanhua District. I think it's the oldest part of Taipei, but it's hard to tell with the constant tearing down and building up all over the city.

Zoning is a joke in Wanhua. Futuristically textured green office towers with solar paneling abut older buildings with birdcage bars over the windows and rust smears running down the grey concrete outer walls like parrot droppings. Webs of television, telephone and electric cables wind all around the upper floors for blocks and across streets.

I pushed my moped down a narrow alley crowded with incompetently parked cars and piles of bricks, stones and other building materials. There were little gaps in the piles where people had helped themselves to a tile or five.

The alley tightened up even more, leaving barely enough room for me to walk my moped. Corrugated aluminum was used piecemeal to patch walls on either side of me, and algae-stained ridged-plastic strips that jutted out overhead served as rain gutters. It was like walking through a forest of trees with leaves made of crinkle-cut potato chips.

There were fewer prostitutes on the street than there used to be, so in that sense the neighborhood was improving. Commercial sex now happens at the all-night barbershops and the upscale karaoke joints, abbreviated around here as "KTVs."

The alley opened up into a concrete parking lot, and I walked by a group of guys in their twenties and thirties, *jiaotous*, leaning against a BMW with smoked windows. In LA you wouldn't think much of men in flowery shirts and flip-flops, but in Taipei they are the local enforcers. Everybody has their own "corner leaders" to protect the neighborhood against *jiaotous* from other areas.

It wouldn't be right to call *jiaotous* "gangsters." They are more hyper-local outfits. They don't own more than a few blocks. Most of their money comes from running the local temple—a major source of tax-free income—and bars and nightclubs. They're laid-back guys, happy to collect protection money and keep the temples looking good for festivals.

Full-on Taiwanese gangs are much different. They're run like businesses, and their members are disciplined and professional. It's in the genes. The nationwide criminal organizations of today were founded by army brats whose fathers lost the Chinese Civil War to the Communists in 1949. They grew up training to "retake the mainland," as the slogan went, and transferred that focus to "taking the money."

The heads of Black Sea, for example, all hold engineering degrees (which come in handy for those rigged construction bids and contracts), and many graduated with honors from American schools. It seems fitting that gangsters on an island that values overachievement are also scholarship material.

Black Sea has politicians in its pockets, and some regional leaders cut out the middleman altogether and run for local offices. Once elected, they make sure to get on the commissions overseeing crime and fire police captains who are too clean or too greedy.

MY FAMILY HAD NEVER been seriously bothered by *jiaotous*. We paid the late-night parking fee and other fees. When I was born, the local leader, German Tsai, had presented my parents with a congratulatory basket of fruit and a lucky money tree. My parents paid German for his trouble. After all, he had a bunch of little brothers to look after, and he wanted to get them something to eat, he had said.

That old gambling debt of my grandfather's, the one that sat inside me like an abscess, was once owed to German's father, who'd had the foresight to have a lawyer draw up the loan as a promissory note. Now the debt was what I owed to German.

I looked over at the men, looking for German's distinctive mole on his upper lip, which looked like a Hitler mustache. He wasn't here, but the guys on the sidewalk were his boys.

They looked nothing like the young, pop-star-pretty boys who had portrayed local gangsters in the hit film *Monga*, which was shot in the Wanhua District and had turned some neighborhood locations into tourist destinations. Suck down a bubble tea in the alley where Mosquito stabbed Monk in the side. Instagram the warehouse where Dog Boy was murdered by having his mouth and nose sealed shut with glue.

I could have been an extra in *Monga*. I was approached in the street by a production assistant who told me that I was a good-looking guy and asked if I minded taking a light kick in the neck. I shouldn't have turned down the offer. I never say yes to the right things.

In reality, *jiaotous* are older than the actors in the movie, and they look like a regular bunch of guys. They don't run around shirtless, and you don't want to see them that way. The film got one thing right, though. They were mainly dangerous to one another rather than to the general public.

The only time a tourist would encounter a *jiaotou* is probably at one of the smaller temples. You might notice that the guys sweeping the floor and cleaning the joss-stick urns have scary tattoos on their necks and arms. They'll show you where the gods are, how to worship them and where to leave your donation. You don't have to worry about your safety. As long as you're respectful, *jiaotous* will always be polite.

For example, look at the *jiaotous* waving to me as I walk by. Why, they look downright friendly. I waved back but maintained my stride and kept the moped between us.

One guy called out, breaking away from the car. He pushed up his sunglasses and pointed his Longlife cigarette at my throat as he approached.

"Hey, you! You're Ming-teng's kid, right?"

"That's right," I said, finally stopping. This is how every conversation with the *jiaotous* started.

"How come you're still riding this crappy old moped? How about we get you a new one? Maybe even a motorcycle?"

"That's okay. I still like this one."

"I gotta tell you, chicks like men on motorcycles."

"I can't afford one right now."

He shook his head and smiled, showing teeth stained red from chewing betel nut. "Ming-teng was a good man. A great man. We all miss him a lot. We're glad you're keeping his business going."

"I don't know if my father was a great man," I said. "He was too busy to even be a dad, really."

"Hey, at least your father stuck around." His smile faded a little.

"Do you want money?" I asked, my hand going to my pocket. My father always told me to pay them whatever they asked, because they prevented other people from coming into the neighborhood and asking for even more.

"Christ, no! Put that shit away! I was just thinking that maybe you and some of your friends who have food stalls might want to come sing karaoke at the Best Western KTV. We just opened. The mics are shaped like guns, and the girls dress up like Indian princesses. You should come. We'll treat you right."

"You know I work at night."

"Take a night off. Relax already. First round is on the house. Okay?"

"Okay. Thank you, *ojisan*." I'd always heard my dad use the Japanese term for "uncle" when talking with German's father.

He laughed. "Don't call me uncle! I'm your older brother! You're my *ah di*!"

"Some other time. It's been a long night."

I kept going. This was how the scam worked. There wasn't money handed over in the street. I had to blow a wad of cash at the KTV, making a legitimate transaction at a legitimate business.

German and his boys weren't merely leeches on the community. The guy really did take an interest in how people were doing. He wouldn't take money from businesses that were struggling. Also, I deeply appreciated that he brought huge banners and flower arrangements to my parents' funeral, along with more than a hundred people and a troupe of professional mourners who had wailed for hours with abandon.

I walked along a stone-and-concrete wall almost as tall as I was. It was topped with shards of broken glass that stuck up like small stegosaurus plates. Older property walls from Taiwan's martial-law era were all topped with glass or metal spikes. People must have been so paranoid back then.

When I reached an off-center iron gate, I swung it open and pushed my moped through before me. I made my way down a short concrete walk to the house. The hinges were tilted for the gate to shut by itself, which it did with a click.

I refused to look back. When I was a kid, I used to imagine there was a monster standing there, holding the gate open. Its teeth, dripping with saliva, made the click sound as they clamped on a human bone.

I STILL LIVED IN the three-room, one-floor building I had grown up in. Considering that the place was constructed illegally, it was well built. It was painted white on the outside and was pushed up against a larger residential building, like a pop-up toaster against a kitchen wall. At one point four people had lived there, including my grandfather. How had we all fit?

I went into the bedroom, disrobed and wedged my feet into a pair of sad plastic slippers. I clicked on my stereo amplifier, spun the balance all the way to the right and put the right speaker in the doorway, pointing out. On my PC I cued up a bootleg of Joy Division playing one of their last shows, in early 1980. I started it near the end of the regular set. It was the right soundtrack for two in the morning.

My bathroom is set up in the traditional Taiwanese style. No sit-down toilet or bathtub. Just a ceramic oval on one side of the room and a recessed drain in the center of the tiled floor. I ignited the gas heater to warm up some water and listened to the lumbering, feedback-strewn "Atrocity Exhibition."

I stopped up the sink and poured hot water in, then ran the cold water for a few seconds to offset it. I soaked my one-foot-square towel, rubbed it all over my body and lathered up with a green-striped soap bar. I dunked a little bucket in the sink, stood over the drain and rinsed myself off.

Ian Curtis wailed from my bedroom, powerless against a world where fate overruled everything and bred indifference among the living.

Julia.

I could see her face, her tough but graceful jawline. Maybe that was a strange thing to admire in a woman, but I knew it well because she loved for me to kiss her neck. When I held her, I was in awe of her physical and mental strength. She always thought her eyes were too small, but they could light up like a two-star constellation, particularly during the several times we escaped to love hotels. We felt like we were running away to another world. Even after the sex, which we usually did right away and one more time before leaving, we lay there and lied about how great our lives were going to be together.

Love hotels are a hallowed institution that don't exist in the US. They are the only places young couples can be intimate, because Taiwanese live with their parents in small apartments until marriage. Even after marriage, one might still need a love hotel for trysts to break up the average workaholic day.

I should consider myself lucky to have the whole house to myself. I could have as many parties and women over as I wanted, only I didn't really want to have parties, and the few women I had slept with since returning to Taipei I hadn't wanted to bring home.

The concert recording ended with drums crashing wildly. From what I've read online from people who were supposedly there, this was the show that ended with Ian having an epileptic seizure and tumbling over the cymbals and bass drum.

I felt trapped in the sudden silence.

I thought about my parents, Dwayne, Frankie the Cat and the *jiaotous*. As exhaustion took hold of my body, I felt my skepticism slip away from me. What if we were all fated to be what we were when we were born? I was meant to be operating the food stand, no matter how well I did in school or what I studied. I was also probably supposed to spend my life alone.

Like Ian Curtis, I had control of little to nothing in my life. The singer had been married to a woman he no longer loved but was too stigmatized by the shame of divorce to leave her for his mistress. Complicating things, his fits were increasing in frequency and severity. His medication sent him on wild mood swings. Curtis found a way out, though—he hanged himself the night before the band was to embark on their first US tour.

I shivered and wrung out my towel over the drain.

I WOULD BE LYING if I said I had never contemplated suicide before tonight. The first year alone was probably the worst time ever in my life. For some reason I couldn't shake off the jetlag, and I was struggling at the stall. People heard that both my parents had died and, while they were sympathetic, they avoided my "cursed" booth.

In my weakness, I allowed Dwayne to set up a small shrine at work with photos of my grandfather and my parents. What really got me was how worried Dwayne looked. The big guy was shaking in his sandals. I'd never realized how much he needed this job. We kept joss sticks burning on one of the corner shelves, and he was always paranoid that they had gone out.

I told myself there was absolutely nothing religious about the shrine. It was just a sign of respect, not ancestor worship, and there were no idols. I never bowed when lighting the incense. I merely watched the smoke waft around and remembered the three of them. None of them ever seemed very happy with the way I cooked, but maybe negative reinforcement was their way of training me.

I knew I had hit rock bottom when I bought a bulk pack of joss sticks. I was buying into a system I despised. What a hypocrite.

Desperately, I began to yell out to tourists in English to eat our food. I am an introvert by nature. I hate calling attention to myself, which is basically what I started doing. The "Johnny" persona was born. It worked better than I expected. I learned how valuable English fluency was as the skewers flew from our grill like greasy sparrows.

The first profitable week we had, Dwayne was so relieved he tried to wrestle me to the ground. That was when the nightly matches started.

The business wouldn't have made it if I hadn't made a concerted effort to pull in tourists who knew nothing about me, my family or my stand. Random strangers saved us, and I never forgot it. I tossed out the shrine and returned the photos to a desk drawer back home. Dwayne said I was courting disaster, but not even he could deny that our sales remained strong.

MY FAMILY HADN'T BEEN cursed by angry spirits and gods. My parents were haunted and hobbled by the debt accumulated by my grandfather decades before I was even born.

When my father first nervously sat me down to tell me the whole story, I was worried he was going to try to explain sex. It turned out to be something even more immediately intangible to a ten-year-old.

Not long after my grandfather came to Taipei with my grand-mother to set up Tastes Good with a single charcoal hibachi grill, he found he had some free time in the late mornings and early afternoons. The night market was a lot smaller back then and had far fewer tourists.

The two of them were already living in this toaster building in the 1950s, when the Wanhua District was primarily a red-light district. It was probably a "pretty girl" (the term my father used instead of "prostitute") who first brought my grandfather into a gambling parlor that was open at all hours of the day.

The cops, many of them former soldiers, left the joint alone. Martial law was still the rule of the day over all of Taiwan, and the gambling operated under the guise of buying "patriotic bonds"— money that would go toward outfitting the army to "retake the mainland."

We don't know what games my grandfather lost at, but he never seemed to win at anything. He considered fleeing to Japan, a typical refuge for those who had grown up in colonial Taiwan. But my grandmother told him she was pregnant. The news renewed his spirit. Unfortunately, he believed his luck had turned. My grand-father exchanged the deed of the toaster building for a bundle of patriotic bonds and proceeded to lose them as fast as if he had fed them into a fire. He returned to the gambling parlor with his set of knives and the singular hibachi, seeking to hock them for more bonds. The teller called out to the boss, German's dad.

"You can't exchange these," the elder *jiaotou* had said, "because I already own them. After all, I already own everything in your house."

Still, German's father had a heart. He recognized that my grand-father was an honest guy who had gotten in over his head. At this point most men fled or killed themselves, but this country bumpkin from rural central Taiwan didn't even know enough to do that.

The *jiaotou* handed back my grandfather's belongings and told him to go back to work and never gamble again. German's dad brought the signed deed to a local bank and had papers drawn up to reflect a sale-leaseback deal on the house and a promissory note.

I wasn't familiar with the term "continuous compounding," and neither was my grandfather, because he signed the papers, which allowed his expanding family to stay in their home. He had no choice, really. That was why we owed German a total amount that was probably four times what our house was worth.

My grandfather's big mistake was not going to a loan shark who would have bailed him out on more generous terms. It was a matter of preserving some pride. He wanted as few people as possible to hear about his situation.

"Don't ever let pride get in the way," was how my father summed it all up. I nodded, though I didn't understand. To the end of his days, my grandfather would fly into a rage if The Debt—or any debt—was mentioned. My father didn't even have the balls to tell me how bad our situation truly was until after my mother was dead.

I FLOSSED AND BRUSHED my teeth until my gums bled. In the heat and humidity of the night, my skin never dried off completely, and I was covered in a glistening sweat by the time I rinsed my mouth out. I finished with a cheek full of stinging mouthwash.

In my bedroom, I replaced my speaker and clicked on *Unknown Pleasures.*

When I was a kid I used to think it was so ghoulishly cool that Ian killed himself. I could read into his tortured lyrics and see that he had shamanistic insight into life and beyond. After I read some English-language books about Ian, the image faded. His wife's account was particularly damning. They had married young—in their teens—and in only a few years he felt he was outgrowing her artistically and intellectually. When he noticed his wife, Ian treated her with contempt.

Maybe Julia and I would have suffered a similar fate should we have married. I had no illusions whatsoever that I was as smart as she was.

It was time for a reality check before bed. There weren't any more updates on my phone, but maybe there was something on one of the twenty-four-hour news stations.

I turned on my little Sanyo television, hoping they would have realized there'd been a misidentification. There wasn't any more about Julia. The news cycle had moved on to celebrities leaving their spouses and animated reenactments of an armed standoff in the American Pacific Northwest that ended with five dead. One station used special effects to turn a television presenter into a transparent ghost as he hungrily ate up a bowl of steamed fish and rice in a segment that went on way too long.

I shut off the TV and stereo, zapped the lights and slid across the mattress. A hot breeze from the street felt good across my slick, naked body.

A light orange glow from the street prevented my bedroom from ever really being dark, even with the shades down. I looked over the contours of my useless hands and sighed.

In my heart I knew the dead betel-nut girl was Julia. In the morning I should go to see her parents at their apartment. The trip would give me final confirmation. Maybe then I could cry.

CHAPTER FIVE

I was still asleep when someone grabbed my left shoulder and tried to drag me out of bed.

I woke up in a fright, but then I realized that it was my own right hand doing the pulling.

It was about nine in the morning and the sun was fully up, but it was still an hour earlier than my alarm was set to go off. So annoying.

I stretched out, experiencing a feeling I hadn't expected.

Relief.

I didn't have to keep saving money because I didn't have to go back to UCLA because I didn't have to keep my promise to Julia any longer.

For a moment I felt a light giddiness, as if my entire body were hollow. But despair quickly seeped into the vacuum.

What was I living for now?

I reached for my phone and began to scroll through the news. A Japanese right-wing group had erected a shrine on the largest island in the Tiaoyutai chain—the latest move in the ownership dispute between China, Taiwan and Japan. A group of undocumented Vietnamese women had been arrested as they arrived at a whorehouse. They said they thought they were coming to Taiwan for arranged marriages.

Nothing about Julia.

I was concerned she had been swept under the rug, but I wondered if it was better this way. I wanted the killer caught, but I didn't want the entire island examining her corpse.

My thoughts were interrupted by some people shouting in the street. I went to the window.

Two compact cars, a Nissan and a Toyota, had swished to a halt just outside my gate. Both cars were pretty beat up, so if a fender bender had just happened it was tough to tell. Two middle-aged women standing at the side of the street were yelling insults at each other. Both were Taiwanese and both were screaming in Mandarin, but one had a heavy accent, giving herself away as someone who primarily spoke Taiwanese. It was a classic confrontation.

YOU COULD SPEND ALL day talking about the history and culture of the people in Taiwan. We have twenty-three million people, the same population as Texas, packed on an island slightly bigger than Maryland. If familiarity breeds contempt, then the people of Taiwan are very familiar with each other. On top of that, our long and complicated relationships with larger and more powerful countries have created an interesting entrée.

I wish I knew how to make *zongzi*, the glutinous rice dumpling packed with a bunch of different fillings and wrapped in dark green bamboo leaves in a tetrahedral shape (think of a soft, three-sided pyramid). I love them, and I also feel they sum up Taiwan as it is now. *Zongzi* are served fresh from the steamer or boiling pot, still tied with twine. Cut or untie the string and slowly unwrap the leaves. Contents will definitely be hot. Try to avoid getting your hands too sticky from the melted pork fat that has permeated everything and is now leaking through the leaves. Once the *zongzi* is fully peeled, spread out the leaves to keep the table surface clean. Admire how the rice and other fillings retain the tetrahedral shape.

There's no neat way to eat *zongzi*, but whatever you do, chew slowly and taste everything in there. You can sense all the separate and sometimes contradictory components, and how they come together as a whole.

Taiwan is like a compact *zongzi*, tied up together whether

we like it or not. The rice is the land. The melted pork fat is the humidity and precipitation. The yams are the *benshengren*, the "home-province people," descendants of people who came to Taiwan from China before the Japanese colonization in 1895. *Benshengren* actually refer to themselves as "yams," because Taiwan is shaped like one.

The taros are the *waishengren*, or "outside-province people," people who came to Taiwan after the Chinese Civil War ended in 1949. They are also known as "mainlanders," even later generations born in Taiwan. They say China looks like a spade-shaped taro leaf, the Bohai Gulf corresponding to the indent by the stem.

The fungus and salted eggs are the Hakka, probably the only distinct ethnic group of Han Chinese that hasn't been assimilated into the larger population. They are known for their hearty food and hearty people. Traditionally farmers, Hakka never bound their women's feet, as they needed everyone to be mobile and working. Although Hakka can be *benshengren* or *waishengren*, those identities are secondary.

The pork represents the native Taiwanese, as the various tribes who lived here centuries before any Chinese arrived hunted wild boar, among other animals. They weren't all hunters, of course, and most of them are gone. They make up only about 2 percent of the country's population now. Dwayne's people, the Amis, are one of fourteen recognized tribal groups. The government says the rest are extinct or too integrated to matter.

All of these groups have historically fought and struggled against each other over the years, and new events make sure that the pot's stirred frequently. Announcements of new major highways might bring condemnations from the Indigenous Peoples' Action Coalition of Taiwan if any sacred lands are involved. They usually are. Hakka are roused to action whenever the Hakka language (and dialects) are excluded from public discussion, or when their culture is marginalized. *Benshengren*, the yams, take to the streets whenever the subject of closer ties to China is brought up, as they are mostly against the idea that Taiwan is really a province of the People's Republic. *Waishengren*, the mainlanders, are indignant that none of the other groups thank them for the economic miracle that has unfolded over the last forty years. They also don't understand why nobody seems to appreciate the transition to democracy that they presided over—after the era of harsh martial law they had imposed.

My family was *benshengren*. My grandfather and grandmother had left the farms of Taichung County near the middle of Taiwan's west coast in 1954, headed north for Taipei and started the food stall.

"Damned mainlanders," my grandfather would call the *waishengren*. He would call them worse names, too. I asked him why he sold them food if he hated them so much. He told me to be nice to anyone who put money in my hand. It was the best advice he ever gave me.

It was difficult to take his hatred of mainlanders seriously, though. Most of our neighbors in the Wanhua District were *waishengren*. Also, grandfather's number-one employee wasn't my father: it was a mainlander, Frankie the Cat.

Julia and her family were also yams. Dancing Jenny was a Hakka. Song Kuilan and her family were mainlanders. Dwayne was a native Taiwanese and had taken his English name from Dwayne Johnson, with whom he shared Pacific Islander heritage.

Of course I didn't think of my friends in a categorical sense, but then again, we never really had serious political discussions.

The mainlanders are mostly associated with the Kuomintang, or KMT, the political party that lost the Chinese Civil War and still claims it is the legitimate ruler of not only Taiwan, but its definition of China, which includes Mongolia and Tibet. The KMT was in power in Taiwan from 1945 until 2000. That was when the DPP, or Democratic Progressive Party, which is mostly backed by yams, won the presidential election. The DPP is known for seeing Taiwan as an independent country from China, and the eight years the party held office were the most combative with the mainland. The KMT came back to power in 2008, and China was happy again. Even though the Communists had fought a bloody war with the KMT, they were united in the view that Taiwan was an inalienable part of China.

Political candidates from these two major parties, the KMT and the DPP, know they have to appeal to anyone and everyone for the presidential election, so they soften up their stances and appeal to the four major population groups through endless campaigning and giving away food and prizes. The candidates say that they won't declare independence for Taiwan and will seek more trade agreements with China to keep the mainlanders happy. They tell the *benshengren* in the Taiwanese dialect that they are native sons and daughters of Taiwan. They proclaim haltingly in Hakka that they carry the mountain songs in their heart as they help dye fabrics in the traditional blue. After donning aboriginal clothing, the candidates conclude that modern Taiwan still has much to learn from its original communities. They all promise to do something about the undocumented workers from Indonesia, Vietnam and the Philippines. Then after the election, we all go back to being our parochial selves.

But what are we, really? Do we have a broader identity that covers us all? Someone came up with "New Taiwanese" as an umbrella term to include everybody, but that phrase fell out of use, mainly because it just sounded stupid. We are people who work hard and disagree about a lot of things. Luckily for me, everybody loves to eat, and no one ever says the food in Taiwan sucks.

THE SHOUTING OUTSIDE REACHED a new pitch. I drew back my bedroom shades and saw that the women were now each restrained by a stoic, silent man.

German Tsai, accompanied by one of his boys, came between the women and spoke too softly for me to hear. Open hands slid out from the sleeves of his linen jacket and gestured at one woman and then the other. He took off his sunglasses so they could see that he was sincere.

His underling produced two plastic bags. I couldn't believe what German pulled out of one of them. A wrapped *zongzi*. He held it up in the sunlight as if it were a prism. He smiled and gave each woman a bag of *zongzi*.

The situation was defused by two bags of *zongzi* German had picked up for his crew. I'm sure that he could get another two bags with no problem.

—

I TURNED AWAY FROM the window. Now that I was wide-awake, I felt the weight of what I had to do. I wet a towel and wiped my face. I dressed in my least-wrinkled buttoned shirt, black slacks and good shoes. I didn't eat anything, but I had half a cup of soy milk to coat my stomach. It was something my mother told me to always do because it could prevent stomach cancer. It hadn't helped my dad, though.

It was about ten in the morning now, and I was on schedule to see the Huangs. I rolled my moped out. In the daylight my ride looked old and dirty. There was a big tear in the seat that I hadn't noticed before. Overall it wasn't much better than what I had been riding in high school. I'd told Julia that when I came for her, I'd be driving a red sports car. What would she think if she saw me, a college dropout, riding this thing? What would I think if I had seen her wearing next to nothing, slinging *binlang*?

WHEN THE HUANGS SOLD their Shilin Night Market stall ten years ago, they also left their old ground-floor house to move to an apartment in a new building in the Zhongzheng District, the next one over, east of the Wanhua District. Zhongzheng houses the national government buildings and the Chiang Kai-shek Memorial Hall. The Huangs' building had been banged out during one of the construction booms that come around every few years. It looked impressive from a block away, but a casual observer need only enter the building and walk across the loose porcelain tiles before a number of shortcomings revealed themselves.

The panel to the apartment buzzers was crooked because it was screwed into a frame that was a few millimeters too small. Hammer blows on the protruding edge indicated someone had attempted to cram it in anyway. Luckily visitors didn't have to worry whether the buzzer system was functional or not, because the solid-steel front door was propped open by a plastic bucket with a chipped cinder block in it. The lock was probably out of order, and all the residents probably assumed somebody else had notified the repair service. What did it matter, anyway? Taipei didn't have many thieves, they reasoned, and surely even those few bad men would be punished by the good brothers during the holiday.

I felt odd about simply walking into the building, so I switched my bag to my left hand and buzzed the Huangs' apartment. I heard Mrs. Huang say hello, her voice fuzzy and faint, as if transmitted from Pluto.

"Hello, Mrs. Huang, I am sorry to bother you. This is Chen Jing-nan," I said. The exposed lock made a clicking sound, and I stepped through the open doorway.

In the elevator I had a small anxiety attack and looked into the bag. My pack of joss sticks, some mixed CDs of music Julia liked and a few Snickers bars, her favorite candy. Everything was there.

Whatever I do next, I'm doing only for your parents, Julia. Don't take it personally. Then again, why am I talking to you?

The elevator opened on the thirteenth floor, and I saw Mrs. Huang was holding the door open. She was dressed in burlap mourning clothes. Her hair was noticeably greyer since I had last seen her, at my parents' funerals, an event where we'd held hands but said nothing.

It was tough seeing Julia's mom, because only now did I notice how similar the lower parts of their faces were. Mrs. Huang was looking up to me, fusing her eyes to mine and pursing her lips off-center in the same way Julia used to when she was lost in a thought.

"Jing-nan," Mrs. Huang said, with a trace of joy around her bleary and baggy eyes. "I knew you would come."

There was no doubting that Julia was dead now.

"Mrs. Huang," I said. "I was so sorry to hear. The news just destroyed me." I embraced her lightly.

Mrs. Huang moved away and blew her nose. I stepped into their apartment and slipped off my shoes. Mr. Huang stood at a slouch in the kitchen, looking lost.

"I told you! Look!" Mrs. Huang said to him. I think he coughed.

I was dimly aware that Mrs. Huang was leading me toward the altar they had set up for Julia on a wall shelf by the dining table. A photograph of Julia looked indifferently over the smoking forest of half-burned incense sticks. I had never seen her face like that before, devoid of emotion except a hint of a smile. How mature you've become, I thought. I didn't recognize the striped top she was wearing, either. This photo must have been taken at college.

I felt a tightness around my left arm. It was Mr. Huang's hands.

"Jing-nan!" he said. "It's really you!" Mr. Huang was about as tall as me at five feet eight inches, so among people his age he's a giant. He was the source of Julia's thick eyebrows and vaguely sad and beautiful eyes.

"I am so sorry," I said, briefly embracing him and rubbing his back. "I've brought some things."

"Of course, of course!"

I shook out several joss sticks from my box and lit them in my hands. I formed prayer hands and bowed three times to Julia's picture.

You would have hated this, darling, but I know you would appreciate me doing this for your parents.

My hands shook as I planted the sticks in the holder and placed the CDs on the altar. I had a hard time reaching up to place the candy bars, because I had fallen to my knees and was sobbing. My whole face was raw, wet and salty, like a just-popped blister.

"No, no, no," I babbled in English.

The Huangs helped me over to the couch and propped me up on some cushions. Mr. Huang pressed a damp and mildew-scented towel to my forehead. I had to cry it out before my sobs stuttered and slowed.

When I was able to talk again, I said, "Thank you."

Mrs. Huang handed me a cup of hot barley tea, pumped from a hot dispenser. She sat down to my right and swung her knees away from me.

All three of us were quiet for a few minutes. For the first time, I could pick up the soft sound of the *Amituofo* chant from an electronic Buddhist chant box plugged in behind the altar.

Mrs. Huang touched my right arm. "The police brought us in to identify Julia's body," she said. "Still beautiful. Looked just like she was sleeping. Part of the back of her head was . . . gone."

I sucked in my lips and nodded.

"I made sure it was her by feeling the calcium deposit near her right ankle. You know, it's just like a little knob. Always had to get her low-cut shoes, or else they hurt."

"She always carried corn cushions," I said.

"When was the last time you saw Julia?" she asked.

"Right before we left for college."

Mr. Huang took a seat to my left in an armchair covered in a pill-infested fabric.

"We know you told Julia not to talk to you," said Mrs. Huang. "She said you didn't want to get in touch again until you were going to ask her to marry you."

"That's right," I said. "Sounds stupid now."

"She thought it was so romantic. I did, too."

Mr. Huang grunted. It wasn't clear that he meant to indicate approval.

"Everything was doomed by the way you two left Taiwan," said Mrs. Huang. "You didn't ask for Buddha's protection. You didn't ask Mazu for a safe return to Taiwan. Now look what's happened. You abandoned them, so they abandoned you and Julia!"

Now was not the time to argue about this. I took a sip of tea.

"This is the wrong way to talk," said Mr. Huang. "We're all in shock. We have to appreciate each other."

"If it would have made a difference, I would have done it," I said. "Believe me."

"We'll never know now," she said.

Mr. Huang cleared his throat and moved to the candy bars on the ground. "I'll put these up," he said.

"Jing-nan," said Mrs. Huang, "I know you and Julia meant a lot to each other."

"Yes, we did." I drank more tea. It had a pleasant, roasted-grain flavor.

"She told me about the times you went to love hotels."

Barley tea nearly shot out of my nose, but I managed to swallow and say, "She told you?"

"We were very close. We had no secrets, mother and daughter, until a few years ago."

I nodded. I didn't want to say anything upsetting. She knew we were sleeping together the entire time! I caressed my puffy eyes and kept quiet.

"I think my relationship with my daughter started going a

little wrong around the time your parents passed away, Jing-nan," Mrs. Huang said. "I asked her if she wanted to come back for the services, but she insisted you wouldn't want her here. She felt so terrible for you! She was crying like crazy. I told her that under the circumstances, the deal was off. You two had to talk to each other. But she insisted you would see it as a broken promise."

I nodded.

"That was really something. It was the first time she wouldn't do something I told her to. My little girl was slipping away. Pretty soon we were talking less on the phone. I could hear it in her voice, no more emotion. Then she told us about the expulsion from NYU, at the end of her junior year. Daddy went crazy."

Mr. Huang spoke up. "I was very upset," he said. "I left messages and cursed her. I told her she wasn't good enough for you."

"She never called Daddy back," said Mrs. Huang.

I let a few moments of silence go by before asking a question. "Why was she thrown out of NYU?"

"She cheated," said Mr. Huang. "She plagiarized from a book for a paper."

I couldn't imagine Julia cheating. She wouldn't look at another student's paper, not even in cram school, where everybody developed serious cases of giraffe neck. It must have been a huge misunderstanding at NYU. A missed attribution. A footnote gone astray.

"I don't believe it," I said.

"We didn't want to believe it, either," said Mrs. Huang. "But she told us she did. She was taking too many classes and tried to take a shortcut. She only copied a few paragraphs, but it was a serious enough violation."

"When did she come back to Taiwan?" I asked.

"We don't know!" said Mrs. Huang.

"I thought she would try to get back in to NYU," said Mr. Huang.

"You had no idea she was here?"

"We had no idea she was in Hsinchu City!" said Mrs. Huang. "Less than an hour away all these years."

"Maybe it was my fault," said Mr. Huang. "I was too harsh. That's why she didn't call us again."

"Who else's fault could it be?" said Mrs. Huang. "If you really cared about her, you would have told her to just come back to Taiwan and finish her degree here!"

I knew Julia wouldn't have wanted to do that.

Mrs. Huang launched another attack on her husband. "If you really loved your daughter, you wouldn't let this go. You would make the police find out who did this! Make the murderer pay!"

Mr. Huang rubbed his hands. "What do you want me to do?" he asked.

"Call them every hour!"

"That's not going to do anything."

"See? You still don't care!"

I spoke up. "Is there anything I could do to help?"

"Jing-nan!" Mrs. Huang looked me over like I was the last chocolate in a box. "Help us! The police don't care about Julia. They haven't done anything! Not one person brought in for questioning."

"You have to give them a few days first," said Mr. Huang.

"Not even one person! They should bring in everybody who works at that betel-nut stand! The police won't even tell us which stand it was."

"They probably don't want us to interfere with their work."

"They're not working!" Mrs. Huang thumped her fist against her breastbone. She sounded empty. "They just want everyone to forget about Julia! The owner of the betel-nut stand must have bribed the police! The news stations don't even talk about her any more, just two days later!"

"That's true," I said.

"There's nothing keeping the pressure on! Jing-nan, you have to do something!"

"Don't put Jing-nan in this position," Mr. Huang pleaded.

"What position? Her father won't do anything, and Jing-nan is the closest thing to a husband Julia had!"

Mr. Huang shook off the sting and said matter-of-factly, "Jing-nan hasn't even seen her in years."

"Wake up! He never bought a ticket, but he got to ride the bus when they were still teenagers!"

I was spurred to speak up. "Please, I want to help," I heard myself say. "I know two people who went to NYU with her. I can talk to them and see if they might know something." I wasn't really friends with either of them, then or now.

"Thank you so much, Jing-nan," said Mrs. Huang. "We appreciate your help."

"Anything you could find out would help us a lot," said Mr. Huang. "We haven't known our daughter in a long time, and as you can see we're losing touch with each other every day."

"When is the funeral?" I asked, feeling my mouth go dry.

"We aren't having a funeral," said Mrs. Huang.

"Is it because you couldn't find anybody to handle it?" Undertakers are loath to handle funerals during Ghost Month because they are unlucky to stage—they're unlucky to even attend. Many of the wandering ghosts never received proper rites and burials, so a funeral could incite their wrath and turn it upon everyone involved.

"We could have found someone," Mrs. Huang snapped. "The problem is that she had her beliefs, just like you. We could have had a very proper Buddhist ceremony, but I knew what Julia's final wish was. She wanted to be cremated and her ashes to be scattered at sea, so that's what we did this morning."

I took a deep breath and sank lower in my chair. So I wouldn't get to see Julia one last time.

In the Huangs' silent apartment, the light seemed to dim and time became lumpy.

Julia and I had made so many plans. They changed a little bit every time we discussed them, but we already had a basic narrative established.

We'd had a few ideas as to what sort of job I would have when it was time for me to come for her. Engineering was the traditional Taiwanese ticket to America. Americans hated studying math and science, so there was always a shortage of engineers. Best of all, the starting salaries among engineering majors were the highest you could get for an undergrad degree.

Yet I really enjoyed poetry, both English and Chinese.

I hadn't declared a major yet when I left UCLA, but I had aced the freshman coursework for all engineering majors, and I also did well in a survey class of American poetry of the twentieth century.

Julia was certain she was going to study political science, and that she was going to see it through to a doctorate degree.

Since I was probably going to have less flexibility in landing a job than the brilliant and eminently admissible Julia, who would have her pick of grad schools, when I came for her we were going to get married in a civil ceremony and settle in to whatever town I was already working in. She was going to transfer to the nearest big university and continue studying until she had her master's degree.

Somehow we were going to get permanent residency cards or US citizenship. We didn't know what the climate for immigration would be, but we figured our English was good enough that we could blend in well with ABCs.

Then we were going to have two kids. Well, sometimes we thought just one. By that time, with a number of years of work experience under my belt, I would probably be in a position to kick back a little bit and help more with raising the kid or kids while Julia focused on her PhD. She would also probably have to teach a few undergraduate classes. Maybe Mandarin, too. At some point she would be done with her PhD. She would either hold on to a post in academia or open a consulting firm and do . . . whatever those consultants do.

We would be in a holding pattern for a few years until our kid or kids were old enough to attend college at Julia's university, since the tuition would be heavily subsidized or entirely free. If they wanted to go to another school, they'd better have Julia's smarts to get a mega-scholarship.

Once those kids were done with college, I could quit my job and open up a little music store. Not one that stocked racks and racks of major-label, deluxe-edition, reissued vinyl I personally didn't care for but sold to make money. If I was going to have a business like that, why bother selling music when it could be power tools? My store would focus on Joy Division and associated acts. I also wanted to carry a select inventory of contemporary indie bands I liked, and I would probably like quite a few of them by that point since I would have more time to listen to music. I still wasn't sure if it should be a physical store or an online one. Maybe an online one would be better, depending on how much storage space we had in our house after our kids left. That's how it is in the US. They don't wait to get married before they move out. I know we had a lot of pipe dreams and fuzzy definitions baked into our expectations, but we were crystal clear on one thing. Although we would maintain our fluency in Mandarin and Taiwanese, and even make the odd trip to the island to visit (we couldn't cut off family entirely), we were never going to live in Taiwan again.

Yet here we were, reeled back in by our respective bad circumstances. Maybe Julia, like me, had been planning to save money and get back to the US. When I came for her, we could've laughed about how we had to go back to Taiwan for a little bit before resuming our American lives.

We had never planned out our deaths, though. I actually hadn't known Julia wanted to be cremated, as in so many Taiwanese funerals. Most don't choose to have their ashes scattered, though—the preservation of ashes has led to the construction of condo-sized columbaria up on the sides of mountains.

Julia and I had thought we were going to have long and happy lives together, but fate had other plans. When my parents died, what kept me going was the knowledge that I would see Julia again. What a foolish, false hope! How stupid and prideful it was for me to refuse to reach out to her for the sake of plans made by teenagers!

What would have happened if I had called her in New York, told her I would be stuck in Taiwan and that she had to go on without me? I don't think she would have been able to abandon me. She loved me so much, she would have ditched everything and come back to Taiwan to be with me. It would have had to come down to me to set her free, and I would have had to act cruelly.

I'm sorry, Julia, but I'm calling to break up with you because I love you. You'll have to go down that great path alone . . .

"JING-NAN," SAID MRS. HUANG. I had been mumbling to myself out loud.

Mr. Huang was bringing in people I didn't know. Mrs. Huang stood over me and touched my shoulder gently. Time for me to go.

"You loved each other so much," she sobbed.

I could only nod as I rose to my feet.

"Go talk to them, your old classmates. Find out if they talked to Julia when she came back."

"I'll find out what I can," I said.

I RODE THE ELEVATOR down and hit the ground floor with a thud. The door lurched open, and I had just managed to step out when it closed with a slam.

How could Julia have told her mother everything? She hadn't promised not to, but I assumed she would be like me and only tell her parents the parts of our relationship appropriate for the general public. For example, our impending marriage.

"Still going to marry Julia, huh?" were among my father's last words to me. It was as close as he could come to expressing approval.

I grabbed my helmet and leaned against my sun-baked moped seat. I hadn't been in touch with my high-school classmates Peggy or Ming-kuo in years, and I wasn't sure they were two people I wanted back in my life. Funny how I needed to get in touch now. Maybe it was time for me to start a Facebook account.

Peggy Lee was from a well-off mainlander family. Her great-grandfather had been a confidant of Chiang Kai-shek, and their family had privileged status when the Generalissimo established the capital of the Republic of China on Taiwan after bravely retreating in the face of inevitable failure.

Peggy's family had a fancy house that Japanese officials had once lived in, the nicest one I knew of in Wanhua District. It had clay roof tiles that ended in slightly upturned corners. Every few feet there were fanged and horned demon faces making agonized expressions. I can only describe the roofs because I couldn't see anything else over the exterior wall. Apparently Peggy's family had a private garden with stone lanterns and a pond with kumquat-colored koi as long as your arm.

Mainlanders who didn't come over with money or connections grew up in *juancuns*, military residential communities hastily built on public land for families of low-ranking officers and soldiers.

People from every province were thrown together—something the normally clannish Chinese weren't pleased by—as those *juancuns* were meant for temporary housing. Chiang Kai-shek's Kuomintang party and Republic of China Army were going to launch that counterattack any day, after all. That day never came. Several generations of families ended up living in *juancuns*, patching up crumbled cinder blocks in their walls to keep the rain out. Meanwhile, Peggy grew up leisurely feeding the same koi in the Lee family pond her father and grandfather had cared for years before.

Today, most of the *juancuns* are gone. It wasn't the typical *waishengren-benshengren* politics that pushed them out—it was money politics. Condos had to go up.

And Peggy's family had a lot to do with that. The Lees were big in real estate and helped the government "monetize" the land. Let's face it. The *juancuns* were a major eyesore. Gangs like Black Sea were originally formed by disaffected mainlander youth living in those blocks, but a lot of those kids made it out and did something with their lives, including Ang Lee, the film director, and Teresa Teng, the immortal and yet dead singer. Supposedly Teng's lifelong asthma was caused by childhood exposure to asbestos in a *juancun*.

After a public outcry to preserve *juancuns* as historical sites, the Lees recently turned their wrecking ball against their own antique Japanese house. A hotel stands there now.

THE LIGHTNESS I HAD been feeling earlier was gone. Thoughts of Julia weighed on me again. I had been tasked by her parents to find out more about her mysterious return to Taiwan.

I saw I had received a news text on my phone. The member of the Black Sea gang who had made allegations about the CIA and drugs was recanting his story, saying he was completely wrong. What an asshole.

I searched online for Lee Xiaopei—Peggy's business name.

Surprise. She had decided to play it close to home. Peggy was a senior vice president of Lee & Associates, her family's hedge fund. Of course it was headquartered in the most expensive office space in the country—the eightieth floor of the gigantic Taipei 101 building.

The phone number was right there, but I took a breath and hesitated.

I'll admit Peggy had striking looks. Even if Peggy's family wasn't rich, she'd still have attracted a lot of attention. She had a sharp nose, a sharp chin and a sharp tongue. A lot of boys liked her. They left things on her school desk—candy, flowers and notes in fancy envelopes. But the only guy she was into back in high school was already in a committed relationship—me. You always want what you can't have, and there was very little Peggy couldn't have.

I looked at my phone again. I had to call her. Peggy might know something about Julia's return to Taiwan. That information might provide some comfort to Julia's parents. If not, I wouldn't tell them.

I was reluctant as hell to open that door again, but still I'd rather call Peggy before trying to get in touch with Ming-kuo.

I hit the number and waited. An automated voice menu answered. I wasn't a current client, so I guessed I was a prospective one. Why else would anyone call? I pressed 2.

Soothing light jazz began to play. Was I scheduling a dental appointment? Oh, I should probably schedule a dental appointment.

As if reading my thoughts, a man wearing cheap sunglasses and a grey linen sports jacket approached me slowly. He was a big man, almost two meters in height, and he had a crew cut. I thought he was Japanese, but he gave himself away when he smiled. Straight, white, American teeth. I looked at him, but he kept a respectful distance while I was on the phone. An operator took my call.

"Hello, thank you for calling Lee & Associates," a man said. "You seem to be calling from a mobile phone."

"Hello, I am calling from my cell. I'm actually trying to get in touch with Ms. Lee Xiaopei, please."

"I'm sorry, if you're not already a client, we don't accept calls from mobile phones. You have to come in person or call from an office."

"That's ridiculous."

"Have a good day, sir." The son of a bitch hung up.

I crossed my arms as the man approached me. "Are you done with your call?" he asked. His Mandarin had an American accent.

"I'm done. What do you want?" I'm usually not this curt with strangers, but I was still annoyed by the phone call, and this guy wasn't a customer of mine. He lifted his sunglasses and regarded me. The man seemed too young to have those bags under his eyes.

"I just want to see how you are. No big deal."

"I'm doing fine," I said.

The sunglasses dropped back down and he headed into the Huangs' building. Man, some strange people lived there. "Take care, man," he said in English over his shoulder.

Now, did he say "man" or "Jing-nan"?

I had about an hour before I had to be at Unknown Pleasures. That wasn't enough time to go to Peggy's office. That would have to wait until tomorrow.

I was frustrated and annoyed, and buying new music was my usual coping mechanism.

The music stores around National Taiwan University, known as Taida for short, were the best. No one bought mainstream, conventional CDs anymore, so the stores survived by stocking limited editions from indie labels, imports and bootlegs of live shows.

I rode east into the Da'an District. The big government buildings and wide sidewalks of the Zhongzheng District gave way to the residential buildings, churches and MRT stations of Da'an. The smell of incense grew heavier. A small hatchback drove by with a young boy and a girl crawling around in the rear cargo space. It made me think of Julia and me as small kids—until the girl gave me the finger. I had to smirk as I thought about what my father used to say: younger generations had no respect for their elders, and Taiwan was in danger of backsliding and becoming as uncouth and boorish as China.

Taida is the best university in Taiwan. Like a lot of Taiwan's best institutions, it was originally established by the Japanese during the colonial era.

I parked near the Gongguan MRT station on Luosifu Road, which was the way they chose to render "Roosevelt Road" using Chinese characters. Bunk racks of parked bikes marked the edge of campus. It was summer, but Taida was buzzing with activity. The academic calendar was twelve months long. Classes were always in session. It sounds grueling, especially to my American college friends, but we never had such a thing as summer vacation all my years of school and cram school.

Taida students oversee the PTT, the Professional Technology Temple, an online bulletin-board system. It's like America Online, only it remained cool and influential for marketing and networking. Older people thought it was only used for idle chatter and dirty jokes until Typhoon Morakot slammed into Taiwan in 2009, and the PTT organized hundreds of volunteers to haul supplies to disaster areas. Those kids were better than the government at responding to the deadly storm. They also set up blood drives and other public service opportunities that young people are into.

There are a lot of good things about the PTT, but I haven't been on it in years, since I was chased out of a music discussion group when I said the former members of Joy Division shouldn't have carried on as New Order after Ian Curtis killed himself. Sure are a lot of New Order fans in Taiwan. All of them came after me over the entire system, in every discussion I entered.

The first time I heard Joy Division and New Order (which I perceived to be the lesser band by far at the time) was at Bauhaus, a store on Luosifu Road that caters to Taida students with good taste in music. It's the first CD store I go to when I'm up for a big shopping trip. I have a history with the place.

When I was still a kid, I went through a Black Sabbath phase. I think all teenage boys do. Bauhaus had been having a grand-opening sale, and I went in to check it out. I couldn't find a single Black Sabbath or Ozzy CD. I went up to the guy working at the counter. He must have been a student at Taida, because he looked relaxed. Once you got into a school that good, you could finally ease off the pedal a bit. After graduation, you were set with a decent job. You could even sleep in on the weekends for the first time in your life.

"You don't have any Sabbath?" I asked him.

He stroked both corners of his mouth with his thumb and index finger. "We don't. We're a *music* store," he said, looking like he wanted to spit on my school uniform. "I'm going to do you the biggest favor of your life, kid." He stood up and grabbed a CD from the rack above the cash register. "I'm going to allow you to buy this. It's the in-store playing copy, but we can get another one."

The CD cover art matched his shirt: a bunch of lines that looked like undersea mountains. It was *Unknown Pleasures*. He wasn't kidding—it really was one of the biggest favors anyone ever did me. The music scared me in a way Sabbath never had. I studied English harder so I could understand the lyrics beyond surface-level literal meanings. There was a whole world hidden in those squat and loose-looking written words. Maybe Ian had encoded the secrets of life and death in the lyrics before committing suicide.

My English bookshelf expanded beyond two Shakespeare plays to include five costly paperbacks about Joy Division that had been printed in England.

I bought a black trench coat like the ones the band members wore in pictures. I soldiered on with it in the face of heat, humidity and open mockery from other students who didn't get it. Julia was worried that I looked like a gravedigger, but she understood after I played her the music and explained the songs to her.

Early in senior year I sang "Love Will Tear Us Apart" for the karaoke competition and won. A picture of us was laid out right in the middle of the yearbook, me on stage during the instrumental break, reaching down to her outstretched hand. It was the most triumphant moment of my life. When I think about it, I see myself in the third person, looking down from the balloons on the ceiling at my perfectly poised body on that stage. I couldn't have known then that it would all be downhill after that.

Time claimed the coat not long after. The sleeves and the lining were fraying, and mold spots popped up on the back before the fabric essentially disintegrated. I didn't get another one, because by that time I didn't have to flaunt my attachment to Joy Division's music. It was already deep inside me.

IF I HADN'T GONE into Bauhaus that day and met that guy, I might have ended up as a pimply dude in his twenties who didn't know much English. I would probably still be working at the night-market stall, but I certainly wouldn't have as much style.

I never actually cared for Bauhaus, the band the store was named after. I didn't like the theatricality of the guy's voice and the lyrics were too "art school."

Still, there was no denying Bauhaus the store was a great place. I stepped around an offering table on the sidewalk and admired a sticker by the door handle that read, "This is the way, step inside." Those words were taken from the lyrics to "Atrocity Exhibition," the first song on Joy Division's second and final album, *Closer*. I did as the sticker instructed.

I noticed right away that there was a 10-percent-off sale on Japanese-import CDs. The Japanese editions of CDs often contain bonus tracks. I can understand how from the listener's point of view that's better—more songs. But it also destroys the artist's intention; what was meant to be a cohesive piece is cheapened by tacked-on singles and B-sides.

I remember reading about how Matt Johnson, who recorded music under the moniker The The, had to campaign for years before the song "Perfect" was removed from the end of the album *Soul Mining*. I enjoyed the entire album for the longest time, having no idea of the distress he felt about the song being there. "Perfect" is a great song. It's also unusual for a pop song in that it features an accordion, a vibraphone and a trumpet solo. On top of that, the music strangely remains the same through the verses and choruses.

I started humming "Perfect," and then out of the corner of my eye I caught a movement. The woman behind the counter had been looking at me but tried to turn away before I noticed. A swish of her hair betrayed her. From the back of her head and smooth right arm I could tell she was young, maybe younger than me. Her ears stuck out perpendicularly to her head, like an elf's. They looked cute. I wondered what her face looked like and, then I felt suddenly ashamed.

I had just come from meeting Julia's parents. Had I forgotten all about her already?

I slinked to the Joy Division section, which was chock-full of CDs. I removed several of them to make it easier to flip through the bin. This is what the pros do.

It's true that the band only recorded two studio albums, but their label went on to issue several compilations of singles and B-sides, not to mention reissuing the proper albums with bonus live CDs. There were bootlegs, too, of concerts and unreleased studio rehearsals.

It was possible to download it all, if you searched hard enough and had the necessary bandwidth, but it's cool to have the tangible, physical object.

I came across a CD I had never seen before. It was a split release by Joy Division and New Order playing the same two Joy Division songs, the last two the band ever wrote—"Ceremony" and "In a Lonely Place."

That was odd. No complete take of Joy Division recording "In a Lonely Place" was known to exist. Only a fragment of about half the song was uncovered and included in the 1997 box set *Heart and Soul*. The bassist Peter Hook had found it on a rehearsal cassette. Yet this CD purported to have the song in full.

I looked at the price again. In the past I have paid the full price for a CD in order to get a single song I didn't already have. I began rationalizing. Containing only four songs, the CD was fully 25 percent new to me, so I probably had to buy it.

I brought the CD up to the counter.

"Is this for real?" I asked the woman. She looked up and in a synchronized motion both hands brushed her hair behind her ears.

She was indeed younger than me, maybe finishing her undergrad degree. She had a full, round face, bright as a caramel sunflower. I was glad she wasn't one of those girls who huddled under an umbrella to keep her skin pale. Why pretend you don't live on a Pacific island that lies on the Tropic of Cancer?

I noticed she had a scar the size and shape of a clipped pinky nail above her left eyebrow.

"It's real," she said. Her eyes were infinitely black. "It's a bootleg, but it's copied from a legitimate release that was only on vinyl. One of the Record Store Day releases, only in the UK."

I tried to imagine what it sounded like, but it was useless. "Perfect" was embedded in my mind, just like the woman's face.

"How is the sound quality?"

"Let me play it for you." She gingerly took the CD, careful not to touch my hands. "You want to hear Joy Division playing 'In a Lonely Place,' right?"

"Yes. Is it really the entire song?"

"It really is! I feel shivers when I hear it!"

We smiled at each other, enjoying our shared enthusiasm.

I broke into a light sweat as the song played over the speakers. She caught my eyes, and I stopped breathing as the song went into the lost third verse, where Ian sings of a hangman and a cord, foreshadowing his own suicide.

When the song was over, I said, "I'll take it."

"We also have the official vinyl release," said the woman. "If you're interested."

"I don't have a turntable."

A sly smile came over her face. "I thought a big music fan like you would have one."

"How do you know I'm a big music fan?"

Her smile slid to the left side of her face. "You've forgotten me. My name is An-Mei, but you can call me Nancy. I know you're Jing-nan."

"I'm sorry, I don't remember meeting you."

"You were a senior when I was a freshman, but we both were in the karaoke contest."

"What did you sing?"

"I sang a Pizzicato Five song in Japanese, but people didn't seem to like me very much. You sang 'Love Will Tear Us Apart' really well and you won!"

I smiled. "I would have remembered you."

"I didn't look like this. I had braces and I was bony." She cupped her elbows and her face flushed. I felt compelled to touch my fingers to my lips. I know from taking a psychology class at UCLA that most communication is nonverbal. Something was happening here. We might not even be fully aware that our actions were saying we liked each other.

I see a lot of people up close at the night market, but I only rarely see a woman as cute as Nancy. She had music savvy, as well. Did she have a boyfriend?

Wait. Not now. This was the worst time to be Meeting Someone New.

I looked at her and bit my lip. I tried to think of something complimentary that didn't seem like I was hitting on her.

"You're still really skinny," I offered.

"I remember you always had headphones on. Even if you only had a minute free between classes, you spent it listening to music." She spoke quickly, but she had a worried look on her face. Maybe she thought she was saying too much.

I pretended to look past her at the Killing Joke poster on the wall. *Act like you're busy.* I took out my wallet. "I'd like to pay for that CD now."

"Oh, sure, I'm sorry."

I felt a pang of guilt handing over the cash. Bootlegged and pirated CDs and DVDs were mostly made and distributed by organized criminals, including Taiwanese gangs like Black Sea. By buying the CD, I was doing my small part to help fund what was essentially a corporation that pushed drugs and smuggled in Cambodian women and children for sex and cheap labor, not necessarily respectively.

I needed that song and CD, though. And it wasn't like if I didn't buy it those horrible things would grind to a halt, or even pause. I was just one guy. What could I do, anyway?

"I don't need a bag," I told Nancy.

"Okay."

The CD in my hand, I found it difficult to walk away. "You're new here, right?" I asked her.

"It's my first week."

"You know a lot about music."

She nodded and shifted from foot to foot, probably wondering how long it was going to take for me to ask her out.

I was sorry to get her hopes up. My hopes, too. I really shouldn't let my eyes linger on her face.

"Well," I said, "I'll see you around."

CHAPTER SIX

I found myself driving east past Taida's campus on Xinhai Road, a *sansenro*, three-lane boulevard, feeling confused and lost. Looking around didn't help.

When I came back to Taipei after living in California, every block looked strange. I had gotten used to seeing LA's uniform, concrete sidewalks—not that anybody walked on them—and thematically linked groups of buildings.

By contrast, Taipei's businesses and residences were haphazardly placed. Walking on a typical block, one could pass by the steamy mouth of a weed-strewn side alley crowded with low, rusty shacks, and then fifteen feet later feel the blast of cold, dry air from the lobby of a new Japanese-built hotel. You were sure to hit a 7-Eleven or Family Mart before reaching the corner, and there could be a lonely office lobby with an elderly attendant in a rumpled uniform sawing away on the strings of a whiny *erhu* to pass the time.

The sides of Taipei's taller buildings are often scarred by the outlines of former neighbors that have been torn down, rebuilt and sold, and then torn down again because at times the land is more valuable with nothing on it.

Sidewalks vary wildly from door to door in terms of elevation, material and condition. Some are carefully crafted stone blocks, others hastily and unevenly laid adhesive kitchen tiles slapped on top of unfinished concrete.

Considering Taipei's state of near-constant construction and lack of maintenance, it was a minor miracle that the densely populated city hadn't suffered worse during 921, a huge earthquake that rocked towns in central Taiwan on September 21, 1999. Only one major building in Taipei came down, a large residential building that took more than ten years to build back up because the contractors went bankrupt twice. The original builders had stuffed walls and pillars with newspapers and plastic bottles instead of bricks.

The residents who weren't killed claimed the building fell apart in only a matter of seconds. They tried to sue the city for its lax construction codes and largely imaginary enforcement. One good thing that came out of the lawsuit was that the government promised it would pay one million NT, or $30,000, as compensation to families for each victim killed by the earthquake. Once that valuation was set, the government knew how much each life would cost in other natural disasters such as Typhoon Morakot and mudslides.

Back then, I thought I'd be worth a million bucks, or even a couple million in America. But my self-worth had crumbled like the Taiwan stock market whenever there was a global slowdown in technology sales. Shit. Who would they even pay the $30,000 to? I'd say let Frankie and Dwayne split the money before German Tsai and his boys got a piece of it.

I SWUNG NORTH TO Jianguo Road. If I stayed on it, I would go right by the noodle shop I'd been in when I read about Julia.

At a red light, I absently registered that "Jianguo" meant "Build a Nation." The major streets in Taipei are named after nationalistic and Confucian sayings. Hearing and seeing the names continually was supposed to drum the beliefs into everybody's heads, but instead their constant use stripped them down to everyday words, detached from any higher meaning, the same way that Presidents' Day and Labor Day in the United States conjure images of retail sales rather than the historical events behind the holidays.

Sometimes Taipei's street names have a comic effect.

Renai Road, literally "Benevolent Love Road," named after

the primary concept of Confucian humanistic thought, is often blocked by political demonstrators. Xinyi Road, named for "integrity" and "righteousness," has been marginalized by jackhammers and roadblocks for more than nine years as delays continue at an under-construction MRT station. The KMT named Guangfu Road during the martial-law era to express the idea that the "recovery" of the Chinese mainland from the Communists was in the near future. Guangfu, which intersects both Renai and Xinyi, often sees bumper-to-bumper traffic at rush hour. Commuters probably most wanted to "recover" with a beer in their hands.

I ROARED DOWN BUILD a Nation Road, anxious to get to Unknown Pleasures and blast the CD. I rarely listen to music at work, but a newly discovered Joy Division track was an event. I was going to play it as a dedication to Julia, even if she hadn't exactly shared my enthusiasm for the band.

As I neared the outer boundaries of the Shilin Night Market, I slowed to navigate around the double- and triple-parked vendor trailers. This mess would drive some people crazy, but I felt at ease here at the noisy, cluttered night market. There was honor in running a stall, my father had said. We merchants upheld standards and served the public well, or we heard about it right there and then. We couldn't get away with filler ingredients or second-rate meats, because our kitchens were on full display to the public. We were more accountable than politicians, because every day was an election day, and the people voted with their feet and money. If your stand charged too much or the food wasn't good enough, you were forced to improve or pack it in. Hiring pretty women in shorts and tight tops as counter people would only delay the inevitable.

Here's a tip for night-market patrons: the best stuff is at stands run by physically unattractive people in grease-covered clothes. The food speaks for itself. I wouldn't have been able to rebuild our business with the Joy Division imagery alone if Dwayne didn't cook like an Iron Chef. Don't forget to make sure the vendor's breath smells like the stall's food.

I watched as vendors at adjacent stalls helped each other load in.

Ah, yes, the night market is my world. This is where a truly diverse Taiwanese community exists, in this place and at this time.

When the sun goes down, Taipei comes alive. Even during the more reserved Ghost Month, people come in, eat out and loosen up. It's all right to talk loudly and be expressive. The buildings fade into dim shadows as the night lamps highlight the colorful food, clothes and people. It's a happy time. It's a fantasy time.

Look up. There's the moon grazing on cotton.

Maybe Julia will come round a corner and I'll hold her and tell her I miss her.

If Taipei comes alive at night, it reverts to undead during the day. Workaholics walking by ghostly grey buildings and breathing in air that's like gauze.

Give me the night any day.

I FELT A SLIGHT headache. Atmospheric pressure was up. That meant a rain was coming. It was going to be hard and fast.

I parked and walked over to Belle Amour.

Dancing Jenny was wearing a neo-*chipao* made of metallic fabric as she attended to an offering table in front of the store.

"I think this dress makes my tits look like Christmas-tree ornaments," she said, holding her chest out.

"Is that bad?" I asked. I didn't mind the mild flirting from her. What really unnerved me was a genuine connection, like what I'd felt briefly with Nancy.

"Depends on what the wearer's trying to say with her body." She lit up a cigarette and used it to light a few joss sticks placed in front of a carton of cigarettes, holding off on her first inhale until the incense was going strong. "This is for my dad. He was a big smoker."

Jenny put her hand behind my right ear and scraped something off the lobe with her fingernail.

"You've got a dry patch there," she said. "You're not drinking enough water."

"I'm avoiding water," I said. "The good brothers might try to steal my body if I go near that stuff."

She let go of my ear and slapped my shoulder. "Ha, I know you don't believe. But tell me something, Jing-nan. Would you mind if I kept burning money for your parents? When the economy's bad, it's even worse in the spirit world."

"Are you doing this for them, or for you?"

"It's for them and for you, too. Just in case it works."

"Jenny, it doesn't work."

"How do you know? You can't tell me millions of people following this tradition have been doing it for nothing."

"I do think it's useless." I felt something like a little cut inside my nasal passage. I rubbed my nose.

"Then all those people who have died are gone forever? As if they never existed?"

"Do you remember, Jenny?" I asked, feeling tears sliding down my face. "Do you remember Julia?"

A worried look came over her face. "The girl whose family ran the fruit stand here? Of course I remember her, your little girlfriend! How could I forget!"

"She's dead. She was the betel-nut girl who was murdered!"

Jenny hugged me. "I'm so sorry! What a terrible thing!"

Jenny had never felt so soft and warm. As I stood in her arms, sobbing, I missed my mother.

"I used to give that little girl clothes for her birthday, but I never saw her wear them," said Jenny, holding me and sighing.

Julia's mother had made sure they went straight into the trash, calling Jenny a whore and a pedophile.

"Julia was always a little funny about clothes," I said haltingly. "She liked a certain fit."

When I was cried out, I washed my face in Jenny's bathroom and held a cold, wet towel to my closed eyes.

After a few minutes, I met up with Kuilan. I wasn't as close with her as I was with Jenny, so she had never known about my master plan to make it big and marry Julia. She thought I merely wanted to get back to the US and finish college.

"I have to burn money for your parents," said Kuilan. "All the masters say the spirits are having a hard time right now." The Taoist and Buddhist masters on TV, anyway.

Kuilan waved a sheaf of coarse bamboo paper. I think she

wanted to show me she was using the higher-denominated notes with gold patches rather than silver patches.

"It's my gift to them, Jing-nan. I would like to do something nice for your father and mother."

How could I fight her on this?

"Thank you, Kuilan."

"All of us are going to burn money, me, my husband and definitely Ah-tien. We want him to do as many good things as possible for his karma."

Ah-tien glanced at me with accusing eyes. Because of me and my parents, he was going to have to wait in line at some temple and flop around for a bit.

"Ah-tien shouldn't have to go," I said. "He didn't even know my parents."

"Nonsense!" said Kuilan. "Ah-tien insists on going! It's so long since he's been to a temple. He's a stranger to the gods. No wonder so many bad things have been happening to him. So much unnecessary trouble."

Ah-tien was openly glaring at me now. I had embarrassed him by allowing his mother to complain about him in public.

Kuilan's husband approached the stand with a sack of flour on his back. "Good to see you, Jing-nan!" he called, grunting as he flipped the sack to the ground.

"Sir, that's much too heavy for you to be lifting on your own!"

"It's a good workout, don't worry."

"Of course it's too heavy," Kuilan said. "My good-for-nothing son won't even do the smallest tasks for his father."

"I said I would do it!" Ah-tien grunted. "He didn't even give me a chance to!" Then he bared his teeth at me. "What's so great about you, huh? You think you're so smart and rich you can go to America? Look at you now. You've got the same job as me!"

"You apologize, you little ingrate!" said Kuilan's husband. Kuilan herself brandished a rolling pin in an obviously well-rehearsed gesture.

"Jing-nan doesn't have a police record!" she yelled. "He doesn't have obscene tattoos all over his chest and back!"

"It's all right, Kuilan," I said, moving away. "He was only

kidding." I nodded to Ah-tien, but the gesture wasn't returned. If I shared an elevator ride with that guy, only one of us would make it to his floor.

"WHAT ARE YOU DOING?" Dwayne asked as I untied the power cord to the boom box on the shelf.

"I'm going to play some music and psych myself up."

"The CD function's busted, boss."

"It worked fine the last time I tried it."

"Wait, let me see it first." He reached out a hand slick with meat runoff.

"No way!" Dwayne would rather smash the entire stereo system than listen to Joy Division again. I clicked open the lid and found another CD in it. Dwayne swooped in and quickly palmed it.

"Just play anything but you-know-what," he said, as he managed to stick the bare CD in a back pocket.

"I'm the boss and we're going to listen to my music." I examined the playing surface of my CD for scratches out of habit and then popped it in and cued it to "In a Lonely Place." The funereal synthesizer sounds washed over all of us.

"For Christ's sake," moaned Dwayne, "do you really have to play this mopey-motherfucker music?"

"It's good," I said.

"This is a problem. Don't you get it? The singer hanged himself! This music scares all the girls away. That's why you don't get laid! Ain't that right, Frankie?"

Frankie the Cat took a drag on his cigarette and wiped his mouth with the back of the same hand. "You can get used to it," he offered.

"No, this has to go," said Dwayne. "We've listened to this lousy band five hundred times already. Let's just switch it to the radio. Or turn it off."

MUSIC HAD CHANGED DWAYNE's life.

He had been a star baseball player as a kid. Outfielders backed up to the fence for him. My father told me if Dwayne had played on a stronger team, he would have been bound for Williamsport,

Pennsylvania, for the Little League World Championship. Taiwanese teams have won the title there seventeen times over the years.

He downplays it a lot, but Dwayne's smart. He can do math faster than me. With his grades and athletic ability, Dwayne could have gone to almost any college he wanted to; apparently some college in Japan wanted to recruit him.

In 1994, though, Taiwan's native community suddenly found worldwide fame. The German electronic-music group Enigma had a global hit, "Return to Innocence," that sampled a recording of an Amis folk song about drinking. Aboriginal culture became trendy.

That summer Dwayne went to a week-long retreat at an Amis village in Taitung County in the boonies in Taiwan's southeast. He met other high-school kids like him who were out of touch with their culture. Dwayne learned some Amis words, wore a headdress, stepped through some dances and made his own shoulder bag.

When he came back to Taipei, he had changed completely. Dwayne told his urbanized parents he wouldn't be going to college; he wanted to explore his lost heritage and understand who he was. Dwayne spent his days listening to indigenous reggae and hip-hop while studying the Amis language on CD.

Dwayne moved out within a year. He was determined to join an active Amis community and reject modern Taiwanese society. Aboriginals shouldn't have to be a part of the society foisted upon the island by the descendants of Chinese immigrants— whether they were mainlanders or yams. Even baseball, which used to be all Dwayne loved, was a game that had been brought in by the Japanese colonizers. There were other, authentic Amis activities he could be doing. There had to be.

Dwayne made his way back to Taitung County and headed to the Amis village that was the site of his reawakening. He was in for a shock, though.

The village's main source of income was the busloads of tourists streaming in. Men and women danced in their native costumes for the cameras, and then backstage they would smoke cigarettes, drink beer and listen to American or Japanese heavy metal.

After the shows the performers changed out of their Amis wear and into their street clothes, which meant jeans and T-shirts, before

a night of Hollywood movies on VHS or hitting the bars in Taitung
City.

This was what life was really like in the village. "Being Amis"
was just a job. The high school retreat Dwayne had participated
in was something the management level of the village had come
up with to show there was a socially redeeming value to the whole
enterprise. It helped preserve the corporation's nonprofit status
with the government.

But there was plenty of profit. The managers drove nice cars and
lived in homes built in the mountains nearby. The performers, who
ranged in age from the teens to the sixties, were housed in dorms
on the site. They had come from all over the island. Some were
runaways. Some were army veterans. Only a handful of them said
they could speak the Amis language, and all of them declined to
teach Dwayne.

"Too much trouble," an older man said, not specifying which
party would be more troubled.

The managers liked Dwayne's physical build. They offered him
a position in the chorus of the harvest dance. As he hopped around
bare-chested in the steps being taught to him, he began to feel
slightly ill, and then after a few days, angry. Dancing for tourists
like a trained monkey wasn't something a real Amis would do. And
despite all the talk about how Amis culture is traditionally matri-
lineal, all the managers of "the village" were men.

After spending a fitful night in the dorms, Dwayne went to the
older performer, the one who wouldn't teach him the Amis language, and told him the performance was a sham.

The old man nodded and like all the other actors—because that's
what they were—continued to eat his breakfast of fried dough,
soupy rice, peanuts and eggs.

When Dwayne suggested the performers unionize to earn better
wages, the old man put down his bowl and chopsticks.

"That is an idea," he said.

About an hour later, Dwayne was forced into a van and driven
to the Taitung City station. He was put on the next train north and
warned never to come back.

After Dwayne got back to Taipei, he put on weight and lost his touch at baseball. Odd jobs led to working at the Shilin Night Market, and that led to working for my father.

I TORTURED DWAYNE BY playing "In a Lonely Place" twice before turning off the boom box. "I'll save this CD for more discerning ears," I said. "You want to put your Amis language CD back in here?" He handed his CD to me without a word.

"It was a good song," Frankie offered as he sliced squid into rings.

"You can't be serious," said Dwayne.

"Most music is too happy."

"You want me to play it again?" I asked.

"No," both Frankie and Dwayne said.

"I went to see Julia's parents today," I offered.

"That was good of you to do," said Dwayne. He patted my back. "How was it?"

"It was sad, but it was fine." I wheeled out the front grill to the street.

"Her folks are pretty religious."

"Yeah." I didn't want to mention that I was going to do some digging into Julia's past. It probably wasn't going to amount to anything, anyway.

"So, how are you doing, Jing-nan? Are you sure you're up for working? You know me and Frankie can handle the stand ourselves."

I smiled as hard as I could. "There's nowhere else I'd rather be, Dwayne. I want to keep myself busy."

More customers came up, and I was busy right until close. It was the second night of Ghost Month, and people were a little less subdued. Of all the activities typically shunned, eating wasn't one of them. I met some Jewish friends in college who told me they fasted during some holidays. I was surprised to hear of such a thing. Starving yourself on purpose would never happen in Taiwan.

DURING A SMALL BREAK in the action, I looked around to the other three corners of the intersection and took it all in.

Kuilan's Big Shot Hot Pot was really packing it in. It looked like some students were having a dumpling-eating contest, while in another part of the dining room a bunch of tourists were taking pictures and yelling as one of them ate a bowl of pig-brain soup.

"Man, it's like a freaking *brain*!"

"How can you put that in your mouth?"

Then, without even a clap of thunder or flicker of lightning, rain plunged from the sky. A group of young women coming out of Belle Amour stood under its narrow awning and waited. I once went home with a girl that way, by walking over and offering her an umbrella. I hadn't meant to pick her up. Just happened.

Guilt began to gnaw at me. *Well, Julia, I wasn't betraying you because I never said I'd never sleep with anybody else. I certainly have never loved anybody else. That's for sure.* I tried to picture that last woman, but I kept seeing Nancy's face.

Rain fell as thick as metal chopsticks, and water sizzled on the pavement. The owner of Beyond Human stepped out, looked up and frowned. Business had never been too good, and the Ghost Month specials weren't moving. His grotesque demon and dragon sculptures sat in his front display cases, as ugly and undatable as his target demographic.

Dwayne stepped out into the rain, umbrella in hand, for a walk and a smoke. Frankie put out the octopus skewers, our most perishable ones, for prep grilling. If they didn't get bought today, we could put them in a stew tomorrow.

Frankie always kept himself busy.

IN THE WANING DAYS of the civil war in 1949, when the Communists won land as quickly as they could march through the Chinese mainland, people who were aligned with the Nationalists escaped to Taiwan by plane, if they could afford it, or by boat. The island was one hundred miles away from China and looked like the last refuge available.

Many families weren't able to come over intact. Some children were sent over by themselves. Soldiers brought over their women.

Frankie was only eight years old when his teacher led the class out of school and onto a navy vessel. Most of his classmates eventually reunited with their families in Taiwan. Frankie never saw his family again and grew up in a group home in a *juancun* village, singing songs that glorified the KMT and foretold the death of all the "land bandit" Communists on the mainland.

Frankie was told Mao's soldiers had killed his mother and father and jailed his older brother. When he was only twelve, he left school to train in a brigade set up by the KMT comprising orphaned kids—a group that trained as hard as adult men because they had a personal vendetta against the Reds.

Frankie was the standout. He could run the fastest, shoot the most accurately and hold his breath even longer than his commanding officer. Before he met Chiang Kai-shek at a special inspection and dinner honoring the boys, he had his arms tattooed to match those of the KMT veterans: "Kill Zhu and Weed Out Mao" on the left arm and "Anti-Communist and Anti-Russia" on the right. Frankie broke protocol when he rolled up his sleeves to show Chiang. The Generalissimo was stunned, and then offered one of his tight-lipped smiles of unbreakable resolve and gave Frankie an arms-length hug on the shoulders.

"This boy!" was all Chiang said.

Frankie and the other top orphans joined the elite frogmen for suicidal propaganda missions. KMT boats brought them to within two miles of China's coast. The frogmen swam the rest of the way into Fujian Province. They planted the KMT flag on the tops of difficult-to-climb cliffs and blew up power stations. They tried to avoid detection, but killed Communist guards when it was unavoidable. Most of the frogmen were killed by enemy fire and by drowning.

In 1960 Frankie was allowed to march in the parade that welcomed Eisenhower.

The next year, he turned twenty and it all fell apart.

KMT intelligence discovered that Frankie's brother had not only joined the Communists, but was an officer. How would it look for the KMT to use Frankie as one of its public faces when his very own brother was a high-ranking Red?

They arrested Frankie in the early morning, before he had a chance to get dressed. He never even had a trial. Frankie was transferred from cell to cell, finally landing in Green Island, the infamous offshore prison that housed inmates judged to be the most dangerous. Frankie was there because of his tactical skills, but other prisoners were influential human-rights activists who had organized against the KMT regime.

My father told me that for several months Frankie was kept in a cell that filled halfway with seawater at high tide.

After more than a decade of imprisonment, Frankie was released. The KMT had discovered that his brother wasn't a Communist officer at all. He was actually living in Burma with other Chinese refugees. The mix-up was that the wife the brother had abandoned had remarried a Communist officer.

The military offered to take Frankie back, but he refused. He attended an official discharge ceremony in Taipei and then wandered through the city until it turned dark. He came upon the Shilin Night Market and saw crowds of people eating and laughing. Happy people. He stopped at a stand called Tastes Good run by a father and son and asked how to set up a food stall. It turned into a job interview, and my grandfather hired Frankie. It was the three of them for many years, until my father got married. We hired Dwayne when my grandfather got sick.

My father told me Frankie had a Vietnamese wife he didn't talk about and that I should never ask him about the woman.

DWAYNE CAME BACK FROM his break and showed Frankie and me a video he'd just shot on his phone of an elderly man playing a nose flute to a group of people taking shelter under a canopy.

"Sounds like two flutes," said Frankie.

"That's pretty neat," I said.

"It helped my ears recover from your crappy music," said Dwayne. "That guy's from the Paiwan tribe. They were bad as hell, man."

"Is there a Paiwan stall now?" I asked.

"Naw," said Dwayne as he chuckled a little. "When he was done playing he launched into this whole thing about how Ghost Month was offensive to the one true god and that we were all welcome to join the Presbyterian Church."

The rain began to taper off and we got back to work. I got a group of Canadians to come over. To my surprise, I found out that they grew up on farms and had no problem coming in and chowing down on stewed pig intestines.

You meet all kinds of people at the night market.

Everybody from everywhere is here. I've met people from Egypt and even North Korea. But no matter where you're from, you learn immediately to walk slowly, try everything and take your time.

It's annoying to see anybody in a rush and getting pushy, more so when a young man does it with his face and neck smeared in blood. It was still fairly early in the night, around 10 P.M., when he showed up on my stretch of the night market. The rain had stopped by then and he was skidding on water, shoving aside anyone in his way. He was on Dabei and approaching my business.

The man's black T-shirt was covered in dark splotches. His baggy black slacks didn't do him any favors. When a pocket in the crowd opened up, he ran through but tripped when the material got caught in the tines of a knee-level sales rack and a wall of iPhone accessories crashed onto his back. He went down but scrambled back to his feet, throwing off the rack like a cartoon turtle ditching its shell in order to run faster.

When the man got to the intersection, he turned right on Dadong and squatted down. I kept him in view and tried to see whom he was running from. Dancing Jenny was making her way over to me.

"That guy's head is slashed!" she yelled.

"Wow, what the fuck!" shouted Dwayne as he came out to the street.

My guess was that the man had tried to shoplift and got more than he had bargained for from the store owners. Dwayne marched over to him and Jenny and I followed.

The man was tired out. He slipped from his squat and sat on the wet street, panting. He seemed to be about twenty years old, and it had been a rough twenty years. He was probably living the same sort of *liumang*, petty-criminal, life that Ah-tien had been. So it was probably fitting that Ah-tien was calling out to him.

"Yang-yang! Yang-yang!"

Dwayne stood over Yang-yang. Jenny and I were behind him. I became conscious that we were holding hands tightly. Ah-tien made his way to the other side of Yang-yang and touched his shoulder. Blood was seeping through the collar of his shirt, as if Yang-yang's head was the end of a roll cake filled with strawberry jam.

I heard a commotion coming from behind us and it became pretty obvious that a number of people were after him. Men were yelling to be let through.

Three beefy guys wearing shades and black, short-sleeved oxfords muscled their way from different areas of the crowd and fell upon him. Cops. People who ran less-reputable carts covered their pirated DVDs with T-shirts and pieces of cardboard.

One of the cops elbowed Dwayne, possibly on purpose, and grunted, "*Gan ni niang!*" Literally, it means "do your mother," but the figurative meaning is decidedly worse.

I thought Dwayne was going to punch the guy's lights out, cop or no cop. It would have been a fair fight. But the guy had two equally big friends. Dwayne crossed his arms and flared his nostrils. The runner scrambled to get up, but one of the blackshirts, a guy with a bruise on his left cheek, kicked his feet out from under him. I noticed Ah-tien had split.

"Thought you could get away, huh?" the bruised guy yelled down at the runner. He and another man picked up their quarry and each twisted an arm back as they hustled him away. The third man, the one who had elbowed Dwayne, followed behind.

"He's a criminal!" the elbower yelled to the crowd. "We're here to take him away! Don't let it ruin your evening! So sorry!" When he passed by Jenny and me, I noticed he was wearing a vest under his shirt.

The crowd melted away. Dwayne bent over and picked up the iPhone-accessories rack for a grateful older woman. She patted his arms and said, "Fuck those cops. Don't pay any attention to them."

Everybody thought the three men had been policemen until a cop actually showed up about half an hour later. I was already back at my front grill.

The cop was a thin veteran with short, white hair bristles and a chip on his shoulder about not having been promoted from his beat by now. He came up to me and tapped his keys against the glass of my sneeze guard.

"What did you see happen over here?" he asked.

"Some guy came in, and some other guys picked him up and took him away," I said.

The cop was staring at some beef-tripe skewers and tugging at his windbreaker as if ready to molt. "These any good?" he asked.

"They're the best," I said, tilting my head. "If you *buy* two, I'll throw another in free."

A pained look came over his face. "I'm on duty now, I really shouldn't eat." He licked his lips. "Anybody else I should talk to?"

"Talk to Dancing Jenny over there." I pointed my tongs at Belle Amour.

"Oh, her," he sighed. "Never mind, I know where I should go." He strode off to Big Shot Hot Pot.

"Jing-nan," said Dwayne. "Go see what this guy is up to. Something's up."

I followed the cop, who had gained a confident swagger by the time he entered Kuilan's business. He pointed at Ah-tien. "Hey, you little hooligan, what happened here tonight?" he boomed.

Ah-tien wiped the chopped garlic chives from his hands. "I don't know," he said.

"Some *liumang* came running through here, but the gang of heavies caught up with him, right? I'll bet they were people you know, or at least recognize."

Ah-tien didn't even look up to reply. "I didn't see anything. Go ask somebody else."

"I'm asking you, little cocksucker!"

Kuilan stepped up as her husband crossed his arms. "Leave my son alone, officer. If he says he didn't see anything, then he didn't."

"Leave him alone, huh? What about the time I had to come over to your house to break up a fight between your husband and this little dirtbag? You begged me to help you then! I took him in to jail for a night to scare him straight, didn't I?" The cop smiled and rocked on his feet. He was getting off on this.

"I didn't ask for you to beat him up!" said Kuilan.

"Nobody beat him up. As I tried to explain to you before, the kid knocked his own head into the wall to make me look bad. Anyway, it seems to have worked a little. It's nice to see him all cowed like this." I had forgotten how bad cops could be. There was this guy in Wanhua District who used to harass my friends and me while I was growing up. The *jiaotous* helped us by showing us shortcuts through alleys and building basements where we could lie low for a while. For the most part, cops didn't seem to be around, unless there was a huge demonstration. They liked to stay in the air-conditioned station rather than walk beats and prevent crime with their presence. One block in the Ximending area of Wanhua District had been classified as a high-crime area because of a karaoke bar frequented by members of different gangs who wanted to drink and fight over girls. There had been shootings in the street outside. Instead of posting officers there, the police merely installed more security cameras. It was safer for the cops to investigate *after* whatever assault had occurred by reviewing footage.

No wonder the Huangs weren't happy with the investigation into Julia's death. With faulty camera footage, the police probably had no idea how to go about solving the crime.

As I watched the cop leer at Ah-tien and Kuilan, I felt someone brush up against my right elbow. It was Jenny. She was always good about keeping one eye on the street.

Ah-tien was still chopping up chives with a metal cleaver. It was pretty clear that if the cop continued egging him on like this, Ah-tien's next chop would be just above the knot of the officer's dark blue tie. The cop knew what he was doing. He had one hand on his truncheon. I hadn't thought they carried those anymore.

"Ah-tien, do you like being here?" the cop taunted. "I think you're quite suited for women's work."

I didn't say anything. Maybe a part of me wanted to see Ah-tien cut the guy. But Jenny spoke up. "Hey, you lousy cop, leave him alone! He doesn't know anything!"

He whirled around. "Oh, it's you, huh? Still doing porn?"

Jenny put up her phone and began to record video. His smile died instantly.

"Well, if any of you hear any more about this incident, then please call the station. Good night." He nodded and marched down Dabei Road.

"Are you all right, Ah-tien?" Jenny asked.

He shrugged, still chopping in a detached manner. "Yeah," he said.

"Thank you, Jenny," said Kuilan's husband.

"That was very smart of you, to use the phone camera," Kuilan added.

"The lens is broken, but it still makes a good prop."

"I know it's probably best not to get involved," said Kuilan's husband, "but do you think we're safe here? What if the *liumangs* come back?"

"It's no problem," said Kuilan as she also took up a cleaver. There was no such thing as having too many chives. "The whole thing started somewhere else, and they just happened to run here. Nothing to worry about."

"Well," I said, "I'd better get back to the stand before Dwayne kills me."

Jenny muttered to me, "This cop was sent to hush things up, not to figure out what happened."

"Seems like it. What a fucking asshole he was to Ah-tien . . . and to you!"

"Jing-nan, I never did porn. It was nude modeling. They tried to . . . anyway, the judge threw it out."

"I believe you, Jenny."

"I wasn't underage or anything."

"Jenny, I'm sure you were doing the right thing."

She smiled and gave me a big hug. "Stay safe," she said. I watched her walk away and wondered what sort of life Jenny had had.

CHAPTER SEVEN

Traffic on the way home was light as people were still avoiding routes along the water. There didn't seem to be any more ghosts than at any other time of year, but I did notice a modified black pickup truck keeping pace with me. I slowed down a bit, and so did the car. I sped up, and its red lights zoomed past me. It pulled over and stopped on the shoulder. I nearly flipped my moped trying to brake in time.

A man got out of the passenger side. It was the American who had confronted me earlier in front of the Huangs' building. Now he was wearing a dark suit that rendered him nearly invisible in the night.

"Jing-nan," he said. "You're poking your nose where it shouldn't be."

"Is this about the *liumang*?" I asked.

"Don't get smart with me, bitch!" Typical conceited Taiwanese-American asshole. "You stay away from Julia's family and the investigation!"

"What are you talking about?"

"I know for sure you saw the Huangs this morning. Let's make it your last visit there."

"They're family friends. Julia was my girlfriend."

"I'm giving you one warning. Do you know how easily I could

have knocked your sorry ass over into the river? Might happen next time."

I crossed my arms and felt my skinny biceps. "Who are you?" I asked.

He shifted stance so his feet were even with his shoulders. "I'm a guy with a gun. That's who I am."

"What happened to Julia?"

"She's dead. Unless you want to join her, stay far away from the Huangs."

"I get it," I said. It lacked conviction, but it was good enough for him. The American got back in the car, which eased away from the shoulder before peeling out. I got back on my moped like a little fucking boy.

It wasn't until I was taking the highway exit home to the Wanhua District that I started shaking. I'd never had my life threatened before by someone who could possibly back it up.

Looking into Julia's story was dangerous. Who the hell ran the betel-nut stand she'd worked at? Gangs? Cops? Americans?

Who was the Taiwanese-American, and why was he watching the Huangs' apartment? He knew who I was. If he really wanted me dead, he'd already had a few opportunities to pop me. But why would he? He had already written me off as a shadow from Julia's past. A love-sick schoolboy chasing a ghost. I was something to brush aside, not a threat.

MY HOME DISTRICT, WANHUA, is the old part of Taipei, settled by Chinese from Fujian Province after the Ming Dynasty fell in 1644. I say "settled" in the American sense: the Chinese immigrants drove the natives from the land. The Mandarin name "Wanhua" is derived from the name the indigenous aborigines had given it, which was closer to "Banka," the Taiwanese pronunciation. Taiwanese also called it "Monga," and that was the source of the title of that blockbuster gangster film that has made Wanhua a tourist destination.

Many areas of Taipei still have the names given to them by people who were subsequently forced off. Two of Taipei's biggest districts by population—Shilin, which has my night market, and Beitou, famous for its hot springs—still carry names derived from the extinct Ketagalan language. The Ketagalan homeland was unfortunately in the same footprint as the future Taipei, and they were pushed out as Han Chinese arrived and built out the city. The Japanese after them claimed even more land when they renamed the city "Taihoku." When the city reverted back to "Taipei" at the end of World War II, there weren't any Ketagalans left to push out. We killed them off and took their land, but at least we kept their place names. That was an American thing to do.

I felt bad about the way aborigines had been treated over the years. I wasn't alone. The government had made small but symbolic concessions to Taiwan's first people. Long Live Chiang Kai-shek Road—seriously, that was the name—in front of the Presidential Building was renamed "Ketagalan Boulevard" in the 1990s. The Generalissimo's reputation had slipped by then from Savior of the People to The Wedge That Continues to Divide Us.

The Ketagalan aren't even one of the fourteen tribes recognized by the government. Taiwan doesn't acknowledge their existence, but they are still here, somewhere. The early Chinese immigrants to Taiwan were almost all men, and they hooked up with native women. Around the Taipei settlement, that would mean the Ketagalan.

The Japanese administration recognized the tenacity of Taiwanese aborigines after fighting many deadly skirmishes against them. In World War II, Japan organized native peoples as the dogged Takasago Volunteers. How dogged? The last holdout of the Imperial Japanese Army to surrender—in December 1974—was Amis, like Dwayne. When Private Teruo Nakamura, whose Amis name was Attun Palalin, was brought out from the Indonesian jungle he had been hiding in, his years of resigned solitude came to an abrupt end. Palalin said he had kept his mind off his wife (who had remarried) and son (who was born after he left Taiwan in 1942) by focusing on gardening.

My story wasn't too different from Palalin's. I was living and working among other people, but it was a solitary existence. Julia's death had dragged me out of my crude hut to reality. I was stunned, naked and blinking back at the world.

—

I DROVE BY LONGSHAN Temple, a gigantic open-air complex built in 1738, probably the top foreign-tourist destination in Wanhua. Taiwanese people come here in droves, too, to flop in front of Guanyin, the goddess of mercy, Mazu, the goddess of the sea, and other idols.

The temple stood here when the British invaded Taiwan in 1840 during the Opium War. It was here when the French invaded in 1844 during the Sino-French War. Longshan Temple was already one of Taipei's oldest temples in 1885, when Qing Dynasty China finally decided that Taiwan was indeed a Chinese province and not merely a "ball of mud." When the Japanese took over Taiwan in 1895, they wisely decided to leave Longshan be, although they destroyed other temples that featured Chinese folk deities in a quest to desinicize the island. The temple survived World War II, when the US bombed the shit out of it, convinced that Japan was hiding armaments among the idols of the immortals. There were stories of miracles the goddesses performed during that war. In 1945 believers witnessed Mazu materializing in the sky, spreading her skirts to deflect most of the bombs from US planes away from the temple. Despite her efforts, the main hall was completely destroyed. But underneath the rubble, the Guanyin idol, eyes still closed in meditative serenity, was completely intact. People see these incidents as proof of divine intervention. I see it as proof that the people operating the temples will spread such stories in the name of preserving their livelihoods.

Lit up by the moon, lanterns and streetlights, Longshan, literally "Dragon Mountain," looks just like a temple should. Even a nonbeliever could agree to that. Dragon sculptures in full color prowl around the tiled roofs and columns while phoenixes and other supernatural-creature pals do their best to keep up. The walls and ceilings are covered with painted, carved wood and stone. Angry guardians painted on open doors warn evil spirits not to enter. For Ghost Month, the temple hangs lanterns and bamboo hats to guide lost spirits to Longshan.

The temple was the last place I wanted to go when I was a

kid. We had a smaller one on our block that my parents bypassed because it only had Taoist idols. They brought me to Longshan for their weekly stop to ask the blessings of the gods and goddesses, every single last one of them. "The most forgotten ones are the most grateful," my mother often said. I think my parents expected me to bow and pray with them to each idol as we made our way through the inner courtyard, where there was a new god or goddess every few meters, but I just stood by them and waited. So many old people came to the temple, there was never a seat available. One time, out of frustration and out of view of my parents, I discreetly gave the finger to Mazu, the sea goddess, the mother of heaven and essentially the patron deity of Taiwan. Nothing bad happened to me. Well, not immediately.

The Longshan visits were more than a waste of time. I found the energy of the miserable people at the temple to be completely draining. Most people weren't regular visitors like my parents. Most people only came to beg the gods for help because they were suffering from health or money problems, or their loved ones were. Maybe some people had come to give thanks for their good fortune, but they were drowned out by whimpering elderly people begging for forgiveness before death and muttering young people who had just been laid off.

Most galling of all—and even my parents found them offensive—were the slick characters rolling dice before the altars, thinking one of the iterations of Buddha or a Taoist demon would give them winning lottery numbers.

On certain days my parents left wrapped pieces of candy at the pedestals and altar sills. Those were good days for me, because I would swipe most of them and hide them in my pockets for a sugar boost later. I was scared the first time that I would be punished for stealing a treat left for the divinities.

I asked the oldest kid I knew at the time.

"Dwayne, is it true the gods can punish people?"

"Not for taking candy, Jing-nan. The gods exist, but they don't really interfere down here for minor infractions. My ancestors prayed to our gods to make the Han Chinese go away, and look what happened. You guys took over. Maybe we weren't good enough to our gods." Then he laughed. "Hell, maybe you people are our punishment for not being pious enough!"

THE FAMILIAR STREETS WERE dark and empty from the temple to my house. Not my house. My home. This was my home. I stopped at a red light for nobody and got mad.

Who the hell did that Taiwanese-American asshole think he was to threaten me? Now that I was back on familiar turf and my antagonist was long gone, I was feeling brave, even cocky.

I wasn't going to back off one bit, you motherfucker. I was going to find out why Julia came back and tell her parents everything.

He made me think about all the mean American-born Chinese and Taiwanese, the ABCs and ABTs, back at UCLA, who used to talk around me as if I didn't understand English just because I had the slightest accent. I ended up being best friends with pretty much every other kind of people, because they didn't shun me for the way I spoke.

Let any of those fake Asians try to speak the same languages their parents did. They'd choke big-time.

That American asshole should be ashamed of his Mandarin, instead of thinking he was superior and had authority over me. I was going to show him. I was going to keep one eye on my rearview mirror, but I was going to keep going forward.

I bathed and instead of drying off completely, I put on a shirt and boxers to absorb the water and walked around in the damp clothes. It was one way to beat the heat. They helped cool my body as the moisture evaporated.

It was a hot night, but that was hardly breaking news. Every night was going to be hot until November. Only then would the temperature dip back down below twenty-one degrees Celsius.

To do this right, I had to put myself in the right frame of mind. I was going back to high school, after all.

I pulled out a bottle of Kirin from my squat refrigerator and drank it as quickly as I could. I didn't drink that often and a single beer would hit me harder than a lot of people. I only wanted to numb myself a little. Two beers would send me straight to sleep.

I fished out my cloth high school yearbook from a storage box under the dining-room table and brought it into my bedroom, which had the best lamp. I switched on the Teco fan that had been my grandfather's prized possession and one luxury. I sat on the edge of the mattress to read.

After a few pages of the wallet-sized individual pictures of students came several dozen pages of stats. Class rankings, grade point averages and finals scores for each semester. ESPN would have been proud to have such detailed figures. I cringed every time I saw my name because of how far down the page I had to go to find it. I was in the top three for only one class, English. I was in second place. Julia, of course, was in first.

Hmm. Look at that. There was Cookie Monster, Wang Ming-kuo, in third place. I didn't know he had done so well at English. Rich little Peggy Lee Xiaopei was in fourth. I guess it makes sense that we all went on to American universities—and the three of them on to NYU.

The fan, groaning, shook its head sadly from side to side and sent over a breeze to turn the page on my accomplishment and expose my next shortcoming.

Each successive class ranking saw my name bobble to the lower half of the top ten. That's actually pretty good, but at the time I remember thinking I was so dumb. After all, the name at the top of the page was always valedictorian Julia Huang, except for in Military Education and Robotics. She couldn't handle the rifle training with live fire and slipped to sixth place. I was in fifth, thanks to the written test and tire run, which I was oddly good at. The guy who came in first, Tseng Wen-chen, was a small, meek sort of guy, so it was surprising he'd taken to guns so well. He even outshot the teacher, who had served in the army. Tseng went on to win a national shooting competition, and now he's some sort of advisor to the Australian film industry.

Look at Ming-kuo, taking second in Physics. You go, Cookie Monster!

Lin Cheng-sheng. There's always some Lin in the way. I was always so jealous of him, and now I can't remember why. He was taller than me, but he wasn't better looking. That's for sure. He took the top grade in Circuits, and I'm sure he's some engineering whiz at a chip company in China. I'll bet he never thinks about me.

The less important parts of the yearbook, including the social activities, were near the end, but they weren't detailed with the same precision as the students' grades. There, on the karaoke-contest spread, was the record of my one moment of triumph in years of academic struggle. The picture made me look even more heroic than I remembered. There I was, kneeling down and touching Julia's hand.

And there, right behind Julia, was the girl I met today at Bauhaus, also reaching for me. The young Nancy, a waif wearing a too-big dress, was still in her larval stage. I could see the potential in the photo, though.

Why was I looking at Nancy more than Julia?

I tore through a few pages to get to a poem I wrote, based on a dream in which I was floating over Taiwan, a premonition that I was going abroad. The editors titled it "New Pledge of Allegiance."

Taiwan, you monsoon-pissed-on yam of the Pacific Rim! How many nations have sought and fought to possess you in a game of hot sweet potato! The Republic of China, the diplomatically shunned nation of my birth! You seismically challenged tiny leaf trembling at the real China's doorstep! Formosa, you humid-as-a-bamboo-steamer island nation of workaholics! Takasago Koku, don't forget to clean off the Shinto shrines for Qingming, because your Jap gods need love, too! You land of the brown robbers, I hate you for what you've made me—a man with no country, no identity and no future!

I shouldn't have put the Japanese slur in there. Hell, I shouldn't have written the damned thing at all, much less had it published in the yearbook. It was prescient, though. I was a man with no future.

I'd written it down to sort of get the words from the dream out of my head and stuffed it into the yearbook committee's mailbox anonymously. Some people were pretty outraged by it. The faculty advisor, Mr. Shen, stood by its inclusion, saying the poem was written by one student but spoke for many. Good old Mr. Shen. I heard he opened a bicycling-tour company down at Sun Moon Lake.

The back section of the yearbook detailed our college destinations. Those going abroad were listed after even the lowliest Taiwanese schools.

Julia had gotten into Columbia and Yale, but NYU had offered her a scholarship to cover everything, and she took it. I knew Peggy Lee Xiaopei and Wang Ming-kuo had also gone to NYU, but I wanted to double-check to see if anyone else had gone. Anyone would have been nicer than Peggy or more normal than Cookie Monster, but there was nobody.

WHEN I WAS REALLY young, that mainlander Peggy told me I was a Jap because my grandfather was a Jap. I made the mistake of asking him if he was.

"What!" he yelled, spraying me with betel-nut juice. "Who dares to call me a Jap?"

"A girl at school said you were. You read Japanese newspapers."

"Just because I can read and speak Japanese, that makes me a Jap? You're learning English in school. Does that make you English?"

I wiped my face, which was now slick with his spit and my tears.

He slid over a bucket of organs to me. "This is your punishment. Wash all the shit out of those intestines!" he growled before stomping away from the stall.

I burst into open sobs until I felt someone grab my shoulder. It was Frankie the Cat. He winked at me, then took the bucket and began cleaning.

Peggy played pranks on me as we got older, everything from tripping me to spraying me with perfume. In high school her antagonism morphed into a mildly obsessive crush that I found unnerving in its consistency. When there was a seat free next to me, she'd be in it. When I stepped away from my parents' food stall to walk around the night market, no matter how late it was, there was Peggy walking next to me, her shoulder pressed against my arm.

It didn't stop until Julia slapped her in the girls' locker room. We could hear the commotion from the boys' locker room.

Funny how Peggy also chose to go to NYU. Her family had the money to send her to any school she wanted to go to and, after graduation, set her up anywhere in the world.

I couldn't believe her stupid company wouldn't take my phone call. Now I had to see her in person. Maybe she was better now, mellower and married.

Ming-kuo was a different case. I had no idea where he was or what he was doing. We used to call him Cookie Monster because he was obese and had googly eyes. Both his parents worked long hours, and his grandmother let him eat junk food all the time. He didn't look anything like the scholar he was. Even the teachers called him Cookie Monster when they cited him for doing exceptionally well on a test. He would just take it with a stupid smile, thinking the people laughing the hardest were his friends.

I searched for him online but found nothing. He had to be up to something. Nerds who were teased in school always became successful in the end, right? Look at Bill Gates. Maybe he was a reasonably well-adjusted head of a start-up in Silicon Valley who worked out regularly, the ugly duckling far in the past.

I wrote an email to NYU's alumni coordinator, asking for Ming-kuo's whereabouts. I figured at the very least he and I could exchange some emails and I could find out about Julia in addition to the radical transformation he'd hopefully gone through.

I WOKE MYSELF UP in the middle of the night, unsure if I'd swung an arm or a leg out to defend myself from some dream-world menace. I fell asleep again in an instant. In the morning all but the vaguest details of my imagined struggle were left in my head, and after I yawned even those were gone.

My phone had a news alert on the body of a young man found floating in the Shuangxi Creek, which was just to the north of the Shilin Night Market. Victim unidentified.

I got on my computer to look up a corresponding story. The only other significant detail was that he was wearing a black T-shirt, like that guy who had been running through the night market. I searched for more about Julia. Nothing.

I searched for our old classmate Peggy Lee. She was still a

secondary player within her family, only mentioned as a daughter
of her mogul father.

I ate two bowls of unsweetened instant oatmeal while sitting at
my PC in my bedroom. Having spent my whole life around food—
I'd learned how to walk by balancing myself between dividing
walls of food stands—I found my own tastes tended toward the
bland side.

What I really devoured was music. I was somewhat aware that
I was chewing and swallowing as the sound of a Cocteau Twins
bootleg played over my stereo speakers. It wasn't actually their best
stuff. It was from late in the Cocteau Twins' career, the early 1990s
when they were already on a major multinational label. Some fans
called it a sellout move when they left their little indie label, but the
music was still good.

Joy Division was the only band I listened to for years. For the
longest time, I even refused to voluntarily listen to a single note of
successor band New Order, on principle alone. That was the same
stubborn kid who made the crazy promise to Julia.

I don't remember how I changed, but it came slowly. Hearing
New Order's song "Regret" at random was a major turning point.
It really stuck in my head. I loved everything about it—the snappy
drumming, the trebly bass and the catchy guitar riff. After that
I had to have everything New Order did. Now I do have some
"regrets" about dissing the band online on the PTT.

I listened to a lot of bands now. I even liked what I heard from
the burgeoning Taipei indie scene. If I didn't have to work nights, I
would be at those concerts.

I didn't get out much, or rather, at all. I'm sure it was the same
for many of my old classmates, and one in particular.

Out of respect for the professional nature of Peggy Lee's office
building, I dressed in a buttoned, collared shirt and slacks. My best
shoes hurt like hell, but I carried a pair of Converse in my moped
pack to change into after.

I drove to the Xinyi District in the southern part of Taipei,
the capital of shopping malls and American chain restaurants. I
continued east on Xinyi Road, embracing the "integrity" and
"righteousness" of its name and my mission to find out what had

happened to Julia. The looming Taipei 101 skyscraper observed my approach as shorter, older buildings between us seemed to scurry away. I'd disliked Taipei 101 the first time I saw it; it looked like a stack of green soup containers. It grew on me, though. Now I appreciate the segmented-bamboo aesthetic.

I entered the building and had to push past the shoppers swarming the upscale retailers and teeming to get to the escalators to the food court. I found my way to the office elevators and shot up to the eightieth floor. It was almost noon, and the elevator cars going up were less crowded than the ones going down stuffed with hungry office workers.

Lee & Associates' double doors of chemically antiqued wood were weighed down by two oversized, gold-colored metal plaques. Replica ancient Chinese-lion knockers were set on each door near the center. I brought my hand near the right knocker, tripping an invisible sensor that caused both doors to swing open.

A young man wearing a headset over his windswept hairstyle looked directly into my eyes. "Welcome to Lee & Associates. How can I help you?" He leaned slightly to one side, showing off a sunken cheek and enhancing his famished look.

"Hello there. I'm here to see Peggy Lee."

His eyebrows shot up. "Do you have an appointment?"

"No, but could you tell her Chen Jing-nan is here?"

"Chen Jing-nan? Do you have a more familiar English name, Mr. Chen? A business name?"

"No, I don't."

"I'm sorry, Mr. Chen, Ms. Lee is booked today through the . . ." Suddenly he sat upright, held on to the headset with both hands and stared straight ahead. "Oh, all right," the man said into his microphone. "I will tell him." He looked at me with a newfound sense of respect and fear. "Ms. Lee will be right out to see you."

He had barely spoken the words when Peggy strode out from the far right hallway. She hadn't changed much. She still wore that hurt, indignant expression of a soap-opera heroine. Still wore a pantsuit. The top button of her blouse looked like it might have just been unbuttoned.

"I knew," she said triumphantly, "that you would come crawling back to me someday, Jing-nan!"

Peggy shook my right hand and clapped me on the shoulder. I wondered if she could feel my reluctance.

"Peggy, it's not like that at all," I said.

"C'mon, Jing-nan! I'm just joking! We're old classmates, we should hug!" She pulled me in tight and I could only smile to the greeter, who was staring at us. "Loosen up a little," Peggy chided.

She hooked my arm and dragged me through a maze of potted bonsai and antique landscape scrolls to her office overlooking the city. We walked by a pool filled with kumquat-colored koi and surrounded by a guardrail.

"I was just thinking about you," she said, kicking her office door shut with her heel. "Our horoscopes probably line up better now."

I gave a nice fake laugh. Taiwanese liked to consult with advisors to find auspicious days for weddings, business relationships and investing. Peggy would have to be well versed in astrology and mythology for her family's hedge fund to be successful. It would be lousy to call on a client on a Bad Day. Then again, if you were a good talker, and had the proper Taoist charms and mirrors, you could transform that Bad Day into a Good Day by reversing its evil.

"I don't know much about the stars," I said. "I've been too preoccupied by the news, anyway."

"You mean Ah-bian?" she asked. She used the nickname of Chen Shui-bian, the former Taiwanese president who was now in prison for embezzlement. It seemed that every week he was pulling another stunt—hunger strikes and alleged medical conditions that required hospitalization. He had recently tried to hang himself with a towel.

I looked at Peggy's face. As always, her eyes seemed guileless. It was impossible to tell whether she was pretending not to know about the murder. All I could do was sigh and prepare myself to ask her about Julia. But she interrupted my thoughts.

"Sit down, sit down!" she cried. "Do you want tea? Hey, maybe you want whiskey instead?"

"I'm not ready for a drink," I said, settling into an ergonomic chair that felt like a big piece of boneless meat. Peggy swung into her Aeron and leaned across the table, splaying out her cat claws.

"You know what, Jing-nan? You look like you've never been to America." Peggy cut off my objection. "I mean that as a compliment. You look like a contemporary Taiwanese right there.

"This building, Taipei 101, they didn't finish it until we were away at college, but I was here for the opening over winter break freshman year. It was the tallest one in the world for six years! That's something to be pretty goddamned proud of, right? Our politically marginalized, pissant island showed the rest of the world up for a little while. When my father moved the Lee family headquarters into the building, I was like, 'Fuck, yeah!'"

She got up and stretched her arms over her head, pulling the material of her suit taut. Had she gotten new boobs?

Peggy smiled, approving my glance at her chest. Then she stepped away from the window and tapped the glass.

"That's Taiwan out there, Jing-nan. Come over here! I want you to take a good, hard look at it!"

I pulled myself out of the chair a little awkwardly and nearly fell to my knees. I stumbled over to the full-length window. She put her hand on my shoulder and rubbed.

"What do you notice about the buildings out there? The best ones were constructed by the Japanese while they colonized us. That was seventy years ago! Honestly, it is embarrassing as hell that our Presidential Office Building was originally built for the Japanese governor-general. You think the American president would live in a house built for the king of England? No way!

"Look over there, up in the hills. You see all of those crappy houses? Those are illegal houses, Jing-nan. They're eyesores. Tourists from all over the world are looking down at them from the Taipei 101 observation deck, and they're like, 'What the hell are those?' People who live in illegal houses should all be sent to jail."

"Peggy," I said, "I never really cared much for architecture."

"You have to admire this building. It's a remarkable human achievement."

"I like Taipei 101, but sometimes I think it lacks some heart."

Peggy slapped her forehead with the back of her hand and fell back into her chair in an exaggerated motion. "Oh, I forgot I was talking to *you*! Mr. Joy Division! Of course you have an eye for the negative aspects of everything! Hey, you could leverage that pessimism—start a bearish fund. Maybe clean up a little bit."

I returned to the boneless chair and put my hands tentatively on the edge of my side of the desk. "Actually, Peggy, I am here on rather depressing business."

"Julia," she said, looking down at her open palms.

"You know."

"Of course I do. It was all over our school Facebook page. This was like two days ago."

"I'm not on Facebook."

"You're not, eh?" she said, crossing her arms. "I thought you were just blocking me."

"I wouldn't know how to do that."

Peggy turned her chair, leaned under the table and shrugged. She came up with a bottle of Yamazaki Single Malt and two glasses. "So, you wanted to come here to talk about your old girlfriend? You didn't really want to see me, after all." She poured and made two amber slits dance in the glasses.

"I still don't feel up for a drink," I said.

"They're both for me," she snapped.

I spoke as she took a long sip. "Peggy, you went to NYU with Julia. What can you tell me about her time in school?"

"Well, what do you think?" Peggy eased her chair back and banged a drawer shut. "With a face and a body like that, what do you think? She was popular. Everybody liked her. Guys wanted to take her out—even the Americans. Girls wanted to be her friend. But you know her nature. Study study study all the time." Peggy emptied the first glass and shoved her chair forward until the edge of the desk bit into her waist. "Julia made things as hard as she possibly could for herself. She was a double major."

"What did she study?"

"Political science and something else."

"What else?"

"I don't remember."

"You remember."

I saw her teeth for a second.

"I didn't see her that often. You know we were not friends, Jing-nan. The only time I ran into her was at the Japanese market or at the library, one of the few times I went."

"When was the last time you saw her?"

Peggy shook her head and picked up the second glass. "Back in the US," she said, sipping her drink.

"You didn't know Julia was here?"

She gave me a long look, her eyes half-closed. "I. Had. No. Idea. What?! Do you think I killed her?"

"No, I don't think that." But you probably don't mind that she's dead. "Please, just tell me about when you saw her last."

"The day she was kicked out of NYU, the end of junior year. Six years ago." Peggy sipped some whiskey and snorted. "She cheated. You knew that, right?" She arched an eyebrow that seemed to question Julia's lifetime academic record.

"That's what I heard, but I have a hard time believing it."

"You'd better believe it. She was dumping most of her stuff right in the street. All she was going to take back to Taiwan were two tiny, tiny suitcases. I asked her what had happened, and she told me they had caught her cheating. The double major was too much work, and she had taken one little shortcut. All she did was copy one paragraph and they were throwing her out. It was a bad scene. She had me crying, too!"

I folded my arms. Crying with laughter, I'll bet.

"You knew, Peggy, that I had a serious agreement with Julia."

"The two of you were going to stop seeing each other and one day you would come for her like a knight riding out of the mist. Blah blah. Who didn't know about it?" She finished the second glass and her face twitched.

"We never imagined things would turn out this way."

"No one knows the future, right?"

I felt something at my ankle. It was Peggy's foot. With some effort I shifted in my seat and pulled my feet underneath my chair. "You know what happened to me, right?"

"I heard, Jing-nan. There was a big chain email going around our old classmates. I was a part of the group that sent a banner and flowers to the funerals."

"I'm sure you were the one who spearheaded the gesture, so thank you." She nodded and folded her hands in front of her. "Listen, Peggy. Julia's parents have asked me to help find some more information about her murder. They say the cops aren't helping at all."

"Nobody wants to take the blame for an unsolved crime, so nobody will take it up. Cops won't do anything unless the victim was someone important, someone rich or famous."

"Julia was murdered."

For the first time, I saw a sympathetic look in Peggy's eyes. "I know. It's just unbelievable."

"It would have to be a gangster or a cop—someone who had access to a gun."

"It could be an aborigine," she offered. "They're allowed to carry firearms for hunting and maintaining their culture."

"I didn't think about that."

Peggy looked thoughtful. "A betel-nut girl is essentially a prostitute," she said. "I don't mean to speak ill of Julia, but she probably did turn a few tricks, right? Just to get by."

My hands curled into two fists on my thighs. I had to admit that it was a possibility. If only I had backed down from my big plan and swallowed my pride, she could have stayed with me in the toaster house. She wouldn't have had to do any of it. I'm sure her parents wouldn't have been happy about the living arrangements, but we'd be happy, and Julia would be alive.

We could have just gotten married, anyway. Did it matter that the two of us would be back at the night market, living the same lives as our parents?

Doesn't matter.

Thinking of my father's favorite phrase rubbed the wistfulness away.

"You want me to tell her parents that their daughter was a hooker?" I said evenly to Peggy.

"Hey, they probably half think it themselves but don't want to believe it. Maybe you, too."

I crossed my arms.

"Jing-nan! We really need to consider everything possible."

"Maybe it was a waste of time for me to come here."

"You have an issue with me, don't you, Jing-nan? You always did. Don't think I can't tell."

"This is the issue: you never respected my relationship with Julia."

Peggy sprung from her chair and pointed at my nose with the white-star end of her Montblanc pen. "You hate mainlanders! You hate me and my family, right?" She put on a smug smile.

"I came here to see if you knew more about Julia, about her life when she came back to Taiwan. I'm an optimist. I thought maybe you might have set aside your animosity and become friends with Julia. I thought you two might have been in touch by email or through Facebook."

"If it were up to me, we would have been friends," said Peggy. "When my parents made me a VP I wrote to Julia to offer her a job—an important job—and I told her I didn't care if she didn't have a college degree. She completely ignored me. Can you believe that?"

"When was this?"

Peggy visibly stiffened. "Two years ago. I guess you missed the press coverage. I was the youngest female vice president ever in the securities industry."

"How did you reach out to her?"

"I wrote to her NYU email. It was still good, and I know she read it because I had a read receipt on it." She splashed more whiskey in her first glass. "Am I really such a horrible person that I don't deserve a reply?"

"What sort of job did you offer her?"

"I was going to make her my top researcher—reporting directly to me."

"I can't see why she didn't respond," I said, leaking sarcasm.

"Wait, Jing-nan, why can't we simply be decent with each other? It's been so long, after all."

"It has been a while."

She slapped the desk and grunted like an old man. "Do you know what's been going on with me? Do you care? It hasn't been all good for me, either, you know."

"I'm sorry, I never even asked about you," I said as sincerely as possible. "I just assumed you were doing well because . . . you seem to be. How have you been?"

"I married a guy from Switzerland after graduation. A banker."

"You have my congratulations."

"We got divorced six months ago." She fixed the shoulders on her pantsuit. "It was over before then, but you know how it is."

"I'm sorry to hear that."

"My parents won't get off my case. They say I should have found a good mainlander boy. Guess I'm cursed, huh?"

She looked sad. The world doesn't need another sad person.

"Peggy, I've changed my mind. I will have a whiskey. A small one."

"I'll get you a clean glass."

"I'll just use this one. Alcohol kills germs. And anyway, we're old friends."

It was nice to see her smile for real.

"You wouldn't happen to know," I asked halfway through my shallow drink, "where Cookie Monster is, would you?"

She spit on me when she laughed. "Oh my God, I'm sorry, Jing-nan!"

"It's all right." I wiped myself with my hand.

"Wow, I have no idea where he is now!"

"He might be better. You never know."

She shook her head. "Say, Jing-nan, have you been seeing anybody?"

"Oh, no." I felt a lump in my throat spiral upward. "I was still going to, you know, marry Julia. Are you seeing anybody now?"

"No. My life is all about work."

"Your family has all these business connections and you know all these people—a lot of guys, I'm sure."

She smiled bitterly. "Do you think any of us are free to see each other? We all work eighty-hour weeks!"

EVERY ELEVATOR HAD SEEMED to be going down when I arrived at Taipei 101, but when I stepped out of Peggy's office they all seemed to be coming up.

I had forgotten how straight whiskey could burn. I felt like my throat and nose had been cauterized. I rubbed my tongue against the roof of my mouth. I needed some water.

Finally the elevator arrived. It was empty, save for the smell of burning cigars. Or was it incense?

I rode down, thinking of Peggy's words: "If it were up to me, we would have been friends."

Julia was just like me, I thought. After my exit from UCLA, I completely avoided messages from all my former roommates and classmates. I didn't want to field their sympathetic emails or explain exactly what had happened. It had been too much for a newly minted orphan to deal with. After a while, people stopped asking, stopped emailing. I'm sure I was no longer even in their address books.

I rode the elevator alone. The car slowed as it approached ground level, and I could hear a disturbance outside. As the doors opened, two big men in overcoats, one wearing shades and one wearing a floppy rain hat, shoved their way in and blocked the doors before I could exit.

I quickly recognized the guy on the left as the American who had accosted me at the Huangs' parking lot and on the highway. I looked into his shades and he greeted me by throwing the back of his hand against my face. Before I could react, the man in the hat jabbed me hard in the gut with an umbrella handle. My body involuntarily folded in on itself, as if I were a startled armadillo. I staggered to a corner of the elevator and propped myself up. That bastard had gotten me good in the middle and I couldn't inhale. Behind my assailants, an old woman tried to enter the elevator.

"I'm sorry, auntie," the man in the hat said. "This car is going out of service." Unlike the American, he was a yam and spoke Taiwanese. She nodded and stepped back.

The men opened up their umbrellas, I observed, to block the security cameras. There were a few awkward seconds before the doors closed. There was little I could do apart from trying to get my halting breaths under control as the elevator shot up.

The American turned to the side and activated a switch on the elevator panel, possibly with a key. It was hard to see his actions clearly from the floor. I still couldn't raise the upper part of my body. The car slowed and then stopped. An emergency light on the panel began to blink, and a prerecorded message began to play loudly.

"We apologize for the delay. The car should be moving shortly," a woman's voice said in English, Mandarin and Taiwanese, then what must've been the same thing in Hakka and Japanese. Her message kept looping through the languages.

The Taiwanese was clean-shaven but had bad skin. Pockmarks on his face glistened with sweat, looking like the crust bubbles on a pizza slice after the cheese has slid off. He seemed to take his cues from the American. Maybe he'd been the one driving last night; he would know the roads, being a native of the island. The fucking Green Hornet's Kato.

The American spoke, showcasing his bad Mandarin. "Jing-nan, I told you to stop asking about Julia. How come you didn't listen?"

I gasped for breath and whined a little, unable to speak.

The Taiwanese cradled my chin roughly. "Little Jing-nan, a friendly poke couldn't hurt you this badly." He spoke bad Mandarin, too, but I was more interested in the piece of rope he took out from a back pocket. I quickly assessed that it could wrap around my throat twice and have enough left over for two fat fists to grab.

"Hey, come on! No need for that," said the American. "He gets it now. He's a smart boy. Aren't you, Jing-nan?"

The pockmarked man let the rope dangle from one hand. "We should kill him right now," he shouted over the sound of the prerecorded woman's voice. "That way we know for sure he won't keep talking."

"We don't have to kill him," said the American, laughing a little bit. "He just didn't know how serious the matter was. Now he knows. Isn't that right, Jing-nan?"

"I'll be good," I said breathlessly. "I didn't know." I felt stupid and weak for wishing Dwayne were there to stick up for me.

"See? We don't have to do anything to him. He'll stop right now. He knows he can't fool us anymore."

"Let me have just one punch," said the Taiwanese as he wrapped the rope around his right fist menacingly. "One in the gut. It won't leave a mark, I promise."

The American looked up and petted his own neck thoughtfully. "Jing-nan, my friend is upset because we had to buy these umbrellas for six hundred NT. Each. I think if you agreed to pay for them, he would calm down considerably."

My right hand shot to my wallet. I managed to stand upright and paid the exact amount. Twelve rose-colored hundred-NT bills, all featuring a portrait of Sun Yat-sen, the father of the Chinese revolution and the one man unreservedly loved on both sides of the Taiwan Strait. Sun's engraved likeness somberly reprimanding me for all my wrong actions leading up to this moment.

Shit. Twelve hundred NT. I probably grossed ten times that on an average night, but a thousand NT was my allotted weekly disposable income, after I paid off the debt and interest.

"You still have enough to eat?" the American asked me as he held up the folded bills. He looked contrite and seemed ready to peel off a Sun or two and hand them back.

"He's got that fucking food stand!" objected the Taiwanese. "He could still eat if we took his whole goddamned wallet. If you still don't get it, boy, guess where we're going to show up next!"

"Stop," growled the American. "You don't know when you've gone too far." He released the emergency tab. The elevator rose for a few seconds and then slowed. The Taiwanese looked meaningfully at me and tapped his temple. *Don't forget this warning.*

The doors opened and the men filed out, snapping their umbrellas shut. I lunged at the panel to close the doors and then pressed the button for the ground floor. The smells rising up from the food court—so different from a night market and so appetizing not even an hour ago—now made me nauseated.

The worst thing about the encounter, I decided later, was that despite the fact that the emergency stop had been on for a few minutes, no one had broken in over the intercom. Typical blasé Taipei thinking: alarms only go off by accident.

I WASN'T GOOD AT hiding things from Dancing Jenny. She freaked out when I finally gave her the brief version of events, from Julia's parents to the guys who had warned me off and roughed me up.

She raised her hands and called up to the sky. "Oh, Mazu,

Mother of Heaven," she said. I could see Jenny's nipples darken and push against her nearly transparent bra and cheesecloth shirt. "Are you badly hurt?"

"Naw, I'll be all right."

"Lift up your shirt," said Jenny.

"Why?"

"I want to see something." I complied and she gasped. "It's as bad as I feared. I can see auras, you know!"

I bent over and saw a baseball-sized splatter of purple.

"*Gan*," I whispered.

"I know you don't want me to, but I'm going to be praying for you, Jing-nan. I'm going to ask for all the protection you can get!"

"I don't need help from gods. I just need a gun."

Anger flashed in her eyes.

"Hey, I'm kidding, Jenny!"

"I've had enough guns in my life. Don't even joke about it, Jing-nan."

"Okay, okay."

"Make sure you drink a lot of liquids. Your body needs to wash out the damaged tissue."

"You know best."

I left and went to Big Shot Hot Pot. Kuilan was away, so I said hi to her husband. Her son was chopping chives in the back, and he didn't break from his hacking motion even when I waved to him. I'm glad my grandfather had the sense not to have a dumpling-and-soup business. The fillings are cheap because they're mostly vegetables, but you have to spend a lot of time chopping.

"YOUR COLOR DOESN'T LOOK good," Dwayne informed me.

"You never liked my color," I said.

"I'm not joking, kid. You look sickly. You feeling okay?"

"Two guys threatened my life today, Dwayne." Fuck it. I told Jenny, how could I not tell Dwayne, the guy I talked to more than anybody?

"What!" he thundered.

"But everything's all right now, I'm pretty sure."

He stared at me, a knife erect in his right hand. I could tell from his eyes that his mind was set to "kill." "Who threatened your life?" Honestly, I was touched he was sticking up for me.

"Two guys. Not *jiaotous*. Probably affiliated with big gangs."

"You think they were Black Sea?"

"I'm not sure. But one of them was a *taiyi* asshole."

"You got pushed around by a Taiwanese-American! On your own turf!"

I lifted my shirt and exposed my bruise.

"Gan!" Dwayne and Frankie shouted.

"It's not as bad as it looks."

"I'll make that guy's face look worse!" Dwayne vowed. He threw the knife into the sink for emphasis.

"Let's forget it for now," I said. "C'mon, let's focus on work."

"Not yet!" Dwayne pointed at Frankie. "You! Have you been doing your duty?"

Frankie's face tightened just the slightest. *"You're* questioning *me?"*

"I can't think of a reason why else our young boss here was accosted by gangsters, Mr. Cat."

Frankie said, "I've been keeping him out of trouble."

Dwayne sighed and said to me, "I don't know what to say."

"Don't blame Frankie," I said. "This didn't happen around here. They got me at Taipei 101."

"God, I hate that place. The Han Chinese built that thing to give the finger to my people. So they roughed you up, huh? Shit."

"I also had to pay them twelve hundred NT."

Dwayne whistled. "Next time you get ripped off like that, you goddamn call me and I'll show up and kick some ass!"

"I would've called you, but I was too busy trying to breathe."

"What did they say to you?"

"They want me to stop looking into Julia's death. I was asking an old classmate for information. Somehow they knew."

Dwayne rubbed his stubbly chin. "What are you going to do?"

"I have no choice." By that, I meant I had to keep on going.

Dwayne nodded. "I think we should report this to the Black Sea people, Jing-nan. Frankie has connections with those guys."

"Shouldn't we report it to the police?"

"Naw, it's faster and more effective if we go straight to Black Sea."

"I'll handle it," said Frankie as he patted my right shoulder. "Don't worry." He walked off.

"Hey, I didn't tell you the details, the circumstances!" I called after him.

"I heard enough."

"It can wait, Frankie!"

"No, it can't. Right now I'm just going to take a leak, Jing-nan! I'll talk to Black Sea later."

IT WAS A BUSY night, and I didn't notice Ming-kuo's email on my phone until we were closing. The alumni office had forwarded my email and he was excited that I was getting in touch. I felt a little bad reading his note, because he thought we were going to resume an active friendship when there hadn't really been one to begin with. Ming-kuo seemed to think we'd had a lot of good times together. I couldn't remember even talking to him for more than thirty seconds at a time.

Shit. Cookie Monster was still in Taipei, and he sounded needy, if not flat-out desperate. I wondered how he would react when he found out I just wanted to pick his brain for info on Julia. I wished we could have done so via email. There was no way to avoid an in-person meeting now.

Wait. I wasn't even giving the guy a fair chance. High school was a long time ago. It might be fun to hang out with an old classmate and laugh a little about the old days, back when I was the king of the world and he was Cookie Monster. Hadn't things ended nicely with Peggy? My conversation with her, anyway, not the aftermath.

WHEN I WAS DONE with work, I drove home keeping one eye on the rearview mirror.

I sent Ming-kuo a short reply with my phone number, saying it was great to hear from him. I was tired now from work, I wrote, but I would love to talk late in the morning or early in the afternoon, whichever was better.

I took off my shirt and noticed that the bruise had expanded into an ugly nebula of blue, purple and red jam. I didn't know injuries could be so colorful. I went to the bathroom mirror to admire my bruise in full.

My phone rang.

I didn't recognize the number, but it had to be Ming-kuo. Did he just skim my email? It was like three in the freaking morning. Didn't he know how late it was now? Shit. If I didn't answer now, I'd have to call him back at some point, and it would never be enjoyable. Why draw it out?

"Hello, is that you, Ming-kuo?"

"Jing-nan! It's good to hear from you again! I wasn't sure if you were still here in Taipei!"

"I've been here a long time, Ming-kuo."

"I'm sorry for your loss," he said, clearing his throat. "I was sorry to hear about your parents. I didn't know you stayed. I thought you would have gone back to UCLA." His voice was the same. Squeaky and fast, like a gerbil on a sugar high.

"Yeah," I said. "There was a lot for me to take care of here."

"I heard about Julia," he said.

"You did?"

"Jing-nan, it was all over the TV!"

"Ming-kuo, where are you? It sounds like there's a big commotion over there."

"I'm at work." He chuckled to himself. "I have a late shift at the front desk of a love hotel."

Damn, and I thought I had it bad. Think of the scumbags and lowlifes he had to deal with.

"Is something really funny there? I hear people laughing."

"A guy is checking in with three girls. They're all pretty drunk."

"That explains the terrible singing."

"Do you want me to send you a picture?"

"No, I don't need that."

"They're leaving the lobby now. Boy, this job is crazy sometimes."

"Ming-kuo, are you working two jobs?"

"No, this is my only job." I heard facial stubble brush the phone as he switched to the other shoulder. "Who would have thought I'd end up here? This economy sucks. What do you do, Jing-nan?"

"I work the night shift at a restaurant. It's sort of a menial job."

"Oh," he said, unable to disguise his disappointed tone. "Look at us. The smart guys in high school stuck with these dumbass jobs."

"Maybe we should talk later, Ming-kuo. I don't want to bother you at work."

"No, don't worry! They don't care if I'm on the phone. It helps keep me alert."

This could be my break. If he could help me over the phone, I wouldn't have to see him in person.

"Let me ask you something. Were you in touch with Julia through college?"

"You know, Julia was really busy at NYU. Every time I ran into her, she was in a rush to go somewhere, whether it was the library or to an afternoon nap."

"She liked to keep herself busy." And away from Cookie Monster.

"I saw her when she was working at the betel-nut stand, only a few months ago."

"Did you talk to her?"

"I saw her from the car a few times. It was by an exit, so I drove slower. I got a good look, but I wasn't absolutely positive it was her. Until, you know, after the news."

"Where exactly was the stand? The news didn't say." I looked out my window into the haze where ghosts were supposedly slipping by, looking for bodies to possess.

"It was out in Hsinchu City, the second exit on National Highway One." Less than an hour away by car to the southwest of Taipei, right on the coast. "If you get to the intersection with National Highway Three, you've gone too far. When you get out of the exit, there are about seven betel-nut stands. She was at the one that had sort of a little parking area. None of the other ones had one. It might have changed."

"What sort of *binlang* stand was it? Did it seem sort of rinky-dink?"

"Not at all. It was a classy place. That whole area is, actually. You try to offer money for sex and no one will take it."

How desperate were you, Cookie Monster? There are plenty of

red-light districts right in Taipei, unless you got yourself banned from all of them. I fumbled around with a piece of paper on my desk and wrote down the directions. Second exit to Hsinchu, place with parking lot.

"Were you working in Hsinchu City, Coo—er, Ming-kuo?"

"No, no. I wasn't working at the time. I was driving around, trying to figure out what happened to my life. This job fell into my lap not too long after. Life wasn't fair to any of us, Jing-nan. We were the smart ones! You, me and Julia."

"Peggy seems to have done all right."

"Her family's rich! Fucking mainlanders stole all the money from China and made out here like bandits!" It was the first time I had heard him angry. "You know how stuck-up she is! Whenever I saw her in college, I turned the other way. I wouldn't give her the time of day."

"Speaking of which, it's late for me, Ming-kuo."

"Yeah? Wow, it's three thirty in the morning."

"I have to sleep."

"Hey, let's hang out real soon!"

"Sure we will."

I chucked my phone into my pillow. I hated how he lumped Julia and me into the same sad sack he put himself in. It might have been an appropriate comparison, but he shouldn't have assumed he and I would have this sudden camaraderie. I was so glad I hadn't told him I worked at a food stall in a night market.

I picked up my phone and threw it back into the pillow again. Damn it! This was the worst thing possible. My life was in danger and Cookie Monster and I were reunited! I slapped my forehead.

Well, he was at least good for something. I sort of knew where Julia's betel-nut stand was.

I was riled up and afraid I would be up all night. After I washed I turned the volume low on the stereo and played Joy Division's cover of "Sister Ray" by The Velvet Underground. The song had been my introduction to that great '60s band and Lou Reed's music. The original recording was a seventeen-and-a-half-minute narrative about a party with drugs, drag queens and a murder, with a noisy groove repeated in the background. In concert, The Velvets could extend the song for more than half an hour, but the seven-minute Joy Division version was enough for me.

Unfocused anger and frustration combined with my physical pain to give me a vivid sexual dream. I was in a love-hotel bed, trying hard to hurl myself through a woman on all fours. I couldn't see her face, just her ears poking out from her tossing hair. She reached back and pulled my chin up and in the mirror I saw that it was Nancy, the girl from the music store.

I woke up gasping. Maybe I needed this girl to offset all the recent horrible people and events in my life.

Maybe I just needed her.

CHAPTER EIGHT

"I was hoping I would find you here," I said to Nancy. She was wearing a light green blouse and a knee-length blue skirt. I loved her big black shoes.

"Here I am," she said with a smile and a shrug.

Bauhaus was busier than I had hoped it would be. A string-bean male student in a short-sleeved knit was looking over the rare releases under the glass at the front counter—close enough to hear every word we said. I felt self-conscious.

"I was thinking, Nancy," I started.

"Miss?" interrupted the man. "May I see the *Goth Box*?"

It was out of print, and the store had one used copy that was kept under the register in a display window.

"Certainly," said Nancy. She slid the cabinet back open and handed the item over to the student.

"Anyway, Nancy," I said.

"Excuse me, miss," said the student. "The CDs aren't in here."

"You can see the track listing from the back of the box," Nancy said.

"I want to check the backs of the CDs for scratches."

"Our CDs are guaranteed. If there's a problem, you can bring them back for a refund."

"It's a lot of money. I'd rather not go through the trouble of coming back if I could just make sure before."

"I'm going to have to take the CDs out of the file cabinet. Are you willing to wait?"

"Yes," said the bean pole. "I have some time."

Asshole, you don't even dress like a goth. You should be doing *buxiban* commercials. "Hey, kids! Even a skinny dweeb like me was able to get into a great university like Taida because I went to the best cram school in the country! You can trust Old Wang & Sons to steer you right! *Jiayou!* Let's go!"

Mentally, I prepared myself for the time it would take for him to look over each CD, which he would spear on his index finger. I had no doubt he would ask Nancy to play a few songs on each, just to make sure, before he decided whether to buy or not.

I was willing to wait however long to ask Nancy out, though.

Nancy crossed her arms. She wasn't as patient.

"I get a break at twelve thirty," she said to me. "Meet me at Sicily Pizza a few minutes after, say twelve forty."

"I'll be there," I said, leaving the store in two hops.

I had been with two other women since Julia. Those passing encounters meant nothing to me. That's how I had been planning to explain them to Julia when the time came. Of course, if she had also had flings I would have been heartbroken. I'd been handling any inconvenient urges in the usual, solo manner. My extensive work hours had kept my ego and my sex drive down for months at a clip.

I think something related to my survival instinct was kicking in. Now that I knew my original mate was gone for good, my mind and body were searching for another. Now I only had to wait until 12:40 P.M. , a little more than an hour from now.

Ordinarily, I would spend this time at Bauhaus. I wasn't good at killing time outside of a music store.

Well, I hadn't expected an immediate date with Nancy. I thought I would ask her out for another day and then swing by the Huangs' place and tell them what I knew so far. It sure wasn't much, and it wasn't going to help the police, because they might already know.

The incomplete information could wait another day.

I strolled into a 7-Eleven, glanced at the wall of differently flavored chips and bought a cold can of Mr. Brown coffee. Little sticks of milk that had settled and congealed along the bottom of the can floated along the surface. Now that the can was popped open, it was too late to shake it, something I had neglected to do. I drank it anyway, wincing a little bit when one of those gross milk blobs washed up on my tongue.

A rack of newspapers at the front screamed something about how the body found in Shuangxi Creek had been a member of a faction of the Black Sea gang. I went back in and bought the paper. I stood on the sidewalk, drinking my chewy iced coffee and reading the story about the dead guy. An anonymous source said he might have been seen running through the Shilin Night Market the night before, but the police department couldn't confirm it.

I noticed a bunch of kids hanging out in the alley two doors down from the convenience store. They were smoking and laughing. When I approached they stopped laughing and gave me hard looks. *Jiaotous* in training. Delinquents today, corner leaders tomorrow and in the river the day after.

I finished up my coffee and continued to walk, holding on to the empty can and folded newspaper. Outside of the night-market areas, Taipei doesn't have public garbage cans. In Los Angeles and probably all over America, you can leave your trash by the side of the road to be picked up. That wouldn't work in Taiwan. The heat, humidity and relentless vermin would reduce each block to a swampland. We have to buy blue garbage bags from shops approved by the Taipei City Government. It's not cheap, either. A twenty-pack of twenty-five-liter bags (half the size of the American standard thirteen-gallon kitchen bag) runs 225 NT—almost eight dollars US! Some people buy counterfeit bags, but it's easy to get caught, because the official ones have holograms and ultraviolet characters on the sides as security measures.

We keep the bagged garbage in our homes until the trucks come in the night. The yellow truck in the lead flashes lights and blares cheesy versions of "Für Elise" or "A Maiden's Prayer" like a smelly music box. When the music plays, we have about a minute to run down to the street and personally throw our garbage into the truck's compactor. The less adorned, silent trucks that bring up the rear take glass and other recycling. If you miss the trucks, you're kinda screwed, since they don't come every night. Many people will wait on the sidewalk in the rain so they don't miss their chance.

I'm never home when the garbage truck comes. What little trash I generate I bring to the night market and use the receptacles there. I must have one of the smallest waste footprints in the city.

I grew up carrying around my garbage, a habit that was suppressed while I was at UCLA. Someone said I looked like I was homeless, walking with a bag of trash.

I MET NANCY AT Sicily Pizza. As we sat down at a table on the front patio, a waiter brought us water and disposed of my newspaper and coffee can. I took in the restaurant's sign. The word "Sicily" was printed on a boot that was supposed to be Italy, while the island of Sicily itself wasn't represented. The top part of the "P" in "Pizza" was the long nose of what was supposed to be an Italian man, while the descender comprised his long moustache or his nostril hairs.

A small crowd of students had gathered on the sidewalk near us to admire a souped-up bright red sports car parked at the curb.

"You like that car?" Nancy asked.

"It's not really my kind of thing," I said. "Too flashy."

She narrowed her eyes at me. "I thought all guys liked sports cars."

"It might be fun to drive a few times, but it would probably get boring if you did it every day. The mileage probably sucks, too."

Nancy smiled. "I think you're right," she said.

We ordered a combo—two sodas and a medium pie with vegetables and curiously crispy pepperoni slices. The tables were small, and there was barely enough room for the pan and our Cokes. The cheese smelled like the hot glue the shoe-repair guy in the night market used. I shook extra crushed red-pepper flakes onto my first slice to compensate.

Nancy chomped away. She tore off a second slice with a vengeance.

"It's good, huh?" she asked.

"It's not bad, but in all honesty, the cheese is really weird," I said. "Pizza is a lot different in America."

"I've never left the country. What's it like in the US?" She twirled a loose strand of cheese on her plate with her finger.

"What's *what* like?"

"What did it feel like, being there? I remember hearing you say it was so much better than 'stupid Taiwan.'" She put up her fingers for the quote marks.

I had to laugh. "I did say 'stupid Taiwan' a lot, didn't I?"

"Yes. The younger students debated whether you were serious or not."

"It's sort of fitting that I'm stuck here now." She knew my parents were dead—that had been on the school's Facebook page, too. I talked about the night market, and she continued eating until she finished her fourth slice.

"Please have another," I said.

"Those are supposed to be your slices."

I had only eaten two slices, and that was probably all I could take. The pizza wasn't awful, but I found that I couldn't eat in front of Nancy. I was content to look at her. I did the Taiwanese thing and slid the last two slices on to her plate.

"*Ai ya!*" she said, but she smiled.

"You can do it. These slices are thin."

"I'm sorry you don't like the food."

"It's fine. I'm not too hungry now."

Nancy stuck the cheese sides of the slices together and took a bite. After she swallowed, she said, "You didn't answer my original question. What did it feel like being in America?"

"Honestly, it's not too different. Maybe I wasn't there long enough, or maybe people are the same wherever you go."

"It sounds like you didn't really have a good time there."

I sipped my soda and tried to search my feelings. "I guess I didn't have the greatest time," I said. "I guess I was expecting to become different myself. I was ready to change." I thought about how the ABCs had treated me, and I felt my right hand tighten into a fist. "Some people weren't really nice."

Nancy finished the fused slice and brushed her hands over her plate. "I'm sorry America wasn't what you expected, Jing-nan. Are you happy living here now?"

"I'm not happy," I started.

"Yes, of course, about your parents and now Julia! I shouldn't have said that." She reached out and touched my shoulder briefly. A small gesture, but even if the city is full of love hotels, public signs of affection are rare. Everything's supposed to happen under the table, in a hotel room or in the dark.

I reached over and petted her hand on the table. Wow, we were moving fast.

"Before anything happens," said Nancy, "and I'm not saying anything will, I want us to be as honest and up-front as possible. We went to the same high school, so we owe each other that." She rubbed the knuckles on her right hand.

"Now is when we trade deep dark secrets? I might disappoint you."

"No. Now is when we trade the truth about who we are. Who are you, Jing-nan?"

I took a deep breath and slapped my thigh. Was this some crazy personality quiz to see if I was going to be a fling or something serious?

"You know I'm an orphan. You know I run my family's food stall. You know I never finished college. Anything else I can tell you?"

She raised her eyebrows and rolled her right hand in a circle. Tell me more.

I wasn't sure where to go. I had a lot of compartments in my head, and none of them seemed waterproof anymore.

"I still like Joy Division a lot," I offered, "and other bands, too."

"What about your recent love life?"

"Oh, that?" It was my one cut-and-dried area. "Nothing to speak of, really." I played with the straw in my drink. "To be really honest with you, Nancy, the only girl I ever loved was Julia. I've never even considered anybody else. If she hadn't been murdered, I would have spent the rest of my life trying to make something of myself and get back to her."

"Oh, God, that is so heavy." Her eyes filled to the brim with tears and quivered, threatening to overflow. "So romantic, too." Nancy grabbed the table as if it were slipping away.

I patted her arm. I felt bad for traumatizing her with my life-lived-in-vain story, but it was only right to be up-front.

"I really wasn't expecting something like that," Nancy said. She dabbed her eyes with the edges of her napkin. "I once thought about going to UCLA because you went, but they jacked up the tuition for foreign students. I could never afford that."

My heart sank. I wondered how much tuition was now. I could never afford to finish my degree there. I brushed some crumbs off the table.

"Now it's your turn," I said. She probably had an asshole-boyfriend story.

"My story is pretty simple. As you know, or maybe you didn't know, I had the biggest crush on you in high school."

"I didn't know, but I'm very flattered, Nancy."

She hunched over her soda but kept her voice at a conversational volume. "Well, after school, during my first year at Taida, I became a mistress to an executive at a laptop manufacturer. He bought me a really nice condo and gave me a lot of money and even some stock in the company. All the officers had mistresses and did the same. The company was doing really well, taking market share away from all the American computer makers, and Ah-ding's career was taking off."

She coughed and rubbed her nose before continuing.

"Of course he had two kids—they must be out of college by now—and his wife was so mean. He used to play me her messages and she'd be screaming at him for being out at night."

She rubbed her eyes with both hands and cleared her throat.

"Anyway, Jing-nan, my junior year, Ah-ding was arrested for supposedly bribing some officials for government contracts. He was sentenced to fifteen years in prison, and that ended things between us."

I looked at her askance, and she took that to mean I wanted to hear her academic record.

"Also, I finished undergrad this year with honors and now I'm in the graduate program for biomedical electronics and bioinformatics. Well, it's all biomedical engineering, in simple terms."

I laughed out loud when she was done.

"That's a funny one, Nancy. Did you make up all that just now? The biomedical stuff is too involved to say off the top of your head, but the rest was very creative."

She crossed her arms. "I didn't 'make up' any of it."

Two minutes ago she had been ready to cry her eyes out. Now she looked ready to gouge mine out.

"Wait, everything you said was true?" I asked.

"Of course!"

"The whole mistress thing?" I whispered.

"I was!"

"You don't reveal all this to many people, do you?"

"No. I usually just say my family is rich. In fact, my family isn't rich and I don't talk to my parents anymore. I'm telling you the truth because I thought we had some history and a good vibe between us." She pointed at my nose. "Then you have the nerve to question my honesty."

She picked up her purse.

"Please don't go," I said.

She undid the snap and took out her keys. She showed me a small black tab and pressed a button.

The souped-up sports car chirped and flashed its lights.

"WAS I RIGHT? DOES this get boring?" I asked from the passenger seat. She chuckled and eased the car away from the curb. It moved as smoothly as freshly ground soy milk and had the restrained power of a stalking lioness.

"Only when there's traffic. Even then, it's not so bad."

I touched the dashboard and tried to remember the last time I'd been in a car. It sure was a quiet ride. "You don't usually park this on the street, do you?"

"No, I usually keep it in the garage under my building. I was thinking of driving into the country after work." She glanced at me. "You're not free, are you?"

I shook my head. "I'm not. I'm a prisoner of the night market."

"Oh."

"Nancy?"

"Yeah?"

"Can we continue being really honest to each other?"

"Of course," she said, tightening her grip on the steering wheel.

"I think it's really amazing that I ran into you again and I think you're really incredible. But I don't think I'm ready to begin a relationship right now."

We slid to a stop at a red light.

"Well, I'm definitely not ready. In fact, I don't think I've ever been in love."

"You had a crush on me, though, right?"

She shrugged and touched her throat, drawing my attention to her chest. "When I saw you in the music store again, everything came back like a wave. I was lifted up." The light changed and we were moving again.

"Did you love Ah-ding?"

"God, please don't use that word for him and me!"

We turned the third corner of a big loop.

"I'm glad we're both not ready to start anything serious," I said. "It would also be bad luck during the holiday."

"I don't believe in good or bad luck or ghosts. I thought you didn't either."

"I don't."

"Jing-nan, you know I had a schoolgirl crush on you. I guess I still do. What do you think about me?"

I wormed the tips of my fingers into my front pockets. "I think you're very beautiful, Nancy."

She scoffed. "No, you don't."

"I do so!"

"I don't believe you."

"You don't? Well, listen. If you didn't have to get back to work, I would take you to a love hotel right this very moment."

She kept her eyes on the road but raised her chin, challenging me. "Oh, you would, huh?"

"Of course. Look, it's almost one thirty. I guess we should have skipped the pizza and just had sex. Too bad." I was feeling playful and lucky. I could see us having sex at some point. I already dreamed of it.

We hit another red light. Nancy licked a finger and wiped something off the rim of the steering wheel.

"I might have two hours off for lunch," she offered casually. Ah, she was trying to call my bluff. I could keep it up longer than she could.

"Oh, look over there," I said. "There's a love hotel up on the left. Why don't we go?"

"You wanna go?"

"Yeah, let's go," I said. "Right now."

She scratched her right knee. "Oh yeah?"

"Yeah."

Nancy crossed her arms. "You're scared," she said, showing me her clenched teeth.

"So are you."

We laughed. She lurched the car to the right.

"I'm parking."

I tapped the clock on the dashboard. "We better hurry. You only have an hour."

"It's a perfect fit—right here." She shut off the engine and I unsnapped my safety belt first.

"Let's run in like we have no time, Nancy!"

She undid her belt and narrowed her eyes. "I'm warning you," she said. "They're going to think we're boyfriend and girlfriend."

"Let's tell them right up-front that we're only sex partners."

ONCE WE GOT IN the room, Nancy said, "Are you sure you wanna . . ."

I cupped the back of her head with my left hand, kissed her forehead and moved down from there as we did a stunt fall to the bed. I was dimly aware of slipping off my shoes and then my pants.

Suddenly Nancy stiffened.

"What is that?" she asked, her face right next to the bruise. It seemed bigger than this morning and somewhat oblong. The original baseball-sized injury looked like it was splitting in two now.

"I got that from work. A crate slammed into me."

She touched a finger to it. "Does that hurt?"

"No."

"How about this?" she asked, jabbing it playfully with her thumb.

"Ow! *Gan!*" I yelled and laughed, grabbing both her wrists.

Laughing was a big part of the release. So was crying. We shivered in the cold air from the blasting AC. I pulled the sheet over us. I held her to me and told her I was broken inside.

"You were in love," she told me.

"I was," I said.

I came after her anew.

I was giddy as I hopped on my moped, but my mood darkened as a light rain began to fall.

Damn. I had planned to see the Huangs this afternoon to tell them what little I had found out, but instead I had chosen to go to a love hotel to fool around with a young woman.

Was I done with Julia so quickly?

First thing tomorrow, I'm going to see the Huangs, I promised. It would probably be the last time ever.

When I dismounted at the night market, I realized how sore I was. At least the rain had stopped.

Jenny was tied up with some business types at the counter, so we shared a wave and mouthed greetings.

Kuilan offered her condolences for Julia and held both my hands.

"I was talking to Jenny, she told me all about it. It's not fair at all. That poor little girl. I'm going to pray for her and her parents. They were good people."

I nodded somberly, feeling even guiltier for my romp with Nancy.

"Thank you, Kuilan," I said, firmly shaking the clump of our four hands.

When I stepped into Unknown Pleasures, Dwayne cast a look at me. "Jing-nan?" he asked.

I made an innocent face.

"You're half an hour late! You get your pubes trimmed?" Dwayne was referring to the illegal and legal houses of prostitution that operated behind barber-store fronts.

"No," I said, putting my hands in my pockets. "Not *there*, Dwayne."

"Are you serious?" He threw down a pair of skewers on the grill and they sizzled with indignation. "Can you believe this, Frankie? We're busting our humps here and little Jing-nan goes out for an afternoon of planting his sugar-cane stick."

The Cat nodded and smiled, not missing a beat in his prep work of cleaning out intestines, removing veins from shrimp and squeezing out beaks from squid.

"Dwayne, I'll be back in about half an hour," I said.

"Now he's going on break already!" Dwayne shook his head in mock indignation.

"Relax. It's work-related."

About once a month, I go on a pre-opening market inspection. I walked south on Daxi Road, made a right on Danan Road, a left on Xiaoxi Road and finally onto Jihe Road. One big zigzag south. Jihe Road essentially took me straight to a bi-level indoor area under a giant roof. The building had an inhuman, generic strip-mall feel. Taking a good look at it now, I had to admit the building resembled something straight out of LA. Over the facade that faced Jihe Road were giant letters reading "Shilin Market" in English under four big Chinese characters saying the same. This open-air building was more than one hundred years old and had reopened in December 2011 after a ten-year renovation. For a decade the vendors were in a temporary spillover market, a *juancun* for food. Some tourists think this is the Shilin Night Market itself, rather than just a part of the larger beast. The soul of any night market is walking in the open air and being with the crowds. You just can't get that indoors.

The ground-floor outlets weren't my competition. These stands sold fresh-cut fruit, T-shirts, watches and boxes of candy perfect for tourists to bring home for gifts.

I stopped at a fruit stand to get a cup of chilled and cut *atemoya*, which is a type of *cherimoya*, that prehistoric-looking fruit that resembles a small human head painted dark green, with the drips of paint still visible. The *atemoya* is literally called "pineapple Buddha head." Breaking the fruit open yields milky-colored flesh and black pits staring back like multiple Mickey Mouse eyes.

A middle-aged woman, wearing a bamboo farmer hat for authenticity, brought me a small plastic bag along with my cup of *atemoya*, peeled from the thick rind and cut into wedges. I picked up the first piece with a long toothpick and slurped it up. It was so ripe I could feel the grains of sugar on my tongue as the flesh readily broke up. The overall taste was close to vanilla pudding flavored with pear juice. As I swallowed, I stored the seeds—as big as playing pieces in the board game *Go*—in my right cheek. I spit them into the bag I was provided with. It's a perfect fruit: sweet as dessert, and it comes with fun seeds.

I hungrily ate up the rest of the fruit as I made my way to the escalator to the below-ground level, where things were literally cooking. About a hundred stands were arranged into blocks separated by narrow walkways. Reflected light from illuminated menus pooled on the metal ceiling as ventilation panels loudly sucked in their breath.

Many vendors didn't have English translations, but for most of the food, that wasn't a problem. Still, people who couldn't read Chinese would have a hard time figuring out the small-bun-wrapped-in-large-bun stand. The woman at the counter takes what looks like a fried fillet, partially covers it with something close to a flour tortilla and crushes it with a mallet. Then she reopens it, sprinkles some fibrous crap into it and rolls it up. She couldn't tell an American that the fried fillet was filled with shredded pork and that the stuff she sprinkled on was dried shredded pork and that the whole thing was delicious. At only one US dollar each, it wasn't worth her time to go through the effort to explain in English. There are Chinese and Japanese tourists right behind you who have no problem reading the menu, and they'll probably buy a lot more than you.

"Dude, that looks cool, but I don't know what it is," I overheard some Americans saying.

Music to my ears. I—or rather, Johnny—moved in for the kill, giving them directions in guy-talk to Unknown Pleasures as they stepped away from the pork-bun lady. Johnny is that friendly, English-speaking bro you want to bring your money to. Some guy recorded a video interview with me last year, but it hasn't shown up online yet.

Along one stretch the air became thick with stinky tofu,

which—and I know from direct experience—smells exactly like a beer-soaked garbage can outside a UCLA frat. The stinky tofu gets its smell from fermenting in various brine formulas and can be prepared a number of different ways. Eating it straight-up is strictly for the hardcore. The most popular way is to deep-fry the squares of tofu, snip them into cubes and then serve them with a topping of pickled carrots and radishes. They can also be skewered and brushed with meat sauces and then grilled. Eating stinky tofu in a hot pot was popular with the early arrivers to the night market. Kuilan would never serve such a dish at Big Shot Hot Pot. She hated stinky tofu with a vengeance. I sort of burned out on the taste as a kid. Contrary to what you might think, even though it smells like garbage, stinky tofu has a mild taste.

Right in front of me, a man trying stinky tofu for the first time turned to spit it out into a garbage bag. Dude, you have to breathe through your mouth when you eat it! Another guy Johnny could help out.

As I rode the escalator up, I realized my phone had run out of power. More people were coming in now and my return trip to Unknown Pleasures was crowded with annoying potential customers.

Dwayne grunted as a greeting. Frankie merely glanced at me. I plugged my phone into the wall and started pitching our skewers to a group of people checking their guidebooks to see if the market was indeed open yet.

After about two hours, I went to the communal bathroom for a quick break and took my phone. I walked east on Xiaobei Street. It was mildly amusing that the nearest bathroom was on Xiaobei, which literally means "Little North." The street name sounded a lot like *xiaobian*, which means "to piss."

One phone message and two texts from Cookie Monster. All within minutes of each other. C'mon, Ming-kuo, gimme a break!

The extended texts read like a sad little kid writing to an absent dad, talking about the things we could do together and the places we could go.

I had never even seen this guy outside of school. In fact, I remembered seeing him trying to hang out with the security guards after classes were over.

I shuddered as I pressed play on his voicemail. It was only fifteen seconds long, and I wanted to listen to it just in case he had remembered something about Julia. If not, I wanted to forget about it as soon as possible. I heard bus-interior sounds before he started talking.

"Jing-nan! Did you get my texts? I forgot to mention that I think I saw you! Were you in a fancy sports car today? With a beautiful girl driving? Was that you, Jing-nan? You always get the hot girls, right?"

Wo kao! Holy shit! He was stalking me! Stay the hell away from me, Ming-kuo! Or, rather, let me stay the hell away from you!

A lot of people were out on Xiaobei Street, but I didn't have a hard time getting through until I reached Everybody's Everything Electric, a gadgets shack across from the restroom entrance. About a dozen vendors had abandoned their adjacent stands to gather and watch a breaking-news report on the projection TV, which was using the street door to the restroom as a screen. I stepped to the door and people started screaming at me to get out of the way because I was disturbing the picture. I backed up and watched the report with them.

The bodies of two young men had been found in an OK Mart dumpster in Datong District, just north of Wanhua District, where I lived. Knifed to death.

Datong has been hammered by the recession more than any other district, and since the landmark Chien-Cheng Circle food market closed in 2006, it hasn't really had a viable business center. Things were so dire in the district that the yams' political party, the DPP, was allegedly able to recruit local down-on-their-luck gangsters to register as members for five hundred NT, or twenty dollars, each.

A gangster's life is cheap in Datong District.

Security cameras outside the store had mysteriously been shut off before the bodies were placed there, so the police didn't have any leads. The two store clerks on duty said they hadn't noticed anything unusual, but neither had been outside.

The sensationalist twenty-four-hour news channel we were

watching, *TV Now!*, made sure to close in on the dead men's faces. It wasn't a pretty picture, as their ears and noses had been hacked off.

"*Ai!*" and "*Yo!*" mumbled the crowd, but none of us turned away.

One of the *aiyu*-jelly guys pointed at the screen with a hand encrusted with dried lime pulp.

"Those hoodlums were in Black Sea!" he declared aloud. After realizing that it probably wasn't a good idea to be blabbing, he dropped his voice. "They had their ears cut off because they didn't listen! They had their noses cut off because they caused the gang to lose face. Why don't they ever report the relevant facts on the news?"

Other people watching made noncommittal grunts. My hairs stood on end. Black Sea sure was coming up a lot in my life.

The next story was about the growing phenomenon of women pole-dancing and stripping at funerals for those who wanted to go out in a memorable fashion.

I felt bad for the two dead men. They looked like boys, really. It was hard to imagine what they had done to deserve such harsh retribution. If this was indeed the gang taking care of their own, there was no way the police would interfere, because there was nothing to gain. The public figured the kids had gotten what they deserved. The parents had probably been absent or inadequate. They might even see the murders as a sad but inevitable conclusion. The gang definitely wouldn't want the murders investigated.

I wondered whether Julia had been mixed up with something or was just an innocent bystander. Either way, I couldn't let her story end with nobody paying for the crime. Julia deserved better, and so did her parents.

I thought about that big Taiwanese-American and his pockmark-faced buddy. Who the hell did they think they were? They couldn't stop me from seeing the parents of my dead fiancée! They didn't have a legitimate reason to hurt me, much less kill me, like those two gangsters in Datong were rubbed out. I wasn't a drug dealer or a pimp. I didn't collect protection money. I didn't know anything I could blackmail someone with.

Oh, wait. Ming-kuo had mentioned something to me that wasn't known by the general public. He had told me approximately where Julia's *binlang* stand was in Hsinchu City, near a highway exit.

I licked my lips. This was dangerous knowledge. Was someone watching me? I looked around at the other people watching the television. I didn't recognize most of these people.

THE VENDORS WERE ALL aware that paying a local *jiaotou* group for "protection" was included in our common charges. Was this group collecting it for themselves or for a larger organization, such as Black Sea?

About a year ago, several of us met up in a cafe on Jihe Road in the early afternoon to talk about a number of things, not just the protection money, which really wasn't very much at all. Frankie the Cat got Unknown Pleasures a nice discount since he'd become good friends with actual criminals who'd been serving time on Green Island with him. He also got us top-quality food, and I didn't ask where it came from.

I certainly didn't bring that up at that meeting on Jihe Road. We talked about other things, our lives and the good and bad of working at night every night. Then it became a bit of a moan-fest. Things weren't bad, but we had issues we never talked about and it was good to get them off our chests.

We all thought the lousy water fountain by the bathrooms in the common area leaked more water than it spouted.

We all knew *benshengren* from the deep south didn't know how to drive their trucks and always caused fender benders.

We all agreed we shouldn't have to pay any protection money to the gangs, since there was a police station in the boundaries of the night market.

We all laughed at the end and agreed we should meet more often.

The next day, Frankie warned me never to meet with those people again. I think they all got a similar warning, too, because nobody ever brought it up again.

AS I CONTINUED TO watch the Datong District report on the television, I thought I recognized a woman standing to my left. She

might have been at that meeting on Jihe Road, but she didn't seem
to recognize me.

The story was playing in a loop, and they were at the part where
they interviewed the two store clerks again. On the second viewing,
they seemed scared, which was understandable, considering the circumstances. But it also seemed like they were lying.

What was the truth about those poor dead kids? Would anybody ever know?

Would I ever know the truth about Julia? How about her parents?

I looked at the ground as the television screen went back to the
bodies. There had to be more to Cookie Monster's story about
Julia that I could squeeze out. If I was going to see the Huangs one
last time, I wanted to go with everything I could get.

AFTER TAKING MY DELAYED bathroom break, I returned to
Unknown Pleasures. Although I tried to focus my thoughts on
Julia, my mind began to wander.

I began to feel guilty but also excited about the physical-therapy
session with Nancy. I have never considered myself a lustful person,
but I couldn't wait to be with her again.

About halfway through the night, a sudden storm broke out and
the entire market was drenched. It was a good thing Frankie had
already unfurled our canopy. We were able to shelter more people,
and I sweet-talked them into buying skewers with a sob story about
how business was going to be bad that night.

As the rain let up, groups of people began to break away. I
restocked the front grill and stared at my phone. I wondered what
the politics of calling Nancy were. I knew she would want a call the
next day, but if we had sex in the early afternoon, should I call her
at night or early in the morning?

I was a little lost in thought, so I didn't recognize Ming-kuo
right away when he walked up to the stand.

"I knew it was you!" he said, pointing at my chest. "I recognize
the shirt from this afternoon!"

Cookie Monster had slimmed down but retained all the fat
around his neck and head. He still had the stupid crooked smile.

He looked like a doll that kids use to learn how to dress themselves, what with his blue snap-button uniform shirt and the displayed zipper of the puckered front of his jeans.

"Wow, Ming-kuo!" I said. "Is that really you? You look great!"

I came out from around the grill to shake his hand.

"Jing-nan, after all these years, it took a tragedy to get us back together!"

Man, had he been eating stinky tofu? I hoped so. Having a guy like him standing in front of Unknown Pleasures could hurt business.

I gestured to a table in the back.

"Say, Ming-kuo, could you take a seat at that table for little bit? I just need to help these customers in back of you."

He shook his head and cracked both sets of knuckles in well-practiced rapid succession. "I'm actually on my way to work. I thought I would stop by. The love hotel is near Tianmu, so I inter-act with quite a few foreigners, just like you!" He pointed tactlessly, full arm extended, at a Latino man taking pictures of the front grill.

Tianmu was the part of Shilin District where a lot of American expats settled. The international schools, including Taipei Ameri-can, alma mater of the half-Okinawan, half-Taiwanese matinee idol Takeshi Kaneshiro, were in Tianmu. Those kids always had a lot of money to spend. I liked them.

Ming-kuo continued. "My hotel's right over the Shilin Bridge."

I broke out in a sweat. That was only about fifteen minutes away. He could swing by the night market any night, any time.

"Why, we practically work in the same place," I told him as I tried to smile.

"Can you believe how close we are?"

He shuffled his feet a little. We were stuck in that little dance people do when the conversation is over but neither party wants to leave first. Actually, there was something I wanted to know.

"Ming-kuo, how did you know I was here?"

"You told me you were in the Shilin Night Market!"

"I don't think I did." I was sure I hadn't. I knew I'd told him I was working at a restaurant and not at a night market. We weren't close enough in school for him to know my family ran a stall, and certainly not which one.

He shrugged, creating a bib of flesh under his chin. "If you didn't mention it, then someone must have told me. What does it matter? We're back in touch, old friend!"

Had someone on Facebook tipped him off? Maybe he'd Googled me and found out about the family business.

Like my father would have said, doesn't matter.

Ming-kuo wiped his face, and I felt the sweat when he shook my hand again.

"Jing-nan, I'll go for now, but I want to compliment you again on that girl you were with. Set me up with one of her friends!"

When he was gone, Dwayne came up to me.

"Who was that sad sack of shit?"

Dwayne has a way of sizing people up quickly.

"An old classmate. I don't like him, so that's why I didn't introduce you guys."

"Call him back! I'm going to tell him what you said."

"No!"

Dwayne put me in a headlock. "Are you going to call him back?"

"No, I'm not."

We danced around in a giddy struggle. It was dangerous because the floor was still slippery from the rain and the hot grills were on three sides of us. Someone could get seriously hurt, but the danger just made it funnier. I managed to wedge my greasy ear between my head and Dwayne's hairy forearm and slipped out of his grip.

"Too easy this time," I chided him. Dwayne moved back to his station and covered it like third base, his legs set wide and bent at the knees. His hands were ready to grab a grounder and throw to second to kick off a double play. The guy was always ready to play.

I WAS AT THE sink later when Frankie came up to me. He took a dirty pan, turned it upside down and threw the cold-water faucet on. The resulting sound was the perfect white noise to cover a private conversation.

"Jing-nan, there's some streamlining going on at Black Sea." His blank face added nothing.

"It's strange that you use a business term to describe a gang."

"They are a business. A conglomerate. They're liquidating a

troubled subsidiary. One of their leaders is hiding in Cambodia. His son was promoted to the head of a faction. The younger guys, they're not seasoned enough to be in a leadership role. Too impatient and hotheaded. They stepped up the high-margin high-risk stuff—stolen credit cards, pushing drugs. They've burned a lot of Black Sea's bridges with other businesses and the authorities."

"Thanks for looking into this, Frankie."

"One more thing. This out-of-control faction is responsible for killing Julia."

My body reacted by having a coughing fit. I scooped a handful of water from the faucet and drank it to help myself recover.

"Are you sure?" I asked him.

He tasted his front teeth without opening his mouth. "Yes."

"Can't we go to the police with this?"

"No. Can't prove anything, even though it's true. She's dead, Jing-nan. Nothing can bring her back. Believe me, Black Sea will punish every last person in this faction."

"Does this have anything to do with those guys shot in Datong District and the one found in the water?" I expected him to say he didn't know or something else vague so as not to alarm me.

"Probably. They would want the bodies to be found in a public way as a warning to anybody else in the organization who was thinking of making their own rules."

"Why did they kill her, Frankie?"

"I don't know. The only people who know are on the run right now."

He touched his front pocket and felt his cigarette box. I hoped he would take questions before his smoke break.

"Do you know anything about a big Taiwanese-American guy going around?" I asked.

"There are always some ABCs or ABTs going around."

"Frankie, can I ask you a question? Are you a member of Black Sea?"

He chuckled and put a cigarette in his mouth. "I was in prison, Jing-nan, during martial law. You know that. It was a tough time. The Generalissimo said it was better to kill ninety-nine innocent people than to let one guilty man go. He applied that thought to jailing people, too." He faced me and looked right through my eyes. "On Green Island I met a lot of people who did bad things. I also met many people who were like me—completely innocent. If we had had fair trials, or even crooked trials, we wouldn't have been in there. When innocent people see they're treated the same as criminals, do you think that once they're released they'll be on the side of the law?"

"Well, you are. Aren't you?"

He blinked and the look in his eyes told me he was back in the present. "I *understand* both sides of the law. Sometimes one is right. Sometimes the other is."

Dwayne looked over at us, but decided to leave us alone. Even though the water was still making a racket, I moved in closer to Frankie.

"Frankie, the Huangs wanted me to look into Julia's murder. They said the cops aren't doing anything. One of our old classmates saw her at the betel-nut stand in Hsinchu City fairly recently. I was thinking of going there to find out what really happened."

Frankie smiled gently and touched my shoulder. "Be reasonable, Jing-nan," he said. "You're not going to find out any more than I did, you're only going to put yourself in danger."

"I'm already in danger. Those guys yesterday warned me to stop looking into Julia's murder."

Frankie took the cigarette out of his mouth and looked down into the sink. "You're lucky you even got a warning, Jing-nan. Stop everything you're doing. Right now." He stared at my wavering reflection in the pan as the water played over it.

"I know you're right. I just have to do one more thing. I have to see the Huangs and tell them what I know."

"Be careful."

"I definitely will be."

Frankie grunted and turned off the faucet. He plunged his hands into the water up to his wrists to clear the drain.

"Frankie? Is it true that when you were on Green Island, your cell used to fill up with seawater?"

His left eyebrow rose slightly. "Who told you that?" he asked softly.

"My father."

"Hmm," Frankie said noncommittally and put the cigarette in the left corner of his tight mouth. He was done talking.

CHAPTER NINE

I texted Nancy when I got into bed.

STILL THINKING ABOUT YOU, MY LITTLE SEX PARTNER. We had agreed to call each other that. It sounded practical and yet playful. "When do you sleep?"

My phone vibrated seconds later.

Her message read, I CAN'T SLEEP WITHOUT HEARING FROM YOU. HOW IS YOUR BRUISE? SIGNED, YOUR SEX PARTNER.

I looked down. The color was becoming more consistent and was turning dark blue. That meant it was healing, right? I touched the splotch in the center and it didn't hurt as much as it used to.

I took a flash picture of the bruise and sent it to Nancy with the caption, PLEASE KISS IT. I put the phone down and looked out the window. Clouds were passing under the moon, sending grey wisps crawling up and down building walls.

My phone rang.

"Hi, sexy," I said as I answered.

"Ummm, Jing-nan?"

"Ming-kuo. You sure are calling awfully late, again."

"Do you always answer your phone like that?"

"I was joking. I knew it was you." I groaned as I saw that Nancy was trying to call me.

"Jing-nan, who was that girl you were with? Is that your wife?"

"No, she's a friend. She's actually trying to call me now so I have to . . ."

Cookie Monster wasn't getting it. He continued chatting as if we had all the time in the world.

"I was thinking I could take you to lunch tomorrow?"

"You're going to tell me all you can about Julia, right?"

"Didn't I already? Well, we have so many other things to talk about, anyway. It's been so many years, Jing-nan. We should sit down and meet properly."

"I might have plans already." My phone buzzed with Nancy's call.

"If that doesn't work for you, then I can come to your stand and hang out for a few hours at a table until you're free."

Nothing could be worse than that.

"You know what, Ming-kuo? Let's do lunch tomorrow. I'll clear my schedule."

"Great!"

I got him to agree to meet me at a Korean place with wait staff who don't let you linger.

Nancy hadn't left me a message. I called her back and got her voicemail. I texted her, IS IT TOO LATE FOR YOU TO COME OVER AND COMFORT ME?

ADDRESS PLEASE, she texted back. I'M A LITTLE TIRED. I'LL TAKE A CAB. I sent her the information. I hoped she wasn't too tired.

My ear canals began to itch, so I used a small bamboo spoon to scrape the wax out. I brushed my teeth again, making sure to brush my tongue thoroughly.

Most importantly, I set up my PC to play my personal mix of songs culled from Joy Division's best live bootlegs. I wanted Nancy's first impression of my house to be a good one. She hadn't said much about her place, but I was sure it was nicer than mine.

It was almost two thirty in the morning. As a last-minute thought, I put out a pack of dried mangoes, a pack of roasted cashews, one Kirin and one Asahi.

She texted me to say the cab was nearby.

I stepped outside wearing a pair of flip-flops, shorts and a T-shirt that featured the drummer-boy cover of Joy Division's *An Ideal for*

Living EP. She had to know that one. I swung open the gate and stood on the sidewalk.

Even though Ghost Month spooked most people into staying indoors at night, younger people seemed more blasé about it. I saw a car of joyriding kids go by blasting AKB48, a best-selling Japanese girl group that, despite the name, had almost one hundred members. Girl groups like AKB48 and the Taiwanese equivalent, TPE48, were destroying minds with their synthesized, sunny songs that all had choruses with "baby" in them. Everything's happy! Everything's fun! Nobody's sad! Nobody gets murdered!

I watched the car with contempt as it turned the corner and left. Those kids would be safe during Ghost Month. The undead would flee from that music.

A cab swung up to me from the other side of the street, and I reached for my wallet. I knew I couldn't beat Nancy to taking care of the fare, but I had to make a good effort. Her window was down and she smiled at me.

"I have it," I said, showing her a few bills.

"I've already paid, Jing-nan." She popped open the door.

"Hey," said the cabbie. "Don't you guys want to go out? I know the best clubs!"

I ducked my head down and looked at him. He seemed to be about thirty years old. Maybe he knew the best clubs from a decade ago. Anyway, Nancy and I weren't into club music. That little snippet of AKB48 was already more than I needed tonight.

"We're tired," said Nancy, stepping out and straightening up. She was wearing a Magazine shirt that featured the cover art of the reunion album.

"Next time!" the cabbie said. He pushed his card onto me before pulling away.

"Any problems getting here?" I asked as I guided her to my toaster house.

"No, it was very easy. Longshan Temple is a good landmark, and you're only three blocks away."

"Did you see the homeless people in Bangka Park?"

"That's the place right across from the temple, right?"

"Yes."

"I've seen the park on the news before. I feel so bad for them."

The most recent controversy was that the city was hosing down the benches and concrete platforms late at night and early in the morning, ostensibly to clean the park. The workers evacuated the park before spraying, but the homeless men couldn't return to sleep there while it was wet.

"My father used to point to them and tell me I was going to be one of them if I didn't study hard enough."

As we stepped into my house, Nancy sighed. "We have it so good, don't we? Shouldn't we be helping the homeless?"

Shit. This was the wrong thing to be talking about, and it wasn't going to lead to anything good tonight.

Luckily, the music changed the subject.

"Wow," Nancy said. "This is the first song on the second side of *Closer*!" She stepped into a pair of slippers I had set out.

"'Second side'? You have this album on vinyl?"

"Yes. I'm not a big audiophile or anything, I wanted it mostly to have the cover art full-sized."

"You want some snacks or beer?"

She sniffed. "Did you cook something?"

"No, I didn't. What do you smell?"

"Smells a little like something fried."

"You're probably smelling my clothes in the hamper. I stink after coming home from work." I touched the back of my neck and winced. I'd been alone so long I didn't realize that my place stank.

She stepped into the minuscule kitchen. "I think it's something else."

I didn't want to admit that at home I rarely cooked anything other than instant ramen, so I said I would clean up better before she came over again.

I was glad Nancy wasn't the shy type. She burped while drinking her beer and it made her laugh. When she first stepped into the bathroom, she squealed that the toilet was a squatter and not a sit-down.

I didn't want to, but we went through my yearbook. Man, why had I left it out? We stopped on the spread of me singing while reaching out to Julia with Nancy right behind her.

"I liked you, but I was scared of you," she said. "You always wore that big trench coat. It was menacing. People said you robbed graves."

I laughed as I tore a dried mango slice. "I was just trying to dress the part. I didn't mean to scare anybody."

"The younger girls loved it. We all called you Ian."

"Oh, really?" I said, unable to suppress a smile. "I didn't know I had made such an impression."

"I think the fact that you were with Julia was a big part of it. You, as a man, become more attractive to women because you are already partnered with a woman."

"What are you talking about?"

"It's a matter of social selection. A woman has selected you as a mate, and that means there's something worthy about you, you're better than the pool of single guys. So other women would rather try to mate with you than waste time with potential losers."

"Nancy, does this somehow tie in with your bioengineering studies?"

"It's more like psychology, but I like psychology. When you study human behavior, sometimes it's hard to distinguish individual choice from what we're hardwired to do. Maybe we really can't exercise much choice in our lives."

"You did choose to come here, didn't you?"

She dropped her slippers, pulled her feet up on the couch and placed the back of her head in my lap.

I played with her funny little right ear a bit. Who was this woman on the couch with me? She seemed to be on her own, although she had alluded to her estranged family "down south."

Had she come back into my life because Julia was gone for good? Had I somehow willed myself to find her? Maybe this was supposed to happen.

But things couldn't be meant to be, could they?

Nancy began to murmur along to "Twenty Four Hours," the hardest-driving song on the mid-tempo *Closer*. I thought about the lyrics, in which the speaker tries to make sense of an illusory world in the wake of a relationship that has come to a jarring end.

Too close to home.

I rested my head against the couch's backboard and felt the furious drumming thunder through the house.

Could anybody else in the world really understand and love me except for Julia? After all our time apart, though, our relationship had become theoretical in nature. I could see that now as I sat here on the couch with this woman. I felt more alive than I had in years. I even seemed to be able to breathe more deeply.

All those wasted, loveless years of living in exile! I was the Chiang Kai-shek of love. But things were looking up for me now.

I moved my hand down to Nancy's chin and she teasingly licked my index finger. I chuckled. She could do so many surprising things.

"Twenty Four Hours" ended, and now we were at the last two songs on *Closer*, mid-tempo curtain closers that pushed the boundary of what post-punk was at the time.

"What do you think of 'The Eternal' and 'Decades,' Jing-nan?" Nancy asked.

"I think they're great," I said. "I think Joy Division ended at their peak. Everything built up to this."

"I have to confess something," said Nancy. She sat up on the couch and held her hands. "I remember when you ripped on New Order on the PTT."

I instantly thought of all the stupid talk online.

"Oh, that," I said. "Ha!"

"You said the surviving members of Joy Division shouldn't have gotten together again."

"I was wrong to post that. I really like New Order now," I said, putting my empty bottle down. "Well, it was all over, in a way, right? Why did they start up again?"

She crossed her arms. "They wanted to go on! That's the only reason to do anything."

"At the time I was mad that they didn't stop."

"Because you think they owed it to Ian Curtis to stop?"

"That's right."

"Do you think you can't love someone else after Julia?"

I looked at the floor, although I didn't see anything. "I don't know," I said. She touched my face and I looked into her eyes. They were lovely. "I didn't think so."

"Let's just be happy," she said. "I haven't been in a long time, either." I reached over and closed my hand over hers.

"Nancy, you must have guys all over you!"

"That's not a good thing! It gets really annoying."

I felt her little knuckles. "Let me know if I annoy you."

"How could you?"

The album ended and I became aware of the time. It must be after three.

"What time do you have to be at Bauhaus?" I asked her.

"I never have to go back," she said, shifting on the couch. "It was just a temp job while somebody was on vacation."

"Damn. I was counting on you to get me a whole bunch of music!"

"You can download almost anything. I can buy you the rest."

"I don't need you to buy me stuff."

"That's true." She pointed to my bookcase overflowing with CDs. "You probably have too many things already."

"I have more CDs in the bedroom."

She looked directly at me. "Ah, I'm not falling for that line."

"I swear, it's not a line!" I stood up and opened the fridge. "Do you want to cool off by splitting a can of Apple Sidra?" It's a Taiwanese sparkling apple cider. I used to think it was misspelled, but it turns out that *sidra* is "cider" in Spanish. Why Spanish? Some things about Taiwan will always remain a mystery.

"It's not that hot out here," said Nancy, "but I'll have a few sips."

"We could move to the bedroom. There's a fan there."

She stood up and brushed her hair behind her ears. "Again with the bedroom, huh?"

"I don't want to wear out the couch."

I popped open the Apple Sidra and led the way.

After playing bumper cars for a while, we fell asleep.

I had a dream that Julia was trying to tell me something using only her right eyebrow. I wasn't sad when I woke up. Just confused.

I didn't tell Nancy about it. She left without showering because I didn't have a shower and she didn't want to wait for the hot water to boil for a bucket bath.

CHAPTER TEN

Ming-kuo had dressed in a shirt, tie and jacket. In the bright lights of the Korean restaurant, he looked like a chubby variety-show host minus the microphone and charm.

"This isn't a job interview," I told him.

"I wanted to look professional," he said eagerly. "My mother always said that even though I wasn't good-looking, I could at least dress well." Man, was she right.

"Your mom was wrong," I said.

"I don't dress well?"

"You are good-looking," I said as I wiped my mouth. I delved into the menu so I wouldn't have to look at him.

"Thank you, Jing-nan! You're a good-looking guy yourself!"

"Say, Ming-kuo. If I take you to Hsinchu City, do you think you could point out the stand Julia was working at?"

"I don't know if I could. It's been a few years and it was dark. No, I definitely couldn't."

"A few years? I thought you said it was a few months ago."

He smiled and nodded. "Ah, you see how bad my memory is?"

"So which was it, a few months or a few years?"

He gave me an exasperated look. "Jeez, you're making me feel like this *is* a job interview, putting all this pressure on me!"

I mashed my right foot into the ground. "Ming-kuo, could you please get serious about this? I'd like to know any details you can remember."

"Well, then I guess we can choose something in between. Let's say it was a year ago."

"Last Ghost Month?"

"Sure, let's say that."

Gan! Could I believe anything this guy said? I sipped some water and swished it around my mouth. "Ming-kuo, I'm going to level with you. I'm actually asking for Julia's parents. I'm seeing them after this and I'm going to have to tell them I couldn't come up with anything useful."

His eyes bugged out and he cracked his knuckles again. "You're asking for her parents, Jing-nan? I thought you were trying to get to the bottom of things for yourself. I mean, you two were practically married."

"Only in our minds." I noticed that our silently furious waitress was standing at the ready. She took our orders for *zhajiangmian*, wheat noodles in bean sauce, without saying a word, and returned with several appetizers, ranging from salty to spicy, and steamed to chilled. There are a lot of different ways to make *zhajiangmian*, but for my money the best one is a dish that originated in the ethnic Chinese communities living in Korea. This variety includes a thick black paste made from roasted and fermented soybeans and tiny chunks of pork. The only place to find this type is in Korean restaurants that include Chinese items on their menu. Apart from that I didn't know much about Korean food, and I knew even less about the little snacks. I didn't want to ask our waitress about them because she was already mad enough that she had to serve us. It also didn't help that Cookie Monster was looking at her like she was the daily special.

Classy as ever, Ming-kuo craned his neck and stared at her ass as she left.

"It's not a crystal ball," I said.

Ming-kuo sighed, shoved his elbows up on the table and cradled his head. "I'm not like you. Looking is all I get to do."

"You haven't been dating?" I asked, suppressing a laugh.

"Every few months I work up the courage to approach a girl, but I strike out every time."

"I'm sorry, Ming-kuo."

"I'm a virgin," he said with exasperation.

Gan! Or rather, non-*gan!*

"That's an honorable thing, Ming-kuo. You're saving yourself for marriage."

"But how do I get to marriage if I can't even get a date?"

"What a situation you're in. You work at a love hotel and everyone else around you is getting laid."

He dug his chopsticks into a cold dish of sprouted beans and threw them into his mouth. "You don't have to rub it in," he said with his mouth full.

I sampled some silvery fish that looked like crumpled foil candy wrappers with eyes. "I'm just making an observation. I'm not making fun of you."

"You're laughing at me."

I bit into the inside of my left cheek. "I'm not laughing."

"This is a fine way to treat your old classmate."

A different waitress brought our *zhajiangmian*, snipped the noodles in our bowls with a pair of plastic scissors and left without saying a word. This would have been a huge breach of etiquette in a Chinese restaurant. Sure, shorter noodles would be easier to eat, but the noodle represents one's existence. Breaking it means shortening your life. You're supposed to have the entire noodle in your mouth before chewing it.

But it was just another stupid superstition. Why pay attention to it?

Ming-kuo's face was ashen.

"She didn't even ask if she could cut the noodles," he said to the table.

I picked up my chopsticks and mixed the bowl. The bean sauce was impressively thick, like tar.

"Ming-kuo, you scared that first waitress away. This one probably has it in for you as well."

The minor calamity wouldn't stop Cookie Monster from eating. I'm not even sure a major one would. The dejected look on his face didn't perk up, but he began to feed. At least he used a napkin. "You think she saw me look?" he asked.

"Of course she did! Women see everything."

"I'm sorry I don't have the experience that you do. Nobody was ever in love with me, all right?"

As I ate, I continued to stir up the noodles. You have to. The sauce is so thick, it can only penetrate the ball of noodles one layer at a time. The greasy black gravy made slopping sounds like someone chewing with his mouth open, as Ming-kuo was. The poor bastard.

"Look," I said. "I'm going to help you, okay? I'm going to fix you up."

"With whom?"

"A pretty girl."

"She has to be smart."

Don't make it tougher for me, I thought.

THE *ZHAJIANGMIAN* WASN'T SITTING right in my stomach, and the little bumps I hit on the way to the Huangs' apartment sent strands of noodles whipping around inside.

It felt like a final act. This part of my life was over. This was the goodbye.

I wasn't worried about the big Taiwanese-American. If I ran into him, I'd say I was here only to pay my respects to Julia's parents one last time, and I was never going to see them again. Even an uncouth Taiwanese-American would understand that.

I pulled up to their building. I would give it to them plain and simple. I had tried asking Julia's NYU classmates but neither of them had anything useful to offer. That would be enough for them.

But was it enough for me? Damn, Ming-kuo's words were stuck in my head now: "You two were practically married." Any husband whose wife had just been murdered would not rest until the killer was prosecuted—or he'd go out and kill the guy himself.

At least that's how it is in the movies. I didn't know if I could hold a gun in my hands, much less shoot someone.

I put my hands in my pockets and rode up the elevator. The doors made a hard scraping sound I could feel in my molars as they opened. Strange. The ride had been quiet last time. The place was falling apart.

I rang the doorbell and stood back. I saw something block the light of the peephole.

"Jing-nan!" Mrs. Huang shouted through the door. "What are you doing here?"

Odd. She sounded unusually surprised and maybe a little scared.

"Hello, Mrs. Huang, I just wanted to talk to you a little bit," I said.

"It's all right. Everything's okay. Don't need to come here anymore!"

"What?"

"Go home or go to work. Just go away."

Just go away? Now that was just plain mean!

"Mrs. Huang, are you all right?"

"Get out of here now and stop bothering people!" I heard her stomp away from the door.

"You won't even let him in?" I heard her husband say. "That's rude!"

My thoughts exactly.

"Doesn't matter!" she yelled at him, before apparently dragging him off to their bedroom so she could yell at him some more.

I was stunned. Out of all the phrases she could have used, she had to pick that one. It was the most hurtful thing anyone could say to me.

I crossed my arms and walked gingerly to the elevator. I felt the way I used to as a kid when my grandfather would reprimand me for transgressions I didn't know I had committed.

Was I somehow at fault here?

Maybe they had been expecting me to call every day with updates? I hadn't wanted to talk on the phone because it wasn't respectful enough.

Maybe I should have come to Julia's altar every night? No, they knew neither of us was into such a thing.

Then it hit me.

Someone had gotten to the Huangs. That Taiwanese-American and the goon who had confronted me at Taipei 101. I subconsciously covered my stomach with my hands.

The bad guys were probably watching the Huangs' apartment. They probably saw me come in.

I continued walking cautiously down the hallway, but the sound of a door closing on another floor spooked me. I broke into a full run to the elevator, which was jammed open with the light off. Reluctantly, I ducked into the stairwell and began the long walk down. The smell got to me immediately. It wasn't just putrid garbage. It was the stink of rotted and maggoty meat run-off. A few people must have missed the garbage truck and hurled their kitchen waste into the stairwell.

I tried to get out at the next floor, but the stairwell door was locked. A nearby sign said that all the doors were locked from the stairwell side as a security measure. I had no choice but to continue.

I looked down and saw something that made my heart stop. The lights were out to the ground floor.

I heard another stairwell door open somewhere above me and slam shut. Then came the sounds of steady footsteps and a solid-wood sound tapping the floor—a baseball bat?

The goons had been waiting for me. I had already been given my last warning. This was where they were going to finish me, making me yet another victim of an unsolved murder.

Using my phone light as a guide, I walked down quickly and cautiously.

"Hey!" called out a gruff man's voice. "I hear you down there! Don't try to run away!"

I stumbled down as fast as I could. Soon I was on the ground floor. I shone my phone light around until I saw the shiny metal handle of the door.

The damn thing was locked.

The footsteps continued to descend from above at a deliberate pace, heavy with authority.

"You've run out of room, eh?" the man taunted. He slammed the bat hard on the ground. "Like a little cornered rat, ha ha ha!"

There was nowhere to hide. I stood with my back against the door, waiting for the inevitable. I was going to find out how long a pair of fists could last against a baseball bat.

A beam of light from the stairwell poked around my feet.

"I see you! You're gonna get what's coming! You shoulda listened to my warnings!"

The light zipped up to my face, blinding me. I did the bravest thing I could think of. I brought my two fists up into the light.

"I'm not going to go down easy!" I yelled.

"Huh, what's this?" the voice asked. "Who are you?"

"I was just here visiting someone," I stammered.

I heard the sound of a large ring of keys rattle.

"Get away from the door," the man commanded. I moved to the side. A dull light poured in as the man wedged the door open.

He was a big guy in his thirties, and his uniform said he was the maintenance man. The crooked fingers of his right hand were wrapped around the middle of a wooden axe handle.

"Sorry, fella. I thought you were one of those kids messing with the elevator. You know, they jam up the doors by putting crates and bricks in the door so it can't go anywhere. Eventually the thing shuts down, and I have to call in the elevator guys." He swung the axe handle to his shoulder. "I was just trying to scare them. I wasn't going to hurt anybody."

"Are you going to do something about that smell?"

"You smell something?"

I WALKED OUT INTO the lobby and pushed the building doors open with shaking hands.

I got on my moped and started the engine. I sighed as I drove in slow, lazy loops around the parking lot.

I had been warned not to ask questions about Julia and even taken a beating for it. I was ready to provide what little closure I could on the whole sad story. Unexpectedly, Julia's parents had closed the books on me.

Doesn't matter, huh? Your only kid doesn't matter? I went through hell and it doesn't matter?

Anger coursed my body, but as I got madder, I also softened. I thought about the kid I had been and the girl Julia had once been, too. They were so in love. Sure, they were stupid. What was wrong with that?

What would that stupid, love-struck kid do right now?

He would go to the police. Of course! Sure, the Huangs had given up on the cops, but older people don't know how to talk to authority figures. They're too deferential, and that never gets you anywhere. Jenny had shown me the way. Stick the phone in their faces and make a video.

Besides, the Huangs had been bugging the wrong people. They had been harassing the Taipei City cops when they should have been sticking it to the Hsinchu City police.

When I marched into that hick police station, confident and cocky, they would know there would be no peace until they solved the case. Those stupid, lazy cops would have to set down their coffee cups and bowls of Hsinchu *ba-wan* meat dumplings and get off their asses for a change.

I cracked my neck. This was Johnny talking.

CHAPTER ELEVEN

Hsinchu is a city on the northwest coast. It's not too far from Taipei, but it doesn't get a tenth of the tourist traffic. Many foreigners in Hsinchu are strictly there for business, most likely related to semiconductors.

I thought about Nancy's Ah-ding for a second, then let it go.

They call Hsinchu the Windy City for good reason. I huddled over my handlebars as best as I could, but I was still blown around on the highway. After half an hour, I knew I was about halfway there when I saw the exit signs for Taoyuan Airport.

Hsinchu was also known for being the capital of chip production, but I drove past a few abandoned factories and former research parks. A lot of the manufacturing and circuit-design jobs had relocated to China, a real sore point during elections. Politicians always vowed to bring the jobs back home and railed against the unfair trade practices of Chinese companies. But when all the votes were in, all the bravado and tough talk fell off, and more trade pacts with China were announced.

In another half hour I found the first exit to Hsinchu. Ming-kuo had said it was the second exit, which came up fairly quickly. I didn't know how reliable he was, but it was as good as any place to start. I turned off the main highway, and my heart leapt when, just after the taking the exit, I saw several glass-enclosed betel-nut stands lined up like neon-lit ice cubes.

Even in the daytime, the multicolored lights sparkled like the set of a cheap cable game show. As I got closer, I saw barely clothed women on display through the full-length windows. I had caught the *binlang xishi* during a lull. Two women in skimpy tank tops and skirts that were little more than belts were standing in stilettos, talking animatedly to each other.

One girl with her hair in braids sat on a stool by herself at a translucent-plastic desk. As I coasted by, she stood up, revealing inflated breasts straining against a lacy teddy. She tapped the glass with her right hand and brushed down her flimsy skirt with her left.

I looked up at the sign. EVERYTHING BEAUTIFUL. There was nothing special about it. Just another betel-nut stand like any of the others down the road. JADE EXPRESS. CHINESE GIRLS 2. MOUNTAIN BEAUTY.

I kept going, looking for the little parking area that Ming-kuo had spoken of.

I pulled up to a stand named Fragrant Beauty, the last *binlang* stand on this stretch.

A girl who couldn't have been older than seventeen strutted out in mommy's high heels. She brushed her blonde extensions away from her black bikini top.

"Hello, how are you?" she asked in street Mandarin.

"Hi," I said. "I was wondering if you knew anything about a betel-nut beauty who was murdered somewhere around here."

Her hands shot to her hips. If she had been wearing jeans, they would have been shoved in her pockets, but her flimsy miniskirt offered no such refuge.

"I don't know anything about it!"

"She was shot and killed in Hsinchu City, near one of the highway exits like this one."

"Why are you talking about crazy things like this?" she cried. "Don't you know what month this is?" Her hands cupped her nose and her eyes filled with tears. I reached out a hand to comfort her, but she ran away.

I could see I wasn't going to get far by interviewing people. I had no choice but to go straight to the authorities.

I had the locations of Hsinchu's three police stations in my phone. I mapped them out to find the closest one.

THE STATION WAS A block-long, rounded brick building with the entrance on a corner. I swung the door open, and before I had taken ten steps a young information officer whose badge read PENG stopped me. Phonetically, the surname "Peng" sounded exactly like "friend." I hoped he would be.

"Can I help you?" he asked. A reflection of the bright ceiling lights looked like a shiny hook in his slick, combed hair. He was about my height, and he looked directly into my eyes while wearing a friendly non-smile.

"I'm here to see what progress you're making on a certain investigation."

"Could you please be more specific, sir?"

"Well, I wanted to know more about the case of the murder at the betel-nut place."

His pupils narrowed. "Are you a family member?"

"Sort of."

He crossed his arms and cocked his head. "You either are or you aren't."

"I was going to marry her," I said.

He searched my face and then nodded. "But you didn't actually get married?"

"That's right. You see, we were old classmates at school."

"What's your family name?"

"Chen."

"First name?"

"Jing-nan."

"Mr. Chen, we've already coordinated with the Taipei City Police, and they've contacted the family. She only had her parents. Nobody mentioned a boyfriend or fiancé."

"Well, here I am."

A female information officer stepped over to us, but he waved her away with a childlike hand gesture.

"Mr. Chen, just because you knew the girl from visiting her at the betel-nut stand doesn't make you her boyfriend."

I chuckled. "Look, Mr. Peng. I really knew her very well."

"Okay," he said with a slight lilt in his voice. "I believe you, Mr. Chen. Why don't you come with me and I'll let you talk to one of the detectives?"

"Thank you very much," I said. Things were moving along.

He led me down a long, brightly lit corridor painted light blue. We passed by the female information officer, who stared at me while clutching a clipboard to her chest. I smiled at her.

"This room, please," said Mr. Peng. He opened a door and made a sweeping gesture. It looked like an interrogation room. There were four chairs and a suspiciously scarred wooden table. It wasn't the ideal sort of place to meet, but at least it was discreet.

I sat down, expecting Mr. Peng to come in, too.

Instead, he closed the door behind me and locked it. I couldn't hear what he said to the other information officer. The room was soundproofed, and the only word I could pick out clearly from the hallway was "crazy."

He thought I might be the killer. Of course he believed my actions were suspicious! When a guy comes in off the street and says he was going to marry the dead girl, he must be crazy. I pounded the table. How stupid of me!

I got up, intending to try the door. *Ai ya!* No knob or handle.

I stayed on my feet for a few minutes, until I heard several people coming down the corridor. Don't act crazy. Stay calm and explain yourself.

The door swung open.

"You guys are making a huge mistake!" I screamed to an older man in street clothes.

"No mistake," he said. "We know who you are now. I just talked to Mrs. Huang." The man took a seat and pulled the table to his waist. "Jing-nan, please, let's talk."

I sat down across from him and looked over the dry patches of skin on his forehead. Spindly white hairs clustered around his earlobes. I turned and noted that the two information officers and a high-ranking man in uniform were standing behind me.

"I didn't kill Julia," I said.

The older man leaned his face in to mine. "We know that. By the way, could you show me some ID?"

I took out my wallet and unfolded it. He glanced over it and nodded.

"Every minute you waste on me is another minute the killer gets to be free," I said as I shoved my wallet into my pocket with as much indignation as I could manage.

The man coughed into his fist. "Mr. Chen, we know the Huangs probably sent you here to bother us about their daughter. I understand that on an emotional level. As a parent, I would do anything to find out who killed my child. But as a veteran detective, I can tell you that pulling stunts like this only makes trouble at our station and delays our investigation."

"I wasn't trying to pull anything! I was only asking."

"You're not a family member. You don't have a right to know."

"Just tell me you're going to find the murderer!" I pleaded, my voice breaking.

The man sighed. "We're doing everything we possibly can. Look, Jing-nan, in the realm of the betel-nut business, there are all these tangents to nefarious characters."

"Maybe I could help in some way."

"So you wanna help, huh? Well, I wasn't insensitive enough to ask this of her parents, but we would love it if you could name all the guys she was turning tricks with."

I sprung up with one arm cocked, but the man was experienced. He smiled calmly as he shoved the table into my gut. I crumbled to the floor. The edge had cut right across my bruise.

"See that, Peng?" he said as I struggled to inhale. "That's how we deal with people who waste our time!" He stood over me and shouted down, "And you. Get back on your shitty little moped and get the fuck out of my city!"

They showed me the back door, and I managed to struggle out to the street on my own power.

CHAPTER TWELVE

Jenny's stand was closed. I was relieved. She would have forced the entire story out of me. I was in pain and too distressed to give a genuine smile.

I could fake talk with Kuilan. She asked me if something was wrong, and I told her I missed Julia badly.

I had to fess up fully to Dwayne, and he let me have it.

"I used to think you were smart, Jing-nan," he said. "Now I know you're dumb. Don't you know the cops are just as bad as the crooks? No, make that worse!"

I thought I had recovered from taking the table in the gut a few hours before, but now I couldn't stand up straight. It was messing with my head, and I couldn't slip into my Johnny personality properly. When I shouted out to passersby, the effort left me gasping for breath.

"Look at him, Cat!" Dwayne continued. "You think people want to eat at a stand where the barker looks like he's ready to drop dead?"

Frankie glanced at me and pronounced, "He'll live."

I dragged a chair to the front grill and dropped into it.

"I just need to rest for a minute," I said, closing my eyes and bracing my hands on my knees.

"You need to work out and toughen up. You're the first person I ever heard of getting beat up by a table."

"The table had some help."

Someone reached down and touched the back of my neck with soft fingers.

"Nancy!" I said as I looked up. I came face-to-face with Peggy Lee. Her eyebrows were raised and her mouth was screwed tight.

"Nancy?" she asked. "Who's Nancy?"

"She's a friend of mine," I said.

"You were expecting her?"

"Sort of. More than I was expecting you."

"I'm glad I caught you during your break. I was thinking you could grab a bite with me."

"I'm busier than I look, Peggy. Some other time."

"Oh!" exclaimed Dwayne. "I know you! You were the little bird who used to come after Jing-nan all the time!"

Peggy brushed her hair over her right ear. "It's true," she said. "But things are different now."

"Seems like you have the same crazy look in your eyes."

In a futile gesture, I put up an open hand, blocking Dwayne's face. "Peggy, I want to apologize for Dwayne's comments. He likes to incite people. I'll meet up with you some other time, I promise."

"Don't worry, Jing-nan. I like to have fun, too. I wasn't offended." But the look in her eyes said she would have pushed Dwayne off the curb and into traffic as soon as his back was turned.

When she was gone, Dwayne came up to me and said softly, "Do you know how expensive that necklace was? It was a Tiffany!"

"Now you whisper?" I said.

"I have a cousin in the jewelry business. The chains on that thing." He shook his head. "You don't wear something like that to a night market." Dwayne mimed picking a pocket.

"That was probably the cheapest thing she had."

"Listen to me, man. You don't want a girl like that. Find a humble girl who knows the value of work. The old ways of getting people together were better. Your grandmother was bought and adopted by your grandfather's family and grew up working on the farm. When she was old enough, she married your grandfather."

"She was fifteen when she married my grandfather."

"Things weren't perfect, but they were better than now. Girls chasing money only lead to trouble." Dwayne covered his mouth and added, "Look at what happened to Julia."

"Don't blame the victim," I said. "I'm fucking serious."

Dwayne threw his hands up. "I can't talk to you when you're like this." He suddenly put a smile on his face. "Why, hello, miss! How can I help you?"

I turned to see Nancy. She was wearing an old, outsized Echo & the Bunnymen T-shirt over Uniqlo shorts. A heavy bag—probably filled with LPs—was slung over her right shoulder.

"Hi, Jing-nan," she said. "You never answered my text. The vinyl pop-up store had a lot of great stuff!"

"I'm sorry, Nancy. I was so busy."

"Looks like you're sitting around talking!"

"This is Nancy!" boomed Dwayne.

"Hello."

"Nancy, this is Dwayne, who should be working, and that is Frankie, who is actually working." Frankie gave a small wave.

"Nancy," said Dwayne, "how about you take Jing-nan out of here for the night? He's not feeling well."

"No!" I said. Taking a sick day was for the weak. It would call my manhood into question.

"What's wrong?" asked Nancy.

"I'll explain later. I'm not hurt badly." I struggled to stand up and knocked the chair back by accident.

"He's out for the night," said Dwayne. "Don't worry, Jing-nan, we'll cover for you!"

"Now it looks even worse!" exclaimed Nancy. She poked my bruise.

"Ouch!" I said. "Stop it!" Despite the teasing, most of my pain from earlier in the night was gone. Who knew sex was better than physical therapy?

"I can't believe you got beat up by some hooligans and then the cops . . . and in the same spot!" She turned on every light in the room to get a better look at my injury.

I piled two pillows behind me, sat up and looked around the room. "This is one of the plainest love hotels ever," I said.

"It was close by. Some other time, when you're better, we can try one with a jail theme, with the cell and handcuffs. I can pretend to be a police chief and hit you some more."

"You would be a good cop."

"Hey, I take that as an insult."

I grabbed her and licked her ear. She laughed.

"It's interesting to be with a young guy."

"Oh?" I turned on my side to face her and winced.

"Ah-ding would have been long asleep by now, and it seems like you're raring to go again."

"Say, Nancy?"

"Yes?"

"Have you been with a few guys?"

"What, have I slept around a lot? Is that what you want to know?"

I thought about the Hsinchu detective asking me who Julia's johns were.

"Hey, I didn't mean it like that! I certainly haven't done this very often at all."

"You think I do? That's the second time you've insulted me tonight!"

"Nancy, I just felt jealous when you mentioned Ah-ding. That's all."

"You don't have to be jealous of him. There weren't deep emotions involved."

"Just like us," I said, quickly adding, "Well, so far."

Her lips quivered. "Yes. Exactly."

I brushed her hair back behind her ears.

"Still, though, it's all right now to say we care about each other."

"Do you still love Julia?"

"A part of me does. The younger part of me, with all the memories."

The phone rang.

"I didn't even know the phones worked in this place," I said. "I wonder who it is. Nobody knows we're here."

"It's probably the front desk."

"We still have at least twenty minutes!" Feeling my annoyance surge, I answered the phone with an attitude. "Yeah?"

"Didn't we warn you, Jing-nan?" said a voice that matched mine for exasperation. It was the Taiwanese-American. "Didn't we say to leave it alone? Now you've gone and done it. That was so stupid of you, going to the Hsinchu police."

Every emotion ran through me. I felt like a frozen fillet of fish dropped into a deep fryer—bubbling and crispy on the outside, thawing and slimy in the middle and solid ice at the core.

I was scared as hell that he'd found me. Furious that he was calling me when I was with Nancy. Tickled that I had pissed him off.

Strangest of all, I felt hopeful. After the Huangs cut me off, the Taiwanese-American was my sole connection to Julia. If anybody knew anything, it was him.

I licked my lips. If I pushed his buttons, he might tell me something useful.

"You're that American guy," I said. "I can tell by your stupid accent. Are you in Taiwan to work on it through immersion in Mandarin?"

I heard him cough, holding back his rage so he could speak and not scream. "Oh yeah, Jing-nan? You're gonna be talking a lot funnier than me when I break your fucking face in half!"

"Why don't you shoot me, the same as you shot Julia?"

"I didn't kill Julia!" He was indignant, but he also sounded like he was telling the truth.

"You're my number-one suspect," I spat, pointing my finger at the receiver.

"You have no idea what's going on!"

He hung up. I laughed with relief and nervousness. My hands fumbled as I tried to replace the receiver.

I looked at Nancy. She was sitting up with the sheet gathered over her body, looking sexy and scared.

"That was one of the *liumangs*, right?" she asked.

"I lied to you about my bruise," I said. "It wasn't from work." I told her all about my run-ins with the Taiwanese-American. She stiffened.

"How did he find you?"

I instantly knew the answer. "It had to be the clerk," I said. "They have all these love-hotel staff members on the payroll. How else do you think these gangsters blackmail businessmen and politicians?"

"I don't feel safe here," she said. Her legs did a scissor kick over the mattress to find her panties.

"You're right. Let's get out of here before he shows up with his friends." I tore through the sheets, looking for my boxers.

"I hate rushing," said Nancy as she snapped on her bracelets, left then right. "I forget things when I rush."

I pointed at the blotch on my stomach. "Look what they've done to me. It's going to look a lot uglier on you, Nancy."

"Who are they? Just a bunch of low-life hooligans, right?"

"Can't be. The guy coming after me is an American."

WE TOOK NANCY'S SPORTS car to my neighborhood. It wasn't subtle, of course, but it was safer than my moped. We circled my block twice, looking for a spot, but as expected we attracted unwanted attention.

"Pull up to the curb there, Nancy," I said.

"We can't park there."

"We're going to talk to that guy waving to us."

"Is he a friend?"

"He's a *jiaotou*, a big brother around here, so he is a friend."

Nancy rolled down her window. German Tsai loped over, smirking. His crew cut of white hair looked like a fuzzy halo, and his Hitler mole gleamed in the light from the streetlamp. He took the toothpick out of his mouth, snapped it in half and dropped it.

"Hello, German," I said.

"Is that really you, Jing-nan?" He was too dignified to lean down to the window, so he widened his stance and bent at the knees to get a good look at us. "Just the other day you were on your sad little bike. Now you're here in this beautiful car with an even more beautiful girl. You been rubbing Buddha's belly?"

"German, this is Nancy," I said. He gave her a respectful nod. "We're about to head home, and we're looking for a parking spot."

"Calling it a night already?" asked German. "It's not even nine. You should take Nancy out for some fun. You need to show off a beautiful girl like that."

"We've had enough excitement for tonight."

"You two should go to my KTV, Best Western. It opened a month ago, Jing-nan, and you still haven't come by. You have to give me some face. I've known you since you were a bump in your mama's stomach!"

"Some other time, I promise."

German settled things with a loud whistle. "Jing-nan! You, girl! Get out of the car!"

Three little brothers came over to the curb. Nancy squeezed my left hand.

"Are we in trouble?" she asked quietly.

"It's all right," I said to Nancy under my breath. "They're *jiaotous*, but they're my *jiaotous*."

"I still need to park," Nancy pleaded with German.

"We'll take care of that," he said. "Leave the keys in."

Two of the little brothers stood guard by the car, ogling its curves with their mouths open. We followed the third guy, who turned his head every so often to spit *binlang* juice. I wondered where he got his betel nuts from.

The little brother brought us near the Ximending neighborhood of Wanhua District. Ximending literally means "West Gate District," as it used to be the wilderness outside the west gate of Taipei. It was the home of movie theaters and shopping for young people. Japanese culture is big there. So are lesbian, gay, bisexual and transgender interests.

German Tsai's turf didn't extend to Ximending itself. The little brother brought us to a side alley below the southern boundary. The building entrance was set back from the sidewalk to make room for traditional guardian-lion statues sporting cowboy hats. Old-time wagon wheels leaned against their flanks. BEST WESTERN KTV, read an oversized sign that ripped off the font from the American hotel chain.

The little brother handed me a coupon. "Give this to the cowboy with the arrow through his hat. He'll take care of you."

"Thank you," I said. He slipped away back to the street. To Nancy I said, "That guy was looking at your ass."

"He was only looking. There was no touching."

"Still."

Nancy leaned against me and grabbed my hand.

"We'll be safe here," I said. "German wouldn't give us away."

"Singing together might be fun."

"We don't have to go in if you don't really want to. We could go back to my place."

"I do want to go in. I haven't been to karaoke in more than a month."

THE BEST WESTERN LOBBY was crowded with artificial cacti with right-angle elbows and microphones and drinks clamped in their prickly mitts.

Something light landed on my head. I pushed back the brim of the foam cowboy hat and stared into the cleavage of a hostess wearing a feathered headdress and a short leather skirt.

"I want a blue hat like his," complained Nancy.

"Blue is for boys," said the hostess, "pink is for girls. Time for you to check in with the sheriff now." Her fringed sleeves shimmied as she swept her arms forward.

"I'm Sheriff Chang," said a stocky man wearing a large hat that featured the word "Coyboy" embroidered in misspelled English. There was indeed an arrow through it. "What are you laughing about? When you come into my territory, you best be behaving yourselves!"

He didn't seem to be acting very coy, which only made me chuckle some more. "I'm supposed to give this to you," I said, handing him the slip from German's little brother. Sheriff Chang lightened up immediately.

"You're special guests!" he announced. "First round of drinks and first hour are on the house." The sheriff moved in like he was going to hug me, but felt me up instead, including up the insides of my thighs. "No weapons allowed in the territory," he offered, winking at Nancy.

KTVs are infamous for drunken fights, sometimes with knives and pipes. Even the toughest guys in the world feel vulnerable to criticism when they sing.

Sheriff Chang unlatched a box and opened the lid, revealing a pair of pistol microphones.

"Here you go, kids. Take the Shootout at the OK Corral Room, right through there."

We walked down the corridor, which was decked out with rickety planks, fake torches and plush canaries in cages.

"You get it, Nancy?" I asked. "We're supposed to be in a mine."

"They did a good job!"

Surprisingly, the inside of the room wasn't adorned at all. It looked just like any other twenty-year-old KTV. The videos were old as hell, too. The songbooks didn't have anything from this century. Which was fine with the two of us. Once we'd flipped past the country and western songs, it was the best of the '80s, including Joy Division, New Order, Echo & the Bunnymen and The Clash, who Nancy gushed over.

"They were so cool!" she said. "They had a real political message, too!"

"All these bands . . . are English," I said. "Maybe that's why this place is called 'Best Western'! Everything's from the West."

"Does that bother you?" asked Nancy as she cued up "White Riot."

"I just wish Taiwan had a band with that defiant vibe. Instead they all go for cuteness, like those girl groups and boy bands. They don't even play real instruments. You know what I mean."

"I do. You might like that band Boar Pour More. They never officially released anything, but they played a bunch of shows."

"I've heard of them, but I've never heard their stuff."

"They have a MySpace page."

"I don't use MySpace."

Nancy stomped her foot. "It was my band."

"I'll check it out, Nancy. Were you the singer?"

"I was the drummer. Actually, we were really bad. Maybe you shouldn't check it out."

"But I—"

She cut me off by handing me a gun mic. "C'mon, you have to help me on the choruses!"

Once you've done "White Riot," you have to do "London Calling," "Rock the Casbah" and "Train in Vain." The songs were all

KTV extended mixes, calculated to make you stay longer and pay more because you're renting the room by the hour. Next thing you know, it's three in the morning and you're all lining up at the ATM in the KTV.

Three quick knocks came at our door and before we could say anything, in walked a woman wearing a rhinestone-studded bikini, cowboy boots and a big smile.

"Howdy, partners," she said in English before continuing in Mandarin. "Can I get you something?"

"You mean drinks?" I asked.

"Or food or cigarettes?"

"I thought we weren't allowed to smoke in the rooms," said Nancy.

"We could all step outside and share a smoke."

Was this lady a house prostitute or just pushy with the amenities?

"We're fine for now," said Nancy. "We'll call if we need you."

The woman whipped out a phone camera from somewhere.

"Smile! I want to put you two on our wall!" We obliged.

"Adios!" the bikini lady said cheerfully. When she was gone and the door was closed, Nancy slapped my shoulder.

"Her boobs are fake, you know," she said. "You don't need to inspect them that closely!"

I showed Nancy the open palms of my hands. "She was bending over, pushing them into my face!"

"You could have moved away!"

"You're jealous!"

"I'm angry!"

"Don't be mad at me. You're the only one I love." I backpedaled immediately. "I mean, the only one I could love."

She blinked and I saw her pupils darting around. "You have to sing 'Love Will Tear Us Apart' for me," she said.

"If it will make you happy, I will."

I was kidding around, being as melodramatic as I could, but halfway through the song I felt my stomach tighten, and it wasn't because of the bruise. I looked into Nancy's eyes and saw she was still that girl in high school with a crush on an upperclassman.

When I was done, I shut off my mic.

"I can't fall in love with you, Nancy," I said to the floor.

"I wouldn't let you fall in love with me," she said. "Not until you're done with Julia."

"Maybe I'll never be done with Julia."

"Maybe," she said, turning to the songbook and studying the titles intently. "I'm a little thirsty now. Why don't you pick up the phone and call your friend?"

"She's your friend, too."

I ordered two Kirins, and a man dressed as a cowpoke brought them in. "They sent him to even things out for us," I told Nancy. "Feel better?"

She grumbled. Julia would have never grumbled at me. I liked how Nancy was honest about how she was feeling.

Nancy gave Joy Division's "Transmission" a shot, singing it probably two octaves above Ian Curtis. It lent the song a feeling of innocence, and the lyrics about the societal alienation of the individual were recast as the narrative of a child asking why his parents never really loved him and now they were dead.

"You're crying, Jing-nan," said Nancy.

"That song makes me cry sometimes."

I changed the energy in the room with the dancy "Bizarre Love Triangle" by New Order.

It was right that they'd decided to carry on. It was right that they chose to do what they loved.

After a while, I became irritated at the mix of the song. It must have gone on for fifteen minutes—most of it instrumental. I made Nancy jump up and down with me while we pretended to shoot our guns into the ceiling. I forgot all about our panicked flight from the love hotel earlier.

After what seemed like only a few more songs, we stumbled out of the room and handed back our gun mics. Sheriff Chang rang up our bill.

"That's six thousand NT," he declared.

"Hey, wait a second," I said. "We were supposed to get a deal."

"Yeah, the first hour was free and so were the beers. You were in our best room for two charged hours, and I'm rounding down, too." A hundred US dollars per hour. What a scam. I wondered how many times German would strongly encourage me to visit.

Nancy handed over her credit card.

"Now, little lady, I quoted you the cash price. I'm sorry, but I have to add another ten percent for credit."

"That's fine. Also, put in another two hundred NT for a tip for the waiter," she said.

"I like your style," said Sheriff Chang. He swiped her card and handed it back. To me, he said, "I like your friend. What's her name?"

"You just saw her card, sheriff," I said. "Her name's Nancy."

"No, I mean your other friend. The one with the car-crash bags." He cupped his own breasts, which were, truthfully, impressive in their own right.

Suddenly I couldn't breathe.

"You mean the girl in the bikini?" asked Nancy. "She doesn't work here?"

"I *wish* she did! She came in looking for you, Jing-nan!"

"I'll tell her you like her," I managed to say.

"She's got a job here, if she ever wants one!"

Nancy signed her receipt and we walked out.

"I wonder what this all means," she said.

"It's bad," I said. "Now that they've got a picture of you, you're mixed up in this, too."

We met up with German and his boys, who were still watching over our car. He thanked me loudly for visiting his KTV. Then he put his arm around me and walked me to a poorly lit section of the street.

"I have bad news, Jing-nan," he said. "You've pissed off some pretty powerful people."

"It's Black Sea, isn't it?"

"The only thing I know for sure is that the Americans are involved." He turned and spit into the road. "You're in some serious shit."

"They already warned me." I put my hands in my pockets.

"Then lay off, already. I don't know what you did, but just stop doing it."

"I did stop."

He put his hand on my shoulder, not in a menacing sort of way, but like a little-league coach. "Stop even looking like you might do it again."

"Who told you, German?"

"I heard through the grapevine. People saw you go into the Best Western. I don't want you to bring any trouble there, you got me? It's a legit business, and I'm keeping it clean."

I cracked my back. "Trouble's been following me."

"Stop bringing it into the neighborhood, because then it becomes trouble for me and then I have to take care of it. Then it's going to cost you. Understand?"

"I got it."

"Here's what I suggest. You and Nancy get in the car and go somewhere else tonight. Don't ever bring that fucking car back here. You two want to come back to your place, take your shitty moped or the train."

I looked over at the car. It looked like it had been Photoshopped into a picture of this worn-out block.

"The car's pretty conspicuous, right? The Americans will know when we're around because of it."

"Fuck the Americans," said German with a scowl. "I'm just noticing my boys like that car too much. I can't watch over them twenty-four hours a day, and a car isn't the biggest thing they've made disappear."

CHAPTER THIRTEEN

Nancy lived in a luxury apartment complex in the Da'an District. We pulled up to one of the entrances and a skinny man in a red uniform stepped out immediately and opened Nancy's door.

He chirped, "Good evening, Miss Han," with his head down.

It must have been four in the morning, but he was as lively as if it were four in the afternoon.

"Hello, Yeh-jung," said Nancy. She left the engine on and stepped out of the car. I didn't think the man could see me under the low brim of his hat, but he nodded to me over the car roof as I exited.

Another man in a uniform with the same build as the first attendant spun the revolving door for us as we walked through.

"Good evening, Miss Han," said the man.

"Hello, Chao-tang," she said.

Chao-tang brought his head up and looked at me casually.

"Hello," I said.

"Good evening, sir." I thought I heard his heels click.

We walked the length of a giant salt-water aquarium to get to the elevators. A bright yellow fish shaped like an uncut starfruit kept pace with us before giving me the eye and darting away.

"This building looks really familiar for some reason, even though I'm sure I've never been here before," I said.

"We were on the news a few times," Nancy said with some weariness in her voice. "Whenever people want to protest, they come here to target the rich and politically powerful. The last group was that anti-nuke group who said that when the New Taipei City reactors leaked radiation we'd have to abandon our luxury apartments. One guy tried to grab my collar when I was walking out."

"Seems like a small price to pay when you live like this. Do you realize how underdressed I am?"

"Don't be silly. The men who actually live here dress like slobs, because they don't care about trying to impress anybody. The women are different, though."

I looked over the walls near the elevator doors. The only things I saw were smooth tiles and my confused face reflected in the mirrors.

"Where are the buttons?"

"It's sensor-driven. We call the elevators by just standing here."

On cue, the door in front of Nancy slid open as a chime suspiciously close to the default ring of an iPhone sounded. As I followed her into the car, another elevator opened up to my right. I turned around in time to see our doors close on a woman focusing an accusing glare on us.

"Do you know her?" asked Nancy.

"You don't recognize an old schoolmate? That's Lee Xiaopei. Peggy."

"Your year?"

"Yeah. I was too surprised to wave."

Nancy pulled me in close. "Well, you guys can talk later," she said.

Gee, I'd thought Peggy and I were cool. Something was up.

NANCY DIDN'T HAVE A lot of stuff in her apartment. Not to the naked eye, anyway. Every five feet of wall space concealed some kind of storage bin that opened with a handle and folded away seamlessly in the wood grain.

"I like how there's no clutter," said Nancy as she gestured to the wall, "but everything's right here at your fingertips." She slid out a CD rack and vinyl album shelf to show me. She lifted up a panel and pushed it in to reveal a home-theater system. Then she bent down to open a bottom drawer before exclaiming, "Whoops!" and slamming it shut before I got a good look at it.

"What was that, a pet cobra?"

"It was just something. I don't open that drawer often."

Nancy fast-walked to the bar area. "Want some ice water?" she called.

"All right." I went over and fiddled with the wall that had the forbidden drawer. I could tell where the handle was, but I couldn't pop it out. "Nancy, how do you open this thing?"

"You're so nosy," she grumbled as a piece of fancy machinery let out a metal mouse whine and scraped crushed ice into a glass.

"Show me," I said.

She came over and gave me my drink. "This is mountain-ice water. It's never been brought down to room temperature since it was harvested."

I took a sip. It tasted like any other glass of water I've ever had, although it was impressively cold.

"Nancy," I insisted. "Show me."

She sighed and lifted the handle while twisting it. The drawer opened, revealing stacks of folded men's socks and briefs.

"Ah-ding's, right?"

"Yes."

"Still hoping he comes back, huh?"

"No. I just don't feel right throwing away his things."

I took too big a gulp of water. It slit my throat lengthwise like a steel sword.

She shifted the cup of water in her hand and stood on her tip-toes. "You said you didn't want to fall in love."

"I'm not talking about that," I said. "I just think it's weird that you're still attached to this guy, weird on a purely intellectual basis. You said you don't love him."

"I feel obligated to him. After all, he did buy this place for the two of us to hang out in."

I held my glass with both hands, feeling my palms and fingers begin to burn from the cold. "You did more than just 'hang out,' Nancy."

She flapped her arms twice. "I get it. You're making a stand for morality."

"Not so much morality, but personal dignity."

"*Dignity?* You've been taking me to love hotels! What a hypocrite you are!"

I wasn't sure who'd slipped me the stupid pill or when it began to take effect, but the way I was going it was going to be a quick, lonely ride down to the lobby. What an asshole I was being! I put my glass down on what looked like a coaster on the closest side table.

"I'm sorry, Nancy. I've been talking like a crazy person."

"Don't forget who paid for KTV tonight."

"Thank you so much for taking care of me. I'm such a chump."

"You're jealous of Ah-ding, aren't you?"

"Yes, I am jealous. I just wanted to be alone with you, and his boxers suddenly popped up between us, like a fucking spring-loaded crotch."

That made her smile. She punched my arm just hard enough to hurt.

When a Taiwanese woman is mad at you, if she is able to forgive you, she will punch you. If she remains quiet and doesn't hit you, you are in big, big trouble. Death-penalty big.

I put an arm around Nancy and tried to pull her to me, but she twisted away in the same practiced way that I broke free of Dwayne's holds.

"I want to show you something special," she said. She opened a drawer, took out a box the size of a birthday cake and ducked into what I assumed was the bathroom.

I sat on the designer couch and toyed with my phone as I waited. No voice messages, but there was an email in my junk folder from a Gmail address I didn't recognize. I heard a clicking sound from the bathroom before the door opened.

Nancy came out in a red teddy thinner than a facial tissue. She had a pair of red-plastic horns on her head. She sashayed over to me and sat on my lap.

"Do you like this? It's my devil-girl outfit."

"It looks uncomfortable. We'd better take it off."

"Hey, you have to get me into the mood. You were mean before, and I was thinking that I should probably go straight to sleep."

"What do you want me to do?"

"I want a good, hard massage."

"All right."

"My entire back and my legs."

"I've never massaged legs before."

She sighed. "Well, you're going to learn. Trial and error, but make the errors minimal."

"Back first," I said. She slid onto the coffee table and stretched out. No wonder the top was padded. I put my hands on her shoulder blades.

"Not like that!" she exclaimed. "Wash your hands first! Use hot water!"

"All right," I said, heading for the room she had changed in.

"And get the oil! On the shelf under the sink!"

I turned on the water in the sink.

"Warm up those fingers, Jing-nan! Nothing's a bigger turn-off than cold hands!"

It might be a long night, but I was sure it was going to be worth it in the end.

I DREAMED I WAS in a shadowy hall in a temple, standing before a fiery brazier. I heard Julia tell me to do something, but I didn't want to do it. I looked down at my hands. They were full of reams of bamboo joss paper with small patches of gold foil in the center that were traditionally burned to send money to deceased loved ones. A Western Union to the dead.

I peeled off a sheet of paper and a friendly flame caught in the middle, below the gold mark. I saw letters in the soft little light, but I couldn't read them. What did they say?

Julia was now standing above me, pointing at the paper in my hands and indicating that I needed to feed it into the brazier. A breeze began to blow, and her full-length, translucent dress flowed back like a jellyfish in a current.

No, I won't. That would be playing into the whole myth of the underworld I refused to believe in.

She insisted.

I love you, Julia, but I can't.

The wind picked up. I hung on to the single fiery sheet. Everything around me was being swept into the mouth of the brazier. Now I had a howling wind at my back.

I realized there was only one way I could prevent this joss paper from going into the brazier.

I folded it like a flour tortilla and fought to shove it into my mouth. It became soggy. I began to choke.

I woke up and yanked the sheet out of my mouth.

IN THE MORNING I slid out of bed, trying not to wake Nancy up. I checked my email and my phone promptly died. I fumbled and dropped it on the wooden floor, making the loudest sound in the world. Nancy didn't even flinch. I had been planning to clean my face in the kitchen sink, but since she was in such a deep sleep, I decided I could wash up quickly without bothering her.

Nancy's shower fixtures were American, and her shampoo and soap were Japanese. I came out and dried myself off with a big quick-dry towel. My skin had never felt this soft. Even my bruise was looking better. Maybe it was time to ditch the old house, or at least get a new bathroom installed.

I dressed and touched my lips lightly to Nancy's. In her sleep she reached up and rubbed off my kiss.

I rode the MRT back to the market around noon. I was glad to find my moped where I'd left it. I shouldn't have been surprised. Cars and motorcycles made much better joyrides. Frankie and Dwayne weren't due for a couple hours, so I went into a Family Mart for a strawberry milk and sipped slowly as I charged up my phone.

The main market wasn't open yet, but I picked up a fried chicken leg from a sidewalk vendor and took a few bites. It was old and tasted like it had been fried three times. The meat had hardened into jerky. I soldiered on because I only rarely experience bad food. As I ate, I had an almost transcendent experience. I didn't register how much I cared about the food we served at Unknown Pleasures until I realized how deeply ashamed I would be to serve something as terrible as this chicken leg to my customers. I picked the bones clean, undeterred by a strip of calloused flesh that lodged between my molars. I even crunched down and ate the cartilage that connected the thigh and leg bones. My disgusting little snack had given me oil-trap breath but left me feeling extremely satisfied. A little bit proud, too.

I checked my email as I walked down Daxi Road to Unknown Pleasures. Nothing in the inbox. Just that one that had popped up in the junk folder last night. The subject line simply read, WARNING. It didn't offer a Nigerian lottery prize or Viagra, so I opened it.

I will call you soon, read the email.

Creepy. I shrugged it off and opened up the metal gates to my stand.

I took a deep breath and scratched the end of my nose. Suddenly, my nostrils were tickly. It could only mean one thing. I cranked out the three canopies all the way.

Seconds after I finished, raindrops fell in moving sheets. I stood and watched the animated dot-matrix impacts make a story in the empty street. In fifteen minutes, the sun was out again and the air smelled of hot garbage. Or maybe it was stinky tofu.

Frankie the Cat came strolling down Daxi Road and nodded to me. Silently, he unloaded boxes of animal parts from the hand truck he was pushing. Despite the fact that I was never at the stand this early and that I was wearing yesterday's clothes, he didn't ask me a thing. Hell, he had probably put all the clues together already, so there was nothing for him to ask.

I helped him wash out grisly intestines and stomachs. Dwayne came in about half an hour later.

"Whoa, Jing-nan, what are you doing here so early?"

"I'm the owner," I said. "I have a responsibility."

"If you're so responsible, then how come you haven't changed clothes? Look at him, Frankie. What a dissolute man! Carrying on with women during Ghost Month! What nerve! Jing-nan would make the Eight Immortals keel over and die with his insolence!"

Frankie walked to the street and lit up a cigarette before speaking. "The kid's getting laid and you're not. Deal with it."

The rain never came back, and throngs of tourists choked the streets. I called out to a middle-aged male tourist wearing a Clash shirt from the *Give 'em Enough Rope* era and told him that Joe Strummer should have begged Mick Jones to come back.

"I saw that last tour without Mick, and it sucked!" he roared.

"Mick went on to do great stuff, though," I said. "Big Audio Dynamite's first album was awesome."

He smiled and waved his whole group of six over. Three couples of old punk rockers. The Clash guy came around the grill and hugged me like an old friend.

Over his shoulder I saw Peggy Lee in a black linen pantsuit enter and sit at one of our tables. I had a pet peeve about people putting their bags on empty chairs, and she indulged my annoyance when she plopped her Louis Vuitton down next to her. When I glanced at her again, she was holding her lipstick in a fist and smearing it on.

The group bought up a lot of stuff I wouldn't normally be able to trick white people into trying: chicken hearts, gizzards, whole cuttlefish. They settled in at a table near the back.

I sat down next to Peggy as soon as I could.

"Did you just get out of work, Peggy?" I asked.

"I did. It's quite a quick car ride here," she said. "Could I get a napkin, Jing-nan?"

I swiped some from under the front grill and handed them to her. I thought she was going to kiss off the excess of her lipstick but instead she lifted her bag, wiped the seat under it and then put it back down.

"Are you hungry, Peggy?"

She raised her eyebrows. "Do you want to go somewhere?"

"You can have anything you see here."

She rolled her eyes. "I'll get something at home."

I drummed my fingers on the table. "Speaking of which, funny seeing you this morning," I said.

"Yes, funny seeing you in my building."

"It was almost five in the morning. Pretty late for you to be going out."

"I was going in to work. The market closes in New York at four A.M. our time, and the most relevant financial news comes out shortly after." She folded her legs under the table and kicked me, maybe by accident. "I need to be up on the latest news before the Asian markets open."

"I'm sorry I didn't have a chance to say hi or introduce you to Nancy."

"You two seemed to be in a rush." Her eyes narrowed as my silence fed her imagination. "Are you having something serious with her?"

"Peggy, I don't see how she's any of your business."

"I'm here to save you." She lowered her head and whispered, "You know about her, don't you?"

"Sure I do."

"She's not a good girl."

"I think she is."

"You don't have money, but you do have morals. You would never have cheated on Julia."

"That's right."

"A girl like that has no standards," said Peggy as she folded her hands in her lap. "How do you think she lives in a place like that even though she doesn't have a real job?"

"Peggy, Nancy is a graduate student, and I know about her past." I put my hands together and built a small wall of fingers on the table to shield myself.

"Look! I don't want my old classmate to be seen associating with a call girl. Wang Ding-yu would come to stay with her. You know who he was, right? That tech executive who went to jail two years ago?" She slapped my finger fortress hard. "He's married, and his kids are almost as old as us!"

"Ow! *Gan!* Well, so what, Peggy? Nobody's perfect. Look at you! You're divorced. There's a stigma to that. Look at me! I've been living with a ghost, and this was years before Julia actually died." I planted my elbows on the table as reinforcements. Even though I was talking to her, I was really speaking to myself. "You can plan on living a great life with someone you love, but that doesn't mean it's going to work out that way."

Peggy's hands shot to her bag and tore open a pocket. Why was she opening an eyeglass case? Oh, it was a flask disguised as an eyeglass case. Peggy took two quick pulls and grunted. She shoved it at me.

"Do it," she commanded.

I took a small sip. "Damn, that's not whiskey," I gasped.

"It's *soju*."

Korean rice liquor. I wasn't sure how much alcohol was in it, but it tasted like a hundred percent. She took another mouthful and stuck the flask back in her bag before continuing.

"You know, Jing-nan, that dirty Mr. Wang tried to pick me up at an investing conference in Beijing a few years ago. We were having drinks and he thought he could bring it to that next level." A dreamy, happy look came over her eyes. "I was married at the time, too. He didn't care."

"I'm glad nothing happened," I said. "You're not the cheating kind."

"I hate people who cheat. Boy, Mr. Wang got the shock of his life when I ran into him in the apartment building."

"He probably wondered who had set you up there."

Her face reddened and she grabbed my wrist. "Hah! The joke's on him! My family helped to construct that place! Go read that plaque in the lobby!" She shifted in her seat before triumphantly adding, "We still own the penthouse apartment."

I glanced back at the counter and wished hard for some customers to walk up. "Peggy, it's nice that you stopped by, but I'm working right now. Maybe we can do lunch sometime." I meant it, too. Even though we were completely different people and had a contentious past that sometimes bled into the present, I still liked her.

Her eyes flashed at my attempt to bring our talk to an end, and some programmed business instinct seemed to kick back in. "I came here to offer you something special, Jing-nan. Something no one else here is going to have." She fished through her bag again and handed me a stuffed legal-sized Tyvek envelope.

"What is this?"

She dropped her voice and cupped her mouth. "It's a lifeboat for when this night market gets blown out of the water," she whispered. "This whole area is going to be redeveloped into condos and upscale retail."

I regarded the envelope. It was unmarked and seemed to hold about twenty pages of paper clamped with a binder clip.

"They've been talking about that for years, even decades," I said. "It's never going to happen."

"Oh, it's going to happen, big boy. In about a year, give or take a few months of protests." She looked happy enough to burst into song.

"How do you know?"

"We're doing it. My family's company. I'm taking the lead on this project."

I grabbed my kneecaps. The removal of the night market was an on-again-off-again fight that pitted developers like Peggy Lee's family against vendor families like mine that have built up their business over generations.

In the larger scheme, the well-off mainlanders wanted to bulldoze the night markets in the trendy parts of Taipei, even though the night markets were what made the areas so desirable in the first place. The scrappy *benshengren*—yams from the country, like my grandfather—had built the night markets with their bare hands and delighted in the simple pleasures of cooking and eating good food late at night.

Everything my grandfather and my parents did with their lives was sunk into my night-market stall. No business cards, letterheads or office doors carry their names—or mine. Threads of meat from that crappy chicken leg were still stuck in my teeth, reminding me how great a place Unknown Pleasures was. I would have picked up a bullhorn to fight for it.

When I was in eleventh grade, in fact, I remember the night-market merchants staged a huge protest when they got word that the city council was about to approve a rezoning of the area. In front of the night market's Cixian Temple, a man doused himself with cooking oil and threatened to light himself for the news cameras on standby. The developers quickly backed off.

That protester was Julia Huang's father. The grateful denizens of the night market tacked up posters that featured Mr. Huang standing in front of the tank at Tiananmen Square, with his pasted-on head turned to the viewer, *Exorcist*-like. Nonetheless, the Huangs sold their stand fairly soon after that incredible display.

I let out a small sigh. "Don't do this, Peggy."

"Don't worry, Jing-nan. We'll keep an indoor area for many of the vendors. It's another step forward to help internationalize Taipei."

I shuddered. Whenever I heard the phrase "internationalize Taipei," I took it to mean they wanted to do away with lower-class neighborhoods and replace them with Taipei 101 clones. I looked over at Dwayne and Frankie. What place did they have in an exclusive Taipei built for wealthy tourists and rich mainlanders?

I patted the still-sealed envelope. "Now, what's this about, Peggy?"

She kept her voice down and splayed her hand out palm-down on the table, practicing her grip for grabbing the entire globe. "We're going to hold a lottery for spaces in the new retail location." She narrowed her mouth and added, "We could assign you one majorly prime location by default."

"Is this illegal?"

"It's not. We're allowed to designate spaces for the most culturally significant merchants as determined by a nonpartisan committee of which I am the chairwoman." She gave a closed-mouthed smile and picked at the wax crumbs of lipstick in the corners. I crossed my legs under the table.

"Is the entire committee made up of mainlanders?"

"No! It's about fifty-fifty. We were going to vote on potential candidates, but we're finding that it's easier for each member to simply pick one they want. I pick you."

"I'm flattered, but I'm also somewhat disgusted."

Peggy blinked. Her face remained in its neutral position of vague amusement.

"What makes you think you can pull this one off?"

Sure, there would be another ugly public hearing, complete with shouted threats, fistfights, crotch-level kicks and thrown chairs. Status quo won more often than not. But this time Peggy's family was involved, and they were undefeated against little guys.

"History's on our side, Jing-nan. They've already broken ground on the Taipei Performing Arts Center next to the Jiantan MRT Station. That's gonna be done in 2015 or so, but before that you have to ask yourself, are well-dressed and well-heeled people going to want to fight their way through a grubby night market?" She opened her eyes wide for emphasis. "Of course not! Now, before or after a night at the theater, they might consider an indoor dining area that's well-ventilated and clean, not like this." She waved her right hand around.

It was true that the arts center was going to be completed roughly on time. What else was she right about? "Even if I agreed to this, and I'm not going to unless you put a gun to my head, everybody else here is going to hate me for life."

"They won't find out. I promise. I can make it look like you were lucky in the lottery."

"How do I know you'll keep your word?"

"We bought out Julia's father years ago, in anticipation of developing these blocks someday. That troublemaker didn't have too high a price. So, Jing-nan, you can trust me because I've never told anybody that except you just now."

CHAPTER FOURTEEN

I had only taken my first shoe off before I unloaded what was on my mind.

"Everybody thought Mr. Huang was such a big hero," I told Nancy. "My parents and all their friends, too. They thought he sold his stand because he was exhausted from the fight. What a fake! What a goddamn sellout!"

"I'm sorry, Jing-nan," said Nancy. "You never know anybody's real motivation for anything."

Wangba! You bastard, Mr. Huang! I couldn't go much further than that. He would have been my father-in-law, after all.

WHEN I WAS A kid, I thought he was so great. He was nicer to me than my dad was, and his fun side came out when his wife wasn't around to rein him in. Mr. Huang would take pomelos and make big citrus-smelling helmets for Julia and me with the rinds. He showed us kids how to write in lemon juice with toothpicks to create messages in invisible ink.

Most enchanting of all, he stuffed his mouth with wintergreen mints and cupped his hands around his mouth, letting us see sparks flying around his open mouth as he chewed.

"Don't do this after you eat something oily, otherwise your mouth could catch on fire," he had warned. Of course we believed it.

He was the first guy, in direct opposition to my parents, to tell me not to take the gods and goddesses too seriously.

"The priests and monks at the temples pray that people keep coming to give them money," he muttered to me once when his pious wife was in the bathroom. She gave generously to temples of all faiths. "She helps keep Buddha fat," he joked another time.

I must have been in third grade when I asked him why people worshipped so many gods. He had brought Julia and me to eat dessert burritos filled with peanut ice cream.

"I'll tell you why," Mr. Huang said. "People in Taiwan have always been vulnerable to many random natural events. Monsoons, earthquakes. Stormy seas drowned fishermen, and farmers were ruined by too much rain, or not enough. Disaster was historically right around the corner."

He paused to take a bite of his burrito to suck the ice cream through. Julia and I did exactly the same.

"If you feel like you have no control over your life, then you need gods, goddesses and good-luck charms," he said. "But a truly educated people can prepare for the monsoons and earthquakes and predict storms and weather. We are a capable people, but we Taiwanese are too scared to trust ourselves."

Julia and I didn't say anything, but we both thought about what he had said and knew that he was right. He mopped up the melted ice cream on his plate with his tortilla and we imitated him.

"Julia," he said, his voice unsteady, "don't tell your mother what I told you. Jing-nan, don't tell your parents."

Julia and I vowed soon after to wean ourselves from religion altogether. We never blamed Mr. Huang.

"So that's how you got turned on to atheism," said Nancy. She was sitting at the end of the couch closer to the floor lamp, her arms folded across a closed laptop.

"Yeah," I said, bitterly. "I guess I should have known there was something wrong with him because he kept going to the temples as often as his wife. He never had the balls to do and say what he believed as long as she was around."

"Do you think he wasn't a good father?"

"Maybe he was, but he wasn't a real man."

Nancy sighed and lifted her closed laptop to her chest. "It's not right to sit around and rip on Mr. Huang. Jing-nan, I have a long essay due in two days and I haven't really started. It's important. All the freshman science majors are going to read it in the fall. If you want, you can watch TV. I have wireless headphones you can wear."

I dropped to the rug and grabbed her knees.

"Wait, Nancy. I just thought of something. The last time I went to see the Huangs, Mr. Huang was bothered that Mrs. Huang wouldn't even let me in. Maybe he wanted to talk to me. If I can get him alone, he might tell me what happened to change their minds about looking into Julia's death."

"That's a good idea, Jing-nan!"

I licked my lips. "If he's reluctant, I could tell him I know the circumstances of the sale of his stand. If I tell the other merchants about it, when the removal of the night market is announced, they'll march down to his apartment and tear him apart. Man, Kuilan would rip his head off."

"How are you going to get Mr. Huang alone?" Nancy asked clinically. Her anxious fingers remained clasped to her laptop. She really wanted to work on her essay, but I wasn't done thinking aloud yet.

"Mrs. Huang is into temples, priests and shamans." I looked in her eyes. "Will you help me, Nancy?"

"If I say yes, will you let me work on this essay?"

"Sure."

Nancy tore open her laptop and made some tentative keystrokes. "Good," she said.

"After I tell you about this plan."

Not bothering to close the lid, she set her computer aside. "What, already, Jing-nan?"

DANCING JENNY LOOKED NANCY over, her eyes taking in each breast, and nodded slowly.

"You ever think of modeling?" Jenny cooed.

"I'm only five foot six! I'm not tall enough to model."

"Not as a runway model. I can see you as a Victoria's Secret model. You know, for the local ads."

"Let's leave the lingerie talk for another time, Jenny," I said. "How about digging up a *tang-ki* outfit for her?"

"They're not very flattering."

"We just need one that works."

"This might take a while. I need to go to the 'other' section." Jenny turned sideways to slip into one of her stock rooms.

"She's very free spirited," said Nancy.

"Jenny's the best. She's one of my oldest friends."

"Did you sleep with her?"

"What? No! She's like my sister!"

Jenny returned with an outfit. "This is an authentic ceremonial dress of the Paiwan people. There's no 'official' *tang-ki* outfit—just wear this and say you're a Taiwanese aboriginal shaman."

Jenny held up the black robe, which was heavily embroidered in red, yellow and green at the cuffs, collar and borders. The leggings and gloves were made of red, yellow and green fabrics.

"Look at the patterns," said Nancy. "It's like a snakeskin."

"The Paiwan say they're descended from a poisonous snake," said Jenny. "The *paipushe*, the hundred-pacer. If it bites you, your flesh starts to rot immediately and you can't walk a hundred steps before dying."

"Am I going to get bit by a snake if I wear this?" asked Nancy.

"No, this outfit protects you from snakes," said Jenny. "They'll think you're one of them."

I pinched the fingers of my right hand together and moved it around like a cobra's head. Nancy punched me.

"Stop playing games and try this on," Jenny told Nancy. "The sleeves are a little scratchy, but you'll get used to it. Don't forget these necklaces." Jenny handed her two handfuls of coiled beads.

"How many do I put on?" asked Nancy.

"The more, the better. Go to the back room behind the shower curtain and change. I can make some adjustments if we need them."

When Nancy was gone, Jenny asked me, "Did you sleep with her?"

"A little bit."

She pinched my left nipple.

"*Ai!* Damn it, that hurts!"

"I think she could be good for you! Everything about her is fantastic. She's in school?"

"Nancy's a star graduate student at Taida."

Jenny nodded slowly, her eyebrows raised. "A smartie! What's she studying?"

"Bioengineering."

"Ah, what a waste! She should be modeling while she's so young!"

"She needs to use her brains."

"You think models are stupid? There's nothing harder, mentally. Running a business is a piece of cake compared to the days when I used to model. Sometimes I still do, for special clients."

"What are you talking about?"

Jenny only shook her head and waved her right hand in the air between us.

Two high-school-aged girls came in and asked to see maid outfits. Jenny narrowed her eyes and evaluated their bodies from head to toe.

"English, French or Japanese?" she asked. "Well, maybe French for you, because you've got long legs," Jenny said to the taller girl before turning to the other one. "And maybe Japanese for you because you've got such an innocent-looking face."

The girls were still looking through the clothes racks when Nancy stepped out before us.

The outfit looked a bit ridiculous, campier than the costumes the "native" people wear in Disney movies. It was definitely the least sexy outfit I had ever seen her in.

"This is really a genuine Paiwan outfit?" I asked.

"Absolutely," said Jenny. "The gods smile upon anyone who wears this. That's why it feels so uncomfortable. They feel your suffering and your sacrifice."

"It hurts, all right," said Nancy.

"It's painful to look at, too!" I said. Nancy slapped my shoulder.

"It's the real thing," said the girl with the innocent face. "I'm from Pingtung. My grandmother was part Paiwan."

"Really?" said the long-legged girl. "You don't look it at all!"

Jenny's face soured as she looked over Nancy.

"I have to make up for this outfit," said Jenny, shaking her head. "I'm going to throw in a *binlang xishi* outfit. It will help offset the unfeminine lines of the *tang-ki* robe. Nancy will look good in a thong, I think."

"Nancy doesn't need a betel-nut beauty outfit, Jenny."

"You two can do some role-playing games with it in private," she whispered with a wink. I saw that Nancy was smiling shyly.

"Charge us for the *xishi* outfit," I said.

"Please, it's my pleasure to give sexy clothes to sexy women," said Jenny.

"But it's really too much," objected Nancy.

"No, it's not very much at all," said Jenny. "You'll see."

MY PARENTS AND GRANDFATHER were regular temple worshippers, but even they used to make fun of people who went to *tang-kis* until my uncle got cancer.

The shaman they went to spat rice wine on them to cleanse their souls and to clear the air. He lit up a loosely wrapped cigar and went into a trance. My uncle had offended the earth god, Tudi Yeye, by disparaging the farming profession. At the time my uncle was a newspaper reporter, and he had indeed just written a story about alleged fraud in some branch of the Executive Yuan's Council of Agriculture.

After my uncle made a donation to one of Tudi's temples, the cancer went away. My uncle is currently in remission—in more ways than one. After my parents' funerals, his own gambling debts forced him to go into hiding, supposedly in the Philippines. I guess debts run in the family.

I POSITIONED MYSELF IN the front window of a cafe across the street from the Huangs' apartment building. I had a good view of the front entrance, and I watched Nancy waddle into the lobby.

I was suddenly seized with doubt. How could this crazy plan work? So many little things could go wrong.

Nancy was supposed to go to the Huangs' apartment and tell

them that Julia had a message for Mrs. Huang alone to hear. They would have to go to the ancient Guandu Temple in the mountainous Beitou District of Taipei. Nancy could fudge something to tell Mrs. Huang.

As soon as Mrs. Huang was out of the way, I would go up and see Mr. Huang alone.

I sipped my café au lait and picked at a *lu dou peng*. The little pastry was dry on the outside and the baked green-bean filling was like crumbling plaster. You're really supposed to eat this thing with tea, but the waitress hadn't batted an eye when I asked for coffee. Anna, as her name tag read, was a sloucher just trying to make it through her interminable shift, but her body below the shoulders looked so great in her French-maid uniform, I started thinking about seeing Nancy in something like it in the distant future, when everything had settled down.

Look at me. I was already thinking like a dirty old man like Ah-ding. I shook my head and bit into my pastry, sending pieces of the flaky crust flying everywhere. The waitress, who was sitting at the next table over and playing with her phone, took notice of my sloppy eating and sighed. More crap for her to clean up.

A man and a woman sitting by the other side of the door were desperately trying to get her attention by waving politely, but it wasn't working. Tourists from the southern end of the island. This is Taipei, guys. If you want something, you'd better be loud.

I crossed my arms and legs, fortifying myself like the Great Sphinx, eyes fixed on the doorway of the building across the street.

"Excuse me, miss?" called the woman. She was sitting behind the man so I didn't get a good look at her. Not getting a reaction, she called again, louder. Anna the waitress remained fascinated by something on the phone, but I saw the smallest hint of a wry smile crinkle the corner of her mouth.

I drank more coffee and refocused.

"Miss! Please, miss!"

Anna rolled her head, cracked her neck and brushed her fingers through the ends of her limp perm. She looked at the woman and then the man with barely contained jealousy. Maybe Anna was in a bad relationship.

"Miss, I know you can hear me!"

Anna slapped the table hard.

"I'm on break right now," she shot back at the woman. Unfortunately, I was directly in the line of fire. "If you need something, you need to tell the man at the front counter!" She fished a set of pink earbuds from her apron and plugged them in.

I took a measured sip of coffee—my plan was to keep myself alert without needing to head for the urinals.

"Hey, now," the man called to Anna. "I already paid you a good tip! We just want refills on our water and we'll be going."

"Why don't you go now and get a bottle of water from a 7-Eleven?"

The man stood up and brushed off his left and then his right hand. He was about thirty years old and the sort of guy who laughs when he's angry, because he began to smile.

"Do I have to come over there and stand you up myself?"

"Just stay there and be quiet."

"Give me back my tip!"

"Sorry, I can't do that."

"You little bitch!"

During the entire exchange, I hadn't taken my eyes from my target for more than a second, but if I didn't move now, I was in danger of being hit by stray missiles.

I picked up my cup and walked to the corner of the cafe window.

"Look, ugly, you're bothering the other customers!" the waitress yelled.

"You're the ugly one! That man's trying to get away from you!"

"Have some respect! It's obvious that he's lost his job. Look at the miserable guy!" She called over to me with surprising gentleness, "Everything's going to be all right. I was there myself a little while ago."

"Please leave me out of this," I said as evenly as possible to the window. The Dog Whisperer would have been proud. "I just want to mind my own business."

"Ha, you see!" said the man. "Nobody cares about you."

The waitress sprang to her feet and pointed at the couple with both hands. "Get out of my cafe, you stupid lovebirds!"

"We're not going anywhere." He sat down to make a point and picked up his phone. "I know some very important people at the police department. You're going to be sorry."

Great, the cops. Just the people I wanted to see.

I put down a 200 NT note and set the cup on top of it. I was leaving her a decent tip because it wasn't worth waiting around for the change. I stood and faced the waitress for three seconds.

"By the way, I have a job!" I said. I flew out of the cafe and stood in the shadow of a column, never losing sight of that door. After about a minute, I realized that there was one thing I should have done before leaving the cafe.

Now, I've developed several skills from working at the night market. I am an excellent public speaker in two languages (three, counting Taiwanese as its own language rather than a Chinese dialect). I can count money by touch alone—hand me a wad of bills and coins and I know instinctively if you are trying to rip me off.

I can also hold my pee forever.

I regulated my breathing and strategically crossed my legs. I snapped a steady beat with my left hand. Everything was going to be okay. Incense wafted from an offering table farther down the block. Why did it smell like burning dog food?

I saw Nancy come out of the apartment building alone. Damn it! I was about to lose all hope when she turned around and waved for someone to follow her. Mrs. Huang stepped out tentatively, holding a sun umbrella.

All right, Nancy! I don't know what you did or said, but it worked. Good girl!

I watched them get into a cab and leave. The driver must have been superstitious, because he leapt out of the cab and opened the door for the *tang-ki* with his head down. The cab left, but I continued to wait another two minutes just in case the car looped back for a forgotten purse or wallet.

When I was convinced they were gone for good, I skipped across the street and entered the lobby. The lock was still busted on the building's front door, so I swung it open and walked through without bothering to buzz Mr. Huang. I didn't want him to have advance warning.

Knowing that I was so close to a bathroom triggered something inside me. Soon the floodgates would open.

I rode up and rang the Huangs' doorbell. Mr. Huang swung open the peephole and said, "Jing-nan?"

"Yes, it's me. Hello, Mr. Huang. I really want to talk to you and use your bathroom, please."

"You missed Mrs. Huang by a few minutes. She just went out to a temple."

"It was you I wanted to see. I hope you don't mind."

"You're not supposed to be here, Jing-nan. I really shouldn't let you in." His voice lacked resolve, and already Mr. Huang sounded like he was chastising himself for what he was about to do.

"If you could open the door, Mr. Huang, I'd really appreciate it. This is the last time I will bother you, I promise."

A pair of pop and click sounds came from the doorframe.

"You never should have come back," said Mr. Huang as he shook my hand.

I shucked my shoes off as quickly as I could. "I need to use your bathroom," I said. "Right now."

"Go ahead." I heard him snap on the television and crank up the volume.

When I came back into the living room. Mr. Huang held his finger to his lips and pointed to the couch cushion next to his reclining chair. I took the seat. He picked up the remote and cranked the volume even higher on a drama show that was a rip-off of the hit series *Mysterious Incredible Terminator*.

He put his hand on my back and came in close enough for a kiss before whispering, "We have to be quick."

"Okay," I whispered back.

"I know why you're here. You just won't give up on Julia. You really did love her."

"Yes."

Mr. Huang grabbed my knee as he stood up. He pushed back the reclining chair and fished out a box from underneath. It was about the size that could pack a laptop.

"This is the last bit of Julia that I have." He put it in my hands.

It seemed heavier than it should. "She shared her heart with her mother, but she shared her mind with me."

"You knew she was back in Taiwan?"

He wiped his forehead. "I knew, but I didn't tell anybody. Not even her mother." He wrote the letters "C," "I" and "A" in his left palm. "You understand?"

Gan! The fucking CIA!

"That was her job, huh?" I felt my body floating out of itself.

He gave me a curt nod. "I don't know what she actually did, though, so I don't know the story of what happened." He rubbed his left elbow. "What I do know is that she was facing a choice: wait in America for you, or come back here for the job. I told her to just take the job here for now while she was waiting. Julia said it wasn't that kind of job. Once you went in, you didn't come back."

I was so tense I could have pushed my tongue through my clenched teeth. "What did you tell her?" I managed to say.

"This is what I told her," he said, folding his hands on the arm of his chair. "I said, 'You and Jing-nan are in love, and nothing is ever going to change that. But it looks like Jing-nan's not going to make it, stuck at the night market, and he's so stubborn he will destroy himself before he comes back to you.'"

I wanted to kill this man for saying that to Julia. I could have grabbed a knife from the kitchen and torn into him like a pepperoni pizza. But I shouldn't be mad at the guy for telling the truth. He had summed up my situation better than I had, and had given his daughter good advice.

"So she took the CIA job," I heard myself say.

A vein in his right temple throbbed. "Don't say that!" he growled, pointing to his ear and then out the window. I understood what he meant. *This apartment is bugged.*

I nodded to him and patted the box. "What's in here?"

"Some of her papers that she gave to me. After you came here the first time, some people came over, looking to confiscate her personal effects. They only let us keep a few photos. That was when my wife learned about Julia's job." He sighed and adjusted his seat. "I don't know why I did it, but I hid these papers in this chair quite a while ago. I had thought about burning them, but now I know you should have them."

"Did a big Taiwanese-American come here?"

Mr. Huang's eyebrows shot up. "Yes! He seemed to be in charge, but he wouldn't give his name. He told us that they were going to seek justice for our daughter. But he warned us not to ask questions about what had happened."

"I think that's the guy who had someone beat me up."

Mr. Huang looked into my eyes. "He didn't say anything about that. He said he would just talk to you."

"About what?"

"About forgetting Julia."

I coughed. "Mr. Huang, I know about your deal with the Lee family. How they bought you out of the night market."

He sucked in his lips. "Well, so what?" he asked. "I can't sell my business when I want to? I can do whatever I want, all right?"

Originally, I'd had the info ready to use as a final bullet if he wouldn't talk, but he'd turned out to be helpful. I held up a hand to check his defense. "They're offering me a sweetheart deal, Mr. Huang," I said. "They're going to raze the rest of the market and give me a prime stall in the new indoor space. What do you think I should do?"

"You should do it," he said, not hesitating for a second. "You'll be helping yourself. If you don't, you won't be helping anybody at all."

He made a lot of sense.

Mr. Huang then cleared his throat. "Get the hell out of here!" he yelled. "I never want to see you again, you ugly son-of-a-bitch!" He winked at me and slapped my shoulder. I got up with the box under my arm and hustled to the front door. Mr. Huang cut across the floor and swung it open. I stepped out into the hallway. Mr. Huang slammed the door shut before I could raise my hand in thanks.

I rode down to the lobby and looked for a side or back door. I didn't want to be caught with the box Mr. Huang had given me. I found a workshop room that led to a back exit. I had to tiptoe past the maintenance man, who was asleep on a cot.

WHEN I WAS ON the sidewalk, I turned on my phone to see if there was an update from Nancy.

Ming-kuo had sent two emails only an hour apart and a follow-up voicemail that seemed to have been left in one breath.

"Hey, Jing-nan, I don't know if you saw my emails, but I wanted to see if you were free for a meal sometime during the week or weekend. I don't know what days are better for you. Every day is pretty much the same for me. I work at night like you do and I just want to be with old friends to break it up a little. I know you're busy, so if you can't get back to me, I'll try to catch you again. Talk to you soon!"

Even as I held the phone in my hand, it rang. Give it a fucking rest, Ming-kuo! There was no way in hell I was going to take this call.

I started banging out an email response: *Sorry I've been missing your calls, Ming-kuo. I seem to have caught a little bit of a cold, and it's really hard for me to actually speak. I'll drop you a line when I'm feeling better. See you soon!*

I shuddered as I read over the email. Talk about a stock kiss-off message. If he had any social awareness, he'd never try to call me again.

Wait. Did I really want to send him this message? Was it really so horrible for me to hang out with him? Here he was, trying to reach out to me as a colleague with a common history. Or as a boogeyman from my past who was relentlessly pursuing me.

The truth was, he and I both lacked real friendships.

Then again, who in Taipei had time for friends? Who didn't have an interminable workday? Who ever got enough sleep?

Not me, not Nancy, not Peggy and probably not Cookie Monster.

I sent the email and didn't think too much about it after.

CHAPTER FIFTEEN

I met Nancy in the lobby of her apartment building two hours later. She had already changed into her latest indie outfit—cut-off stove-pipe denims and a new T-shirt that sported a graphic of Ian Curtis's left eye blown up to cover her entire chest.

I saw one of the doormen cringe as her cheap wooden sandals clacked against the tiled areas of the floor.

"What's in the box?" she asked as we waited for the elevator.

"Let's talk when we get into your apartment," I said. I must have looked scared, because she didn't say anything else.

When we were in her place, I waited until the door was closed, locked and chained behind us before talking.

"Nancy, when I saw Mr. Huang, he turned up the TV volume and said he wasn't supposed to have this box."

"What's in it?"

"I don't know, exactly, but it's Julia's stuff. I haven't opened it yet."

"Why did he turn up the TV volume?"

"Julia was working for . . ." I thought about how cautious Mr. Huang had been and also spelled out "C-I-A" on my palm. Nancy gasped. "People are monitoring them."

"That means they're monitoring you, too," she said. "And also me."

I patted her arm. "You've got doormen downstairs to protect you."

"We're not really going to be safe until we know what's in there." She tapped the box, which was wound shut with duct tape, forming crosses on the top and bottom panels.

"Can you get me something to cut this with?"

"What if there's a head in there?" she asked.

"Look at the shape, Nancy. Only SpongeBob SquarePants's head could fit in here."

Nancy went to the kitchen and brought back a steak knife.

"Everything seemed to go smoothly with Mrs. Huang, right?" I asked as I hacked away at the tape.

"It was so easy to make her come with me. I told her I had a message for her from Julia and that she had to come to the temple to hear it. She couldn't put her shoes on fast enough. Mr. Huang looked pretty skeptical, but he didn't dare say a word to stop her. The only thing that held us up was the elevator."

"That elevator sucks," I said. She nodded. The duct tape was strong as hell and as fibrous as an unripe mango. "I saw you guys get in the cab."

Nancy sat down and grabbed hold of herself. "Mrs. Huang covered her face and cried in her hands the entire time. I felt really guilty, like I was tricking a little kid." Nancy wrinkled her nose. "Also, I realized that it was pretty racist for me to be wearing a Paiwan outfit. I wanted to tell her it was all just a trick to get her away from the apartment."

I managed to cut through one of the duct-tape bands on the top. "You didn't tell her anything, did you?"

"No, of course not. I was resolute about carrying out the mission. Anyway, when we entered Guandu Temple, something weird happened." She rubbed her hands and arms as if spreading lotion.

I put the knife down. "What happened?" I asked. "Did Mrs. Huang start freaking out?"

"Not yet," Nancy said. She was now rubbing her knees. "I felt something walk right through me. From my back to my front. It felt like a cool breeze, only it went through my body, not just over my skin. It was definitely a spirit."

"There's no such thing as ghosts." I put a hand on her back. "You were just nervous."

She sat down and turned away. "It was definitely something. It is Ghost Month, right?"

I went back to the box. "Nancy, Santa Claus isn't real, either. It's just stuff for a holiday." I severed the other end of the tape band. Now I just had to slit the tape along the flap edge.

"*I* don't believe in ghosts, Jing-nan. Honestly. But it was really something. Anyway, Mrs. Huang was walking in front of me and all of a sudden she froze, as if that thing had just walked through her, too. She began to shake, and then she screamed that Julia was there."

I put the knife down again. "Are you serious, Nancy?"

She nodded hard. "Mrs. Huang knocked over a table of incense burners—on purpose, I think," Nancy continued. "Then she started pushing people, saying that the Americans killed her daughter."

"That must have really freaked out all the worshippers," I said. Temples were noisy with cell-phone ringtones and yelled prayers for help, but nobody touched anybody else. "What did Mrs. Huang do when you told her your fake story?"

"I never got to tell her, because they took Mrs. Huang away."

"Who took her away?"

"Policemen. There were signs up that undercover cops were around because people have been breaking into the money boxes. I thought the signs were just for show. She was acting so crazy, it took two men to grab her and carry her away."

I almost wished I could have seen it. The only time I had seen Mrs. Huang flip out was when someone stole some fruit from her stand. The thief wasn't a big guy, but he probably weighed twice as much as her. She followed him as he tried to scamper away, but the market was too crowded for him to bolt. Mrs. Huang screamed and slapped him repeatedly until he dropped everything he had stolen that night from all the stands.

How could such a plucky person also have a vulnerable side?

Poor Mrs. Huang. I felt a little bad that we had tricked her, but I had no idea that she would be so susceptible to a plan that hinged on a costume. Then I thought about how mean Mrs. Huang had been to me the last time, and I felt less bad.

"I hope they didn't do anything to her," I said, renewing my fight against the box.

"I didn't stick around," said Nancy. "I just took the MRT home after that."

I had just cut the last bit of tape holding the box shut, but I hesitated before opening it. I crossed my arms and sat back.

Nancy came over and put an arm around my waist. "Jing-nan," she said. "Open the box! I'm dying to see what's inside!"

I pulled all four flaps open and something fluttered inside. The box was packed with papers, some in binders and some held with clips. Julia's work for the CIA.

I flipped through some of it. Everything was in English. Essays on the political future of China, Taiwan and the US. A study of potential outcomes if Taiwan were to declare independence. None were good. Most tantalizing of all was a thesis project about military intelligence on both sides of the Taiwan Strait. The abstract noted that China would recruit more Taiwanese officers as spies not only to check the island's military efforts, but to stymie America's Asia strategy, as well. Taiwan was one of the biggest US allies in the Pacific, along with South Korea and Japan, and realistically it was the only base the US could attack China from.

Under that was a report on the head of a Taiwanese chip company who was selling technology to the Chinese government. Nancy snatched it away, and I was about to protest when I saw what was underneath it.

At the very bottom of the box, folded in half and tucked into a flap, was Julia's diploma from NYU. I thought she hadn't graduated. How puzzling. I touched the signatures. They seemed real.

The diploma hadn't been handled with care. It was wrinkled from water damage.

I touched the paper with wonder before I understood. Not graduating was only part of the cover story. Being a betel-nut beauty was another.

I showed Nancy the diploma.

"Look. Julia did finish college."

"Oh, that's nice," said Nancy. She was still reading the chip report.

"Nancy, why are you so interested in that?"

She put the papers aside. "Julia is the one who helped put Ah-ding in jail. Look, she recorded him talking about selling technology to the Chinese in addition to fixing bids on Taipei city-government contracts for laptops."

I picked up the papers and flipped through them. "Looks like she planted a bug in his car! Did Ah-ding chew betel nut?"

"He did," said Nancy, her voice dead. "He went to Hsinchu City a lot, too, of course. Ah-ding had a few plants out there."

"He must have stopped at Julia's betel-nut stand at some point, and that must have been when she bugged his car."

Nancy stared into my eyes. "What was she doing in his car?!"

"Nancy, she probably didn't have to get into his car to bug it! She probably dropped something when she handed him the bag of chews."

She sighed and looked visibly relieved. "Do you know how weird it would be if Julia and Ah-ding had slept together?"

"Please," I said. "I don't want to imagine that."

On my way to work, I had a hard time visualizing anything but Julia with a tag team of repulsive older men with reddened teeth.

DWAYNE WAS IN A bad mood when I finally showed up just a little later than usual at Unknown Pleasures.

"You didn't call, you didn't text," he grumbled. "I was thinking maybe you were hopelessly tied up . . . between that girl's legs."

"I can get out of any hold," I said as I hastily washed my hands. "I get a lot of practice here."

"Yeah, but I don't grab you the same way she grabs you. Right?"

"Gentlemen," admonished Frankie with as much disgust as possible. We swung into position and got to work.

It was a busy night, but not exceptionally so. When I was coming back from the common bathroom, I saw two teenaged boys break away from my moped, trying to stifle laughter. All right, maybe it was the oldest, worst-looking vehicle in the night market, but I'm stubborn, and the flagrant mockery made me even more determined to keep riding it.

Kuilan came over to chat and brought over a bowl of noodles

with one of her new fried-chicken fillets on the side. I thought they were okay. She was touting and shouting about her new organic chicken, but they didn't taste any better than Kentucky Fried Chicken. In fact, the current specimen in the glassine bag in my hand was too heavily seasoned with chili powder. Eating it was like licking the sun.

"Jing-nan, did you hear?" said Kuilan. "There's a rumor that the big move is back on!"

I crossed my legs.

"Are you sure, Kuilan?"

"It's those lousy developers trying to push us out again. They make all of us mainlanders look bad! I've seen them walking through the market with their money buddies from China, checking the sightlines and drawing up the blueprints in their minds." She gestured all around before thumping her fist on her chest. "They don't even see us or our stands."

I took another bite of Kuilan's fiery cutlet and wiped away tears as I chewed.

"Nothing's been announced, though, right?" I struggled to ask. I picked up the bowl of noodles and eagerly drank the pickled soup.

"You know how it works, Jing-nan." Kuilan propped up a foot on the side of my front grill and counted off points on her fingers, taut with patches of healed skin. "They're going to finalize the deals first behind closed doors. Then they announce that they are examining the idea and want to involve the community. The land's probably already been sold and the construction bids already accepted." She closed her hand and shook her scarred fist at me. I drank some more soup to clear my mouth, but it only spread the spicy heat around. "Kuilan," I said, "we can sue them and tie everything up in court. There are a lot of ways to fight this thing if we want to."

Listen to me. Acting all tough even though I had an out with Peggy Lee's company, if I wanted it. I was the new Mr. Huang.

Noticing my watering eyes, Kuilan gasped, "You really do care, Jing-nan! Your parents would have been so proud of you!" She rubbed my arm and went back to her stand.

We sold a broad range of grilled and fried meats, but we didn't sell fried-chicken fillets, and I felt self-conscious about having it on my breath. I swished my mouth a few times with Coke to get rid of the taste. When I wasn't looking, Dwayne grabbed my bottle and chugged it.

"*Gan ni niang!*" I yelled and slapped his back.

"Watch your mouth!" Frankie said, uncharacteristically loud. "There are kids here."

"Then they're out too late."

A big anime convention was underway, and a platoon of Japanese attendees made their way to the night market from the Taipei International Convention Center. They were easy pickings for the stands that had barkers fluent in Japanese. That wasn't the case for Unknown Pleasures, but a lot of Japanese came over because they were Joy Division fans. I always made sure to give them a little extra, and they struggled through English to talk about their favorite songs.

One dude, who was dressed up as a character from the world of *Final Fantasy*, tucked his plastic sword under his left armpit as he showed me pictures of his Joy Division vinyl collection on his phone. He had two copies of their first record, the four-song *An Ideal for Living* EP, and close-up pictures of the matrix numbers scratched in the inner grooves to prove they were genuine.

I couldn't help but shake my head at the Hitler Youth drummer on the cover and the inside sleeve picture of the Nazi soldier pointing a gun at a Jewish boy. Joy Division had taken their name from a fictionalized account of brothels at concentration camps that operated for the pleasure of Nazi officers.

What a bunch of stupid punks, flaunting Nazi imagery only to offend people. Isn't it embarrassing to be confronted with the dumb ideas you had in your youth?

I resolved right then to retire my T-shirt of the Hitler Youth drummer. I couldn't justify wearing it anymore, even if it was the cover of a Joy Division record.

AT THE END OF the night, I counted up the money and was surprised by the amount of cash. We had done better than I thought. I paid out Dwayne and Frankie and said good night.

As I was going over to my moped, Ah-tien, Kuilan's son, caught up with me.

"Hey, Jing-nan?" He tried smiling but looked extremely apprehensive and couldn't stop rubbing the back of his neck.

"Hi, Ah-tien." I had my helmet in my hands.

"Why don't we hang out a little bit tonight?"

"I kinda just want to go home now."

He gave a fake laugh, which required an incredible amount of effort on his part. "If you stay here a little longer," he said through gritted teeth, "we can sit at one of the late stalls together. I know a good place for congealed pig blood in hot pots."

"Some other time, I promise," I said.

Suddenly angry, Ah-tien spat out, "Then go ahead! See if I care!" He stomped off.

Wow, that was really weird, I thought to myself. Maybe he'd always felt bad that we weren't friends and was trying to bridge that gap. I should have met him halfway.

Honestly, though, I'd never liked him or his negative energy, and I was all right with the way things stood now. We didn't need to be buddies.

JUST OVER THE FIRST bridge, my back wheel started to make a lot of noise. Before I could pull over, my bike fishtailed. I managed to jump off before it leapt out from under me, the rear wheel popping off its axle. I tried to land on my feet but only succeeded in tumbling into a forward roll.

Miraculously, my only injury was a scratched-up right palm. I made a fist to make sure none of the bones were broken. My phone was okay, too.

I looked over the wreck. I was too shocked from my tumble to feel anger or disappointment and had only pragmatic thoughts. I resolved to move all the parts over to the shoulder and walk home.

I suddenly noticed a small circle of white light that seemed to fall upon me. It opened up and bathed my entire body. My arms and legs disappeared in the thick milk. Then I couldn't see anymore.

Oh my God. I had died in that accident. Now I was a ghost. I teetered on my feet. I could feel the ground begin to rumble. Was my soul about to be judged?

From out of nowhere, a large pickup truck, painted black as night, pulled up to me and turned off its high beams. A man got out of the passenger side of the cab.

"When are you going to realize that I'm on your side, Jing-nan?" said the Taiwanese-American. "You didn't call me, and you never answered any of my emails."

"I didn't know it was you," I said. "I don't know if I would have answered if I did."

He cocked his head, and I think he smiled. "Did you hit your head, Jing-nan?"

"No."

"Come here. Let's put your bike in the bed. We can sit there, too." I didn't trust him, but I didn't have much of a choice, either. Even if Nancy were awake, it would take too long for her to come by and scrape my carcass off the road. I looked at my dirty knees and my right palm, which I noticed had sprung a small rivulet of blood.

"So you had those little punk kids mess up my bike," I said. "Too bad they didn't finish the job. I'm still alive."

"Actually, they executed it perfectly. We figured the wheel would fall off right around here. And that piece of shit doesn't go fast enough for you to get seriously hurt, anyway."

The road wasn't completely deserted. I made sure that the several cars rubbernecking got a good look at my face in case the American tried to disappear me. I was tired, sweaty and thirsty.

"Could you give me a hand here?" I asked.

Another man popped out of the cab. It was the Taiwanese guy with bad skin who had dropped me in the elevator. "Jing-nan," he said, slapping my back. "Sorry about that thing before." I went to one end of the moped, but the Taiwanese said, "Let me grab that." He lifted the moped onto the truck's bed by himself.

I went back for the loose wheel, expecting both guys to get back in the cab, but the American remained in the truck bed. He really did want to sit with me.

The truck bed had seats built in against the back panel of the

cab. I sat down and noticed circular scrape marks around a grom-
met in the floor for another seat, or maybe a mounted gun. We
snapped on seat belts.

The American tapped the roof of the cab and we pulled out onto
the road. He eased back in his seat and lit up a cigarette. After a
few puffs, he spat over the side. He crossed his right leg over his left
knee and folded his arms behind his head, as if we were in his living
room, which happened to be in a mild wind tunnel.

"You must be a contractor with some American agency," I told
him. I wanted to say "the CIA," but that could escalate things
quickly. "You should be in Iraq."

"Jing-nan, the less you know, the better." He took a quick drag
on his cigarette. The annoyed look on his face told me I had hit at
least a partial truth. "I've been trying to elbow you out, but you
keep coming back in, like one of those tropical bugs that won't stay
squashed."

"I could call the cops on you for what you did to me."

A thoughtful look came over his face, and he wiped his chin
and mouth. "Don't you have enough trouble with the police?"
He chuckled and flicked his cigarette over the side, sending glow-
ing ashes into the wind. I looked at my scraped hand and brushed
gravel bits off of it.

In English he said, "You gotta learn to be more careful, Jing-nan."

I said back in English, "Are you taking me home?"

"We will, but I want to show you something first."

"Are you sure you're not going to shoot me and dump my body
someplace?"

"There are people who want you dead, Jing-nan. They think
you're out to fuck up their operation. But I see you as you really
are: a little lovesick bastard hung up on his old girl. I get you,
because I know some other guys like that."

The Taiwanese driver turned onto National Highway One,
heading east toward Keelung.

"You know that I'm an ABC. I'm here on American business."
Behind his face a steady stream of silhouettes of shacks and factories
went by, an animated story of Taiwan's too-rapid industrialization.

"What kind of American business are you on?" I asked.

"We work best with nondemocratic governments. More stable than governments subject to free elections. That wasn't a problem for most of Taiwan's history. Now that you allow political candidates from all these dissident political parties, and they actually win elections, we've had to partner with, uh, nongovernmental agencies that are more stable and discreet."

A series of double-trailer trucks driving away from Keelung groaned by in the opposite lane.

"Nongovernmental agencies?" I asked.

"Organized criminal groups, Jing-nan. There are gangs here that are three times as old as Taiwan's democracy—gangs that were formed by mainlanders after the Chinese Civil War."

I wanted to know how he fit into all of this. After all, ABCs could join these gangs, as well. "Are you a criminal?" I asked.

He folded his arms and licked his lips. "I handle the relationship with the gangs, Jing-nan, but I'm not a gangster, and I can't control everything they do. The whole Julia thing they're handling in their own way. She was an innocent bystander caught up in an intra-gang power struggle, but her death was not in vain." He rolled his cigarette between his thumb and middle finger and regarded it clinically before tossing it aside. "They're taking care of the guilty parties their way. I don't have anything to do with it, and neither does America."

I felt my throat lock up, but I managed to chirp, "Who killed Julia?"

"Specifically, I don't know and I've never asked. I told you. It was friction within Black Sea, but everything's all right now, or will be soon."

"Black Sea, huh?"

"Oh, fuck. You better just forget I said that."

I interlocked my fingers and pounded my hands against my knees. "I was gonna marry her, you know?"

"Let me guess. You were also going to have two cars, a suburban mansion and two kids going to the Ivy Leagues?" The American laughed out loud before composing himself. To show that he was serious, he switched back to speaking Mandarin. "You're talking crazy, Jing-nan! Look at you! Look at what you do! Look at where you live! I don't want to make fun of you, but take a good look at who you are!"

Both of us leaned into a turn. We were now headed south on Fuxing North Road. We went into a tunnel, and engine sounds echoed around us like lost souls. We came out and whipped through Zhongshan District. Construction barriers narrowed the road, and we were probably driving too fast. Our wheels pounded metal plates set in the asphalt to the one-two beat of Joy Division's "Isolation."

As we drove by assorted works in progress, I thought about how I hadn't really finished anything. Not college. Not my promise to Julia. Not paying off that family debt to German Tsai, which I felt like bringing up, to make my case seem less subject to my personal failings.

I looked at the American. He didn't give a shit what I had to say, anyway. Probably thought all Taiwanese were stupid and simple.

"You know," I said. "I wasn't supposed to end up living such a stupid, simple life."

"Jing-nan, who are you trying to kid? You keep the same schedule nearly every day. You go home, have a beer, wash yourself and sleep. You're entirely predictable."

I turned my body to him as best as I could. "I think you're projecting your life onto mine," I said.

"Oh, no. I'm talking about you. Well, until Nancy started fucking it up a little bit. She noticed the smell."

"What smell?"

The American pointed up at the sky and wormed his finger upward.

"She noticed the frying smell. When we were drilling holes for our surveillance equipment, we used cooking oil as a lubricant. That caused the smell. We figured you wouldn't notice after a long night surrounded by frying meats, but the girl . . ."

The American took out his cigarette pack, had a second thought and stuck it back in his coat pocket.

"We usually use rifle microphones to listen remotely," he continued. "But your crappy little house is built from a composite of scrap metal, rock and concrete. It's completely soundproof!"

He nodded at me with approval and leaned into my arm as we made a right on Heping Road. This would take us to Wanhua District. So they were taking me home after all. Still, they were bastards for what they did to me.

"You bugged my house?" I asked, feeling my hurt hand pulse.

The American put his hand over his heart. "I personally didn't want to, but we did. Everything we ever got from you was completely useless, just like I said it was going to be. You don't even have people over. Except for that one intimate night with Nancy." He winked at me.

My arms shook with anger as I hugged myself. "Why the hell did you bug my house?"

"Don't blame me, Jing-nan. I told you to stay the fuck away and you didn't. You forced us to evaluate your threat level." He pointed at my nose. "Everything that happened was your own fault." He jerked his body away from me and checked his phone.

"I can't believe this," I said. "You destroyed my bike and you spied on me. You can go to hell."

"Don't get mad at me," the American said over his shoulder. "I saved your life tonight."

"You people put my life in jeopardy by messing with my bike! And if you hadn't been there, I'm sure that eventually somebody would have come along and helped."

We slowed down around the Taipei Botanical Garden. The gates were locked, and lumbering palm trees looked down at us like curious giraffes. When we were kids, there were signs that banned the mentally challenged from entering the garden. We used to joke that so-and-so couldn't go on the field trip there. I don't remember all the people that we made fun of, but Cookie Monster was definitely one of them. The Taipei Botanical Garden didn't lift the ban and remove the signs until 2011.

I became apprehensive again. Were they going to kill me and make it look like I had been trying to enter at night, a thief trying to steal rare aquatic plants for his private garden?

"I saved your life by destroying your bike. Right about now, you'd be asleep in bed, right?" I played with my seat belt, unsure if I should take it off now that we had stopped.

"I don't know."

"I know for sure you would be." He waved his hand to the northwest. "Your house is somewhere over there, right?"

You certainly couldn't see my house from here. My little toaster building was blocked by much larger buildings down the block. This road would take me home, though. What was this crazy American trying to get at?

"It's somewhere over there, sure. Ten blocks away. So what?"

He smirked and allowed himself to have that second cigarette he'd denied himself earlier.

"Keep looking."

I crossed my arms. I wondered if he had watched me undress, if he had video files of Nancy and me having sex.

Suddenly, I heard an explosion in the distance and saw a flame flick up in my neighborhood. It flared upward at first, but then steadied to a constant flame.

"That's your little house on the prairie right there, Jing-nan," said the American. "Your ass would have been Cajun fucking blackened right now."

"You're lying!" I said.

He used his phone's walkie-talkie function to talk to the driver and instructed him to go by my house. I was somewhat unnerved that he didn't have to give him my street address. We went past Longshan Temple, which still had lights mounted to help guide lost souls. A block later and I could tell that it was my house on fire before we actually drove by it.

The explosion had been well planned. The destruction and remaining fire were concentrated on the exterior wall—where my bedroom was—and away from the adjacent apartment building, which was buzzing with people yelling and pointing out of their windows.

My records. Records that Julia had once held in her hands. My music files. Even the burned CDs. All gone. I took in a series of halting breaths. All those sounds had been silenced. I didn't care about the actual stereo equipment or anything else in the house. I didn't even care about the house itself. All of that music was now in the hereafter. I'd wasted most of my life putting that collection together.

I reverted to my teenage self. I just wanted to die.

My head was chilly. I ran my fingers over my hair and they came out slick with sweat.

"Satisfied?" the American asked in English. I nodded dumbly. We drove down a few more blocks, made a U-turn and stopped at Longshan Temple.

"This is where you get out, Jing-nan."

"What do I do now?"

"Go walk to your house, talk to the fire fighters. Tell the cops your bike broke down and you caught a ride from a 'depressed friend.'"

"A 'depressed friend'?"

"They'll know. Don't worry about your moped. We'll fix it up and bring it back to the night market."

I snapped off my seat belt and crumpled my head into my lap. "All my things are gone," I moaned.

The American put a heavy hand on my shoulder. "I'm sorry about that. Say, Jing-nan, that box you got from Julia's father was in there, wasn't it?"

I raised my head and stared at him vacantly. The box was still at Nancy's.

He read my expression all wrong. "It's better destroyed, Jing-nan. Believe me."

"Easy for you to say." I stood up.

He touched my left forearm. "Jing-nan. It stops here, okay? You've already found out all there is to know about Julia. Don't go looking for more trouble, because next time, they will kill you."

I was about to make a comment about the diploma, but I stopped myself. After all, it probably didn't mean anything and the American might suspect I still had it. He had saved my life tonight but he wasn't my friend.

I looked down and nodded. Then I hopped out and walked slowly to the burned foundation of my home, the source of the light and smoke pouring up into the night sky.

I WAS HALF A block away when I slowed down to a stiff-legged, undead trudge.

I couldn't bear the thought that everything was gone. All the music I had ever listened to in my life. I also began to miss specific books and certain clothes, such as my Joy Division hoodie. It was cooler because it had a picture of the band and no words to clue in non-fans. The little paperwork I had accumulated at UCLA was gone as well. Julia had left behind more things than I now owned.

I still had the memories of living in that home with my mother, father and grandfather, even though most of them were merely prosaic. Eating, washing, sleeping.

Damn it, if I had only worn my Joy Division hoodie today! Sure, it was too hot for a hoodie, but I could have pulled it off while riding my moped.

As I drew closer to the fire, the air stank of chemicals oxidized into evil spirits that bit the insides of my nasal cavity and the roof of my mouth. I clamped the inside of my right arm over my nose and continued.

The concrete-and-stone wall topped with glass was still intact, but the metal gate was gone, probably already in the hands of a scrap-metal dealer. Even with the obvious gap, the outer wall was in better shape than what had been my family home. The roof was gone and the walls had crumbled. The flames had lost some intensity since we drove by, but they were still going strong enough to throw off heat. I sat on a brick stump and watched embers winking at each other and cackling.

A fire truck had beaten me there, but it hadn't used the siren, or I would have heard. Even more curious, the water hoses remained rolled up behind the roll-down gates on the sides of the truck. Two male fire fighters, one with a helmet and one without, stood at the rear of the truck, both glued to their cell phones.

"Hey!" I said to them. "Why aren't you putting this fire out?"

"Who are you?" asked the man with a bare head.

"This is my house!"

"You're Jing-nan, huh? You'd better talk to General Yang. He's the guy over there." He switched his helmet to his left armpit and pointed to a heavyset fire fighter talking to a man I knew to be a plainclothes policeman and German Tsai on the far corner of the block.

I marched over to the three of them. I saw the so-called general gesticulate to the others that he was going to handle me himself. He was the kind of guy who buckled close to the crotch because he refused to get a longer belt to accommodate the child he was carrying in his womb.

"Jing-nan, I'm Mr. Yang," he said. "I'm glad you weren't home."

"How come you won't put that fire out?" I said.

German Tsai rubbed his nostrils with his right thumb and looked away. The policeman put his hands in his pockets and stared at the ground. "It's more dangerous if we turn on the water, Jing-nan."

"How could it be more dangerous than having an open fucking fire, General?"

I don't know what set him off more, me cursing or calling him "General."

"You live in an illegal house, you know that?" he bellowed. "You're lucky we came at all! Can you smell that? Do you know what that is?"

"A bunch of chemicals, obviously."

"It's tar! The walls of your home were filled with tar and probably some other industrial waste! We can't spray water in there when we don't know what toxic crap we could be spreading around. It's safer to let it all burn away completely."

"That's bullshit! Put out that fire right now!"

German Tsai approached, showing me his open palms in a calming gesture. "Now, look, Jing-nan, everything's pretty much lost already," he said. "I know that things don't look good now, but you and I are going to work things out."

Mr. Yang felt free to add, "This is what you get for living in an illegal construction! This building should have been demolished decades ago."

I headed back to the two fire fighters. "He's not going to put out the fire," I told them.

The man with his helmet on shoved his phone in his back pocket and said to me, "Come here." He brought me around to the back of the truck and popped open a storage door. "Take one," he said, pointing to a rack of dirty shovels.

I picked one with a flat edge and he took one with a rounded blade. We walked toward the fire. I never felt more like a hero, even though it was my house.

The outside west wall had blown apart where most of the fire was concentrated. The east wall—the one next to the adjacent condominium—was merely scorched. The flames had nearly burned themselves out by then. The fireman dug into a dirt patch along the remains of the north wall. He threw dirt across the fire and nodded to me. I went over to the dirt patch and scooped up a shovelful of moist earth.

The two of us were able to smother much of the fire. It seemed too easy.

"Everything that can burn has already burned," the fire fighter said. He held up his shovel and pointed with the handle end. "Look at the pattern of the burns on the floor. Your house didn't catch on fire. This looks like a grenade or explosive hit it here."

"This fire was no accident," I said, resting my foot on the top. "I know it was arson."

"You said something about arson?"

The plainclothes policeman stood right at my elbow. He wasn't a low-level beat cop. He looked impossibly young for his mid-fifties—I knew him from around the neighborhood when I was growing up. I remembered him roughing up would-be delinquents who tried taking a day off from school, one of whom was my best friend who lived in his family's car-repair garage. That garage had been bulldozed years ago and was now an office building filled with dimly lit windows.

"I'm just guessing here, officer," I said.

"You're Jing-nan, right?"

"Yeah."

"I remember you from the neighborhood. You're a decent kid. I never had to knock any common sense into your head. I'm sure you remember me. I'm Ou-Yang."

"I remember you."

"You fell pretty far from the tree. Other people in your family got mixed up in the wrong racket."

"Are you talking about my grandfather?"

"Not so much. Your uncle was the one I was thinking of. I had to run him and his hoodlum friends out of the neighborhood a few times."

"You mean you were working with German and his gang?"

Ou-Yang grabbed my shoulder hard. "Well, forget about all that. So you want to tell me more about the fire? You seemed to know something about it."

"I don't know anything."

"Well how about this, then? It's a little funny how you came home so late, and coincidently after the fire. Where were you?"

"Ah, I was with a depressed friend."

"Really? Who?"

"I said 'depressed friend.'"

"And I said, 'Who?'"

"That phrase doesn't mean anything to you?"

"It means you have a troubled friend. Or maybe you're really the depressed one, and you're projecting your problems onto an imaginary friend."

The fire fighter decided he had done all he could and returned to the truck.

"Ou-Yang, an American told me to say . . ."

"Oh, an American! All right, I get it. Say no more."

"What just happened?"

"You let me know it's all being handled at a higher level." Ou-Yang slapped my shoulder and walked back to German and General Yang.

The fire had died down to the point where I could enter where my front door had been. The whole house looked a lot smaller now that the Sheetrock walls were gone. My bedroom had been adjacent to the west wall and so had my CD rack. I looked down at what used to be my music collection. It looked like a puddle of burned macaroni and cheese.

The smell was worse than when I first arrived. I cupped my nose and mouth with my left hand as I jabbed the shovel around, cracking melted plastic.

My desk had caved in, and my PC was sitting in the middle of the wreckage looking like a fried, deflated volleyball. Nothing remained of my plastic speakers.

The bathroom tiles had disintegrated, so I guess they weren't made from genuine ceramic, after all. The sheet-metal sink had wilted to the side. The only thing that remained unscathed in the entire house was the squat toilet, that oval of porcelain set in the floor. It would probably withstand a missile attack from China, as well. The survivors wouldn't be lacking places to poop.

I stepped back into what had been the living room and saw what looked like a little pile of flour. I poked it with my shovel, and two blackened metal spirals rolled out. I realized that the coils were the remnants of my old notebooks and that my little box of high-school memorabilia was a heap of ashes.

The yearbook with the picture of me and Julia was gone.

I knew I should have scanned it, but I had never gotten around to it. Well, even if I had digitized the picture, it would have ended up as part of the twisted blob that my PC was now, because I wouldn't have uploaded it anywhere.

It also meant my high-school diploma was gone. A sudden realization stopped me in my tracks.

My house had been burned down to destroy Julia's box of stuff. Only my arsonist didn't know I had it stashed at Nancy's apartment. Maybe it wasn't Black Sea who had firebombed my house. Maybe it was the CIA, trying to cover their tracks. I didn't know if I could believe the American.

I gulped in some air and nearly retched. There was a terrible oily taste in my mouth.

A cable-news van pulled up, scraping its guts against the curb as the side door drew back. A woman tumbled out and immediately began to haul out canvas bags of equipment. A man came out of the cab and helped her.

Ou-Yang came up to me. "Jing-nan, get out of there."

"Out of where?"

"Get out of the rubble, it's dangerous, plus you're destroying evidence. There are still some open flames in there."

"It's not dangerous anymore."

Ou-Yang yanked me out of the foundation of my house. He pointed at my nose with the index finger of a hastily pulled-on industrial-strength rubber glove. "Stay the fuck out, you!" He grabbed my shovel and began to root around.

General Yang was also compelled to act before the cameras were turned on. It sure would look bad for the police and fire fighters to be standing around idle at a fire. On a slow news day, the loop could be playing until the afternoon.

Obviously, Ou-Yang had more experience at posing than General Yang.

"How long do you need in there?" Yang asked Ou-Yang, his voice breaking.

"Shut up, fatso!" Ou-Yang replied. "I'm working!"

Yang headed to the fire truck and yelled, "Let's get those hoses out!"

Ou-Yang continued to scrape around. The TV people were setting up.

The driver was also the cameraman. "This place smells like shit," he said as he unwound cords.

"It was an illegal house," said the reporter. "They smell awful when they burn down."

"This was my house," I told her. "Are you going to do a story about it?"

"Maybe," she said cagily. The woman looked me over. "You lived here by yourself?"

"Yes."

"Why did you live here?"

"I used to live here with my parents and my grandfather. They're all gone now."

"I'm sorry to hear that," the woman said with the empathy of an automated voice menu. She was younger than me and also tougher.

Ou-Yang called me over. "Is this yours?" he asked, holding up half of what used to be a digital clock radio.

"No," I said. "We . . . I only had a round clock in the living room."

"This isn't yours?"

"I've never seen it before."

"This was part of an explosive device. The fire radiated out from where I found it."

"Hey," called out Yang. "Are you done in there already?"

"Yeah, go spray it down," said Ou-Yang. He bagged the clock radio and lit a cigarette. He walked over to the reporter, smiled at her and asked if she smoked.

CHAPTER SIXTEEN

Nancy sounded sleepy when she finally answered. I suppose she could have been in bed, considering it was about four thirty in the morning.

"Jing-nan? Why are you calling me on the intercom phone?"

"Because you wouldn't answer your cell phone."

"But how in the world did you call in to the intercom system?"

"I'm in your lobby. Right now. Please tell them it's okay for me to come up. The guy at the desk is looking at me like I'm crazy, and the doorman wants to beat me up."

I handed the phone back to the desk attendant, a tall man with a short temper. He put the receiver to his ear and listened, which seemed to require an enormous effort.

"That's fine," he said to Nancy, "but you have to come down to escort your guest up. It's the policy at this time of night." He replaced the handset and rubbed down his stringy eyebrows. "You," he said to me. "Take your elbows off the desk."

I was so relieved I had been able to get in touch with Nancy. Plan B was buzzing Peggy Lee to ask if I could crash on her couch.

Nancy came down in a zipped-up pink hoodie and cut-off sweat-pants. Appropriate dress for the glacial temperature of the lobby. When she got closer, I saw a few centimeters of a black slip peeking out like snail meat from just under the waistband of the hoodie.

The doorman broke away from eying the soft parts of my throat to leer at her legs.

Nancy smiled at me and signed something at the desk. We walked to the elevators. I waited for the doors to open before saying anything.

"My house was blown up," I whispered. "It's probably on the news right now."

"Oh my God!" she exclaimed in English.

I put my hands on her shoulders. "Everything I have is gone."

She covered her mouth and nose. The elevator came and brought us up.

We got into her apartment and she ran her hands up and down my body, checked the number of ears, fingers and other things.

We sat on the couch, and I explained to Nancy what the American had essentially told me: that I had run afoul of the Black Sea gang, the one that was still cleaning house by getting rid of a faction of dissident members who had killed Julia or caused her death.

"The CIA is working with Black Sea," I said. "They think the gang is more stable than the government."

Nancy pointed at my nose. "Of course the Taiwanese-American's working for the CIA," she said. "It makes so much sense."

I got up, walked into the kitchen and poured two glasses of iced water. "He mentioned something about you," I called from the kitchen.

"What did he say?"

I came out and handed her one of the glasses. "He said you noticed the smell from the cooking oil they used when they installed the microphones in my house." I took a long sip; I hadn't realized until then how dehydrated I was.

"They were bugging your house?" She stared into her glass and turned it in her hands.

"It turned out to be a waste of time, too. I'm the guy who knows the least about the situation!" I gulped more water.

Nancy touched my hand. "Do you think the CIA burned the building down because they didn't want anybody to find the microphones they used?"

I looked directly at her. I hadn't thought of that.

"Ah-ding's company makes specialty chips for intelligence

operations. Ordinarily, if a chip is recovered, you can open it up and read it like a book to see who made it and who was using it. But the specialty chips melt away like solder—you can't even tell what it used to be."

I sucked a small ice cube into my mouth. "I hadn't thought about that at all," I said. "I thought they were only interested in burning the box with Julia's stuff in it. Now I see they saw it as a two-birds-one-stone deal.

"Since my family's gone, it somehow makes sense that our house is gone, too. It was a temporary house that lasted for three generations of Chens, so it did its job." I swallowed the sliver of ice that was left in my mouth. "I'm glad, though, that we got to go through the yearbook together."

"Isn't it funny that the three of us—me, you and Julia—were all in that picture together?"

"She would have liked you a lot, Nancy," I said. She blushed immediately.

Nancy drank some more water, then stood up. "I need to have some shrimp chips," she said. "When I drink iced water, I need shrimp chips." She headed for the kitchen.

"I hope you don't mind . . ." I called after her. "I mean, if it's okay with you, could I stay with you . . . ? Until I have my own place again, of course. It shouldn't take too long."

Nancy padded back from the kitchen and jumped onto the couch with a bag of spicy shrimp chips. "You don't even have to ask," she said. She tore a side of the bag open and grabbed a handful of chips, which were formed into shapes like French fries. As soon as you bit them they'd collapse into shrimp-flavored dust. They were made out of processed wheat and palm oil that was probably poured over a shrimp armpit. A perfect snack for mindless munching.

"These are really bad for you," I said as I shook a few into my left hand.

She blinked. "It's one of my favorite snacks."

"I don't think you should be eating them anymore."

She held the bag open. "Well, if they're so bad for you, then put your chips back in."

"No!"

She tried to grab them out of my hand, but I shoved them all into my mouth. They were hot. I choked a little bit and drank down some water. She slapped my back.

"Serves you right. Making fun of my food." After I managed to swallow she asked a serious question. "Is all your music gone?"

I sighed and fell back on the couch. "Everything was destroyed. Even my toothbrush was melted away."

"Don't worry, Jing-nan! I have all the best music files from the music store. Bauhaus had everything, certainly everything from Joy Division. Now I have them, too." She crunched down some more shrimp chips.

I asked her something I'd been wondering. "Nancy, is Bauhaus owned by Black Sea?"

"Naw, not enough cash flow. Bauhaus is owned by a local *jiaotou*."

"A *jiaotou* who's into Joy Division?"

"Yeah, he's a nice guy."

I walked back into the kitchen to pour two cups of hot decaf oolong tea from the Japanese dispenser on the counter. Had to wash out that hot shrimp-chip taste.

"Are the cops going to help you?" Nancy asked when I handed her some tea.

"They're going to investigate," I said as I eased into the couch. "That doesn't mean shit, though. The American already told me they won't solve this case. Nobody was killed, so it wasn't that serious, and they have their own relationship with Black Sea to maintain. Not to mention that German Tsai's company is the mortgage holder."

Nancy was crunching her way to the bottom of the shrimp-chip bag. "Who do you think burned down your house?" she asked. "Black Sea or the CIA?"

I shrugged. "Or the two of them working together. Why count anybody out?" I drank some tea, which was just the right temperature. I relished its hint of bitterness.

"Aren't you afraid they'll come after you again?" Nancy asked, cradling her teacup in a bird's nest of fingers.

"No. The American said that if I stopped looking for trouble I was going to be fine. I'm just going to stay away from the Huangs' place, that's for sure. German already said he was going to sort everything out for me, because the fire was technically an attack on his turf, but I asked him not to make a big deal out of it on my behalf."

Nancy licked her fingers to get the chip crumbs off them and then stroked my hair. "You lost everything," she said.

"Well, you're going to give me all the music files, right?"

"Oh, I wasn't talking about that. I meant that box of Julia's."

"I didn't lose the box."

She straightened up. "You said everything in your house was burned."

I drank some tea to prepare myself. "Julia's box is here. It's in the hallway closet."

She stood up in fear. "Oh, God, Jing-nan, you have to get rid of it. That thing is dangerous!"

I held two pleading hands up to her. "First thing in the morning, I swear," I said.

"Even before you shower."

"Yes."

"Even before you pee."

"Yes."

She crossed her arms and glanced at the clock. "Man, it's almost five thirty in the morning! I have to sleep!" She yawned into her right elbow. "When I saw you come into the music store, I never imagined I'd be in this situation now."

"Why don't you go to bed, Nancy? I'm going to watch some television."

"It's not like we're going to sleep together every night, anyway," said Nancy. "Keep that in mind for the future. I have lab research to do, you know?"

"I'm so sorry I bothered you so late, but I had a good reason."

She raised her right leg and stood stork-like. "Are you going to be up long?" Nancy asked.

"I still have to calm down a little bit." I stood up and kissed her forehead with my wet lips. She put up her arms like a zombie and did a stiff-legged walk to the bedroom. I couldn't help but laugh. What a funny girl.

I charged up my phone and turned on the television. I flipped through some of the twenty-four-hour cable news stations.

Taiwanese farmers opposed to the importation of American beef pelted government buildings with eggs and manure. Videos don't lie. Farmers have good arms.

The Uni-President 7-Eleven Lions were continuing to struggle after coming off the All-Star break. A Japanese minor leaguer who was a clutch hitter at the beginning of the season was now choking on a regular basis. That reminded me of my early Little League baseball days. They used to call me Mr. Wind Power because I whiffed so much, often spectacularly.

I found a report by the woman who had come to the remains of my house, but it was another story, recorded while there was still daylight: a hard-hitting exposé of a hen with a pattern on its back that looked like the character for "love." The farmer said he planned to auction the animal off for charity, as the character was clearly a message from the gods during this month of spiritual instability.

Another channel showed a blurry camera-phone video of something white hopping by the side of a road. It supposedly was a *jiangshi*, a reanimated corpse that moves by making short jumps and sucks the chi out of living creatures. During the broadcast some joker in the newsroom donned a wig that was a shock of white hair and hopped in the background.

I shivered and rubbed my hands. I was creeped out. Not by the *jiangshi* story, but by the fact that there wasn't one single syllable's mention anywhere of the fire that had destroyed my house.

I was dazed by the revelation that I was up against what seemed like a gigantic conspiracy. All I could do for a while was eat more shrimp chips like a little kid having an after-school snack in front of the TV.

Why would anybody want to kill me? What had I done that was so bad?

I couldn't say that I hadn't been warned, though. If people were willing to track me and beat me up on occasion, my life was probably in danger.

What had Julia done to deserve being murdered? Apparently she was spying on customers of the betel-nut stand, based on how she helped nail Ah-ding.

The American had given me a final warning to back off and lay low. He claimed that he was going to smooth things out for me and convince his clients that even though I was still alive, I had at last gotten the message.

This is where the story should end. I keep my stall at the night market. Maybe I live happily ever after with Nancy. Maybe Nancy finds someone else. Maybe that someone else is Ah-ding when he gets out of jail. Does she still care about him? Why was I thinking about this now? I was the one who had told her I couldn't fall in love.

After some more mindless munching, I lay down on one of the living-room couches and drew the throw blanket over myself. I didn't want to crawl into bed and possibly disturb Nancy more tonight. The soft leather of the couch cradled me, and I rolled into its deep, dark pocket.

IT WAS A SUNNY day, not too humid, and I walked arm-in-arm with Julia, my wife of many years. Who knew where the kids were. We were laughing about something.

People were walking by. We didn't know any of them. A woman ran out of a store and grabbed Julia by the arm, saying there was a beautiful dress inside that was perfect for her.

What can you do when that happens? If I objected, it would be tantamount to saying that my wife didn't deserve a beautiful dress. I followed them into the store. I had to duck under some garments hanging from the ceiling as I followed them to the back.

Julia went into a dressing room and I was alone with the saleswoman, who began to lick the backs of her hands.

"Are you sure this is the dress for her?" I asked.

"Of course," said the woman. "You'll feel like you've never seen Julia before." I saw that she had a tail, and I thought it would be rude to stare at it, so I turned and looked at myself in a full-length mirror. I was dressed in burlap head to toe—traditional mourning clothes.

I gasped.

"Don't be alarmed," said the woman.

"You tricked me!" I growled through my clenched teeth.

"It's no trick. Look." She led me into the dressing room. Julia was lying in a coffin wearing a flowing white dress. "Isn't she beautiful?" asked the woman.

She pressed a button on a remote control and the coffin slid away on a conveyor belt as a furnace door at the other end flew open. Julia suddenly sat up.

"Remember to burn paper for me, Jing-nan," she said.

"No!" I said, pressing all the buttons on the remote. The conveyor belt chugged on. Julia lay back down, and I saw her in the light of the furnace flames, shadows dancing on her chin.

"JING-NAN!" NANCY SAID AS she shook me. "You were shouting!"

I apologized and dropped the TV remote. I had slept on the couch specifically in order not to bother her, and now I'd woken her up a few hours before her alarm. I lifted the blanket and she crawled in with me. After a few minutes of fidgeting, we slunk off to the bedroom for a quickie.

NANCY HAD LEFT BY the time I woke up at 11:30. I had a vague memory of her kissing me and saying I could have something in the fridge, and to get that box the hell out of her apartment. Neatly wrapped in cellophane on the second rack, I found a to-go breakfast of *youtiao*, *shaobing* and *danbing*—deep-fried cruller, baked sesame flatbread and an egg crepe. I ate them with my fingers, and everything was so cold and soaked with grease, it was eerily reminiscent of raw meat. I swept the crumbs on the counter into the sink and ran the hot water over my hands.

That box. I had to get rid of that box. If somebody somehow discovered Julia's CIA papers weren't destroyed in the fire, there could be serious trouble. I didn't need the American to tell me that. What was the fastest way to ditch it? The nearest dumpster, or maybe a river? Throwing the box into a river would be bad luck, though, especially this time of year.

Damn it, there was no such thing as bad luck.

I retrieved the box from Nancy's closet, tucked in its flaps and slipped it into a shopping sack made from recycled bottles. I went down to the lobby, where I discovered that there was definitely such a thing as bad timing, if not bad luck.

"Hello, Peggy." Surprisingly, she was wearing a skirt with her blazer. No pantsuit today. Dressed in navy blue with a white blouse, Peggy looked like a schoolgirl who could kick the principal's ass.

"Jing-nan, how are you?"

I brushed my hair back in an attempt to cover up not having combed it. "I'm doing pretty good."

She made a face at me like I was the ugly new kid on the first day of school. "You look like you slept in those clothes!" She broke into a smile and rocked forward on the balls of her feet in her flat shoes. "Well, I guess it doesn't matter, considering where you work."

I tapped my right foot, trying to come up with something. C'mon! "You're very nicely dressed, yourself, Peggy. Aren't you running late? Well, I guess it doesn't matter when other people do the real work for you."

She crinkled her nose and hid her briefcase behind her back without letting her smile down. "I started today with a conference call. A potentially big deal with Australian investors. I guess you were still in bed."

"I was working early, too." I made a move for the door, and Peggy walked alongside.

"So where's Nancy?" she asked.

"She had to run." I swapped my bag to the arm away from Peggy, but she picked up on its movement.

"What's in the bag, Jing-nan?"

"It's stuff for the stall. New decor."

"Let me see it!" I was walking briskly, but Peggy had no problem keeping up. Man, this was one long lobby. The revolving doors didn't seem to be getting any closer.

"It's not quite ready yet, Peggy. I still need to go through a finalization process with some focus groups."

"But I know all about Joy Division! 'Love Will Tear Us Apart!' You still think I don't know?"

"That's not the issue. It's not good enough for you to see it. I know how demanding you are."

"Did you make it? I promise I won't laugh," she said, contradicting her statement by letting out a nostril-snort chuckle.

I stepped into the building's revolving door, followed closely by Peggy. I used the microseconds I had alone to try to plan my escape from her.

When she swished out into the open air I told her that I had to go.

"Let me give you a lift!" she insisted.

"I'm in a bit of a rush, though."

"My car is right here. I can take you anywhere!"

"I'd rather not take up your time."

"Nonsense!" A black Yukon with smoked windows pulled up next to us. The driver, a big guy in a dress shirt and black tie, jumped out and had a little fight with the building doorman to open the rear passenger door for us. I had no choice but to climb in, keeping the bag tight against my body. The doorman won the fight to close the passenger door, so the driver hopped back into his seat before Peggy had settled in next to me. He adjusted his rearview mirror and I noticed that he raised his eyebrows as he looked me over.

"Birdy, this is my old classmate, Jing-nan," said Peggy. "We've known each other since we were little kids."

"Hello, Birdy," I said. He nodded. I knew what he was thinking. I wanted to say, "I was visiting someone else here last night, not Peggy!"

Peggy didn't care what Birdy thought and didn't attempt to clarify the situation at all. In fact, she further compromised my position by stroking my arm and saying, "Are you busy tonight?"

"You know I am. I work at the family business. Just like you."

We turned off into the street, and Peggy cleared her throat. "Birdy, we're going to make a stop before we go to the office."

"Where do you want to go, miss?" Birdy spoke an earthy brand of Mandarin, the kind you would pick up in northern China working jobs that built up your biceps. Like Birdy's.

"The Shilin Night Market," I said. "Any entrance is fine."

"Too early to go, my man! Still so many hours before it opens!"

We swung out into the street behind a swarm of bikes. The motorcycles were the adult insects, and the mopeds were the grubs.

"Jing-nan runs one of the stalls there," said Peggy with a mixture of admiration and admonishment.

"No kiddin'. I go there sometimes. It's a great place."

"I run a food stall," I said, knowing that it would have been impolite for a mere driver to ask me outright.

"You look like a great chef!" he declared as we swung onto an elevated highway.

"He is, Birdy!"

"I wouldn't go quite that far," I said.

Peggy turned to me and said in a low voice, "Have you thought more about my proposal for your new indoor location?"

I looked at her. From my angle I could see sky and clouds the color of rancid, fatty meat go by behind her head.

"I've thought about it, but I can't see how I can go along with it."

"How can you *not* go along with it? Don't you want your business to do well? Your parents put their whole lives into it."

"Thanks for reminding me of my parents, because sometimes I forget. Of course I want Unknown Pleasures to do well, but it's bad luck to arrange something during Ghost Month, as you well know." I shifted in my seat and played with the seat belt.

"Bullshit, Jing-nan. You don't believe in that crap any more than I do. Julia didn't, either."

I heard the driver cough into his fist.

"Please leave her out of this, Peggy."

"Why won't you let me help you?"

"I don't need anybody's help."

"Then what are you doing with that girl Nancy?"

I thought I saw Birdy eying me in the rearview mirror. I felt self-conscious. Why didn't her car have one of those privacy dividers?

"It's none of your business, Peggy."

"Christ! If you wanted to keep me shut out of your life, then why did you get in touch with me in the first place?"

"I needed your help then, to find out more about Julia."

"And now you don't need me or my help."

"Kinda."

The Yukon slowed as we took an exit back to a ground-level street. I could see we were close to Xinyi Road, which would take us to Taipei 101.

"You don't genuinely care about me at all, do you? All our years together in school add up to nothing, right?"

"Peggy, I do care." I didn't know how to phrase it in a neutral way, so I tried to be as honest as possible. "But I don't care to the point where we have to associate with each other . . . closely."

"Birdy!" she shrieked.

"Yes, Miss Lee?"

"Let me out at the next corner!"

"Are you sure?"

"Just shut up and do what I say!" She turned to the window but directed her words at me. "You probably don't even want to ride in my car with me, so I'll go! I'll make it better for you! I'll make *everything* better for you!"

I touched her arm lightly, and Peggy rammed her shoulder into the palm of my injured hand. It stung.

We came up to the curb, and before we reached a full stop, Peggy broke out and slammed the door.

Without missing a beat, Birdy pulled the car back into traffic.

"Next stop, Shilin Night Market," he called out. We headed down Xinyi Road and then made a left to head north on Jianguo Road, one of my traditional routes to the market.

"Is Peggy going to be all right?" I asked.

"Oh, sure. She'll get a cab for the rest of the way. Don't worry about her. She's good."

"Does this happen often?" I asked.

"Oh, yeah. All the time. The whole family's the same way. Her aunt's the worst. If they don't fight during the ride, then they're asleep or drunk."

"Nobody's drunk on the way to work, though, right?"

Birdy smiled and shook his head. "The horrors that I've seen, you wouldn't believe. I'm scarred for life." He rubbed the back of his neck. "Her ex-husband, the Swiss guy, what a victim he was! She hammered him every day until he assumed the fetal position. That was his only defense!"

"Maybe it was best that the marriage ended."

Birdy coughed hard and made a sucking sound in his nasal passage. "Us mainlanders, you know, we're not all like that. Most of us are regular people. Anybody with money and power acts crazy. You're *benshengren*, right?"

"Yeah."

"I could tell. The way your ears and nose are." He pointed at me in the rearview mirror. "When your ancestors came over, they were almost all men, and they interbred with the native mountain women."

"It was a long time ago," I said. Now was not the time to tell him that the term "mountain people" was offensive to aboriginal people, not least because not all the tribes were from up in the mountains.

"You know I'm from China," said Birdy. He pointed at his mouth. "Way up north. You can tell just by the way I talk. Also, I'm big. You people never get to this size. It's the Mongolian blood."

I leaned back. This could be a revealing ride. I put my hand tentatively against the back of his seat. "Say, Birdy, how long have you been working for the Lees?"

"Couple years. I'm distantly related to them, so they brought me over, hooked me up with this job. I always have to be grateful for that. Decent pay for decent work. All in all, they are not the nuttiest people I've worked for. You want to see crazy, you go to China."

"I think I already saw crazy today."

"Ha!" shouted Birdy. We pulled up to the curb outside the Shi-lin Night Market. "So, right here, is this about where you want to go?"

"I'm fine here."

Birdy unhooked his seat belt and reached back for my hand. "It was nice to meet you, Jing-nan." He was like Dwayne in that he tried to intimidate with his grip.

"Thanks again, Birdy." I left the car and shut the door with a solid slam. He had gotten the better of me with the handshake, so I had to show that I wasn't completely weak, that I wasn't less of a man.

I also had to show him that I wasn't afraid. He knew his *heidaoren* tattoos were visible through the slits in his sleeves.

Tattoos aren't as common here as they are in the US, where almost everybody who is cool or wants to be cool gets them. It was a rite of passage for incoming freshmen at UCLA to get some ink on their arms by spring break.

Not everyone in Taiwan who has tattoos is a criminal, but all *heidaoren*, "black-way people," have them.

The black way is the extra-legal arena where so many political and business deals are forged. The deeds that black-way people do may not be technically legal, but they are socially acceptable. *Heidaoren* had built my home without worrying about getting a permit. *Heidaoren* operate temples, nightclubs and KTVs—all cash-heavy businesses where the accounting books offer only modest approximations. Older *heidaoren* are elected to serve in the Legislative Yuan, parliament, and wouldn't hesitate to throw chairs and punches to get their way. *Heidaoren* and supposedly completely legitimate *baidaoren*, "white-way people," help each other to keep their reputations consistent.

German Tsai was a *heidaoren*. So was Kuilan's son, Ah-tien. But Kuilan and her husband were *baidaoren*. Peggy and her family were *baidaoren* with *heidaoren* connections.

I wondered what the Lees had tasked people like Birdy to do. If I didn't do that deal with Peggy, maybe I would find out.

I WALKED THROUGH THE still-empty streets of the market. It was a little after noon, still a couple hours before the businesses would open.

I could feel the box buckling in the bag, so I perched it on a chained stool and turned the box ninety degrees to distribute the wear and tear on the cardboard. If it broke open, it might be harder to get rid of. I wasn't sure what I was looking for. In the absence of public trash cans, a big bottomless pit would be ideal.

I found a dark back alley that looked as good as any route to explore. I followed it to the sunlight at the far end, where I found myself standing at the edge of the construction site of the Taipei Performing Arts Center.

Several dumpsters squatted around me like giant cakes powdered with dry-wall dust. One of them would be a perfect place to ditch this box and walk away.

Yet I hesitated.

After all, I was about to throw away the last belongings of the girl I had loved almost my entire life.

I shifted the bag to my left arm. It didn't feel very heavy at all, certainly not for something that was supposed to summarize all the most important work Julia had done in her brief adult life.

Yet I had to get rid of it. Nancy and I wouldn't be safe as long as it was around. I set the bag on the ground, put my hands in my pockets and looked around as nonchalantly as possible. A group of workers were down in the pit area, about fifty feet away, while the others were sitting in the shade of a crane. No one seemed to be actively working. I didn't understand what they were saying to each other. Most of them were probably Thai or Filipino and in all likelihood living in the country illegally. They had enough to be worried about already and wouldn't mess around looking through a box full of papers in English. I lifted the lid to the nearest dumpster. It was nearly empty. I didn't need two hands to lift the box out of the bag, but I used both, anyway. It seemed more respectful to do so. I released the box and watched it slide down and kick up some dust. I folded up the bag and stuffed it into my back pocket.

Goodbye, Julia. There's still so much I don't know, but I think I understand everything I need to.

I walked back through the dark alley. I felt at peace with myself. Finally letting her go felt like cutting off a gigantic tumor from my back that I had forgotten I was carrying.

Not a tumor. That wasn't fair. More like a big old burden of failure to keep my promises. Everything was going to be better now.

I cheated a little, though. I didn't get rid of everything.

I kept Julia's diploma. I couldn't bear to throw it away, even though it looked like crap, all crinkled and folded. It still represented an accomplishment. Her success. Her genius. I kept it folded in my wallet so I would always have it close by. Certainly the CIA couldn't begrudge me this.

I WALKED NORTH ON Zhongshan Road and found a used book-
store across the street from Ming Chuan University, where I bought
an American book of short stories. I tried to read them while sitting
at a park bench, but I didn't seem to have the patience to stick with
any of them for more than a page or two. Even though the cover
made no mention of it, they all seemed to be about love. I watched
the elevated MRT line rumble across the street, and it looked so
lonely.

I tried a new drink at Starbucks, and as I slurped it down, it hit
me that I was falling in love with Nancy. How could I be? She used
to sleep with a guy who was more than twice as old as she was,
after all. Was she the kind of woman to get serious with?

I looked into the sad suds at the bottom of my drink and felt
sheepish. She was right to point out what a hypocrite I was for taking her to love hotels and yet pretending to stand on some higher
moral ground.

And what about Julia? The woman I had been planning to be
with forever had worked three-quarters naked as a *binlang xishi.*

What a chauvinist I had been. What a lout. Who the hell was I to
pronounce that being a mistress was immoral? Who was I to judge
that a betel-nut beauty didn't deserve respect? After all, I pimped
food every night with a shit-eating grin.

At about 3:30 P.M., I arrived at Unknown Pleasures and met
Frankie. I told him everything, and he didn't seem surprised by any
of it.

All he asked was, "Did they fix your moped?" I told him that
it was in my usual parking space and that it was in great shape.
He nodded, and we went about getting the place ready. Dwayne
showed up about twenty minutes later.

"What are you doing here so early, Jing-nan?" he asked. "You
weird me out when you beat me here."

"What's wrong with me being early? It's my stall, all right?" I
hosed down the street and brushed a stiff broom over the asphalt.
Damned cigarette butts.

"It's *your* stall? Look at the balls on this one, Frankie!"

The Cat looked up from his task and rolled his shoulders back,
left and then right. "About time they dropped," he said.

I leaned against the broom and looked Dwayne in the eye. "My house was firebombed last night," I told him.

"What?! You're kidding me, right? You mean your grandfather's place?"

"It's just a pile of ashes, scrap metal and rubble now."

Dwayne rubbed his forehead, trying to get the image out of his mind. "I didn't see anything on the news about a fire."

"It didn't make the news," said Frankie.

I held up a fire-scorched wok. "Everything's burned to this color now!"

Dwayne rubbed his eyebrows. "This is some evil-spirit shit."

"No, it's not. It was arson." I brought the broom inside and washed my hands at the main sink.

Dwayne followed me in and pointed both index fingers at me. "You have to repent to the gods, Jing-nan!"

"It had nothing to do with them, because they don't exist."

"Why are you talking like this? Even if you don't believe in them, you don't have to piss them off! You better say sorry to Mazu!"

"Mazu, my ass!"

He closed his eyes and shook his head. I couldn't believe how distraught the big guy was getting. He was acting like a student about to have his hands whacked with a ruler in front of the whole class.

"What is your problem, Dwayne? You don't even believe in her. Mazu is a Han Chinese goddess."

He put his fists on his waist like an old-time wrestler. "But I respect her. You should, too. We live on an island, so you'd better damn well respect the goddess of the sea! And you know what month this is!" He held up his left hand, warning me not to say the forbidden word. "It's Ghost Month!" I said.

Dwayne rubbed his hands anxiously.

"Ghost, ghost, ghost!"

"Jing-nan, settle down now," said Frankie. "You don't like it when people force their beliefs on you, so you shouldn't force your non-beliefs on them."

"Do you know what really gets me?" I said, feeling my arms shake in anger. "The actual cause and effect get buried under all this superstition and incense. Gangsters torched my place, and I know because their American friend told me! That's why it wasn't on the news!"

Dwayne looked me in the eye. "If you were good to the gods, this wouldn't have happened."

"The gods weren't good to me, so why should I be good to them?"

Frankie spoke up. "You're insured, aren't you?"

"We've got some," I said.

The house wasn't formally insured. An illegally built home was nearly the same as a legitimately registered address. Getting an electrical line isn't a problem. Same thing with running water and cable television. You can get your mail delivered there, too. But homeowner insurance? Forget it. Insurance companies were already loath to cover legit homes that were shoddily built; there was no way they would extend policies to people who couldn't even say what their walls and floor were made from.

"I haven't seen the policy in a while," I said. "I'm going to meet my insurance rep soon."

"ONE HUNDRED THOUSAND LOUSY NT!" I yelled at German Tsai. I was too mad to be intimidated by him, even though we were sitting in the front seats of his car.

He seemed amused by my loss of control. "I don't think anyone else would pay you that much for the house in that condition. This also cuts through all the red tape with the insurance company for the building next door, not to mention the lawyers."

I pounded his dashboard. "It's probably worth fifty times that, German!"

"You're exaggerating," said German. "Besides, it's more than you make in three months. Say, I've got your cash right here, and remember that I brokered this deal personally, Jing-nan. Don't embarrass me. The Black Sea are not unreasonable people."

I sighed and stomped my right foot.

"Look," he continued, "if you don't want to take the money, I can just apply this to your family debt."

I felt the blood drain from my head. "I'm still in debt?"

German chuckled. "Hell, yes, you still owe! This whole thing was set up by my dad for your grandfather's gambling debt. The promissory note is as legit as a Sun Yat-sen note." He rolled down his window, spat *binlang* juice and wound it back up. "I sympathize with you, Jing-nan, but this deal was set up before you or I were born, and we inherited the terms."

"I lost all my music in the fire," I said, feeling like a sulky teen. "Do you know how much that cost? That was probably twenty thousand NT right there!"

German put a hand on my shoulder. "I'll tell you what I'll do for you. The debt on the last statement was about three point five million NT, right? I'm going to bring it down to three point three million NT." I could save that much in about a decade, if I stopped eating and buying clothes and gas.

Sensing an opportunity, I said, "Just keep the debt where it is, but drop the interest."

German leaned over, and a dull whirring sound came from his seat as he eased it back almost completely. It meant a lot less money for him, but it also gave me a realistic path to pay off the debt fully.

"All right, Jing-nan," he said. "I think that's fair."

I DIDN'T HAVE MANY albums on my phone, only about thirty compared to the several thousand on my hard drive, which included live performances by Joy Division and New Order downloaded from sites that had wound down years ago. My PC library had also included songs from pre-concert sound checks I had copied from a guy at UCLA. I've never seen them anywhere else. I'd probably never hear them again, especially since the conglomerate corporations that owned the publishing rights to Joy Division and New Order were now vigilant about shutting down sharing sites that dared to post material from either band.

Listening to music was a huge part of my rituals for going to sleep and getting up in the morning, almost as necessary as water for brushing my teeth, washing my face and flushing away my waste. Nancy preferred to only listen to music through headphones. That was fine for me when I was in transit, but in my home (or her home), I really needed to feel the sound moving through the air, as a part of the living world and not just isolated in my ears.

Nancy didn't have a desktop computer or a stereo system. She listened to music on her phone and laptop. I examined her video system, which had speakers that were better than the old stereo system I'd had hooked up to my computer.

I sat on the floor and picked my way though a drawer of cables in the wall unit under the television, as tangles of black cables piled up in my lap like cyborg pubic hair.

"What are you doing?" Nancy asked.

"I'm looking for a cable that will let me connect my phone to the USB port in the television. I lost mine in the fire."

She raised an eyebrow. "Just a second." She went to her bedroom and returned with a portable hard drive the size of a Big Mac. "You can plug this into the TV."

"Whoa, what's this?"

"It's the music files from Bauhaus. I only asked for Joy Division and New Order, but there's a bunch of other stuff on there, too."

My fingers tingled with the excitement of finding Joy Division material that was new to me. "What's on there?" I panted.

"I'll show you my laptop. I already copied the entire drive." Nancy plopped down on the couch, flipped open her computer and clicked on the music folder. She dragged her fingers across the track pad, showing me the names of the files.

It was hard to say what I hadn't heard yet. Live bootlegs rarely listed the dates and places of the performances, and when they did the information was often wrong. I would have to hear them all, and I would.

"I went ahead and corrected a few misspellings," she said. "I get annoyed by that. The best one I saw was the 'Love Will *Tar* Us Apart' twelve-inch single." She looked into my eyes and laughed with her entire face and spirit.

I looked upon Nancy with nothing but love. I had nothing left, and she gave me more than I'd ever had, both musically and emotionally.

"It's a miracle," I told her. "Thank you so much." I got on the ground and hugged her calves tightly.

Unfortunately, the television's firmware wouldn't recognize a portable hard drive of that size. We settled for listening to Joy Division playing somewhere in Manchester over her trebly laptop speakers.

Even though the music's integrity was compromised by the quality of the speakers, Nancy agreed that it was special to hear music move through the air.

"Did you ever go to Boar Pour More's MySpace page?" she asked casually. It was a test. If I asked, "Who are they?" I would have failed.

Luckily, I remembered that it was a band that Nancy drummed for. They had a clever name, a play on *bopomofo*, the phonetic system for learning how to pronounce words in the Mandarin dialect.

"I tried, but it looked like it had been taken down," I said. "I found one picture in a Google search of you drumming, though."

Nancy paused the music and clicked on a bookmark that was supposed to be a shortcut, but a message confirmed the band page was gone.

"Damn it, I'll bet Pei-pei, the singer, took it down."

"How long did you have blonde hair?"

She put a few strands of hair through her mouth and chewed it. "Just a month. I had to try it." Her face sank a little. "Man, I told all these people at Bauhaus to check out our page."

"Sorry you had to find out it was down through me."

"Aw, it's not such a big deal." She was glum enough that I could tell it was.

"Can you play me some of the Boar Pour More song files?"

Her face got even longer. "Pei-pei has them, of course. She was going to have them remastered."

I grabbed her right hand. "Don't worry," I said. "You'll go on to do better things."

"I'm going to start another band sometime soon. Hey, Jing-nan, you can be the singer!"

"No, I'd be terrible!"

"You're a great singer, and you have charisma, too!"

"Well, you don't want to be in a band with a singer who works at night. How would we ever book any gigs?"

"Maybe you don't have to work at night."

"No, I have to be there, Nancy." I laughed nervously.

"You could sell the stand and get a day job. Who cares if you make less, right?"

I took a deep breath. Clearly, Nancy and I would be seeing a lot of each other in the near future. We were going to be in a committed relationship, if we weren't already in one. But it was still too early to tell her about my family-debt situation.

"Nancy, it's not my dream job to run a night-market stand, but it is a dream job for Dwayne and Frankie. I would never want to let them down."

"Are you sure? They don't look very happy there."

"Those are the faces they were born with. I feel bad for them."

I STEPPED INTO AN elevator to find that the air-conditioning unit was broken. I immediately broke out into a light sweat. I had expected more from a high-class building like Nancy's. I was about to step out to catch another when a white-gloved hand reached out and gently blocked my exit, also obscuring my view of the man's face.

"Sir, this elevator was called for you," he said. The voice was familiar, but I couldn't place it.

"So what?" I asked.

"Sir, you need to stay in it." The man stepped in with me and pressed a button to close the door. I still couldn't see his face, because he kept his back to me, but his uniform and cap were in good shape.

The doors closed, and the walls became transparent. Stars surrounded us. Why was I having such strange experiences with elevators?

"Can I breathe here?" I asked. "We have oxygen, right?"

"Sir, of course."

I looked down at the earth. As we rose I saw the West Coast of the continental US beneath us.

"That's where I went to school, for a while, anyway," I said.

"Sir, look over there by that light," said the man.

"Is that the sun?"

"Sir, some people call it that."

We were drawing closer to the light, and I felt the car heating up.

"Can't we do something about the temperature?"

"Sir, only the lady can."

"You mean Julia, of course. Let me ask her for help." I saw her in the distance, asleep on the floor of her own elevator car, also bound for the sun.

The conductor pointed at the emergency call box on the elevator. "Sir, you may ask her for help."

I pressed the button and watched Julia slowly stir in her car and then answer the intercom.

"Jing-nan, is that you?" She didn't bother to cover up a huge yawn.

"Yes! Julia, I need your help!"

"Where are you? Have you been out here the whole time?"

"I'm behind you. Listen, can you do something about the air conditioning? It's broken."

"I could, but I don't have the money to send a repairman there."

"I have money. How do I get it to you?"

"Just burn it and I'll get it."

"Do you mean burn notes as if you were a dead person?"

"It's similar to that. You and I don't believe in such things, but this is how it works out here. There's no other way."

I opened a smaller panel at about waist height, revealing a single flame the size of a tiny pilot light. This was going to take a long time. I sat down cross-legged, threw open my wallet and slowly burned the first bill.

"Did you get that, Julia?"

"I did, but it's not enough. I need another hundred NT."

I had trouble with the next bill because it was wet with my own sweat. As I struggled, out of frustration I said, "This is the worst elevator I've ever been on."

"You're not on an elevator," said Julia. "You're in a coffin, Jing-nan."

I tried to stand up, but the elevator had shrunk to the size of a coffin. I didn't have enough room to even turn my head. Where had the man who was with me gone?

"I don't want to die!" I bleated.

"We all have to die, Jing-nan. I'm just ahead of you. Now burn me money so I can help you!"

"It's just making it hotter in here, Julia."

"If you're not going to send me money, then I'll have to go to work for it." The intercom clicked off.

I looked at Julia. She shed her clothes and then began to swivel her hips around. She was completely naked. "*Binlang, binlang!*" I could hear her cry through space.

I pounded on the wall. "Stop it, Julia! I don't care about the air conditioning! It doesn't matter! Just stop what you're doing!"

The elevator man's face, now upside down, came in close, until we were touching noses. "I wanted to warn you, Jing-nan, but you were destined to take that ride." The man was Ah-tien.

I woke up with my elbows and head pushed up against the head-board.

CHAPTER SEVENTEEN

I stood outside of Big Shot Hot Pot and looked back at the kitchen. I saw Kuilan and her husband Bert. Now where was that—

"Hey!" someone called out right behind me. "You looking for me?"

"Ah-tien, I was looking for you. I wanted to ask you something."

He shoved his hands in his pockets and looked left and right. "Not here," he said. "Follow me."

He brought me to an alley off of Daxi Road that had no name and not a lot of light or air.

"What is it?" he asked rudely.

"Why did you try to stop me from getting on my bike that night?"

He laughed bitterly and shoved two sticks of gum in his mouth. "You think I had anything to do with burning your house down?"

"How did you know about it?" I got in his face a little bit. "I didn't tell anybody about it except Dwayne and Frankie. They sure didn't talk to you."

Ah-tien squeezed his gum into his left cheek and sneered. "You just don't get it, do you, Jing-nan? When someone you know gets murdered, just shut the fuck up about it." I wasn't sure, but I thought I saw tears forming in his eyes. "You think you're the only one who's lost a friend?"

"Tell me how you knew about my house," I said, a little bit more softly this time.

"I hear things." Ah-tien wasn't going to give me anything until I showed him I was in the know. He leaned against a wall and slouched.

"I know that a faction of Black Sea is being liquidated," I said casually.

Suspicion flashed in his eyes. "What do you know about Everlasting Peace?" So that was the name of the faction.

"I know they're killing the members of Everlasting Peace."

He stopped chewing and looked at me hard. "Won't be long now. There are only two left."

"Why did the Everlasting Peace guys kill Julia?"

He folded his arms and sighed. "I don't know, but they ended up signing their own death warrant." Ah-tien made a fist with his right hand and rubbed the side of his nose with an extended thumb. "This is where you stop asking questions about Julia," he said. "Seriously, Jing-nan. You're not safe as long as there are still Everlasting Peace guys out there."

"I thought it was Black Sea that was after me."

"Black Sea just wants you to shut the fuck up. Julia's murder is embarrassing to them. But Everlasting Peace wants you dead. They're trigger-happy young punks just looking for an excuse." He broke away from the wall. "Watch your back," he said.

AT A BREAK IN the action later that night, Dwayne called out to me. "How long are you going to crash at Nancy's? Real men don't mooch." He was at the stove, stirring our heaviest pot, nicknamed Da Pang or "Fatty," which was filled with stewed tendons, spice leaves and bones that needed to be broken down. He ladled out the steaming stew into four smaller pots.

I ignored Dwayne. Three Kiwis had come by because of the sign and decor. Joy Division has always been big in New Zealand. I talked them into sitting down and trying the stew fresh off the stove instead of getting something to go.

Frankie chatted with two giggly Japanese women. I could tell they were going to buy a lot. I assigned myself the task of washing dishes to give Frankie some more time to work on the women.

I washed out Da Pang first. The giant pot was our workhorse, and Dwayne would need it again soon. I ran the spray nozzle over Da Pang. I thoroughly scrubbed the insides of the pot. It was older than me, and I remembered my grandfather treating the pot with great affection. He used to pet it and talk to it gently.

I had just turned the pot upside down when I heard Frankie yell out, "Gun!" I looked up and saw a muzzle pointed at me.

I couldn't think. What was that quivering ring in front of me? I had a vague idea that it was something bad. I should be scared of it. Somebody was babbling something.

A loud noise rang out, and then I couldn't hear. Something slammed into my back. I put my arms out, and my fingers touched the ground. I saw Da Pang, which had saved my life, rolling away in space. Black scissors kicked across the landscape. I struggled to get to my hands and knees. I felt like the tide was dragging me out.

Someone pulled me up and made funny faces at me. Dwayne. That's your name. The Japanese women were screaming and crying. The New Zealanders were running after someone.

I recognized that the torso on the ground was mine. I looked it over. No holes. Good. Dwayne shook me hard, and I focused on his face.

"Frankie pulled the guy's mask off!" He said. "It was your friend!"

"It was my friend?"

"The loser guy you've been dodging! Cookie Monster! Ming-kuo!"

Frankie came over, holding something. "He got away, but he dropped his piece." He held up a loose stocking in one hand and in the other, Ming-kuo's gun, already in a clear plastic bag. "He was too slow."

It was hard to imagine my old classmate as anything but harmless and pathetic. Why was he trying to kill me? "Ming-kuo had a gun?"

"Yeah," said Dwayne. "The thing he tried to shoot you with!"

"Poor Da Pang," said Frankie. The pot now had a dent. A small hole in the brick wall above the main sink showed where the bullet had lodged after the ricochet.

"Cookie Monster," I said stupidly.

"Yeah," said Dwayne. "He was a monster."

FRANKIE INSISTED THAT I let Jenny examine me, as she had experience with medicinal herbs and foods. After taking my pulse, feeling my ears and smelling my breath, she made me drink a room-temperature tea as a preventative measure.

She checked my pulse again when I was done. Jenny then looked deeply into my eyes, searching for something.

"There you are!" she finally declared. I looked Jenny over. I admired her big brown eyes and thick lashes up close. She was treating me with the firm demeanor of a detention teacher.

"He looks all right to me, Frankie," Jenny said. "Now let me do you."

Frankie waved his right arm. "I'm in perfect health, Jenny. No need to examine me."

I walked into the side of a rack of clothes, but before it could tip over, Frankie grabbed the hanging rod and set it right again. The fastest reflexes in Taiwan saved my ass again.

AS WE CROSSED THE street to Unknown Pleasures, Frankie and I both noticed that the bootleg DVD sellers had packed up their rollaway carts and left. It meant that a cop was near.

Closer than near, actually. He was waiting for me at the stand.

"Are you the one who was shot?" the cop asked me as he nervously fiddled with Ming-kuo's bagged gun. He looked young enough to be on the varsity track team.

"Not quite shot, but it was close," I said.

"I called it in," said Dwayne, almost sheepishly. "I know you have a crappy relationship with cops, but I couldn't let this thing slide."

"You're Chen Jing-nan, right?" the cop asked.

"Yes."

"Did you get a good description of the shooter?"

"I know who it is. It's Wang Ming-kuo, an old classmate of mine."

"He's a loser," Dwayne volunteered.

"Okay," said the cop.

"Officer," I said, "I notice that you're not writing anything down."

The cop straightened up. "I can remember what you're saying. 'Wang Ming-kuo.' See?"

Frankie moved to a corner of the stall and crossed his arms.

"If I tell you where Ming-kuo is, will you arrest him?" I said.

The cop shrugged and tilted his head. "At this point it's your word versus his. We have to review the security cameras in the area."

I pointed at the evidence that dangled ever so carelessly in his loose grip. "His fingerprints are going to match the ones on the gun," I said.

"I can't just take his fingerprints, Jing-nan," the cop said through a weak smile. He wiped his forehead and pushed back his snap-back hat. "We have to respect his rights as a citizen. We all have rights, you know."

"*Gan!*" declared Dwayne. "Gimme that gun back, you lousy cop. We'll just go shoot him ourselves."

The cop shoved the gun handle-first into his armpit. "Now, now, let's not get carried away," he stuttered.

"Officer," I said, "what should I do if he comes back with another gun?"

"He probably won't come back," said the cop. "Not tonight. I'd better get back to the station now. Write up this whole incident from beginning to end."

"Get the fuck outta here!" Dwayne yelled. "You can forget about getting any free food, too!"

The cop handed me his card and left, but not before whispering, "Sorry."

"What the hell, you guys?" I said to Frankie and Dwayne. "What would have happened if I had been killed? The same bullshit?"

"We probably wouldn't be able to seat people inside," Frankie offered.

I chuckled and slumped into a seat. Who knew the Cookie Monster could be an assassin? Who knew he could miss an unarmed target from point-blank range?

"You want to take the night off, Jing-nan?" asked Dwayne. "We can manage without you."

"I'm staying. I'm safer around you guys, anyway." I bit my lip. "By the way, thanks for saving my life."

Frankie nodded. Dwayne wrung out a towel that was already dry. "I only did it for the money, Jing-nan," he said.

The DVD sellers crept back in. I slipped back into Johnny mode and didn't worry about anything.

Near closing time I saw people running by Dabei Road to Beefy King, which had an outdoor satellite-TV hookup.

Curious, I followed along. The buzz was that someone was about to commit suicide on a live broadcast.

A large crowd had gathered. The flat-panel television was set up next to the menu, which was branded into a wood sign. The broadcast picture was a little blurry, but it was clear enough to show a man standing at the edge of a roof.

Night-market vendors, including me, Jenny and Kuilan, stood closest to the television, impervious to the waves of beefsteak-grease clouds rolling off Beefy King's grill at eye level. Tourists stood away from the smoke. The guy who sold peanut-candy-scraping crepes was offering 50 percent off to the unexpectedly large crowd and doing brisk business.

"This is disgusting," said Jenny. "Trying to show someone dying on live television."

Kuilan popped a peanut into her mouth. "Well, we're watching, aren't we?" she asked.

"Someone's going to rescue the guy in the end," I said. "No one's going to die on TV."

"Is anybody thirsty?" asked Ranny, the Beefy King owner. He looked anxious to capitalize on the crowd. "How about some Coke or iced tea? Also, closing-time special—Philadelphia cheesesteaks, thirty-five percent off!"

"Turn the sound on," someone yelled from the back.

"If I have the sound on, I can't hear what people are ordering. Not that you're ordering anything anyway."

The channel's ground crew finally got it together and drew up close on the potential suicide. He was standing, holding his head in his hands. Then he dropped his arms.

It was Ming-kuo.

I held my breath. Goddamn you, Cookie Monster. What did you get yourself into?

The frame suddenly shook and drew back, showing that Ming-kuo was on top of a building with probably a dozen floors. He was on Xinyi Road, the main artery of downtown Taipei. I could tell because Taipei 101 was sometimes caught in the swaying frame.

The camera focused on Ming-kuo's full-moon face. It was a good lens. I could have sworn that I saw sweat and maybe tears on his face, which was lit from the bottom, leaving his eyes in darkness. Ming-kuo looked down and drew his arms together, as if preparing to dive. The crowd around me swooned as if they were there in person.

"Don't do it!" yelled Kuilan.

"Help is on the way!" said the crepe vendor.

"Philadelphia cheesesteaks, forty percent off!" yelled Ranny.

Ming-kuo's face twitched. His right hand brought up a cell phone and fiddled around with it.

My ringtone, the opening drumbeat of Joy Division's "She's Lost Control," went off.

The entire crowd turned and looked at me. I checked my phone. It was Ming-kuo. I answered the call.

"Hello, Ming-kuo?" I said tentatively. I could hear the wind whipping around him.

"Jing-nan!" he said. "I'm so sorry! I never wanted to hurt you! I was mad, that's all!"

"That's all right. You know, we're all watching you on TV. Maybe you should go back inside. Okay?"

"I can see the crowds down there. Nobody's ever given me this much attention. I've never felt so powerful before." I saw that one of Ming-kuo's arms was raised in triumph.

"Ming-kuo, you have to go back in now, all right?"

"I was mad at you," he blubbered. "Because I thought we were friends."

"We are friends!"

"But you never wanted to hang out with me! All of you called me a monster back in school—don't deny it. So I became one! I joined Everlasting Peace a year ago, Jing-nan! When they noticed you were making some noise about Julia, I told them I could take care of you. That was even before you emailed me!"

I tried to read Ming-kuo's body language. I couldn't tell if he was going to jump or not. Where the hell were the police and emergency responders? Someone send a goddamn helicopter!

"You know they killed Julia, right?" said Ming-kuo. "The Everlasting Peace guys. I was at the desk of the love hotel when they came back to hide. They were trying to get betel-nut beauties to sell their drugs for them. Things went bad and they shot one. Somehow I knew . . . I just knew it was Julia!"

Keep him talking. Any second there would be people creeping in on either side of Ming-kuo, ready to snatch him and pull him in.

"Hold on, Ming-kuo, how did you know it was her?"

"I saw her, Jing-nan. I actually talked to her a few times. I was lonely. She was always willing to listen to me back in school. She told me she hid a message to you because she didn't think you two would ever see each other again."

Help still hadn't arrived. Ming-kuo sat down. Maybe that was a good sign.

Keep him talking. "Where's the message, Ming-kuo?"

"Maybe at the stand, in the dressing room? The *lamei* might know about it."

Ah, the boss lady, the "spicy sister," might have a message for me from Julia.

"It's my fault, you know," he said. "I blame myself. I took some of the guys to the *binlang* stand to show her off. I told them that I had slept with her." Ming-kuo was sobbing openly now. "I was bragging about it."

I listened to him cry for a few seconds. I hadn't wanted him dead after he tried to kill me, but now I wouldn't have minded seeing him tumble off the building like a dog's chew toy.

"Julia wouldn't deal their drugs," Ming-kuo continued between sobs. "There was some struggle and she was shot—but it was an accident! Now the entire faction has to pay the price. They're going to get me, too, Jing-nan!"

My heart was raging for Julia, but I managed to say, almost to myself, "Stay calm. Everything's going to be fine in the end."

"I know the stand Julia was working at."

"You told me before. The second exit at Hsinchu City."

"I lied to you, Jing-nan! It's the first exit. It's called 'Forever Beauty.'"

"Ming-kuo, come down from there and we'll go together. How about it?"

"It's too late, Jing-nan. I've already lost you as a friend, but at least I've made up for . . ."

The crowd around me screamed, so I missed hearing Ming-kuo's last words. I looked up at the television screen. The camera was now set at ground level, with parked cars mercifully blocking out the spot where he had landed. At the scene, police closed in slowly and awkwardly, like they were in a three-legged race.

I MET NANCY AT her apartment.

"You sounded like a robot on the telephone!" She wrapped her arms around my head like it was going to fly off.

"I feel so strange, *xinai*," I said to the back of her neck. My first utterance of an affectionate name, "beloved," surprised us both.

"My poor baby! Did you talk to the police about Ming-kuo?"

"I can't believe the guy tried to kill me, and then a few hours later he kills himself!"

"It's crazy, right?"

"I told the police that I was talking to him when he jumped. The guy I talked to said they would be in touch. It's sort of a mess, because Ming-kuo tried to kill me in Shilin District and then he killed himself in Da'an District, so those two precincts have to work together."

I hid my hands in my armpits and made an empty cradle with my arms.

"Nancy, he said he tried to be my friend. I wouldn't let him, and that's why things ended this way."

I let the empty cradle bounce against my stomach. I felt guilty, but there was something I had to ask Nancy. She stepped on my right foot to stop my pacing.

"What are you going to do?" she asked.

"Ming-kuo told me which *binlang* stand Julia was working at.

He said she had left me some secret message there and that the *lamei* knew about it."

Nancy's mouth shrank to a disappointed pucker. "I thought you were all done with Julia," she said quietly.

I touched her shoulder. "I have to know what the message says, Nancy!"

"Don't you see how dangerous it is to keep this up? Two people are dead already! Didn't you see the movie where the guy wants to know how his girlfriend was killed, and then he wakes up buried alive?"

"I didn't see the film, Nancy, but if I don't find everything out, I'm never going to be able to let Julia go." I rubbed my face. "Besides, I need your help."

"What do you want me to do?"

"Let me see you in that *binlang xishi* outfit."

Nancy took an uncertain step back. "The one from Jenny? I've never even tried it on."

"That's all right. Let's see how it looks."

After a few minutes, Nancy was twirling in front of me wearing red-lacquer high heels and a short, red-mesh dress over a minimal black bra and G-string.

"It isn't really coming together," she said. "I don't have my lipstick on."

"I didn't even notice," I said. "I think it's going to pass just fine."

Her eyes widened. "You don't expect me to work at that betelnut stand, do you?"

"I was thinking that you could. Get close to the *lamei*, gain her trust and find out what she knows about Julia. I would go right up to her myself, but she might know about me from the American and his buddies. She might shut the door right in my face." Nancy bit her lip.

"It sounds a little dangerous," she said.

"It's not *that* dangerous. There's no way another shooting is going to happen there. I've already talked it over with Dwayne. We'll be checking in on you. Also, if you don't feel safe at any point, just leave. It wouldn't be worth it at all if you were scared for one second."

"You really want to know what Julia's message was." Nancy looked into my eyes. "She meant so much to you."

"It would help give me some closure," I said, crossing my arms. Nancy looked up and wondered at the light fixture. She had a lovely throat.

"Well," she said. "I wonder if I could pull off being a betel-nut beauty. Maybe it will be fun." I was relieved to hear it.

"Thank you so much, Nancy. I owe you a major favor."

"I'd be doing it for me, too. I've already played a *tang-ki*, and that was kind of exciting." She wavered. "Nothing's going to happen, right?"

I put my hands on her hips. "Everything's going to be fine. Like I said, if there's any danger at all, we'll stop."

"I'll try. I'm tougher than you think, you know. Now I need to get out of this." She made a move to go to the bathroom, but I stood in her way.

"Hey," I said, "I was thinking we could take this into the bedroom. I wasn't in the mood earlier, but things have changed."

She giggled. "It's the outfit, right?"

I hooked my thumbs into the waistband of her panties through the mesh dress. "No, it's you."

I DROVE OUT TO the Forever Beauty stand by myself the next morning. It was the third stand in from the first highway exit. I went to the other side of the street and straddled my moped. I didn't want to be too conspicuous. After all, most customers were truck drivers or taxi drivers. Even though I kept my helmet on, I never looked directly at the stand as I pretended to fix my rearview mirrors.

It looked like any other stand. In the light of the rising sun, the green neon and full-length windows made Forever Beauty look like a candy-sprinkled ice cube that encased two nearly naked teenage girls. Both were seated on bar stools. One was wrapping *binlang*. The other was doing her nails. She glanced at me and quickly looked away.

You can undress a Taiwanese teenaged girl and strip her of her modesty, but you'll never take her shyness away. Teenaged boys are shy, too. I blame the Japanese. They did this to us.

A back door in the ice cube opened, and I saw a fully clothed woman come in with a food tray and two bowls. The "spicy sister," as the boss is called, looked more like a sour sister. She was in her thirties and wore a dark blue blouse and slacks. After she set the tray down, she put one hand on each girl and spoke emphatically. Neither girl looked at the boss as they slurped up noodles. Sometimes they nodded in response to the *lamei*.

The boss turned and tapped something into the fish tank. Flashes of silver and gold swam up and collected near the surface.

I was glad the girls were fed before the fish.

The *lamei* stepped out and went down half a block to where a table on the sidewalk was set up with packs of joss sticks, an incense holder and bags of snacks for offerings. She lit up a stick, bowed three times with it and then planted it. She walked back into the stand, pausing to pick up some trash on the ground.

Her whole routine was carried out as casually as if she were walking a dog. I wasn't sure if the ritual was for Ghost Month, a dead relative or the birthday of one of the myriad Taoist deities.

I rubbed my hands. There wasn't much else I could do. I had confirmed that the place existed and that it was still open. I had also objectively determined that Nancy was a lot more attractive than the current staff. The spicy sister would have to hire her.

Almost everything from here depended on Nancy.

I started up my moped and left.

DWAYNE MET US AT Nancy's apartment in the early afternoon. I asked Dwayne to look her over in the *binlang xishi* outfit. He gave her a cursory look and petted the stubble on his chin.

"Not bad," he said. "That's actually pretty close. I've been chewing *binlang* a long time, so I know. The only thing I would say is that your clothes look too . . ."

"Slutty?" asked Nancy.

"Ha, I was going to say too new! I've seen sluttier, believe me. You're going with pretty safe choices here. This outfit would pass at a high school, honestly."

"Dwayne, I know all about you and high-school girls," I said. "But how should Nancy act?"

"These girls," said Dwayne, "they're in not-so-great economic circumstances. Whatever she offers you, just jump at it, even if it's just a few hours at a time or a really late shift, or even if you have to start right away. The *lamei* may even want to dress you herself, but if she tries to make you pay for the outfit, then refuse. A reputable *binlang*-stand owner would never sell stuff to their own girls."

I spoke up. "Nancy, if you ever feel for half a second that you're in danger, get out of there," I said.

"There's always a little bit of danger," said Dwayne. "But there's no way another murder could happen there so soon, you know?"

Nancy lifted her arms and scratched her just-shaved armpits. "I'll try to be as low-key as possible and eavesdrop?"

"That's right," I said. "Who knows what you'll find out."

"Well," she said, "the music probably won't be as good as what we had at Bauhaus."

"It's going to pay a lot more," said Dwayne.

"How much?" Nancy and I both asked.

"You get a regular shift, you can make fifty thousand NT a month."

"Wow, maybe I'll just do this job for the money!"

I touched her hand. "We both know you're just doing this as a favor to me, Nancy. Even if I can't find everything out in the end, I at least want to know more."

"I want to know more, too," said Nancy.

"Here we go, then," said Dwayne. "Nancy, you should change back into regular street clothes. Is the sports car the only car you have?"

"Yes," she said, her face reddening.

"That won't do. You should take the bus to Hsinchu City."

"Ugh," she said.

"Jing-nan and I have to go to work. Just keep us posted with texts, all right?"

"Wish me luck, guys," she said.

Dwayne cocked his head and watched Nancy's ass as she walked away to change. Then he put me in a headlock and jabbed me alternately in the gut and the armpits.

"You're a dirty bastard, you know that? What are you doing, sleeping with this girl, you little playboy!"

EARLY ON IN THE night, Nancy texted that she was at her *binlang* stand and that she was going to begin working immediately because someone hadn't shown up. I said that Dwayne and I would swing by and check on her after midnight. The *lamei* was confiscating her phone for the shift, and she wouldn't be able to stay in touch.

I couldn't focus on work. Frankie nudged me when a loud, swaggering group of Australian men nearly walked by. "Hey, mates!" I called out. "Let me put some meat on the barbie for ya!" They all came over. Naturally, they had a lot of questions—the same ones all young men had. What time did the trains stop running? Where were the best clubs? Did I know any women?

"All the women I know are Buddhist nuns," I said, not missing a beat in getting their food together. "They've already said their prayers and gone off to bed. They're all virgins, too, so don't think about sneaking in on them." I had an answer for everything.

They laughed easily and ate a lot. I liked them. I wondered what it was like to be on vacation in another country, eating and drinking, having a good time.

Instead, I had my life. Here I was, skewering meats that I had lost the taste for long ago while Nancy was potentially putting her life on the line. She said she could pretend she was doing cosplay. For men, that meant donning helmets, full-body armor and swords, but for women it meant wearing lingerie-inspired battle gear.

I wondered if Nancy would be able to retrieve Julia's secret message. She seemed to have a knack for getting things done.

Julia and I had planned out our entire lives together. We knew where we were going and how we were going to get there. I never planned anything at all with Nancy. I never knew what was going to happen the next day.

But I couldn't imagine that next day without her.

Now I was using Nancy to chase a ghost from the past. In all honesty, that's what Julia was. By the time she was murdered, I hadn't seen or spoken to her in years. I didn't know the person she had become. She wouldn't have recognized me. The guy who grew up saying he would never be like his parents was now exactly them.

Maybe this whole thing was a bad idea. All I really needed to know was that I wanted Nancy to be safe and to be with me.

"Stop slacking, Jing-nan!" yelled Dwayne. "I'll stick a hot-pepper suppository up your ass if you keep daydreaming!"

"I'm not daydreaming if it's nighttime, am I?" I muttered.

"Day or night, it doesn't matter. You don't know what's going on, anyway!"

"I'm just thinking about stuff."

"Stop thinking and start selling, already! Move that mouth!"

I tried to get back into the rhythm of things, but I was distracted. Every second I left Nancy at that *binlang* joint was another second that she was in danger. I was relieved when the crowds began to break up early. I turned over the last row of skewers, exposing the charred side of chicken hearts.

"Frankie," I said, "we're going to close on the early side tonight. As soon as we sell these, we're done." It was just after midnight. He frowned. It was a surprise and Frankie didn't like surprises.

"See, Cat, this is how it starts," said Dwayne. "Start packing up early today. In two weeks he's going to let one of us go. A month later, the whole stand is gone."

"You're coming with me, aren't you, Dwayne?" I said.

"Trying to get me to do work off the clock, huh?" he said, even as he folded up his apron.

Frankie stood up. "You two go. I'll handle the shutdown."

"Really, Frankie?" I asked. He nodded.

"The Cat was the first person your grandfather hired," said Dwayne. "He still has that rock-solid work ethic." I saw the light brown blob of his midsection shiver as he tore off his work shirt and pulled on a black polo. "It's my lucky shirt," he explained.

"We need luck?" I asked.

"You always need luck, little brother. See you tomorrow, Frankie."

I fired up my moped, and Dwayne was kind enough to keep his motorcycle down to a speed that I could match. We turned onto the highway to Hsinchu City, and we didn't stop once until we got to the turnoff and pulled in to Forever Beauty.

I saw Nancy's eyes flash for a second after I pulled off my helmet. It was hard not to give her a full smile. Nancy stood up from her stool, but the other *binlang xishi* had already gotten the jump on her. A woman who couldn't have been older than twenty swung open the door and sauntered over to me. Like Nancy she was wearing a short red skirt and a white top. I guessed that was the standard uniform here for the late shift. She had dark skin and beautiful, thick black eyebrows. Although she slouched too much, I'm sure the customers weren't critical of her posture. The girl looked at my neck and asked me what I wanted. I told her one pack of *binlang*, and she turned back to the stand.

Dwayne remained seated but walked his bike next to me, so that my moped and I were between him and the stand. Nancy stood up and stepped out of the stand as my girl held the door open.

"Hello," Nancy said to Dwayne. "What would you like?"

He pretended to be preoccupied with her body. He'd better have been pretending. "Hi there, sweetie," he told her. "How about a date tonight? I can take you for a ride on my big motorcycle."

"No, thank you. I only sell betel nut," said Nancy.

"Well, in that case, just bring me a pack, little girl."

She gave a tight smile and walked back to the booth.

I suddenly realized that my server was standing next to me, clutching a pack of twenty *binlang* chews. "You like that girl better, too, huh?" she asked. "What's so great about her?"

"I was just looking," I said.

The girl's nostrils flared, and she threw down my pack. "It's her first day, all right?" she said. "She's an amateur! I'm the experienced one here!"

"Hey, little girl," Dwayne cooed. "Come over here. I like you better than that other girl. You go tell her I want you to bring out my *binlang*, not her."

The girl crossed her arms but headed back to the booth.

I bent down and picked up the pack and dusted it off. Twenty betel-leaf-wrapped nuggets were packed in a bag featuring an ink-jet picture of a lingerie model.

The dark-skinned girl angry-walked from the stand to Dwayne. Nancy trailed her and then came toward me.

"Are you all right?" I asked her under my breath.

"Yes. Actually, this is kind of fun."

"We'll talk later."

I looked over at Dwayne. He had a hand on the girl's shoulder, and they were both laughing. I handed over a fifty NT bill to Nancy.

"No tip?" she asked aloud. I handed her another fifty NT bill. "Thank you." She walked over to the other girl and handed her both bills. Nancy was about to reenter the cube when Dwayne called out.

"Hey, you girls want to see something funny? Watch my friend here try *binlang* for the first time!" He pointed at the bag in my hand. "C'mon, give it a shot. It's not that bad."

I pulled out a betel nut and popped it in my mouth. Not too bad. A vegetable smell and a hint of lime. It caved in when I bit it, and a foul liquid spilled over my tongue. It tasted like a dead frog had just spit into my mouth. I gagged. Everything came tumbling out onto the ground. Red juice dribbled from my chin into my crotch.

Dwayne, Nancy and the other girl all laughed as I wiped my face with my shirt.

"Girls!"

We all looked over to the stand. The *lamei* was standing in the doorway, hands on her hips, looking sexy and furious. The two betel-nut girls instantly sobered up. The *lamei* observed that her message had been received, nodded once and disappeared. The dark-skinned girl took Nancy by the hand, and the two walked back.

When they got far enough away, Dwayne said, "That girl is from the mountain!"

"What mountain?"

"You idiot. I mean she's aboriginal! I think she's into me, too."

"She was into you because you tipped her."

"Hell, yes, I tipped her! Say, Jing-nan, are you all right?"

"My mouth tastes like shit, but I'm all right."

"Now you know how our customers feel when they eat your cooking, ha ha. How about getting that crap off your chin?"

I wiped my face again. I really needed to wash up at home and soak my clothes to get the red out. "It's fine, Dwayne." I started up my moped.

"More importantly, is Nancy all right?"

I showed him the piece of paper I had found in the *binlang* pack. Nancy had scrawled "OK." Dwayne looked at it, pursed his lips and nodded. We put on our helmets, and I stared at the stretched-out reflection of my face in his visor. I looked like I was in severe pain.

I SHOOK MYSELF AWAKE on the couch and wiped off my mouth. In my dream I had just bitten into a rotten apple. Mouthwash hadn't helped to get the taste out.

"Whoa, calm down!" said Nancy, who towered over me. "That's the last time I'll kiss you while you're sleeping."

I swung into a sitting position and yawned, feeling my jaw crack. "What time is it?" I asked.

"It's about five in the morning."

I put my hands on her hips and felt her body heat through her jeans. "How did you get back?"

"I did what Dwayne said. I took a cab to some *weizhang jianzhu* area in the hills near Taipei 101. Then I got out and took another cab here, so nobody knows where I live."

"That's good, but Dwayne just said to go to some other district. Why did you go to a neighborhood full of illegal buildings? It was probably pretty scummy."

Nancy screwed her face up. "My mother lives in a *weizhang jianzhu*, okay? I grew up in one . . . and so did you!"

I held her hands. "I didn't mean to make you mad. I just thought it was strange. I worry about you, and I want you to be safe."

"I can take care of myself."

"That's why I love you."

She grabbed my chin and kissed my lips. "That kiss went better," she said.

"Tell me that everything went fine, Nancy."

"As fine as could be. The spicy sister is a pain in the ass."

"Did anything funny happen?"

Her eyes rolled to their upper left corners. "Hmm. No, nothing."

"What were the customers like?"

"Truck drivers, cab drivers. A few military guys. They were all perfectly nice. Bauhaus had more weirdos."

"Military guys? You mean soldiers?"

"No, higher-ups. Guys with soldiers as their drivers."

"I see." I gently pulled her down to my lap. "Did anybody try to touch you?"

"They all did."

"What!"

Nancy made a snorting sound. "None of them touched me, silly. 'This is a classy joint!' like the *lamei* says. Other places you get to touch the girls' nipples for one hundred NT. Not us. The other girl says she would do it, though."

"That girl was mean to me. What's her name?"

"She wants to be called 'Xiaomei,' and she's really sweet. She's only mean sometimes to defend herself."

Xiaomei literally means "little sister." It's a nickname for little girls, but some unfortunate women have it as a given name.

"Dwayne says she's aboriginal. Is she?"

"Maybe he's right. I didn't ask her. I don't think someone calling herself 'Xiaomei' is going to give me an honest answer, anyway." I held her closer. A shocked look came over her face, and then a knowing smile. "You're really awake now, huh?"

JULIA AND I WERE riding in the back of the pickup truck. The road was bumpy, and we were holding hands. Then we were lying on a beach, watching the sun rise over our toes.

"Is this what you thought our lives would be like?" I asked her.

"I didn't know we would live so close to a beach. It's perfect."

"I don't miss Taiwan at all," I said.

She laughed. "Well, I don't either, because we're still here!"

"This is Taiwan?"

"Where else would we be?"

"We were going to make it big in America! What happened to that?"

"Those were the dreams of children, and they were beautiful. But not realistic."

The sun was now high overhead.

"What's wrong with wanting to make it in the US?" I whispered.

"Nothing's wrong with that. That was what you chose to believe in."

"You believed in it, too."

"I did. With all my heart. But you and I made a big mistake."

"What?"

"We had no right to put down other peoples' beliefs. If people want to go to temples or *tang-kis* for comfort or consolation, it's none of our business. We didn't have to call them stupid or backward."

"But there are no such things as gods!" I blurted out.

"Maybe for you there aren't."

The sun was now setting behind our backs.

"You know now whether they exist, don't you, Julia?"

She smiled and tilted her head away from me. I had forgotten that she used to do that when she was reluctant to say something.

"It's not for me to tell you, Jing-nan. In any case, only you and I are here right now."

"I should have called you. I should have written to you." She reached out to me and touched my nose.

"I was disappointed that you didn't, especially after your parents passed away. Then I realized that it was your love for me that held you back."

"It was my pride, really, that I wouldn't break a promise."

"It was a promise that you made to me, Jing-nan. Don't you see?"

The only light now was from the moon and its reflection on the water.

"How about we build a fire?" she asked. We dug a pit and threw in a pile of driftwood. Julia gathered her hands together to light the tip of a branch. Soon, the fire was alive and biting the air hungrily like a chained dog.

"All the elements are here," I said. "Earth, wind, fire and water."

"Where's metal?"

"My belt buckle." I checked it. "Yeah, it's here."

"We have both light and darkness, too."

I nodded and shifted in the sand. "What's going to happen now, Julia?"

"I have a letter for you."

"A letter?"

"A goodbye letter, Jing-nan." Her hands seemed to be empty.

I sighed and pulled my legs up. "Well, let's have it, then."

"You have to do something for me first. Burn my diploma at Longshan Temple."

"Why?"

"Because I want to have it." She stood up.

"If I burn the diploma for you, you'll give me a letter?"

"Yes."

The fire grew hotter. I could feel the flames reaching out for my face.

I sensed that she was walking away.

"Wait," I said.

I woke up with the late-morning sun in my eyes and the dream vividly etched on my mind.

I KISSED THE STILL-SLEEPING Nancy on her forehead. Her eyes shot open.

"I had a dream!" she soft-screamed through her yawning mouth. "I saw Julia!"

"What did she say?"

"I don't remember, but she was smiling."

"I had a dream about her, too."

"What happened?"

"She asked me to burn her diploma at Longshan Temple, because she wanted to have it. I, uh, took it out of the box. Must be my conscience getting at me."

"Are you going to do it?"

"Yes. I'm going to do it right now. You stay here and rest, Nancy." I kissed her again. I washed my face quickly and then brushed my teeth. If I left soon enough, I could get there around the time of day my parents used to take me.

WE WERE BOTH NONBELIEVERS, but Julia and I disagreed about temples in general and Longshan Temple in particular. She *liked* Longshan and enjoyed going.

Our two families went to temple together for the big holidays, Lunar New Year and the Mid-Autumn Moon Festival, when the crowds were insane and the temple set up extra decorations and displays in the outer courtyard in an apparent effort to further congest foot traffic.

Sometimes Julia went to Longshan on a whim, merely to see the architecture and contemplate the history, she said. It made her happy to be there, so that was reason enough for me to accompany her several times.

Both Chinese and Taiwanese enjoy the sight of water cascading down rocks, so the temple obliges with waterfalls in the outer courtyard. Approaching the front gate can be intimidating, as you see the multi-tiered roofs and mystical animals leering down from the corners. As a little kid, I would nearly piss my pants as we headed to the entrance. My father told me that I had nothing to fear as long as I was "righteous." When I was older, I knew that the only thing I had to fear were the temple hucksters inside.

As soon as you entered the dragon gate on the right side, the sham began. Counters lining the entire south wall of the temple sold joss sticks, prayer pamphlets and fruits and vegetarian snacks meant to be left at an altar for the gods to eat.

When Americans think of a temple, they probably think about an enclosed area, a building with a roof. Longshan, however, is essentially a large, walled courtyard with a Buddhist main hall featuring Guanyin, the goddess of mercy, in the center and a Taoist hall featuring Mazu, the goddess of the sea, along the north side. The two main deities are both women. The niches along the surrounding walls are altars for lesser gods and folk gods, the divine bench warmers. Everything is so ornate that you'd have a hard time finding an inch of wood, metal or stone that isn't carved, gilded or both.

The open-air design allowed for all the burning incense to waft heavenward to the nostrils of the gods and to pollute Taipei's skies. It used to be worse. Longshan once had open-flame braziers set up for worshippers to burn bamboo-paper notes, but they were scrapped when the Environmental Protection Administration started cracking down in the 2000s. Yet even the EPA knew they couldn't stop incense-burning at temples. It would be like prohibiting bakeries from smelling like fresh bread. Besides, temples made way too much money selling joss sticks. People also bought temple charms to wave around in the incense smoke, to make them more effective when worn.

When I went with Julia to Longshan, I spent a lot of time rolling my eyes and contemplating the sky, pointedly ignoring the idols.

"Jing-nan, that's disrespectful," Julia chided me once.

"I don't have to respect fake gods," I replied.

"I know the gods aren't real and they don't feel anything. But you have to admire the craftsmanship that went into this place. It's almost four hundred years old. Think of all the people who have been through here, nursing their hopes and desires."

"This isn't the original temple, Julia. This is like the third or fourth one on this site."

She punched me in response. "You can't deny that this temple is an admirable achievement by the Taiwanese people."

Followers of Guanyin began to chant loudly and off tempo in the courtyard before the main hall.

"When I come here, I can't help but think, what if all the effort, time and money were put into building something really useful? Do you know how many more MRT stops could have been built?"

"This is a nice place to come to. The MRT isn't."

"Well, if you like it so much, then let's go join in the chanting." I grabbed her arm.

"I don't want to!"

We both laughed out loud as we had a little tug-of-war. Julia wasn't as strong as me, but she was shorter and had a lower center of gravity that worked in her favor. Her little hands had a tighter grip, too. At some point our bodies collided and we were suddenly holding each other.

She then fought to get out of my arms. I held on to her playfully.

An older man confronted us.

"You two kids are being very disrespectful! You should come and beg forgiveness from the goddess of mercy, or go to a love hotel!"

We went to the love hotel. It was our first time, and we didn't really do anything. We were only seventeen. I was sure, though, that going from a temple to a love hotel was a well-worn path.

ENTERING THE TEMPLE NOW, eight years later, I caught a whiff of that mildew smell that comes from improperly dried clothes. I never noticed it at the night market, where the frying smells could cover any odor less potent than a pulp mill. If I rode the MRT, I would definitely notice the smells of the seventh lunar month.

Almost everybody in Taipei usually dried their clothes on an outdoor rack or line, but nobody left their clothes out during Ghost Month. Ghosts could slip into your clothes and then possess your body when you dressed. People resorted to washing their clothes in a tub, hand-wringing them and then draping them in several wet layers across their furniture. The clothes ended up smelling as moldy as the dead.

I tried to focus on the smell of the incense and followed it to the rear hall.

I approached the large metal column before Mazu. I figured that since my dream took place on a beach, it was probably best to let Julia's diploma burn before the goddess who presided over the sea.

I removed the diploma from my wallet and unfolded it. It seemed smaller than I remembered. I drew closer to a large incense brazier, holding the diploma respectfully horizontal with both hands.

The brazier was about twelve feet tall, the bottom half filled with sand with hundreds of joss sticks stuck in it. Four minor gods held a large gold ingot in each hand as a handle to hoist up the top half, which looked like a big brass pith helmet. There was plenty of room to reach in and plant your joss stick or wave a charm through the incense smoke for good luck. The heat coming off was enough to burn paper.

I pulled the diploma taut and waved it over the hot white ash of the tips of the incense sticks. When the paper burst into flame, I would drop it.

Something miraculous began to take place.

Tiny brown squiggles began to appear on the certificate. They looked like bugs at first. Then they grew to form letters and words.

Someone had written on the diploma using invisible ink!

I waved the entire certificate around and made sure the diploma was heated evenly.

A few hundred words were written neatly in English on the back of the diploma.

I retreated to a meditation room on the side of the temple and sat down to read the hidden message.

Jing-nan, you're the only one who could be reading this. You should know that I'm probably dead now, even though I left my previous life years ago. I received this diploma by accident—I wasn't supposed to be issued one. Then I realized that it would make the perfect letterhead for me to write to you. In lemon juice! You would know by the way the paper looked water-damaged! While we were both in Taipei I had to stop myself from seeing you. It would have destroyed us. There was no way you could have found me when you tried to come for me, because I became a contractor for the CIA. They brought me back to Taiwan and let me work on things I believed in, to keep the country secure. Right now I'm focused on stopping people from selling technology to China and also military defections to China. My assignments could change later. I'm not sure you would understand, but I'm happy with what I'm doing. When I arrived in the US, I realized that I missed Taiwan. I wanted to go back immediately. I never felt at peace in America. Maybe you're living there now. I hope you're sixty years old and that you're reading this in your wonderful home and that you've had a beautiful life with a woman who loves you and two amazing kids.

Her penmanship broke down into blobs—probably because the toothpick was wearing away—as she ended with, "I will love you forever."

I folded up the diploma and put it back in my wallet. So this was Julia's secret message to me. Funny. I didn't love America when I was there, either, but I was willing to stick it out for her.

I also wanted her to be happy, though. I wouldn't have wanted to make her sad her whole life so that I could live out my stupid promise. She must have felt bad coming back to Taiwan, even though her father told her it was the right thing to do.

My mouth felt filmy. How could I forgive myself for putting that burden on Julia?

I got my answer by looking up. There, an idol of Guanyin, the goddess of mercy, looked down upon me. Guanyin, whose statue I had turned away from in the park when I first heard about Julia's murder. Tears streamed down my face and leaked into my trembling mouth.

Even if the goddess wasn't real, even if it was just an idol, it represented the idea of forgiveness and let viewers reflect upon their lives.

Was it really so wrong to have temples and superstitions if, in the end, they allowed people to find some inner peace in this horrible world?

CHAPTER EIGHTEEN

I left the temple and stood out front by one of the waterfalls. I called Nancy.

"Hey," I said. "I found Julia's hidden message. It was on her diploma!"

"What does it say?" I could hear crowds of people around her.

"Basically that she didn't really like the US and she missed Taiwan." I put one foot up on a stone fence. "She knew she wasn't going to see me again."

"Did she say she loved you?"

"Yes."

"I see." I heard the sounds of crinkling bags.

"Nancy, what are you doing?"

"I've just bought some more shoes. The ones I wore last night hurt a little bit."

"Hey, wait, you don't have to go back to the *binlang* stand. It's over."

I heard her groan. "But why? I kind of got a charge out of it. It was empowering to try out my sex appeal. Besides, I already moved a research lab day to go again tonight."

The first night had gone without a hitch. Why shouldn't the second?

"Are you sure you want to go? There's no reason to, now."

"Of course I want to go! Besides, you never know what else the *lamei* knows. I could push and try to find out tonight."

"This is the second and last time, though," I said. "We're pulling the plug after tonight."

"Ohhh kayyy," she said. Nancy was thoroughly disappointed. I hoped she wouldn't be all mopey after tonight.

When I got to the night market, I saw that Dwayne was keen on seeing Xiaomei again. We had planned on dropping in at the *binlang* stand again to see how things were going on Nancy's second night, but someone was more prepared than I was.

"Hey," I asked Dwayne, "what did you do to your face?" His upper lip was clean, and his stubble was neatly configured into a perfectly straight line on either side of his chin. It made him look a little devilish.

"I broke out a facial-hair trimmer and did some sculpting." He pointed at his face with both index fingers. "You like it?"

"It doesn't look like you, Dwayne."

"You look smarter," offered Frankie the Cat.

Dwayne winced. "Tell me I look younger."

"All right, you look younger."

I said, "You look more civilized. Less aboriginal."

"You little . . ." He raised his hands and started at me. I dodged to the left. Dwayne stopped and stuffed his hands in his pockets. "You're lucky I don't want to wrinkle this shirt. Or get blood on it."

I chuckled, and Dwayne caught me off guard. He grabbed my left wrist and forced my face up to his mouth.

"Look up here," he said cheerfully and flared his nostrils. "The kit included accessories to trim my nose hairs."

"God, get away from me!"

He let me break out of his grip too easily. He really was worried about his clothes looking good. So worried that he ripped holes in a garbage bag and wore it over his shirt to keep the grill smell off.

"You're going to sweat so badly in that thing," I told him.

He laughed as he tossed charcoal under the main grill with gloved hands. "So what? Girls like sweat. It causes a chemical reaction in their brains when they smell it." I shook my head. "What do you know? You're not a man of the world."

I put my hands in my pockets and walked to the front grill. The inside counter was now between me and Dwayne. "I wanted to tell Nancy to call tonight off," I said. "She's getting her kicks out of it, so she's doing it just one more time."

"What!" said Dwayne as he shucked off his gloves. "After I went through all this trouble to look good!"

"I already know enough about Julia to realize it's all in the past. It's not that she doesn't matter to me anymore, but it's over." I looked up at the sky. "My future is with Nancy." I noticed Frankie smiling and nodding.

Dwayne washed up and began skewering meats. I was surprised by the hurt look on his face. "What about my future with Xiaomei, Jingnan?" asked Dwayne. "Isn't that important? She could be the one."

"You can always go back by yourself," I said.

"I need a wingman," said Dwayne.

I wet a rag with cleanser and wiped down the front sign and counter. When I saw that Dwayne was busy doing the preliminary grilling on the skewers, I snuck over to his Wolf classic motorcycle.

I had to get him back for embarrassing me in front of the *binlang* girls the night before. I pulled off the Prince Nezha statue suction-cupped to the top of the tank. The prince was a boy who had divine weapons, flew around on magical shoes and was featured in the classic Chinese novel *Journey to the West*. Most people these days probably best know Prince Nezha as a costumed character who appears at parades, protests and store openings, dancing to techno music. You can't miss him. He's got five mounted flags stuck in his back.

I stuck Dwayne's idol in my front pocket with Prince Nezha's wind-fire-wheel shoes pointing up. Let's see how Mr. Tough Guy does without his little good-luck charm.

DWAYNE GREW FIDGETY AS the night went on. I think it was the lack of customers. At around eleven I told him that he could head off for the betel-nut stand and that I would meet him there.

I heard him fire up the motorcycle and idle the engine a little longer than normal. I was sure he was freaking out over his lost god.

I had half a heart to hand it back to him, but he eventually pulled out. He must have been lovesick to drive without the prince.

He could to talk to Xiaomei all he wanted. It isn't weird for the beauties to have stalkerish fans who shower them with gifts of money or iPhones. The *lamei* probably wouldn't mind as long as Dwayne kept buying *binlang* and kept his hands off Xiaomei's ass.

At around one in the morning, Frankie and I packed in the stand.

"What are you doing tonight, Frankie?" I asked.

He effortlessly pulled up the heavy rubber mats from behind the main grill. "The usual. Wash my hair, paint my toenails."

"Do you want to go to the *binlang* stand with me and Dwayne?" Frankie piled up the mats in the street, where he would hose them down.

"I stay away from that stuff. Terrible for your teeth. Causes mouth cancer, too."

I wheeled in the front grill. "You don't have to chew it, Frankie. You can just, I don't know, hang out with us."

He wiped his face with the back of his long-sleeved shirt. "I hang out with you two all night! That's enough!"

"But it would be casual, not in the work environment."

"Work is all I know."

Frankie was an older guy, but he certainly lived in the zeitgeist of Taiwan. People live to work and definitely to eat, too, but they never really live, period.

"It might be fun, Frankie."

"I've already had enough fun. You two enjoy tonight. I'll see you tomorrow."

As I rode to Hsinchu City, I wondered how much I would have missed out on by clinging to the past. I was so lucky to have met Nancy. I still had to come to terms with the fact that my first love, my childhood sweetheart, was gone, and I could never replace her.

Wow, I couldn't believe I just thought of Julia as my "first" love.

What else did I need to let go of? Probably this moped.

I could take Nancy around on a motorcycle. We could tour the island like those elderly men on bikes in that bank commercial, trying to live life to its fullest. Well, maybe not quite like them. We could go faster. My father said there wasn't much down south except scenery and ancient history, but I had yet to really get a good look at our homeland, the fields and flooded rice paddies of the *benshengren*.

Maybe I should get a motorcycle like that one parked on the shoulder.

Wasn't that Dwayne's bike?

I pulled up next to it and checked the gas tank. There was a little circle of residue where the prince idol had been. The bike was definitely Dwayne's. Why was it parked here, a few kilometers from the exit to the betel nut stand?

It seemed to be in decent shape. If he had run out of gas, there were stations close enough to walk to, and he probably wouldn't have let it come to that before filling up, anyway.

I became worried. I got back on the highway and took the next exit. I reached a small road where there was no barrier on the sidewalk and walked my moped off into the grass. I saw an unlit building up ahead, but something told me not to simply ride up to it. I parked my moped next to a tree and walked on, staying out of the misty light from the occasional street lamp.

The road I was walking on wasn't part of a real highway. It was an abandoned service road to a semiconductor plant that had closed years before, after China had stolen the jobs. Real-estate information was sloppily slapped on top of the dilapidated original sign. As I approached the parking lot, I heard something up ahead. The squawk of a walkie-talkie.

Plastic barrels were lined up along the near side of the parking lot's border. I peered over them and saw a van about twenty-five yards away. A man smoking a cigarette was sitting on the bumper. He seemed to be playing with something small that made sharp, metallic clicking sounds that echoed around the empty lot. The night was heavy with tropical heat and curtains of humidity. The air kept getting stuck in my throat.

The man dropped the cigarette, took a small package from his pants pocket and put something in his mouth.

I sank to the ground and crawled forward, staying away from

the lapping edge of a pool of light from a pair of derelict lights swaying at the top of a rusty pole.

Taiwanese trees, grasses and weeds, empowered by the humidity and rainfall, were reclaiming the land, busting through the concrete. The site was now being used as an illegal dumping ground. Large, unsalvageable junk items such as old refrigerators and dented car chassis were strewn about.

I kept my eyes on the van, which was parked on a raised, shattered-concrete section that the plants were chewing back into pebbles and sand. I was close enough now to hear grunting sounds from inside the vehicle. Familiar grunts.

Nancy! And Dwayne!

The man slapped the van and yelled, "Shut up!" I wasn't sure if more guards were walking around.

I spat out a bug, but not before it left a taste like a rotten potato. The guy also turned away to spit. When I saw the oval-shaped sweat spot of the back of his tank top, I scurried around the rusted-out hull of an industrial-sized washing machine and moved forward. I was close enough now to hear him spit and clear his throat for another round. He looked my way briefly before hunching over to go for a full-body phlegm purge.

The man, who never stopped chewing, was about thirty years old and seemed deeply unhappy. More importantly, he probably had about fifteen kilograms on me. But all that chewing and spitting probably indicated a lifelong betel-nut habit. The government had warned us since we were kids that a habitual chewer of the betel nut hurt his esophagus, liver, pancreas and lungs. So maybe I could take this guy.

This was crazy. Even though I'd been beaten and pushed around in recent weeks, I hadn't tried to fight anybody since second grade. The last thing I had hit was a Japanese punching-bag game at the night market, which said I had the strength of two pensioners. I had to hope that that would be enough.

I couldn't call the cops because they hated me, and the toughest guy I knew was probably locked up in that van. With Nancy. I saw a pop-up ad in my mind of her opening her mouth and body to me. It spurred me on.

The man continued hacking. It sounded like he was trying to cough out something from his ankles. I drew closer. Soon I had my back against the van, with the man on the other side. I couldn't hear anything from inside the vehicle. I had to hope that they were alive and well.

I needed a gun, but all I had was a belt. I slipped it off from around my waist. Sweat rolled down my back and I shivered. I kept my feet within the van's swaying shadow.

This is it. Here we go. It's do or die.

Repeating the most clichéd movie phrases kept fear at bay as I made my way to the back end of the van. The belt was wrapped around my right wrist, brass buckle dangling. I was close enough now to step on his shadow.

Hit him hard. Hit him fast.

I took a deep breath and on the count of five slowly let the air out.

I swung around the van. He turned in time to get the buckle end of my belt in the face. The guy screamed and stumbled back. Was he really injured or just surprised? I couldn't take any chances. I had to hurt him some more.

My arm slashed through the air as I felt an adrenaline high. Any Taiwanese kid knew there was no defense against a good belting. At some point he dropped his handgun. It landed in a dried-out tire track in the mud. The guy was faster than me, but he made the mistake of diving for it. I kicked him in the stomach before he was ready to aim, and he dropped it again.

My hands swooped to the ground. It was an automatic and seemed pretty easy to use. I pointed it skyward and pulled the trigger. My arm jerked as a bullet rang out. I laughed. Then I pointed the gun at the man crumpled on the ground.

He wasn't there anymore.

Suddenly, a sweaty and muscular inner elbow closed around my throat. My voice box was being crushed. My right hand was pinned against my side, and the gun it held was useless. I looked into the man's bleeding eyes and smiled.

It was a strong but amateurish grip. A puppy could twist out of this one. Years of roughhousing at work with Dwayne had trained me to slip my neck out of nearly anything.

I stomped on the man's right instep and jabbed my left elbow into his gut. His arms flew open, and he hit the ground hard on his back. My buckle prong had gotten him in the left eye, and some of the eyelid was torn away.

"Hey, fatso!" I said, making sure my voice still worked. "I'm going to shoot you if you don't do what I say. Now get up and open the van."

The man picked himself up and said, "Don't call me 'fatso.'"

"Well, you attacked me." He opened one door of the van. It wasn't locked.

"You attacked me first!"

"That's true, but I'm one of the good guys. You're one of the bad guys."

He opened the second door and an overhead light came on. I finally saw Dwayne and Nancy, bound and gagged on the carpeted floor. Dwayne's face was scraped up and bleeding, but the big man didn't seem seriously hurt. Nancy's short skirt had ridden up to her waist, exposing her nearly transparent panties. Her top was little more than a thick bra. One of her lacquer-red high heels had snapped off.

I made a fist with my left hand and bit into it. How did everything get so fucked up so fast?

The bleeding man waddled over and took a seat on top of a knocked-over soda vending machine, holding his shirt to his face. His bared chest displayed brush-stroke tattoos of mythical beasts and naked women.

"Don't move!" I said to him.

"I'm not going anywhere," he said, switching hands on the shirt. A two-headed, arc-shaped dragon quivered above his breasts. "This is so fucking embarrassing," he muttered.

Keeping him in view, I climbed into the van and stepped carefully around Dwayne and Nancy. Their wrists and ankles were bound with hemp rope tied in knots so complicated they seemed to have four dimensions. If I tugged the wrong way, I could cut off circulation. Luckily their mouths were shut with cheap duct tape that slid off their sweaty faces with a tug.

"We have to get the fuck out of here, Jing-nan," said Dwayne. "Black Sea is coming to kill this guy!"

"Dwayne's right," gasped Nancy. "The guy out there is the last member of Everlasting Peace. He was holding us hostage!"

"Hey!" said Dwayne. "That bastard's on the phone."

I looked up in time to see the gangster toss something aside. He slid off the vending machine and leaned against it. I jumped out of the van and pointed the gun at his good eye.

When I got up close I asked, "Did you kill Julia?"

"Who's that?"

"You know!"

"I don't know who the fuck she is and I don't fucking care!"

I felt a sudden rage that tore my scalp diagonally.

"I! Loved! Her!" I grunted, slamming the butt of the gun against his head with each syllable. He dropped his bloodied shirt and turned around to try to prop himself up. Instead, he fell to his knees.

My brain sensed victory, and the adrenaline surge ebbed. My entire body trembled. I tried to catch my breath as my vision dimmed.

I screamed at the stars. Then I looked down at the man. He was sobbing, but I felt nothing for him. I pointed the gun at his head. Kill him. Why not? All his other Everlasting Peace buddies were dead.

Then I noticed a funny red dot dancing on my chest.

"Drop it, Jing-nan!" a voice commanded in Mandarin. It was the Taiwanese-American.

"Is he the one who killed Julia?" I yelled, unsure where the dot and his voice were coming from.

A second red dot danced on my gun hand. Then the brightest flashlight in the world blinded me.

"Jing-nan, it's all over. Drop the gun!"

I looked into the light and brought up my left hand to shield my eyes.

Suddenly there was a commotion. I heard grunting and a cut-off shout. The flashlight was knocked away. I dropped to the ground and crawled toward a group of metal drums, bracing myself for the sound of a gunshot.

Once I was past the drums, I tumbled into a cement ditch. I

could see the Everlasting Peace guy standing in the light, both hands raised but unsure whom to surrender to.

"Everybody?" he said as he looked around. "Don't shoot—I give up!"

Where was the American? How many more people were out there? I had to hope that Dwayne and Nancy were safe in the van.

I grabbed the gun with both hands and stretched my arms out.

I hoped I had enough bullets left to shoot the next thing that moved.

"Okay, okay!" the American said. "Jing-nan, you win! We just want to talk to you." He was speaking English, his voice heavy with resignation.

"I don't wanna talk!" I yelled.

"Look, I know you have another guy out there with our guns, so I'm just going to turn on the headlights with the remote. You'll see we're unarmed."

I had another guy? What the hell was going on out there?

A cone of light materialized. It must have been casual day at the office. The American was wearing a grey linen suit over a white T-shirt. His hands were raised. A big man, his pockmark-faced driver, stood next to him, rubbing his right wrist.

"You did a number on Yang," the American continued. "He deserved it, though. We thought we were coming into a hostage situation and we find you, Jing-nan, and your idiot friends here." He and his driver walked over to where the Everlasting Peace guy stood.

The driver slapped the gangster's head. "It's all because of you, Yang!"

The three of them stood in the headlights of the American's truck. The van with Dwayne and Nancy in it was just behind them. The ditch I was in was parallel to the truck but completely covered by darkness.

There was someone else lurking out there, armed with the American's guns. But whose side was he on? Mine or the gangster's?

I called out from the dark. "Hey, scrape face! Go untie my friends!"

The driver made two fists, but the American gruffly ordered him to do so immediately. Then he addressed me.

"I'm sorry things happened this way, Jing-nan," he started, "but you shouldn't have come down here and put poor Nancy through this."

"The *lamei* is with Black Sea, and she was friendly with Everlasting Peace!" I heard Nancy call out. Her voice was of the perfect timbre to transform the van into a giant speaker. "She gave me up! She had our picture from the KTV!"

The American spoke up. "She's right, Jing-nan. It's a betel-nut stand run by Black Sea, but we have our people there, too."

I called out, "What do you mean, 'our people'?" This was weird. A game of Marco Polo without a pool—but with guns.

"Well, it doesn't matter now, since we're going to pull out, so I'll tell you. A lot of the older military guys go there. They developed a taste for betel nut when they were stationed on the islands offshore China in the sixties. We've incentivized them to come."

"They let the generals touch the women's tits and asses!" Nancy chirped in Taiwanese. Yang smiled and nodded.

"Anyway, a lot of these older guys are in high enough positions to be recruited as spies for China. Unfortunately, China has been very successful at it. We've been running this stand to evaluate them, see who they're associating with, find out more about their lives. Sort of a tag-and-release program. Julia was one of our best. She dug out a lot of information and was personally responsible for rooting out two traitors."

The driver came back into the light with Dwayne and Nancy, who hobbled on one good heel. When she got close enough, Nancy kicked Yang in the stomach and he went down.

Dwayne held her back from doing anything worse. "C'mon, now, Nancy. We're winning right now. Let's not blow it." He took assessment of the situation. "Jing-nan!"

"Yeah!" I said.

"I think we're safer in the van. Just in case." Just in case some bullets start flying.

"You're right!" They both left the light.

"Well," said the American. "I guess this wraps everything up. You got your friends back. We've got the man we wanted. How about we all just leave now?"

I licked my lips and rose to my feet. "How do I know you're not going to come after me again, you lousy American?"

"You're safe now, as long as you go back and mind your own business. If you ever see me again, you're in trouble."

I stepped into the light, brandishing the gun at waist level. "If I shoot you right now, I won't ever see you again, will I?"

He showed me his palms and looked at me dead-on, betting his life that he could convince me to stop. "You don't want to shoot me. You'll start a shit storm so bad it will rip you and all your friends to pieces."

I felt someone touch my shoulder. "Don't do it, Jing-nan," Frankie whispered. He was hiding in the shadow of a car's removable bench seat propped up on its short end. Each of his hands wielded a gun.

"Just get out of here," I said to the men. The driver grabbed Yang roughly, and they walked grimly to the truck.

The driver and the American took Yang to the back and tied him to one of the seats in the truck bed. Ominously, they threw a tarp over him.

"Hey, GI!" Frankie called. He tossed the two laser-sighted guns into the dirt lit up by the headlights. The American scrambled for them.

"These," he said, holding up the guns, "are worth more than your life, Jing-nan." He weighed them in his hands before calling out to the darkness, "Sure, keep the bullets." The truck started up. The next sounds were doors opening and shutting. I saw some movement under the tarp, but once they were on the highway, it could just have been flapping in the wind. The truck lurched away, and in a few seconds it was like it had never been there.

I hugged Nancy in the ugly yellow from the derelict parking-pole light. "I'm sorry," I grunted into her head. "I should never have let you do this." Her hair was a mess, and she smelled like motor oil.

"I wanted to," she said to my armpit. "I'd do anything for you."

I saw Frankie's illuminated shoes walking toward us. "I'm keeping the flashlight," he said.

CHAPTER NINETEEN

I ran into Peggy in the lobby of Nancy's building. She'd been lying in wait.

"Jing-nan!" she called from one of the couches as I stepped from the elevator.

"Why, hello, Peggy."

She rushed over and slapped my shoulder hard. "You and Nancy didn't answer your door!"

"Was that you knocking earlier? We had a lot of resting to do today. Nancy and I are coming off a pretty wild night, if you know what I mean."

"I know what you mean, because you look like crap." It was an honest assessment.

"You look good, too, Peggy. Now if you'll excuse me, I need to get to the night market." I tried to swivel away, but she managed to remain in front of me. Peggy was probably a hell of a good dancer.

"Just a minute. I wanted to talk to you about that."

"Peggy, I've thought about it. I'm not going to go for that deal with you. It's just not right for me."

"Well, fuck the deal. I'm talking about how some media's going to try to interview you today."

I suddenly worried that news of the betel-nut stand, the CIA and the abductions had leaked to the media. "They want to talk to me?"

"Yes! They've traced Ming-kuo's last phone call, and someone at Chunghwa Telecom told the media that it was to you. Some reporters went to your address of record, but apparently they have it wrong. They ended up at an empty lot in the Wanhua District."

I couldn't contain a bitter laugh. "I like to be mysterious," I said.

"Can you take this seriously for once, Jing-nan? A few reporters are going to be waiting at your stall. Don't talk to them."

"Why not? It might actually be good publicity for Unknown Pleasures."

"But it will be bad feng shui for the real-estate developers, you know, the ones interested in signing a deal on the property. They aren't going to want to build at a place tied to a suicide!"

I stopped trying to work my way past her. "He didn't even die there, Peggy."

"It doesn't matter! Just don't talk to them, Jing-nan, and the story will die down. Better yet, tell them it wasn't true. You never talked to him!"

"I have a better idea, Peggy. How about I tell them you tried to get me to sell out early?"

She blinked. "Don't joke around. You don't know what you're messing with." She raised her hand and pointed a finger at my nose. "If you're interviewed on camera, you're going to get a lot of unwanted publicity!"

I smiled, thinking of the American and all his shadowy cohorts.

"Peggy, publicity is what I need. I want as many people as possible to know who I am." I headed for the revolving doors.

"This is your last warning, Jing-nan!"

"You promise?"

A FEW REPORTERS? I think every print, television and online reporter in Taipei was waiting for me. Dwayne had managed to line them up in the order they had arrived in. He had a burst capillary in his left eye, probably a souvenir from last night, and that made him look even more intimidating.

I expected Frankie to be stoically working in the back, but

instead he was talking enthusiastically to a young woman in a pantsuit who was second in line.

"Jing-nan," he said, "this is my niece, Tina."

"Hello, how are you?" I said. I could see why she was on TV. She had a small nose, big eyes and a straight smile. The woman was attractive in a wholesome, save-it-for-marriage sort of way. Had Frankie watched her grow up? How close was he with that brother he never talked about?

The woman signaled to her cameraman and swung directly into interview mode. The man who was first in line complained, but Dwayne cut him off by frowning and putting a finger to his lips.

"Jing nan, what did Ming-kuo say to you as he readied himself for death?"

"He said he was sorry for what he did, Tina. He tried to kill me right here at this stand earlier that night." I looked into the camera. "The Shilin police did a terrible job investigating that."

She didn't go for my aside and instead stuck to the script. "Did Ming-kuo sound afraid, or was he already sober and prepared for life beyond death?"

"Well, I don't know about life beyond death, but he never had a fair chance in life. They used to call him 'Cookie Monster.'"

"Did Ming-kuo have a last secret to tell?"

I took in a deep breath, ready to say everything as briefly as possible. "Tina, he did, in fact, tell me where my old girlfriend was murdered. You remember, the betel-nut girl who was shot, and you people never fucking bothered to follow up on the story? I found out that the CIA was involved. In fact, she was a contractor for the CIA and was on a mission to investigate the Taiwanese military."

But of course I couldn't say that.

What I said instead was, "Ming-kuo didn't have any secrets. He was a young man who never had a fair chance." I crossed my arms. "We all need real friends in life, and I wasn't a good friend to him."

Just when I felt a little emotional, Tina stopped the interview.

"That's it?" I asked.

"I've got all I need," she said in English, with a tight little smile. "Besides, my colleagues still need to talk to you, and I don't want to be a hog."

All the interviews were of a similar length. Camera clicks built to the fury of locusts as I held Da Pang over my head to show off the dent from the bullet.

Only two hours later, I watched myself on the news on the flat screen at Beefy King. I was shown speaking in clips, saying that Ming-kuo was a "monster" who had tried to kill me. It ended with a shot of me holding Da Pang over my head, the news anchor saying in a voiceover that I deserved a trophy for defeating him.

The only good thing about the news segment was that it included a quick shot of Unknown Pleasures' sign.

GHOST MONTH STUMBLED INTO its final days. Solid objects—cars and buildings—wavered in the humidity, lending them a spectral quality.

This is what our world looks like to ghosts, I thought. Soon the weary spirits would retreat into the maw of hell, and the gates would shut for another year and another tourist season.

To celebrate the end of a hellish month, I closed Unknown Pleasures for a few days. Sure, the money lost in that time would probably come back to haunt me, but I needed a break, and so did Dwayne, Frankie and Nancy.

I asked Jenny and Kuilan to keep an eye on the closed stand. They were going to split time displaying Da Pang in their windows. My fame had faded quickly, but the damned pot was practically an idol now. Jenny was even considering making a Da Pang T-shirt.

Dwayne borrowed a car from a friend, and we drove east on National Highway Five to the coastal town of Toucheng in Yilan County. It only takes about half an hour without traffic. I had last been to Toucheng as a kid, when the thirteen-kilometer-long Hsuehshan Tunnel was still on the drawing boards and the drive took more than three hours on stomach-wrenching mountain roads.

"You dirty Han Chinese killed our gods," said Dwayne as we plunged into the eastbound tunnel. "You drove a hole right through them."

"What god was this mountain?" Frankie asked from the passenger seat. I was sitting in the back with Nancy, who had fallen asleep almost as soon as we started driving.

"I don't know," said Dwayne. "I'm sure it meant something to some people."

"We're not anywhere near Amis territory," I said. "You guys lived farther down to the south."

"I speak for all aborigines."

"Then how come you love your little Han Chinese god so much?"

"Goddamn you for taking Prince Nezha that night," said Dwayne as he caressed the idol suctioned to the dashboard.

"Don't start up again," I said.

"If I'd had Nezha, everything would have turned out fine."

"Everything did turn out fine, so let's not worry about it anymore."

YILAN COUNTY HAS AMAZING views of nature. You can even board a boat to go stress out dolphins and whales in their native environment. But the main reason I wanted to go was to see *Qianggu*, a centuries-old rite-turned-contest. "Snatching wandering ghosts" was always held in the last hours of Ghost Month.

My memories of the contest were of teams of men in thongs trying to climb over each other to reach the tops of greased poles as thick as old tree trunks. It looked primitive and seemed to predate written language. The grounds could have been the set of a B-grade National Geographic special on the exotic customs of a forgotten people. I saw bruised and bloodied legs and arms. I remembered that one guy struggled as he neared the top and cried out, prompting the man underneath to look up. That poor guy below was injured when a pair of bare ass cheeks slammed right into his face.

Things were much different now. Gone were the raw braided ropes. Real safety netting was in place. Also, the hundred-foot-high grease-stained poles seemed to be uniform, giving no team—whether policemen, students, retirees or daredevil Australians—an unfair advantage.

The biggest difference was the crowd. When I was last here, I had to dodge the many drunken louts stumbling around. Now there were a lot more women, some of them even pushing strollers.

Banners and sponsorship signs were all over the site. Fifteen years ago, these electronics companies and car makers wouldn't have wanted their brands associated with one of Taiwan's grubbiest events. Now that the tunnel brought in far more tourists and coverage on the Travel Channel, it was an altogether tame affair that could be consumed easily in a one-hour program with generous commercial breaks.

At 11 P.M. Toucheng's mayor and a representative from an energy-drink brand welcomed the crowd briefly. They brought up a Taoist priest, who stuffed lit joss sticks into buns and then, with a flourish, tossed the buns to the ground. The priest then threw around some salt while chanting. A horn sounded to signal the end of the rite, and then a gong announced the beginning of the contest.

All the sanitizing couldn't hide the fact that every contestant suffered. The skinny men lacked muscle and strained themselves. The bulkier ones had a harder time pulling their weight.

A lot of teams made it to the first rack. At that level, the climber can throw down the cakes and cookies that are stacked there. The only other level is the top. The first team to reach the top and cut off a flag with a sickle wins.

"I still don't see why we had to be here in person," said Nancy. "We could have watched it on TV. High-definition, too."

"I haven't been here in years, and you've never been here, Nancy. I thought we should experience it together."

She crossed her arms and scowled. "It's pretty gross."

"If you think it's gross now, you would have thrown up if you had seen this place way back when."

Frankie appeared with a bag of wasabi taro chips. He neatly tore away the top and offered the opened bag to Nancy.

"No, thank you," she said.

"Please," he said.

"All right." She took a small handful. Frankie turned the bag to me.

"Sure," I said as I clawed out two big chips.

"Look at that guy up there, all the way to the left," said Nancy. "He was last, and now he's first."

"I'm glad you're getting into this."

Dwayne came up, clutching a roasted sweet potato. "Hey, Cat," he said. "How come you're eating packaged food? There are some great stands here."

"I work at a stand," said Frankie. "I trust packaged food more."

"What do you know, anyway?" I spoke up.

"He did save our lives, Dwayne. All of us."

"Hostages don't get killed," said Dwayne. "They just wanted to scare us some more."

"Scare ya by chopping off your fingers," said Frankie. Dwayne cleared his throat and wrapped up the sweet potato.

"Thank you, again, Frankie," said Nancy.

"It's all right," he said. "Please stop."

"Leave Frankie alone. He gets embarrassed," said Dwayne. "Let's just watch the contest. I'm pulling for the policemen. They're from the mountain."

"I don't think all of them are," I said. "You're stereotyping cops."

"Don't try to take away my native pride."

It didn't matter that Frankie and Dwayne, two tall guys, were standing in front of Nancy and me. Everybody had to look up to see the show.

When I realized that nobody was looking at us, I pulled Nancy closer and cupped her right breast. She turned to me with a shocked look on her face, and I locked my lips onto hers. She grabbed the back of my neck and stuck her tongue in my mouth.

The crowd roared and we broke away from each other. Some team was near the top, and a particular group of supporters near the front was chanting, "*Jia you, jia you, jia you!*"

"Are you still in love with Julia?" Nancy asked. Her lipstick was a mess, and her eyes were wet. I owed her an honest answer.

"No," I said. "It hasn't been love for a long time. Just my pride in keeping a promise to her."

Another team had inched up on the leaders, so another group, near the back, also began to chant, "*Jia you!*"

"I never came here with her," I told Nancy. "So I especially wanted to come here with you. It's time to try new things."

Disgusted that the policemen weren't contenders, Dwayne threw down his sweet potato, mashed it with his foot and pointed at me.

"This was rigged right from the start to let some Han Chinese win," he sniffed.

"I'm not Han Chinese, Dwayne. I'm Taiwanese. Like you."

He turned around and grunted.

A siren went off. The contest was over. No one on the ground could tell who the winner was. The crowd grew restless and pressed in. Nancy and then Dwayne were pushed into me as I looked up.

High above, the silhouette of a man bathed in light raised one arm in triumph. I shielded my eyes and stared at him hard.

A high-energy hostess came out on the stage in a sparkling dress and announced that some group from Tainan down south was the winner. She mentioned the drink sponsor every other sentence as she congratulated the team, all the participants and beautiful Toucheng in Yilan County.

Dwayne rounded us up like a sheepdog scared of losing its job.

"Look, you guys," he said, "it's one in the morning and there's gonna be a big-ass traffic jam back to Taipei. We have to move *now*!"

DWAYNE WAS DRIVING WITH Frankie sitting shotgun. Both listened intently to a CD of melancholy songs by Jody Chiang, the queen of Taiwanese music.

I was sitting in the back with Nancy slumped against my left side. We seemed to always be in a tunnel, and at times traffic threatened to come to a complete standstill.

"Jing-nan?"

"Whoa, Nancy, I thought you were asleep." We spoke underneath the sound of Jody pouring her heart out to a cold world. Nothing ever made her happy. Wow, is this what other people feel when they hear Joy Division for the first time?

Nancy stirred a little and pushed her head against me to rebalance herself before speaking. "I saw you give money to the people collecting for the Taoist temple."

I stiffened. "I didn't give that much."

"I thought you didn't believe in those things."

I made a pyramid on my right thigh with my thumb and index and middle fingers. "I came to an understanding in Longshan

Temple, Nancy. We're all human. We break promises and screw up our lives, sometimes by design and sometimes through circumstances. It's a good thing that we can find some comfort in goddesses and rituals." Without words, Nancy took my left hand. "Or in music."

"Are you glad," asked Nancy as she traced her fingers across my palm, "that Ghost Month is over and the gates to the underworld are shut again?"

I leaned my head against the window. "The gate is never shut, Nancy. The dead are always with us, because they live on in our hearts. We just can't talk to them."

Nancy wove her fingers through mine. "Some people say that the dead can talk to us in our dreams."

I made a pessimistic groan. "I don't know if I buy that."

"I hear you talking to Julia in your sleep."

"You do?"

"Yes. Every night."

The last dream I could remember with Julia, the one where she told me to burn her diploma, had been about a week before.

"What do you hear me say?" I asked cautiously.

"You usually laugh. Like a little boy. Sometimes you sound sad, and I want to wake you up." Nancy stretched her back briefly before continuing. "A few nights ago, though, you told her you've found someone new, and you sounded happy."

I took in a deep breath and settled back. "I sounded happy," I repeated.

As I was nodding off, our car broke out of the final tunnel, and I looked for home.

The moon pinned a perforated black bowl to the sky. The stars above and the man-made lights of the ancient basin that held Taipei blinked to each other and formed overlapping constellations too close together to name.

ACKNOWLEDGMENTS

Taiwanese people are known for their politeness and tendency to work long hours. They throw themselves into eating and overworking as comfort from painful memories and nagging political questions. Good eats and an office cubicle are tangible and have their own permanence—valuable attributes in an island that is prone to uncertainty in the form of natural disasters and political reckonings as a young democracy continues to figure itself out. It's not always something that can be done politely.

As I write this, there are three major protests rocking the nation. One is in response to the death of a young man serving in the army who was allegedly being punished too severely by superiors. Another is against the construction of Taiwan's fourth nuclear power plant. The third is in response to the demolition of private houses in Miaoli County to make way for planned developments. The path to the resolution of these issues will determine Taiwan's future, even as some unresolved and unresolvable issues continue to fester.

All Taiwanese bear the scars of history. The native Taiwanese were pushed out of their lands and are still marginalized in society. Taiwanese descended from early Chinese immigrants suffered the capricious taxation whims of the Qing Dynasty of China, then colonization by the Empire of Japan and subsequently the brutal early years of the Kuomintang regime. The mainlanders who arrived in Taiwan after the Chinese Civil War were cut off from families left in China; when contact was established decades later, they found out their relatives had been executed, starved to death and tortured. All Taiwanese can relate to the island's history on a personal level.

When my father was a boy, he watched American planes bomb Taiwan during World War II as Japanese anti-aircraft guns fired back. As a young man, he served his mandatory military duty for the Republic of China on Kinmen Island, which is about a mile off the coast of China but controlled by the Kuomintang. China bombarded Kinmen with shells that dispersed Communist propaganda leaflets upon impact. The Kuomintang retaliated by blaring their loudspeakers, encouraging the Chinese people to rebel and promising that the forces of Chiang Kai-shek would provide military support to overthrow the Communists.

My mother's family is from northern China. Her father, my grandfather, was an officer in the KMT, while his older brother was a prominent Communist. If my grandfather's brother hadn't died of cholera at a young age, he would have been one of the revolutionaries they used to sing about in the '50s. When I watched *The Sound of Music* with my mother, she told me that her family had escaped from China like the von Trapp family, eluding Communists block-by-block, all the way to the boat. Ironically, when *The Sound of Music* was shown in Taiwanese theaters, the censors chopped the film in half, lest any viewers compare their lives under martial law with that of Nazi Austria.

My parents met in New York, where my sister and I were born. Even though I have never lived in Taiwan for an extended period, my life is a part of the stories of my *benshengren*-and-*waishengren* family. These have become the stories of my characters.

I'd like to thank everybody in my family for opening up upon repeated questioning.

Thank you, Uncle Danny, for taking care of Cindy and me in Taipei. Within ten minutes of landing, you handed us a rental cell phone, and less than an hour later you had us feasting.

Aunt Lily, thank you for taking us to Din Tai Fung for an incredible meal that remains current in my memory.

Dennis Cheng, thank you for taking us places in your car and in your stories. I'll never be able to eat shrimp again without feeling the need to shoot hoops.

Anna Cheng, thank you for your humor and for translating your junk mail.

Amer Osman, thank you for showing me the ins and outs and ups and downs.

Catherine Kai-lin Shu, thank you for hanging out with us in the night market and for providing a bunch of background info. Some of the best "Inside Scoops" you've ever filed!

If you're in Taipei, Jo Lu and NCIS (Northern California Inspired Sushi, natch!) will rock your world. Check out ncisushi.com.

Thank you, unnamed and anonymous people.

Thank you: Juliet Grames, for your insight and encouragement; Bronwen Hruska, for your vision; Paul Oliver; Rachel Kowal; Meredith Barnes; Rudy Martinez; Janine Agro; Amara Hoshijo; and the entire crew at Soho.

Thank you, Kirby Kim, for being game.

Thank you, Cindy, for your love, your careful eye and your brave heart. And thank you, Walter, for falling into a regular sleeping schedule.

Epigraph from Tao Te Ching, translated by D.C. Lau.
www.edlinforpresident.com
www.twitter.com/robertchow
www.facebook.com/edlinforpresident

GLOSSARY

BENSHENGREN:

Descendants of Han Chinese, mostly from Fujian Province, who emigrated to Taiwan essentially before Japanese colonial rule began in 1895. Also known as Hoklo and "yams," because Taiwan is shaped like one. The "home province people" constitute the vast majority of Taiwan's population—84 percent, according to the CIA's World Factbook—and are concentrated in the middle and southern areas of the island. Although collectively they represent about 80 percent of the island's population, *benshengren* subgroups traditionally had sharp divisions. *Benshengren* originating from rival towns in China made a practice of burning down one another's temples during bloody conflicts. *Orphan of Asia* by Wu Zhuoliu, a novel written in 1945, details the life of a yam villager's hardships under the Japanese and disillusionment during travels through China, embodying the "sorrow of being Taiwanese" half a century before the phrase was famously spoken by then-President Lee Teng-hui. *Benshengren* were once viewed by *waishengren* as people brainwashed by the Japanese who didn't appreciate the sacrifices made by the Kuomintang and the Republic of China during the civil war. The view is more complicated and subtle now, as most of the KMT membership is made of *benshengren*.

BOPOMOFO:

A phonetic system used by those learning to speak Mandarin and also a shortcut for inputting Chinese characters in electronic media. In the song *Rose, Rose, I Love You* by Wang Chen-ho, blue-collar *benshengren* joke that when they struggled to learn Mandarin, "Bopomofo" sounded like "boar pour more." I thought that would make a great name for a band.

CHIANG KAI-SHEK:

The most important figure behind the architecture of modern Taiwan, with a divisive legacy. To some, he was the brave Generalissimo, the president of the Republic of China who defended the island from the clutches of Communist China and inspired his followers' hopes that someday he would unleash his armed forces and retake the mainland. To others, his Kuomintang party oversaw a period of martial law (in 1947–87, the longest imposed in the modern era) marked by ruthless repression and outright assassinations of dissidents. No matter your view, I think you'll enjoy reading the excellent *The Generalissimo: Chiang Kai-shek and the Struggle for Modern China* by Jay Taylor, probably the only objective assessment of the man. In recent years, with the opposition Democratic Progressive Party gaining power, Taiwan has renamed many places that had been named after Chiang. Most notably, the Chiang Kai-shek International Airport is now Taiwan Taoyuan International Airport. Some Chiang statues have been removed from public areas, as well, usually occasioning some high-profile clashes with supporters trying to block the removals. Interestingly, during a three-day trip to Beijing in July 2012, I saw only two representations of Chiang's old foe Mao Zedong. It's especially curious because as the Communist Party of China and Kuomintang have grown closer in recent years, the men who once embodied those respective parties are fading from view. Note that "Chiang Kai-shek" is actually a Romanization of the man's name in the Cantonese dialect, although it's by that moniker that most of the English-speaking world knows him. Jiang Jieshi, written in Pinyin, is the name that Mandarin speakers praise and curse him by.

CHINA:

A large, populous country formally known as the People's Republic of China that is located across the Taiwan Strait, to the northwest of Taiwan's mainland. As one of the world's longest-lived civilizations, and considering its diverse demographics and history of being divided and united countless times, China may be more a continent rather than a country. Through the centuries Chinese culture has greatly influenced Taiwan, along with China's other neighbors. Probably best known as the birthplace of Confucius and the manufacturing site of Apple products, China lives in fear of an invasion by its small neighbor. Why else would it have more than 1,600 ballistic and cruise missiles aimed at Taiwan at the end of 2012, according to Taiwan's Ministry of National Defense? Nonetheless, China has already invaded Taipei in the form of tourists crowding the memorial halls of Sun Yat-sen and Chiang Kai-shek. The strategy of these shock troops is to disrupt solemn changing-of-the-guard ceremonies by talking loudly and using flash photography.

DEMOCRATIC PROGRESSIVE PARTY (DPP):

A political party founded by *benshengren* in opposition in 1986, although it wasn't legally recognized until the next year, when martial law was lifted. Initially, the leadership comprised men and women who had been persecuted, tortured and/or jailed during the White Terror. The party was then bolstered by the return of Taiwanese dissidents from abroad throughout the 1990s. The DPP was founded mainly to advocate for Taiwan formally declaring independence from China, which regards the island as a stray sheep of a province that needs to be coaxed back into the flock—with electric prods if necessary. When the ruling Kuomintang party fractured ahead of the 2000 Presidential Election, the DPP candidate Chen Shui-bian managed an unlikely win. Ironically, warnings from China not to vote for Chen bolstered support for him. Chen served two terms, which were often marked by political gridlock, legislative showdowns and dwindling popularity. After leaving office, Chen was convicted of bribery, further tarnishing the DPP's public profile. The party's reputation recovered in time to nearly take the 2012 Presidential Election.

GAN:

A word in Mandarin. When spoken with the descending tone, it means "to do." When placed before the words "your mother," the phrase rudely suggests something to be done to your mother. *Gan* can also be used alone to express the f-bomb. This usage of *gan* originated in Taiwan but has been growing among Mandarin speakers in China, along with the increased number of Taiwanese expats. Woe to any schoolkid unfortunate enough to have *gan* in their name. *The Last of the Whampoa Breed*, edited by Pang-yuan Chi and David Der-Wei Wang, includes a story about a kid named "Gansheng" by his *waishengren* dad, who was unaware that the name meant "fuck a baby" to the kid's *benshengren* classmates.

GUANYIN:

The Buddhist goddess of mercy. In Taiwan she is worshipped by Buddhists as well as Taoists and adherents to I-Kuan Tao, a syncretic religion that incorporates elements of Confucianism, Buddhism, Taoism, Christianity and Islam. The twenty-foot-tall Guanyin statue in Da'an Forest Park that Jing-nan contemplates in the first chapter has a controversial past. The statue was slated to be removed from the site during construction of the park in 1994, but Buddhist nun Shih Chao-hui staged a hunger strike by the statue until the Taipei city government relented. Why was the statue slated to be removed? There is a longstanding belief among Taiwanese that Buddhist iconography (and Buddhist monks and nuns) should be contained in monasteries in remote mountaintops, away from worldly matters. Taiwanese politicians often set up campaign headquarters in local Taoist and folk-religion temples, according to Taiwan's Ministry of Foreign Affairs. However, a Buddhist temple would never be seen as appropriate for such secular activities.

HAKKA:

Nominally a subgroup of *benshengren*, Hakka have their own language and culture independent of other *benshengren* and *waishengren*. Unlike nearly every other distinct Han Chinese group, Hakka have resisted being absorbed into the melting wok of turbulent history. Their name literally means "guest families," which indicates that they were a people who were constantly on the move. Hakka communities exist throughout not only Asia but the world. Their respect for manual labor gave them the fortitude to establish Taiwan's camphor industry under often-harsh conditions. *Wintry Night* by Li Qiao is an excellent saga about a tough-as-nails pioneer Hakka family just scraping by. As of 2012, one fifth of all Han Chinese, including *benshengren* and *waishengren*, are Hakka, according to the Republic of China's Office of Information Services.

INDIGENOUS GROUPS:

The Republic of China's Department of International Information Services puts the population of Taiwan's first people at 2 percent, or about 520,000, at the end of 2011. Out of fourteen officially recognized indigenous groups, the three largest—Amis, Paiwan and Atayal—make up about 70 percent of all aborigines. The early decades of the Republic of China were marked by political disregard for aborigines, who were insultingly called "mountain people"—no matter where they lived—in official documents. Their sacred lands and burial areas were ruthlessly overturned and developed. In perhaps the most egregious incident, Thao (also known as Yami) living on their native offshore Orchid Island were told in the 1970s that the government was building a fish cannery that would provide needed jobs. The Thao later discovered to their horror that the facility was a nuclear-waste site. The Australian Broadcasting Corporation reported that more than seventy thousand barrels of radioactive waste from Taipower are stored on the island as of 2013. It's no wonder that the Indigenous Peoples' Action Coalition of Taiwan staged a symbolic headhunt of the Republic of China government on its centenary in 2012. Omi Wilang, an Atayal, told the *Taipei Times*, "We have nothing to celebrate, as the aborigines have only suffered under the ROC government." Actually, more than a few people of aboriginal descent have done well. A-Mei, a member of the Puyuma nation, is a huge pop star not only in Taiwan but in Asia as a whole. Like many Asian performers, she sells out shows in the US in those traditional meeting places of the Asian community—casinos. *Cape No. 7*, a 2008 blockbuster, starred Van Fan, who is Amis.

KOXINGA:

The story of this Japan-born son of a Chinese father and a Japanese mother has been exploited by different parties throughout the years to suit their political aims. The Ming Dynasty in China collapsed in 1644 at the hands of the Manchus and their allies. Koxinga, a Ming loyalist, built up and trained troops on islands offshore. He invaded Taiwan in 1661 and expelled the Dutch, who held sway over the island from Fort Zeelandia in present-day Tainan. Koxinga managed to rule over Taiwan until he was felled at an early age by either malaria or a fit of madness. The Manchus and their Qing Dynasty forces soon took control of the island. Centuries later, when Japan colonized Taiwan, Koxinga was upheld as a symbol of the shared heritage of the Japanese and Taiwanese. When the Kuomintang came to Taiwan, Chiang Kai-shek was often compared with Koxinga as someone who would not submit to barbarians on the mainland. Koxinga is hailed by present-day Chinese officials as a man who expelled the Dutch from Chinese territory. Was he really a hero, though? After all, reading about Koxinga and his men raiding the shores of China and the Spanish-held Philippines makes them sound like the common pirates who took refuge in Taiwan over the centuries, albeit well-organized ones.

KUOMINTANG:

The Chinese Nationalist Party, also known as the KMT, co-founded by Sun Yat-sen several months after the Republic of China was declared in Nanking, China, on January 1, 1912. After the collapse of the Qing, China's last dynasty, the opponents to a united China and enemies of the KMT were a colorful assortment of warlords who were incorporated into the revolution or eventually defeated. After Sun died in 1925, Chiang Kai-shek assumed leadership and purged the KMT ranks of left-leaning members as well as members of the Communist Party of China, although the Soviet Union had supported the KMT itself in its formative years. With the help of advisors from Nazi Germany (Chiang's adopted son Chiang Wei-kuo commanded a Panzer unit during the 1938 Austrian Anschluss), the KMT fought a large-scale war with Chinese Communists even as the Empire of Japan sought to expand control of northern China. Infamously, Chiang was kidnapped by his own troops to force him into an alliance with the Communists to fight Japan. While the KMT and Communists allegedly fought a united front against Japan, the Communists perfected their use of guerilla warfare and used it to great effect during the Chinese Civil War, which saw the KMT retreat to Taiwan in 1949 and establish Taipei as the new capital of the Republic of China. Under martial law on the island, the KMT and the Republic of China were effectively one and the same, a cozy situation that enriched the KMT coffers. In December 2001 *The Economist* noted that the KMT was the richest party in East Asia. The party's worst enemy turned out to be infighting, rather than Communists or the independent-minded Democratic Progressive Party. The party splintered ahead of the 2000 presidential election, and some now say that outgoing president and KMT chairman Lee Teng-hui had planned all along to hand the victory to DPP candidate Chen Shui-bian. In the wake of the election, *waishengren* lamented that the sting felt like losing China all over again, as documented in *Remembering China From Taiwan: Divided Families and Bittersweet Reunions After the Chinese Civil War* by Mahlon Meyer. The KMT used its time as an opposition party to build links with its old rival, the Chinese Communist Party. In 2005 officials from the two parties met in China in the highest-level exchange between them in sixty years, to seek peace and to forge trade links. It was an audacious move, as the two sides have never signed a peace agreement or armistice, and from a legal standpoint, the Chinese Civil War never ended. The KMT stormed back into power in 2008 with President Ma Ying-jeou's election; he was re-elected in 2012.

MANDARIN:

A Chinese dialect that was made the official language of Taiwan after the island passed to Kuomintang control at the end of World War II. From 1895 to 1945, the period that Taiwan was a part of the

Empire of Japan, Japanese was the official language. Notably, under the Japanese and the KMT, the Taiwanese language, which *benshengren* spoke at home, was outlawed. The abrupt change in the official language caused problems for the islanders. My uncle told me that when he was a schoolchild, his supposed Mandarin instructor was learning the language at the same time as the class, and that they all read the textbook together and at the same pace. Chiang Kai-shek himself spoke Mandarin secondarily and was most comfortable with his native Ningbo dialect. There are major differences between Mandarin and Taiwanese, which are mutually unintelligible when spoken. Mandarin requires the speaker to sing words in four tones; Taiwanese, which is descended from the Hokkien dialect spoken in China's Fujian province, requires seven tones. Taiwan's Ministry of Foreign Affairs estimates that as much as 15 percent of Hokkien cannot be rendered accurately with Chinese characters, and on top of that, Taiwanese includes borrowed and absorbed words from Austronesian indigenous languages, Dutch, Japanese and English.

MAZU:

Like many gods and goddesses worshipped by Taiwanese and Chinese, Mazu represents a mortal person deified for their perceived good works. Lin Moniang was a young woman who lived on an island off the Chinese coastal province of Fujian a thousand years ago. Her father and brothers were fishermen, and she would aid them in coming home from storms by both mortal means—lanterns—and supernatural means—plucking them from the sea and bringing them to safety while in a dream state. Supposedly she never died, having ascended to the heavens from the oceans while still in her twenties. The legend led to her titles as Goddess of the Sea and Empress of Heaven. As such, she has given safe passage to many Chinese traveling to Taiwan over the centuries. Grateful *benshengren* built temples to her after establishing themselves in Taiwan. The Tourist Bureau of Taiwan notes that Mazu, literally "maternal ancestor," is Taiwan's most popular deity. She is easily recognizable by her black skin and the beaded veil that hangs from her headdress. Taiwan's Mazu islands are named after the goddess. Mazu sits at the forefront of the Taoist pantheon.

RELATIONS WITH JAPAN:

Taiwanese have much affection for Japan and Japanese culture, and Taiwan is Japan's closest neighbor in terms of being cozy with one another. They do not have official relations, mind you, as China and Japan have formal diplomatic ties, and having formal ties with China means you can't have them with Taiwan. However, according to Pew Research Center's Global Attitudes Project, only 5 percent of Japanese surveyed in 2013 viewed China favorably. That's not surprising, considering a dispute between the two over some islands in addition to some historical matters. Taiwan also claims ownership of the islands, known as the Tiaoyutai to Taiwanese, but it reached a fishing agreement with Japan that tables the ownership issue for now. Another Japanese island dispute, with South Korea, has soured relations with that country, and South Korea's insane northern neighbor frequently threatens to turn Japan into "a nuclear sea of fire." And what of Russia? Another islands dispute. So why was Taiwan the only country Japan was able to reach a pact with? Moreover, how can a former colony have warm ties with its former master? Under the Treaty of Shimonoseki of 1895, Qing Dynasty China ceded Taiwan and other properties to Japan. Taiwan at the time was largely undeveloped, and the people of Chinese descent on the island had been treated as second-class citizens by Qing officials. The Japanese built the infrastructure that helped support Taiwan's economic surge in the 1960s and 1970s, long after Japanese rule ended. Even more importantly, the Japanese introduced Taiwan to baseball, and the legacy of that has been world-champion Taiwanese Little League teams and the proliferation of Taiwanese players in Major League Baseball. Unlike Japan's brutal rule of the Korean Peninsula, which seemed to be punitive in nature, its administration of Taiwan was motivated by a need to show Western powers that it could be a benevolent colonial power. Japan built up Taiwan as a showpiece colony and vacation destination for Westerners. Make no mistake, Japan brutally cracked down on insurrections and marginalized dissent. Many Taiwanese who lived through the colonization, however, say that what happened after was worse. These days, Taiwanese and Japanese people rate each other highest in polls that measure sentiment for neighboring countries, and Japan is Taiwan's top source of imports—even higher than China. Visiting Japanese politicians throw out baseballs at Taiwanese games. The Taiwanese airline EVA Airways flies planes decked out with Hello Kitty characters. Japanese words (*ichiban*, *obasan*) live on in common Taiwanese usage, and Japanese underworld culture (tattooing, extorting companies at their shareholder meetings, disdain for guns) remains alive among Taiwan's criminal groups. (For more on that, read *Heijin: Organized Crime, Business, and Politics in Taiwan* by Ko-lin Chin, which will leave you slack-jawed.) If this relationship still seems strange, consider the mutual affection that exists between America and its old colonial master, despite past enmity.

ROMANIZATION:

The Hanyu Pinyin system, which has been used in China since the 1950s and in Taiwan, officially, since 2009, would render the Wade-Giles romanization "Chiang Kai-shek" as "Jiang Jieshi." Of course, not everybody has transitioned to Hanyu Pinyin. In fact, there are at least three other romanization systems that have been in concurrent use, including another type of pinyin. If you can't read Chinese characters, don't rent a car in Taipei, because the roads you're looking for on your map likely won't match up with the street name. To add one more layer of confusion, romanized street names (and other words) are often incorrectly spelled. In a country where standards and identity are in a state of flux, rendering one's name in pinyin in Taiwan could be a political statement. Song Kuilan in this book renders her name in Hanyu Pinyin. As a mainlander who believes that Taiwan is a part of China, she happily uses the Chinese system. Chen Jing-nan, still using Wade-Giles, likes to keep things fuzzier. Adding the "Ah-" prefix to the second character of the given name—for example in rendering "Chen Shui-bian" as Ah-bian—is a colloquial term of endearment. Nancy would call Jing-nan "Ah-nan," but they're not cutesy enough a couple to use diminutives.

TAIWAN:

Concurrently a tropical island, an independent country, a remnant of the Republic of China as founded in 1912, and a province of the People's Republic of China. The population stands at about 23.3 million as of July 2013, according to the Central Intelligence Agency's World Factbook. As a Cold War ally, it is the smallest country, in terms of area, ever to have had a one-on-one mutual defense treaty with the United States. Taiwan sits on the Tropic of Cancer, just over 100 miles east of the Chinese shoreline. Most of the population lives in cities on the plains of the western half, while the scenic eastern half is mountainous, like a bumpy green rind. Over the centuries, Taiwan has been a paradise to headhunting native tribes and a haven for Japanese and Chinese pirates. Flags from the Netherlands, Spain, France, Japan and China have all been planted on its soil. Most importantly, though, Taiwan offers the best and broadest range of foods around. Its night markets are the buffets of East Asia.

228 INCIDENT:

Much has been written about the events of February 28, 1947, and the days after. In short, *benshengren* resentment against mainlanders boiled over, and mass rioting and killing erupted all over the island. Taiwanese students and veterans trained by the Japanese Imperial Army murdered *waishengren*, sometimes after subjecting their victims to tests to see if they could speak Taiwanese or Japanese and so prove they weren't mainlanders. The Kuomintang, which had taken possession of Taiwan after Japan's surrender in 1945, called in reinforcements from China, and through late March went on a retaliatory campaign as martial law was declared. It wasn't an even battle. Far more *benshengren* were killed during the weeks-long conflict and far more Taiwanese leaders eliminated during the ensuing house-cleaning operation than *waishengren* killed in the original unrest. In *China's Homeless Generation: Voices from the Veterans of the Chinese Civil War, 1940s-1990s*, Joshua Fan notes that more *benshengren* died in the first five years of the KMT's rule of Taiwan than in the entire fifty years that Japan ruled over the island. The incident itself was officially banned from history books and the press until martial law was lifted in 1987. In 1992 Taiwan's government estimated that the number of dead totaled between eighteen thousand and twenty-eight thousand. Lee Teng-hui, then president of Taiwan, apologized for the incident officially in February 1995, but it wasn't appreciated; *benshengren* felt the apology didn't go far enough, while mainlanders felt no apology was necessary for reining in an island in chaos. The 228 Incident remains a source of enmity between *benshengren* and mainlanders.

WAISHENGREN:

The terms *waishengren* and "mainlander" refer to those Chinese from all provinces who fled to Taiwan near the end of the Chinese Civil War in 1949. The CIA's World Factbook estimates the population of mainlanders in Taiwan at 14 percent as of 2013. However, these literally "outside province people" are overrepresented at the most powerful levels of government owing to the long period of martial law that favored mainlanders over *benshengren*. The stereotype is that *waishengren* families were all wealthy, and that all of them claimed to have been on the last boat that made it over. In reality, most of those army families and refugees had lost everything on the mainland. Once in Taiwan, non-officers and civilians were housed in hastily built *juancuns*—military villages full of houses with concrete walls and floors; they were meant to be temporary, but some are occupied to this day by old men who never found a permanent home. Those not lucky enough to get housing in a *juancun* improvised. Huaguang Community, which was originally built by the Japanese as a dorm for people working at the local jail and then unofficially occupied by *waishengren*, managed to hang on until it was demolished in 2013. In the film *A Brighter Summer Day* by Edward Yang, who was born in Shanghai and grew up in a *juancun*, the mother of a *waishengren* family scoffs with indignity that barely a decade after they fought the Japanese in China, they have to live in a colonial-era Japanese house in Taipei. How many mainlanders would have wanted to trade places with them to live in such nice houses, which even *benshengren* were largely excluded from! Note that the "mainlander" or *waishengren* identity is distinctly different from that of contemporary immigrants to Taiwan from China, many of whom come over as spouses.